THE
CONSCRIPT

SCOTT BRADLEY

 FriesenPress

Suite 300 - 990 Fort St
Victoria, BC, V8V 3K2
Canada

www.friesenpress.com

ISBN
978-1-5255-8818-1 (Hardcover)
978-1-5255-8817-4 (Paperback)
978-1-5255-8819-8 (eBook)

1. FICTION, SCIENCE FICTION, SPACE OPERA

Distributed to the trade by The Ingram Book Company

THE CONSCRIPT

SCOTT BRADLEY

Prologue

Wade Marshall peered out the cockpit at a reddish-orange light that flickered. *What could that be?* he wondered. *A ship? Way out here?* It didn't seem possible. He looked back at the deep-space freighter, *Oberon,* huge, long and sleek, with a conning tower near the back. Behind it, millions of miles away, was a comet's tail, like a partially open white fan. When the freighter slipped under the comet, it was like a wing on the back of an insect.

"Hey!" Garret Thompson yelled with a winching, pained expression. "Stop your damn daydreaming! We're drifting!" The heavy rattling that reverberated through the excavator's hull abruptly stopped and was replaced by the whir of engines.

Wade danced his fingers over his screen and fired a bolt trailing a long tether from the excavator's hull into the asteroid. It drew taut, pulled the excavator in, and nestled it back into place. The rattling resumed as it ground rock and tossed it into a bin.

Wade breathed a sigh of relief. "We can call it a day soon," he said over the usual clamor.

"There are no days out here, Wade," Garret replied. "Just heartaches." He studied a holographic image that showed the status of the cargo bin. It was full. He detached the mammoth bin and started it on its way back to the freighter. His holographic image switched to an empty container that was approaching.

"Who are you pining after this week?" asked Wade in the relative silence. "Jill? Heather? Or is it Jane?"

Garret smiled. "Not telling. Can't trust you." Using the holograph, he remotely piloted the empty bin into place.

Wade laughed. He had taken on the job and boarded the freighter when it left Cronos six months ago. There were no job opportunities on Cronos, no matter where he looked. The

1

economy was in a planet-wide recession. At least, that's what it said in the news, yet Wade felt it was more profound than that. People were starving. It was more like a deep depression. He had searched until his money ran out and took what he could get. Yeah, it sucked to be away from home for a year, but the money was good. He couldn't complain. When he got back, he'd be able to buy a house, or perhaps, set up a business of his own.

The trip out had been excruciatingly dull, and he had wanted nothing more than to work. Now, he was working fourteen-hour days, and all he wanted to be was off work. The job was wearing him down.

Millions of miles from anywhere, Garret went from one woman to the next.

Wade hadn't found any of them attractive. He often wondered if he should be a little less principled and a little more practical. "Just heartaches," he repeated.

"It's an off the rack world, Wade. You have to pick from what's available."

"Yeah, I know, and I'd appreciate it if you'd stop telling me that." There were thirty-seven crew members, and twenty-six of them were women. He only needed one but not from this rack.

The empty cargo bin slid in front of him and locked in place. He fired bolts into the asteroid, tightened the tethers, and started the grinder.

"Wade," Sue's sexy voice said over the com.

It caught him by surprise. She hardly ever called, and when she did, it was because he'd overextended his shift or quit too soon. He checked the time. Half an hour to go. "Hi, Sue."

"The captain wants you back on board the freighter."

"Why? What's up?"

"There's a ship coming, and it's—well—it's different."

"Different how?"

"Well, it's ah—just get back here, okay? And never mind the questions."

"Well, can we finish filling the bin?"

"Just leave it. This thing's getting close."

"Sue," Garret said, "we can't afford to lose a bin."

"Garret!" She had the roar of a lion. "You're not hearing me! The captain wants you to get back here now!"

Wade shrugged and dropped the excavator's tethers. He backed the craft away from the bin, turned it to one side, and signaled Garret with a quick lift of his chin.

"We can see what you're doing, Wade," Sue said. "The captain wants you to stop screwing around, and beeline it back here."

But Wade had turned the excavator so he could better see the strange ship's thrusters' glare, bright reddish-orange, coming straight at them.

"What the hell is that?" Garret asked.

"No idea," Wade replied, "but it's coming fast. Let's get the hell out of its way."

Wade turned back towards the freighter and punched the thrusters to full. A hexagonal-shaped bay door opened as they approached the starboard flight deck, revealing half a dozen excavators, several empty bins, and two shuttles. He brought the excavator in and put it down.

The bay door closed, and the bay pressurized. They got out and took an elevator to the bridge where half a dozen crew members sat behind consoles. The bridge was broad, and windows stretched across the front below a string of screens.

Captain Hogan, a slim man with hollow cheeks and a uniform a size too large, had his eyes fixed on the main view screen.

The strange ship, a gigantic saucer-shaped thing, was firing its thrusters to slow down. The two cargo bins left behind were like two minnows in the path of a whale. One of them got caught up in the blast from its thrusters and tumbled out of control.

"Should I put out a distress call?" Sue asked, her thin face grimacing and showing crooked teeth.

"Don't do anything to provoke it," Hogan said. "Let's just hope it doesn't take notice of us.

The ship passed by the bins and the freighter at high speed.

"Where's it headed?" Hogan asked.

"Straight towards Cronos," the helmsman replied.

Rose

From where Rose Bashal was standing, the space station, Danae High, was just a small dot of light sitting low on the horizon. She knew the station was seventeen miles wide, a round ring with spokes, and constantly spinning, and she wondered what it'd be like to be up there. It was not a thing she'd ever experience; it was only for the rich.

She turned to look in the opposite direction at the affluent part of the city, Aaronia, where hundreds of skyscrapers stood two hundred stories tall. That was not her world, either.

The street in her part of the city was lined with dilapidated houses and inhabited by the poor. She kicked a tin can and then a paper coffee cup. By chance, she spotted a book, trodden on, the pages curled. She went to it and picked it up. She'd always wanted to know how tokamaks worked and how they can power enormous warships for years without refueling. The secrets of this, the most powerful engine in the world, was in her hands. It had been something she wondered about since she was a child. She remembered back to how her father was beaming with admiration when he showed her the tokamak in the factory where he worked.

She put the book in her handbag, walked to the park, found an empty bench, pulled it out, and started reading. She was a fox, clever and curious. She took a bottle of water out of her handbag and sipped on it as she devoured the pages.

A tokamak, she learned, was a donut-shaped-vacuum chamber. Inside, the fuel, deuterium, was turned into a hot, electrically charged gas. Powerful magnets confined and controlled it. The gas broke down and formed plasma that fused, releasing vast amounts of energy.

She read until it was time to go down the street to the back door of a restaurant that was in the habit of throwing out food—table scraps mostly. She wasn't the only one who frequented this spot. About a dozen in total, the usual patrons were mostly olive-green skinned like her, but there were a few blue-skinned as well.

Today's entree was a salad made of black olives, cheese, onions, and green peppers. There was probably enough to go around, but they'd fight over it anyway. Rose pushed her way to the front and scooped up enough to fill her cupped hands. She found a place to sit and nibbled away at it, like a squirrel. Her salad tasted sour, and she wondered if it would make her sick, but she didn't have a choice—it was this or nothing.

She heard a rustling sound behind her and turned to look. A scrawny man in torn and tattered clothing was swinging something. She ducked but not quick enough, and it struck her on the forehead with a loud whack. She fell over, and her salad scattered.

She moaned. Her world swayed. She rolled onto her back, and as she waited for the pain to subside, the scrawny thief scrambled to collect the bits and pieces of her salad off the ground. A gray-haired woman with wrinkled olive-green skin came running over. "Oh my! Are you okay? That was nasty. Do you need an ambulance?"

"No," Rose said with gritted teeth, gently feeling her forehead. "I can't afford it." When she pulled her hand away, it was soaked in blood. "It'll be alright." In truth, the pain in her head was oscillating from bad to worse.

The woman had a cloth and put pressure on the wound.

"My handbag?" Rose asked, lifting her head.

"It's here," the gray-haired woman said, picking it up and putting it beside her. "Don't worry about that. You have a nasty gash on your head. Does it hurt?"

"Yes," Rose said. She was very woozy.

"Hold the cloth," she said. "You have to keep pressure on it until the bleeding stops."

Rose took it and held it.

The woman opened her purse and dug inside. "Here. Take these." She handed Rose a box of pills. "There's only four left, but they should take the edge off."

"What are they?"

"It's a painkiller called Rend. It'll help."

Rose got her water from her bag and took one of the pills.

The woman stayed with her for a short time, and in that short time, the bleeding stopped, and her headache went away. She thanked the woman for her help, and they parted ways.

Rose walked to the place she called home, a makeshift shelter she'd built against a brick wall from wooden skids and square of tin roofing. She sat with her back to the shelter, and on an empty stomach, she pulled out her book and read.

Slowly, her headache crept back. She crawled into her shelter, lay down on the blankets, and kept still, hoping her trouble would pass. But it didn't. It got worse, so she took another pill.

Gradually, the pill took effect, and her headache disappeared. She crawled out, pulled out her book, and, as she read, her neighbors arrived home to their ramshackle dwellings. She acknowledged them with a nod, read some more, and watched the sun sink into a bruised horizon. When the sunlight faded, there was a comet in the sky, and she marveled at it.

Her neighbors started a fire in a metal barrel drum. Rose went over and stood by it to stay warm.

Tomorrow she'd try to find work and make some money to buy some proper food. Her headache was still there but not as bad. She ignored the pain, determined not to take another pill. She only had two left, and she might need them.

Ebony

The crisp air in Aaronia's most central subway station made Ebony Harding shiver. Something was different. It wasn't just the cold. People seemed to be in more of a hurry, scrambling down the stairs, dragging suitcases, and scurrying into the brightly lit staging area. This wasn't the usual morning crowd on their way to work.

A train bolted out of the tunnel, gradually slowed, and stopped. Ebony got on and cringed at the smell of sweat, perfumes, and weed. She sat in an orange seat that had its back tastelessly taped with a different orange shade, like a bandage. The signal lights next to the tracks turned blue. The train lurched forward and glided into a dimly lit tunnel.

A few stops in, she watched an Athenian lugging a battered suitcase, forcibly push his way in through the jam-packed car. He sat across from her.

She couldn't help but stare. She'd never seen an Athenian before, not in real life. He was grotesque, tall, seven feet at least, thin with stick-like limbs, and draped in a dirty black sports jacket that was too long. He had florid red eyes that peered out from a countenance of desperation, course pink skin, and long greasy white hair that sprouted from his head, his face, the back of his neck, and the back of his hands. He fidgeted, moving in quick jerks as he glanced up and down the car. His eyes stopped on her.

"What's your problem!" he broadcasted across the car's length, like a merchant at a fair.

She didn't answer, looked away.

"You Cronish are all the same," he said. "Can't stand the sight of anyone that doesn't have green skin."

She moved her gaze down and said nothing. He was revolting, like a snake, and he made her skin tingle.

"I don't care what you think," he said, his hands moving in jerks. "Why should I? No one here gives a crap what I believe. That's why I'm leaving."

She pursed her lips.

A big, beefy man sitting next to her addressed him with a grated voice. "You're Athenian. What do you have to worry about?"

"I won't be spared," the Athenian retorted. "I'll be slaughtered with the rest of you."

"But you're one of them," the beefy man said with a skeptical tone.

"I'm not one of them," the Athenian barked, shaking his head. "Look at me. I've been on Cronos for less than a year, and my body has gone soft."

"Spared from what?" Ebony asked the beefy man, wondering what he was talking about.

"You don't know?" the Athenian asked with a glance down the aisle.

She looked up at him and gave her head a slight shake.

"How could you not know?" He held his hands flat out to the sides. "Everyone knows."

Ebony stared at him.

"The Athenians dropped six battalions on Catina last night. It's all over the news. Of course, it's been building up for months. Your wonderful queen," he said, his finger going back and forth between Ebony and the beefy man, "won't give them what they need."

"Catina?" Ebony asked, grimacing. She knew it was on the Southern Ocean. The population there was sparse except for a couple of months in the summer when people vacationed.

He smirked, exposing his canines. "Yeah. Catina. You know Catina, don't you?"

She nodded. The train pulled into a station where bright lights and another mass of people waited.

"You find me repulsive, don't you?" the Athenian asked.

"Just leave me alone," she said, turning her head away. He was repulsive, but she'd not realized her feelings were so transparent. The noise of the train dropped off, and the doors opened.

"Sure. No problem. I'll leave you alone." He sat back in his seat. "But make no mistake. They're coming, and nothing can stop them."

"You're wrong," she said, almost a whisper. "The army will stop them."

More people moved into the train.

"Oh, you think so, do you?" he said, his cynicism ripe. "The Athenian warriors aren't like me. Atheni is a bigger planet. The gravity is heavier. Their warriors are many times stronger. And they train. When your soldiers go up against them, they're in for a nasty shock. It's going to feel like they're fighting super men."

"Super apes," she said under her breath, barely perceptible.

He turned his head sharply towards her and seemed to have to stop himself from moving towards her. "That's quite the mouth you've got there. Say that to the warriors who are coming for you, and you'll lose your head in an instant."

"They'll be outnumbered."

The train pulled out of the station.

He nodded. "Even before the battle has begun, your men are lined up at the recruiting offices. They can hardly wait to get down there, have their fun, and declare victory. But it's not going to be like that. This war is going to be a bloodbath. If I were you, I'd pack your bags and get off this planet."

"This is my home," she said, her body tensing. "You're the one that should get off."

"I am getting off, and you should too. The Athenian way of thinking is different. They have a hierarchy where the strongest take everything, and the weak are eliminated."

"It's the same damn thing here," Ebony rebuked, her heart pounding.

"No. It's not the same here. It's not the same at all." The Athenian leaned forward and bounced his eyes around at the people staring back at him, frozen people, like frightened rabbits. "When I was a young boy," the Athenian said, staring off into oblivion, "my mother got angry and said the wrong thing to my father. The moment she said it, I guess she realized what she'd done, so she stood tall, her arms by her sides, and held her chin up. My father pulled out his longsword and moved towards her at lightning speed, but when he swung, he swung high, just over her head. It scared the crap out of me. My mother told me later that the Athenians respect bravery, and if she'd cowered, he would have killed her.

Ebony peered out the window. The train turned, and the metal wheels screeched in defiance as it moved past a station, abandoned long ago. She could visualize hundreds of ghostly souls still there, still waiting. The train kept turning, and the screeching grew louder, unbearably loud. She considered plugging her ears but decided, instead, to tolerate it. There'd be no sign of weakness from her. The track straightened, the screeching stopped, and the station was left behind. The train went into a tunnel, hummed along, came out of the tunnel, and began to slow.

"When the killing starts," the Athenian said, getting up and moving towards the door, "and the people begin to hear the stories of men tortured, children slaughtered and women raped," he looked back at Ebony, "every Cronish will want to kill every last one of us. You have no idea what's coming."

"The gods protect those who fight evil," Ebony said.

The Athenian rolled his eyes. "Fine, don't listen to me. But be warned. Nothing can save you, not even your stupid Messiah." The door opened, and his black jacket was swallowed up, his greasy white hair bouncing above a sea of olive-green faces towards a graffiti-laced tunnel.

"Do you have a family?" asked the beefy man, leaning in.

"A younger brother."

"How old is he?"

"Eighteen."

"Eighteen?" He turned to look her in the eye. "They'll draft him."

"You think so?"

"Of course, they will."

"But six battalions isn't that many, is it?"

He looked up, his mouth open. "No. It's not, but they'll be more on the way. And that Athenian's right. The way they think is different."

"Different, how?"

"They're true warriors. They think that fighting is a good way to die. The sick and injured are unceremoniously executed. They treat people like possessions, and only the strong are kept around. Females too."

"They're slaves?"

He nodded. "Not all men can take females, only the ones with the will and the skills."

"They fight for them?"

"Sometimes to the death."

"That's revolting."

"Everything about them is revolting," he said, his mouth turned down.

"Do you think they'll get to the city?"

"I can't be sure," he said, shrugging, "but they haven't got all that far to go. Once they've secured Catina, they'll work their way north. Even if the chance is slim, is it a chance you want to take? They're going to kill everyone. They might look at you and decide to keep you, but you'd be better off dead."

"Are you leaving?"

"Yes. I'm going north." He got up.

"Good luck to you," Ebony said.

He nodded. "You too." He sifted through the people on his way to the door.

The train stopped, the doors opened, and the noise of the crowd pounced on them. The beefy man got off, and he, too, was swallowed up by the masses.

Two stops later, Ebony got off and walked to the eight-story apartment building where she lived. Its grounds were littered with fallen bricks, its windows covered with iron cages, and its skinny children screamed as they kicked a ball around in the dirt. In front of the building, the destitute sat on dirty blankets with their belongings next to them.

She went in and up the stairs. The steel railing was missing in places. An old man wrapped in a blanket was asleep on the landing of the third floor. She stepped over him, climbed four more flights, and found her brother's girlfriend sitting on the steps outside her apartment, her head buried in her arms.

"Vicky, what are you doing here?"

"I tried to stop him," she sobbed, showing a tear-stained face, "but he wouldn't listen. He said he had to go. He just kept saying it. I really did try."

"Stop who?" Ebony asked, assuming she meant her brother, and they'd had a fight, and it would blow over.

"Keldon," she said. "I really did try to stop him. Please don't blame me. It wasn't my fault."

"Stop him from what?"

"Joining the army."

"Oh, no!" Ebony shrieked, bringing her hands to her face. "Did he say where?"

"You know. The recruiting office," Vicky mumbled, swinging an arm to point.

Ebony did know. Keldon had mentioned it, but she'd thought he was only toying with the idea.

Without saying another word, she dashed full speed down the stairs, two at a time, out of the building, and straight for the subway. She raced, panting, struggling to go faster, through the streets, down into the subway, and out onto the platform. She waited impatiently for a train, was first on when it pulled in and was first off when it got to where she was going. She flew across the platform, charged up the stairs, and even before she arrived at street level, there were young men, boys, standing on the staircase, four to six abreast.

"Is this the recruiting line?" she asked breathlessly.

"Signin' up for war," declared a boy with an eggshell face.

She darted down the line, searched for Keldon, moved her head left and right, jumped to see the boys' faces, and glanced back to make sure she didn't overlook him. The line went all the way down the street, around a corner, and on for another half a block. When she got to the recruiting office, it was a beehive.

"Sorry, no women allowed in here," barked one of the soldiers at the door.

"I'm looking for my brother," Ebony pleaded.

"You can't go in," the soldier insisted.

Ebony spotted a friend of Keldon's just inside the door. "Jimmy!"

Jimmy turned around and frowned at her. "What do you want?"

"Do you know where Keldon is?"

"He's here," Jimmy admitted, tossing his head down the line, which went deep into the hallway.

"Can you get him for me?"

"Keldon," Jimmy yelled out over the heads of dozens. "Your sister's here. She wants to talk."

Ebony waited. Keldon shouldered his way out.

"What are you doing?" Ebony scolded, grabbing him and hugging him. "You can't do this to me."

"I'm not doing anything to you," Keldon grumbled, squirming free.

"You don't know what you're doing! You fool! This isn't what you think it is. You're going to get yourself killed."

"Listen, Ebony. I know what I'm doing, and I'm doing the right thing. They're approaching Palasia. We can't let them get any further."

"For the sake of the gods, listen to me," she begged.

"You're not going to talk me out of it, Ebony. You need to stop treating me like I'm a little kid. I'm a grown man. I can take care of myself. I've made up my mind. I have to do this." Keldon turned to go back inside.

Ebony threw herself at him and wrapped her arms around him. "No! I won't let you! No!"

Keldon grabbed her arms, twisted, and yanked himself free. "You can't stop me, Ebony." He walked back up the steps to the door.

"The Athenians aren't what you think," Ebony yelled. "They're the creation of the devil. Satanic demons."

Keldon kept going. Ebony ran up the steps but was stopped at the door by soldiers.

"Keldon!" she pleaded as he made his way in. "Please!"

Jimmy winked at Ebony. "I'll watch over him for you." He smirked.

Ebony felt a sharp pain in her chest. "Please," she sobbed. "Please."

She went back down the steps to the street. Her shoulders were slumped, and tears streamed down her cheeks. She walked, this time facing all the young men, not hiding her face. She held her head high and peered into the eyes of each one of them, their faces turning away when they saw her grief-stricken face.

She didn't want to go home. It wasn't the same without Keldon.

The street was a dump. Many of the multi-colored concrete slab houses had boarded up windows, paint peeling off the siding and roofs sagging. Some of the roofs had been ripped off, probably from a hurricane.

As she sauntered along, she realized that people were leaving their homes, walking beside her, carrying children, suitcases, and some pulling carts.

An old couple sat in front of their house on weather-beaten wooden chairs seemingly intoxicated by the events unfolding before them like they were watching a soap opera. The line of boys slowly shifted forward as more frightened citizens spilled into the streets. Yet, a man walked his dog as if nothing was wrong and a young child pulled a wagon behind her mother, who was pushing a stroller.

Ebony wiped the tears from her eyes with the palms of her hands. Her brother had chosen to risk death so that he could feel important. She'd not make the same mistake. She'd go home and get the money she'd saved. She'd use it to buy a ticket north. She knew she had to get out of the city. She wasn't going to let those Athenian bastards rape her. She'd go north, find work, make more money, and go further north if need be. Her brother may die, but not her. She was going to stay safe and wait for the war to be over.

Tears came to her eyes when she realized she'd be going without Keldon. How would she find him when the fighting was over? She knew they'd publish lists of the dead. Would she have to check those lists? Maybe after the war, she'd find him, and he would come and visit her, perhaps even stay with her. She could hope. *Please, may the gods let him live?*

Tears came again, and again she wiped them away.

Rose

Rose stared into the morning fog at a tranquil crowd of maybe thirty, all there to get work. Around her, dilapidated shacks were sheathed in torn canvas and topped with tin roofs that rattled in the stiff wind. A lone sapling stood next to her, a thin pole with a ball of leaves.

Too many people, she thought. *Pointless.* What chance would she have? And besides, her head was pounding. It wouldn't stop. She'd taken another pill during the night, and it had worked for a while, but now it was wearing off, and there was only one pill left. She sat down on a tree stump, pulled the box out of her handbag and studied it. In big block letters was the word REND. The small print was in another language. She took out the last pill, popped it into her mouth and stuffed the empty box back in her handbag. She took a swig of water and washed it down.

The fog lifted and sunlight struck down through curling clouds.

"That's quite the gash you have on your forehead."

She looked up. A man with shaggy-gray hair, wrinkled-olive-green skin, and robust-looking arms stood in front of her. "Yeah, I got clobbered."

"Been here before?"

She gave her head a shake. It hurt when she did it, and she promised herself she wouldn't do it again.

"In a few minutes, a van is going to pull up, and the driver's gonna get out and ask for six people," he said. "That's all. Just six." He smiled. "There's blues in that crowd. He'll pick 'em first because they'll work for less, so I've decided to do somethin' about it. I've already talked to the others. They're with me."

She stood, so she could better see the mob and the Bacchians. They were small people whose skin had a bluish tinge, whose noses were big, and hooked like beaks, and whose hair was a mass of tiny blue curls.

"Do you see them?" he asked.

She acquiesced with a slight nod.

"Just gonna scare 'em. That's all. Watch 'em run." He was grinning now. "So, if the police start askin' questions, I can count on ya to keep this quiet, right?"

She shifted her gaze down.

"Right?" he asked again, louder.

She gave a slight nod.

"Also, when the van pulls up, you're gonna want to be at the front. Ya can't sit back here and expect to be picked."

"I know," she said firmly.

"What's ya name?"

"Rose."

"Vlad." He paused. "Alright, good. I'm counting on ya." He walked back to the crowd, stepped in front of a Bacchian, grabbed him by the sweater, and pushed him back. "Go! We don't want ya kind here! Get the hell out!"

The Bacchian pulled his sweater down, pushed his hood back, and defiantly moved forward. Vlad charged at him and pushed him harder. "You arrogant bastard! Go on!" he yelled, clenching his fists. "Get out of here!"

The man backed away but didn't leave.

Vlad grabbed another one wearing a red pointed hat and pushed him. "You too! Go!"

The one with the hat grabbed the arm of the first one. "Let's go, Belle. Not worth it." Belle shook his arm free. The red hat went on without him. Belle hesitated, moved forward, but stopped, turned, and caught up with his friend.

"You slimy freaks," Vlad bellowed out. "Ya stealing our work. Get out of here. We don't want you. Go!" He pushed another one. The other Cronish in the crowd joined in, collectively pushing and shoving.

A Bacchian woman scampered back close to where Rose was standing and stopped.

Rose, almost twice her height, glared down at her.

The woman turned and walked off down the road, giving Rose the finger as she went. Off in the distance, the sound of a train pulling in to a station drowned out her mumblings. The train stopped. A few minutes passed, and as the train chugged away, a van drove in.

"C'mon," Vlad said, scooping a hand towards Rose. "Right to the front."

Rose pushed her way to the front of the crowd as a man with a beard and glasses got out of the van and opened the back doors. The workers were like wolves encircling their prey. They waved their hands in the air and barked, "Me, me, me."

"Six people, just six. You," he said, pointing to a skinny woman. "And you," pointing to a burly young man.

The crowd was a storm. "Me! Pick me!" they shouted, shoulder to shoulder, their arms thrashing.

"Please pick me and my daughter!" Vlad shouted out. "For the sake of the gods!" He grabbed Rose's arm and held it up.

"You and you," the driver said, pointing to two other people. he paused as if to make an important decision. He glanced over the faces. "You," he said, pointing at Vlad "and you," pointing at a man standing next to Rose.

Vlad and the man got in, and the driver started to close the doors. He stopped, turned, and said, "Our mechanic has decided he'd rather be a soldier. Are there any fusion mechanics here?"

"Me." Rose lied. *Say whatever you have to say to get in that van,* she thought. *Pretend to work on it and tell them it can't be fixed.*

"You look awfully young. Can you fix a tokamak?"

She nodded, stone faced.

"Okay," he said, throwing a hand towards the back door of the van. "Get in."

She climbed in, sat beside Vlad, and put a hand to her head. The doors slammed shut.

"You look like you're in pain," Vlad said. "Are you sure you can do this?"

Rose kept her eyes to the floor. "I need the work," she murmured, pulling the strap of her handbag up onto her shoulder.

The engine revved as the van surged forward.

"I understand," he reassured her. "The Athenians have landed, and you need the money to get out of the city." He grabbed the bench as the van rounded a corner and went over a bump with a bang. The van's engine revved up again.

She opened and closed her mouth. "You mean we're at war?"

"That's right. They landed six battalions in Catina and are moving north. People are scared. They're running from the city."

"What about our army? Aren't they going to stop them?"

"They'll try, but I don't think they'll be able to."

They sat in silence as the van wound its way up what seemed like a never-ending road until, finally, it came to rest. She could hear the driver's door open and close. Moments later the back doors gapped open.

Rose lifted a hand to her face to block the sunlight. It made her head hurt. She followed the others out and saw, for the first time, the view of Aaronia from the top of the mountain. Skyscrapers by the thousands, standing one and two-hundred-stories high, stretched along a coast of rolling cyan colored water beneath a bright yellow sky going to gray on the horizon. Farther from the shore, the rooftops of thousands upon thousands of houses covered the foothills. There were also a few temples mingled into the mix, large majestic and beautifully maintained structures in an otherwise crumbling city. From this distance, the city was almost silent, just a dull hum.

She turned toward the mansion, which was more like a castle, clinging to the mountainside with a dozen pillars and pointed peaks.

"Impressive, isn't it?" asked the old man as they walked up to the side door.

"It's unbelievable. How many people live here?"

"A family of four," he snickered, "but they usually have dozens of guests staying with them as well."

"It doesn't seem right that there could be people so rich."

"It's not right. It's just the way it is."

A line formed at the door.

"What are they doing?" Rose asked as they waited their turn.

"They have a lot of expensive stuff," said the old man. "They'll get you to empty your pockets and search you when you leave."

"What happens if a worker is caught stealing?"

"Depends what you steal. If it's expensive, they'll cut off your hands."

"Cut off your hands!" Rose stammered, feeling a sudden coldness at her core.

"It's a death sentence," the old man said, grimacing.

"It's barbaric."

"They don't care. It's a deterrent and an effective one."

"What's in those crates?" she asked, pointing at a stack of them lined up on a flat clearing.

"They use crates like that to ship food and supplies in from other planets."

"From Talon?"

"Not from Talon. No. There are no farms on Talon. There's nothing but predators and cannibals on that planet."

"What planet then? I thought the other planets were worse off."

"They are worse off," the old man admitted, nodding, "but not because of food shortages."

"So they're selling food to Cronish?"

"Not to Cronish. To the rich."

"It's not right, but that's the way it is," she said sarcastically.

The old man grinned. "You're catching on."

They stood silent for a few minutes while the line shuffled forward. They were searched and directed to walk around to the back of the building.

The line had spread out. "You're not a mechanic, are you?" the old man asked quietly.

"I am."

"I saw the title of your book."

She looked down, and the title stared up at her. She put her head down. "I need the money," she mumbled.

"That wasn't too bright." He shook his head. "What if they find out?"

"I'll improvise."

He grimaced. "That's not going to work. A tokamak is complicated."

"I'll figure something out."

"Yeah," he snickered. "I guess you'll have to."

Leona

"I see we've arrived," Queen Leona said, stepping onto the bridge of the warship, *Leviathan*. The crew sat at consoles littered with screens and blinking lights in front of a command station. On the main screen was Uras, a red planet lacking an atmosphere and too far from the sun to be even remotely hospitable. On one of the many monitors, she saw a few round steel buildings standing on tall pillars scattered across the surface.

The location was ideal for planetary conferences, and that's what the facility was for. It was on neutral territory, owned by no one.

All attempts to de-escalate the conflict through diplomacy had failed, and the Athenian Warlord, Badoni, refused to negotiate with anyone who wasn't royalty.

She was in power. She could make decisions, and no one else. She'd have to end this nonsense herself, face to face.

She'd invited the dignitaries of the other planets to make a concerted effort even though she knew the pact was just a delusion. The other planets weren't prepared to fight a war, but it didn't matter. She could take care of things with or without them. She'd hash it out and settle their differences.

"Your Majesty," Captain Landon said, getting up from his command seat and dipping his head with his arms by his side.

She was wearing her favorite burgundy gown with a plunging neck, long frilly sleeves, and a swarm of bracelets on her wrists. She was escorted by her favorite general, General Steen, in a traditional gray uniform with a stiff collar and red pinstripes. Her attendant, Marina, small, dressed in black, with dark olive-green skin and straight black hair, was also with her.

The Athenian warship, *Sgoinneil,* loomed large on one of the view screens. It was slightly smaller and less modern than the *Leviathan*, yet it had up-to-date plasma cannons mounted on its sleek hull. She shuddered at the sight of it. "Is Emperor Badoni aboard that thing?" she asked.

"I imagine so," Captain Landon replied.

"May the gods help us," she said, looking up to the heavens.

"What do you think he's going to do?"

"I have no idea, but it won't be pleasant."

"He'll try to provoke you," General Steen said. "That's what he'll do. He'll try to make it look like it's your fault."

Leona looked at the other screens to see who else had arrived. The Volian High Priest's passenger ship, *Viper*, had no guns and was sort of rectangular like a crushed shoe box. Except for a few criminals and those who had chosen to become security guards or policemen, they were highly religious, not aggressive, and considered by all races to be neutral, but to her, Volians were spiders, creepy, and repulsive.

The Bacchian light cruiser, *Rahus* was ridiculous, the shape of an elongated fish with two plasma cannons mounted on its sides. It was absurdly small considering the size of their population, but the Bacchian Empress did not need massive warships. Her ships were small and amphibious. She took a defensive position behind an ocean filled to brimming with schools of submarines armed with phantom torpedoes. Her people lived under the ocean floor, like crabs, making them a difficult target.

Talon was a primitive planet, and the Talonian Chief, a giant, didn't have a single ship to his name. Leona surmised he had hired the small merchant ship out of Vole, *Kaskad*, cane-shaped but bulky, adorned with dishes, two towers, six engines, and dozens of square-framed hatches.

"What do you suggest I do?" she asked Steen.

"He's going to try to rattle you, get you angry, and force you into a mistake. What you have to do is ignore his insults, ignore them completely. Let him vent without losing your cool."

"Is my shuttle ready?" Leona asked.

"It is."

Without another word, she headed for the elevator, broad and square, with Steen and Marina falling in stride behind her.

"We've received a report of a strange-looking ship," Steen said as he walked, "from a freighter out in Lupid Belt."

"Strange how?" Leona asked as she stepped into the open elevator.

"The captain of the freighter said it looked alien."

The door shut.

"Don't be ridiculous," Leona grumbled. "There's no such thing. Is it armed?"

"He said he didn't see any weapons, but it's a massive ship, and it's headed for Cronos."

"It can't be Bacchian. Bacchians would never build a ship that big."

"The Athenians wouldn't build a ship like that either."

"How long before it gets to Cronos?"

"We're not sure but not long."

"I thought you said the freighter was at the Lupid Belt?"

"I did. This ship's moving very fast, so it's a question of how fast it can decelerate."

"And what do *you* think it is?" Leona asked as the door opened to the starboard flight deck.

"I don't know what to make of it."

She walked out past sleek needle-nosed fighters, stocky plasma cannon ships, and massive pudgy faced bombers towards her shuttle, her chariot. "Well, figure it out."

"Of course, Your Majesty."

The shuttle was sleek with folded wings and guns sticking out like needles on a pointed head. As they approached, its hatch folded down to provide a ramp.

She went in, found her seat, and thought about Badoni. He was godless and denigrating, a living devil. He complained bitterly about anything and everything. The way he went on, you'd think his planet was on the precipice of extinction. The most frustrating of his many shortcomings was his temper.

His behavior reminded her of her daughter's temper tantrums, the way she'd scream until she turned blue in the face. Yet her daughter, Charline, was shielded by youth. Badoni wasn't. But Steen was right, and she'd have to play it cool. Cool as a cuttlefish.

Leona's chariot lifted off and made the long descent to the surface of Uras and to a roof that slid open. The shuttle dropped down and landed inside the building. They waited as the roof closed, and the bay pressurized. Leona led the way with her entourage in tow. She trudged into the conference hall, filled with people, all talking, all different languages, and the sound was like that of a schoolyard.

There were dozens of Volian guards scattered around the circumference of the room. The ones standing by the door smelled of burnt ash. The walls were smeared with massive display screens, each showing images of the five participants' capital cities. She went straight to her place. The table was a long stretched out oval surrounded by swivel chairs of black leather with high pointed backs.

Leona hated having to travel for two days to a conference, but on the flip side of things, the leaders were all here. Each one cared enough to make the journey, and what's more, there was no gallery swamped with whispering people. More or less, they had the room to themselves. She sat. General Steen and her attendant stood behind her.

Empress Zeta of Bacchus entered. Leona thought she was shockingly beautiful for a Bacchian. Her dress was low cut, soft purple, and gold. She had a broad collar that extended straight out beyond her shoulders and circled her neck with intricate swirling designs. Bulky braids wrapped with flowers and jewelry were piled high on her head. An attendant followed, dressed in black, slightly crouched with his head down. That was the way of the Bacchians. Everyone was a slave. Leona hated them, their ideology, and the blue hue of their skin, everything about them.

The Volian High Priest, the Venerable Father Holla, wore the traditional red robe. His skin was a pale yellow with black creases, and his hands were folded together. He was followed in by two deacons who took their places behind his chair with their hands folded in constant prayer.

The Talonian Chief, more than twice Leona's height, came in alone and sat down, enduring gravity much more substantial than he was accustomed to. He had long hair, an over-sized nose ring dangling from his left nostril, and a vest made of intricate small bones, all tied together, on his chest. She wondered why he bothered to make the trip. He had no army, and no one cared what he thought.

Four warriors of the Athenian Imperial Guard burst through the doors and cleared the way for Emperor Badoni. Dressed in full battle armor, he strode awkwardly down the aisle, the gravity far too weak for his liking. He found his seat, took off his helmet, and smashed it down on the table. He sat down with his warrior escort falling in behind him.

The chairman entered. He was dressed like a monk, but his robe was gray instead of the traditional red. Everyone simultaneously donned headsets for translations.

"I'd like to call the meeting to order," the voice of the translator reported as the chairman began, "and welcome everyone. We'll begin with a brief statement from each of the leaders starting with Chief Eagle Eye of Talon."

There was a moment of silence as the Chief managed to stand on his second attempt.

"We're at the precipice of a crisis," the interpreter translated, "a crisis, not just on any one planet but on all planets. Millions on Bacchus are slaves in a world without light, without hope, and without a semblance of what it is to be human. Hundreds of thousands of Volians suffer from the toxic fumes created by volcanoes and are slaves to a doctrine that prevents them from taking the vital steps to abandon their toxic world. Billions on Cronos are homeless and starving, slaves to a dictatorship that promotes socialism that paralyzes their economy. And finally, millions of Athenians live in a world that's too cold to support life. If praise must be given, it ought to be given, not to those in power, yet rather to the powerless, who patiently bear the brunt of the many misdeeds and indecencies bestowed upon them."

Leona wondered if the Chief had ever been to any of the other planets. He most certainly didn't know what it was like to be the ruler of eleven billion people living in one thousand, eight hundred and forty-eight major cities on eleven different continents. Yes, there were homeless and starving people on Cronos, but that was no fault of hers. Her people were lazy and refused to work.

"On Talon, the people are more fortunate," the translator continued. "They don't live in a toxic world. They aren't slaves to doctrines or dictators. Nor do they have to face a world of poverty. They live a simple life, a life in harmony with the teachings of the Great Spirit. It's my hope that my people, their tolerance, and their lifestyle may serve as an example to the world, an example that will hopefully be sought after and replicated by the leaders of the other planets." He sat.

Good, Leona thought. *He kept it short.*

The chairman spoke again.

"Emperor Badoni of Atheni," the translator said.

Badoni stood. "You'll stop attacking our water tankers," he said as he repeatedly stabbed a finger at Empress Zeta of Bacchus, "or I'll send my warriors down into your rat-infested caves and wipe out your cities. I swear to you, nothing will remain. My people are a proud race faced with extremes. I'll not tolerate any lack of compassion from you or your profit-seeking rodents.

The chairman banged his mallet. "A point of order," the translator said.

"And as for you, Leona," Badoni said, turning towards her. "The Athenian residents of Catina aren't some sort of contagion."

"A point of order—"

"You're to leave them alone," Badoni continued. "They'll make their laws and govern themselves." He stared down into Leona's eyes before sitting.

"A point of order," the translator said. "The Emperor of Atheni will address the chair and not the leaders of other planets, and he will refrain from making threats. The Empress Zeta of Bacchus may speak next."

"Mr. Chair," the Empress said, standing. "Emperor Badoni would have you believe that all he wants is a drink of water, but of course, as we all know, Bacchian water is deuterium rich. It's a natural resource that belongs to Bacchians, and it's not free for the taking! But if the Emperor of Atheni would like to pay for the water, I can give him a very reasonable price. Say, thirty thousand tala per tanker." She sat down.

"Emperor Badoni," the translator said. "You may respond."

He rose. "I'll give you ten thousand tala, and you'll accept my generous offer, or I'll have your head put on a pike,"—the chairman pounded his mallet—"so I can look at you and remember this moment," he yelled out over the pounding. He sat down.

The chairman rose. "I remind you, Emperor Badoni, no threats, please. Empress Zeta. You may respond."

"Ten," she said, not a question, without getting up.

Leona was stunned. How could she cave in so easily?

"Was that an acknowledgment?" the interpreter asked.

She peered up at the Athenian warlord, her face turning ashen. "Yes," she said.

Leona put her hand over her mouth in shock. This was infuriating.

"The Empress of Bacchus has agreed to the terms of ten thousand tala per tanker as witnessed by the planetary council," the translator said. "The Venerable Father Holla, the High Priest of Vole is next."

The High Priest rose from his chair. "I'm truly amazed what a sinful man will do," he said, staring at Badoni. "I'd like to remind everyone that the gods of Uttara are watching. The afterlife will only house one hundred thousand people, and only the most devoted will be accepted, so guard your words, and be kind to those who share our universe. The gods of Uttara will surely punish those who don't follow their commands. Everything is of the gods, and the disposal of anything is sacrilegious." He sat.

Leona wondered if there was anyone in the room that took him seriously? Cronish held the true religion, and everyone knew the afterlife was for those who believed in the twelve gods of Uttara.

"Her Majesty, Queen Leona of Cronos," the translator said.

She stood. "Emperor Badoni dares to suggest that I have mistreated the Athenians in Catina. It's simply not true. They're treated no differently than anyone else, but let me be clear. If they don't like how they're treated, they can go back where they came from. I'm not in the habit of letting foreigners govern Cronos. Cronos is governed by me and me alone. Atheni shall remove their troops from Cronos, or I shall remove them." She sat.

"Emperor Badoni. You may respond."

Badoni stood. "Mister Chairman, Queen Leona's position is untenable. My people are moving to Cronos, not because we want to take her planet away but because our planet is dying. We have no choice. All I ask is that she let my people have their own little corner where they can govern themselves and live in peace." He sat and put on his headset.

"Her Majesty, Queen Leona of Cronos," the translator said.

She stood. "Sir, your people can live on my planet and do it in peace, but just like every other citizen of Cronos, they'll swear allegiance to the queen, pay taxes to the crown, and follow my laws. They will not, under any circumstances, govern themselves."

Badoni tossed his headset, got up, and marched out of the conference hall with his warriors flanking him.

Leona watched him go.

Rose

Drizzle from low lying clouds raked the rocky slopes. Rose sighed deeply as if the weight of the entire mountain was upon her. In front of her stood a shuttle in need of repair, and her head was pounding.

She went up the ramp and into the shuttle. It was brand new, strikingly beautiful, with soft yellow lights, and twelve cream-colored seats. At the back, an egg-shaped tokamak the size of a small fridge sat halfway up the wall embedded in tubular cylinders.

She pulled out her book and flipped through the pages looking for something that might help, but reading was difficult. Her head wouldn't stop drumming. Besides, the book was about how tokamaks worked, not how to fix shuttles. She put it back in her handbag, sat in the pilot's seat, and studied the control panel. She found a button marked *start* and pushed it. The screen filled with brightly lit icons, many of them flashing, none of them labeled. "Low field" was the message on the screen."

Low field. She mouthed the words. What the hell could that be? What field? She tried to reason it out. *The magnetic field,* she thought. *That's what it is. Where's the power plant?*

She knew there had to be a power plant. It generated electricity. She pulled open a few panels and found it—batteries, a gas engine, and a dripping cylinder.

"Hi there," —came a voice from outside the hatch.

"Oh?" she said aloud and put a hand on her chest. An unshaven man with greasy hair wearing a black leather jacket stood in the hatchway.

"Have you found the problem?" he asked

"I found a leak." She pointed.

He stepped in and studied it. "The separator. Well, if that's what it is, we'll have to plug it in and charge the tokamak that way."

Plug it in? she wondered. *Plug what in where?* She wanted to ask, but of course, she couldn't. She'd have to guess. She got up, went to the hatch, and stepped out into the drizzle.

There was a square box on the platform. She went to it and glanced back to see if greasy hair was watching. He wasn't. Not sure if she was doing the right thing, she opened it. Inside was a thick, long electrical cord. She searched the hull of the shuttle with her eyes and noticed a small trap door. Again, she went to it, not sure if it was what she hoped it was, opened it, and found a socket. She ran the cable towards the outlet, but it got tangled, and she had to roll up her sleeves, lift it out of the mud, and untangle it. It was a snake with a mind of its own, and she had to fight with it to get it plugged in.

When she got back on the shuttle, she was wet and covered in mud. Her shirt was clinging to her chest.

Greasy hair was sitting in the pilot's seat, reading her book. He peered at her wide-eyed and held the book up. "This yours?"

She nodded.

"It's kinda strange for a tokamak mechanic to have a book like this."

"I got it for my sister." She lied.

"It's in awfully rough shape," he said cynically. He turned it in his hand.

Rose didn't know what to say, so she said nothing.

"And I see you have an empty box of Rend in your bag."

She pointed to the gash on her forehead. "They're for my head."

He nodded. "You're not a mechanic, are you? You're a drug addict that found a book on tokamaks, and you thought you could come up here and fool us. Well, I'm onto your little scheme, and it's going to cost you."

She considered running, but before she could react, the ramp lifted, and the hatch closed.

"No!" she screamed. She raced to the hatch. "Let me out!"

"Calm down. I can make this worth your while."

"I don't do that," she said, breathless and shaking her head. "I won't."

"It's not that hard. Think of the money."

"Let me out." Her head was throbbing so badly that she felt compelled to hold it with both hands, like a basketball.

He sighed. "The Athenians are going to be here soon. They'll capture you, tie you up, and rape you. You don't want that, do you?"

"The army will stop them."

He laughed. "No, they won't. There's no chance of that. They're already at Palasia. That's not that far away."

He turned in his seat and started the tokamak. All but one of the icons went dark. She glanced back. A band around the tokamak lit up, and a muted sizzling sound quickly and steadily moved up in pitch and volume.

"I told you," Rose said bravely. "I don't do that sort of thing. Let me out." Through the window, she saw a woman come out of the mansion with two children, and an entourage of security guards, maids, and assistants streamed behind like a family of ducklings.

"Your wife's here," Rose said. "Open the hatch."

He glanced out the window. "You could come with us," he said, lifting his eyebrows, "and be my mechanic."

Rose shook her head. "I told you. I don't do—"

"You're a fool." He banged his finger down on the control panel, and the hatch opened. Rose scrambled out.

The foreman was following the family, walking towards her.

She went to him. "The shuttle's working."

"Well done," he said, smiling.

"I want to be paid," she snapped.

"What about that cable?" he asked, pointing at it.

Rose went and pulled it out. She fought with it until it was back in the box, nicely coiled. When she turned around, greasy hair was at the hatch with her handbag in his hand. He held it out, like bait.

She walked up to him and snatched it away.

He didn't say anything. He just smiled—a cynical smile.

Rose walked quickly to the door of the mansion and stood under the gable roof, dripping wet. The foreman came out and paid her. The shuttle took off, and she watched it go up.

"You'll have to wait if you want a ride down the mountain," the foreman said. "The van only goes down at the end of the day."

"Do you have any Rend?" Rose asked. "I've got a dreadful headache."

"You don't want Rend," he said. "That stuff is bad news. I'll get you some painkillers."

"Please."

He came back with a bottle of pills. She thanked him, took the bottle, downed two pills, and started walking. It was a long walk, and the drizzle was continuous. She was cold and wet. The painkillers dulled the pain in her head somewhat but were not nearly as effective as Rend. She needed to find more before she went crazy.

It took her a couple of hours to get down the mountain, and when she got onto the subway, she found it bizarre to be on a train devoid of people. A train going in the opposite direction swooshed by and was packed to capacity.

She got off. People were marching down the street, protesting the war, waving signs, and chanting, "Words! Not weapons! Peace! Not war!" Others were standing on the roadside, watching.

Across the street was a park, an area preserved years ago by the city for trees and leisurely nature walks. Her mother and father had brought her here as a young girl, yet now most of the trees were gone, and the space had been taken over by street people, their homes built from rusty garbage bins, steel doors, plastic siding, or wooden crates covered with plastic tarps.

She asked a beggar, "Do you know where I can get some Rend?"

"Nicko," he said, pointing at a trailer sitting under a tree deep in the park.

She weaved her way across the street and walked past the forlorn people, past barrel drums with fires, and past makeshift shelters, to the trailer. She knocked on the door, and it opened.

Nicko was fat. "Well, well, princess, come in. Let's see what I can do for you."

She smiled, climbed up the two steps, and moved into the trailer. The place was tidy, the bed was made, the small fridge was purring, and a half-empty cup of tea sat on the table. She sat down.

"Let me put a bandage on that ugly gash in your head," Nicko said, reaching to the top shelf of a cupboard. "Looks painful."

Rose waited.

He cleaned the wound up, put some ointment on, and taped a bandage to it. He put his supplies away and wedged himself into the bench seat opposite her.

"Thank you for doing that," Rose said, "and I like being called a princess."

"Well, you do look like her and not just a little, a lot."

"I look like who?"

"The princess. Princess Charline. You know. The queen's daughter."

"Yes. Of course." Rose didn't know. She'd never seen her.

"Next in line for the throne," he said. "About your age too." He was silent for a few seconds. "How can I help you?"

"Do you have any Rend?"

"You got money?"

"Worked for it," she stated, nodding.

Nicko smiled. "That's good. It's not easy to get work. How much did you make?"

Rose brought out her money.

"Whoa! You did well! Are you sure you don't want something little stronger?"

"Just Rend."

He pulled out three bottles and placed them on the table.

"No. The pills."

"Ah, the pills. Let me see if I have any. The liquid stuff is more effective, and if you ration it, it'll last a lot longer."

"No. No. I just want pills."

He got up, searched a drawer, and came back with three boxes.

"There's ten in each box," he said. "Should do you for a while. Forty dollars per box."

"Just one box," Rose said, shocked at the price. "I have to have enough money left over for a train ticket."

"You're going somewhere?"

She nodded. "Because of the war."

"Relax. They'll never make it to Aaronia," he said. "The Cronish army is on the way to Catina as we speak."

"The Athenians are already at Palasia," she said, her fingers combing through her hair. Her head was pounding.

"Don't worry." He raised a hand. "They can't win."

"They *can* win. We have to get out and fast. You're one of the lucky ones. You have money. You don't have to stay here."

"But there's no reason for me to go. This is my home."

"This is no time to get irrational. You can't stay. I'm telling you. Staying is a bad idea. They're coming."

"I don't think so," he said, shaking his head.

Rose took a long time to respond. Her headache was getting to her. She couldn't go on like this. She pushed forty dollars towards Nicko, picked up a box, and ripped it open.

Nicko snatched up the money and got her a glass of water.

She popped one of the pills in her mouth and drank the water. "I don't know what you're thinking, Nicko. You're placing too much value on your possessions, I guess. None of this is going to do you any good if you're dead."

"Where are you going?"

"I don't know, but I'm not staying here." She went to the door.

"Goodbye, princess."

"Goodbye," she said, sure she'd never see him again.

When she got to the edge of the park, she stood and watched as thousands of protesters marched down the street.

Ebony

Ebony peered out over the graying yellow sky and felt the wind beating down on her. She had gone home and got her money. Her brother was gone. Only now did she realize just how attached she was to him and how much of her thoughts, her plans, and her actions revolved around him. She couldn't stop the tears from streaming down her cheeks.

She turned onto a cobblestone street that snaked down the mountainside between houses and came upon a park filled with shelters for the homeless. On the road next to the park, people were marching and chanting. "Words! Not weapons! Peace! Not war!" Over and over, they sang, hundreds of them, in front of a wall of police wearing helmets with visors, gas masks, body armor, and holding shields. A policeman dashed forward, swinging his baton, but the mob parted quickly, the way a school of tuna scurries from a shark.

Ebony stopped. She had to get by them somehow. She had to get to the train and out of the city. She didn't have time for this.

Another officer ran forward, grabbed a man, and swung him violently to the ground. The man struggled to get away. Three other officers raced in, clubbed him, and handcuffed him. Blood streamed down his face as they led him away.

Ebony wasn't sure what to do. She edged forward. In a panic, she bolted, intending to make an end-run through the park, but as she did, the protesters were driven back by charging police, and she found herself among them.

A high pitched pulse blast hit a man and streaks of blue cut through the air above her, like fireworks. The sound was deafening. The people around her scattered. A plasma bolt jolted the woman next to her, and searing pain crossed her face as she fell.

Her body shook briefly, and she lay still. Ebony collapsed to the ground behind her. A plasma bolt ripped a man's neck in half, blood spurting across the pavement as he fell.

Further down the street, in front of an armored vehicle, another wall of police were lined up twenty abreast and three deep. Bolts of blue, sliced overhead, and in the park, people were being scythed to the ground like blades of grass.

Canisters were tossed, and Ebony was suddenly coughing, unable to breathe. Desperate, she got up, started to run, tripped, fell, and scraped her forearms. She closed her eyes, gritted her teeth, and endured the pain. Blood dripped from the small black stones embedded in her forearms. As she struggled to get a meaningful breath of air, there was a cluster of high-pitched sounds and blue streaks.

Then, as the police line moved past her, she managed to get just enough air to believe that maybe, just maybe, she wasn't going to suffocate. A policeman wearing a gas mask grabbed Ebony's arm and yanked her up, slapped a handcuff on one wrist, and, behind her back, the other wrist. A few yards away, they handcuffed a girl with long blond hair, big eyes, and a round face. She and Ebony were both dragged back and crammed into a crowded prisoner transport vehicle.

"Are you okay?" the girl asked.

Ebony lifted her arms and stared at the blood that covered them and dripped on the floor.

"Looks like it hurts," the girl said. She shook her head. "I shouldn't be here." She got up and tried to push towards the door as more prisoners boarded the truck. "Let me out!" she yelled. She was forced back to her seat as the other prisoners pushed their way in. "I need to talk to someone so that I can get out of here," the girl said to Ebony. "If I don't get out of here, I'll miss my flight."

"You're lucky to be alive," Ebony said, grimacing as she picked at a small stone embedded in her arm.

"You don't understand," she said despondently, shaking her head.

"All those people are dead, and you're worried about your flight?" Ebony said dryly, picking out another stone.

"I wasn't protesting!"

"There'll be other flights," Ebony said as the truck started to move.

"I work on a freighter," she said, her eyes glossing over. "It's not going to be back for over a year."

"A year? Wow. That's a long flight. Where's it going?"

"The Lupid Belt. Six months there, a month of mining, and another six months to get back."

"Must be a big ship?" She picked out another stone.

She nodded. "It pays well."

"How much?"

"Eighty-three thousand."

Ebony's jaw dropped. "Really?"

She nodded.

She adopted a sullen look. "What's your name?"

"Mika."

"I'm Ebony."

"It'd be nice to meet you under different circumstances," Mika said. "Have you done this before?"

"Protest? No. I wasn't protesting."

"I mean, have you been arrested before?" She brushed her hair back with both hands.

Ebony hesitated. "Yeah."

"Do the guards take bribes?"

"They'll take your money," Ebony snickered as she picked out another small stone, "but I doubt you'll get anything for it."

"Why would they shoot to kill?" Mika asked, grimacing. "The people were just waving signs."

Ebony gritted her teeth as she backed out a big one deep under the skin.

"It was a peaceful protest," Mika grumbled, holding her hands up in a show of disbelief.

"It was a stupid protest," Ebony stated, taking a break from her self-inflicted pain. "They think if we just give the Athenians what they want, the war will be over, but it's not true. The Athenians won't stop."

"They'll have to negotiate a settlement at some point," Mika insisted. "They can't kill everyone."

"There's no negotiating with the Athenians, and the queen knows it. We have to win this war."

The truck stopped. The doors opened. The prisoners were hauled out like sacks of potatoes and hearded into a brightly lit room. The police removed their handcuffs. The prisoners emptied their pockets, and their possessions were packed away in plastic bags.

Ebony and Mika were placed in a cell with a young woman who had a bandage on her forehead. Her clothes were caked in mud, but she was strikingly beautiful, with a slender olive-green face, full red lips, and dark eyebrows.

The bed frame was made of metal, and there was no mattress. Ebony tried lying on it, but it was tortuously uncomfortable. She sat on the floor and leaned against the concrete wall with the other girls.

"What's your name?" Mika asked.

"Rose," she said.

"I'm Mika, and this is Ebony," she said, tossing a finger.

"Listen," Rose said. "Do you hear that?"

There was the steady rumble of bombs landing somewhere off in the distance.

"I saw an Athenian on a train," Ebony said. "He told me they'd kill the men and rape the women."

"They can't keep us here. Can they?" Rose asked. "They have to let us out, don't they?"

"Don't worry," Mika said. "Our army is fighting them. They'll stop them."

"I don't think so," Ebony said. "The Athenian told me that they couldn't be stopped. They're not like us. When he was young, his mother got into a fight with his father. To avoid being killed, she had to stand up straight with her arms by her sides and let him swing his sword at her to prove she was brave. Can you imagine?"

"Sounds awful," Mika said, shaking her head.

"If we do get out, what are you going to do?" Ebony asked Mika.

"I'll have to go to the spaceport and hope that the ship hasn't left yet."

"Do they need crew?" Rose asked.

"Do you have any training?"

"I'm a mechanic."

"You got a degree?" Mika asked.

Rose nodded slowly.

"What about you, Ebony?"

"No. I don't have a degree. I'm in maintenance,"—she lied —"but I'm a good worker, and I don't care how nasty the job is."

"I don't want to get your hopes up," Mika said, "but if you want, we can go to the spaceport together. You never know. The captain might need more people."

"Okay," Ebony said.

"Me too," Rose said.

"Were you at the protest?" Ebony asked Rose.

"I was just trying to cross the street." Rose shivered and put both hands on her forehead.

"Yeah. Me too," Ebony said.

The conversation stopped. Hours went by. Rose and Mika dozed off, but Ebony couldn't sleep. She missed her brother, and she was worried.

Gradually, the rumblings of the bombs in the distance got louder.

A guard came in and opened the doors. "We're letting everyone out. The Athenians are closing in. We're leaving."

"What about our things?" Rose asked, rubbing her eyes.

"They're on the tables in the next room," the guard said.

Rose jumped up and briskly walked out.

Ebony woke Mika. They followed Rose and found their possessions on the table. Rose pulled a box out of her bag, popped a pill, and held her chin up to get it down. They all paraded out of the police station together.

It was early morning, yet the city's citizens were in the streets, leaving their homes, walking briskly, carrying their young ones, dragging suitcases, and urging each other to go faster.

"C'mon, girls," Mika said with a scooping hand. "We have to hurry."

Ebony glanced back at the early morning sky. The sounds of the battle were much louder outside. Off in the distance, there were flashes of blue and white, like an erratic strobe. She quickened her pace.

They got to the subway, pushed their way through the crowd to the train, and wedged themselves in like minnows in a can. They got off at the spaceport and ran across the terminal floor, dodging in and out of people pulling suitcases. On the other side of a glass window were tall white rocket ships standing beside iron towers. Passengers scrambled to board multi-car buses that went down roads to the towers.

Mika went straight to a counter labeled *Shipping*, where a young woman was waiting. "Selma!"

Selma turned, and upon seeing Mika, smiled broadly. Her black hair was short on one side and long on the other, and she was wearing a black leather jacket, unzipped, revealing a heavy cross on a chrome necklace. "Mika," she hollered, rushing in to hug her, "where have you been? The captain was furious when you didn't show up. He sent me down to find you."

"You mean the ship's still here?"

She nodded. "Engine problems."

"Selma, this is Ebony and Rose," Mika said, putting a hand out towards each.

"Hi," Selma said.

"Rose is a mechanic, and Ebony is a maintenance worker. Can we take them with us?"

"Take them with us?" Selma snapped her head back to stare at Rose's vesture. "I don't think so. The captain might be okay with another maintenance worker, but I don't think he wants a mechanic. He needs a macro fusion engineer."

The sound of a bomb exploding, much closer than the others, rumbled through the spaceport.

Mika glared at Selma apprehensively. "Selma? The Athenians are almost here. Can you make an exception?"

"The captain gave me an order," Selma barked back. "I'm not going to go back with just anyone."

"You can't just leave us here," Rose pleaded.

"We can let Ion take care of things," Mika said.

"Ion's failing right now," Selma stated. "We can't just wing it." She turned to look at Rose with her lips pressed together. "What do you know about tokamaks?"

"Hydrogen gas is ionized by a powerful electric current and controlled by a magnetic confinement field," Rose said, convincingly. "As a powerful electrical current is run through the vessel, the gas breaks down, electrons are stripped from the nuclei, and plasma is formed. The plasma is brought up to one hundred and fifty million degrees. It fuses and releases huge amounts of energy."

"So, you know your stuff?" Selma asked, rubbing the back of her neck.

"Yeah," Rose said. "I know my stuff."

"Okay. I guess you can come. I'll tell the captain—I don't know what I'll tell him, but I'll tell him something. Do either of you have any questions?"

"No," Ebony said.

"No," Rose echoed.

"Alright, we're off." Selma started towards the gate. "Ion taught Harley how to run the engine, so if you have any questions, Ion is the one to ask."

"Is Ion an engineer?" Rose asked, catching up.

"He's not a person," Mika chuckled. "He's the engine's AI."

"Oh," Rose said.

"I sure hope I'm doing the right thing," Selma said, staring wide-eyed at Rose as they walked.

"The captain will think you're a miracle worker," Mika assured her.

Another bomb landed, and the ground shook beneath their feet. Selma gave Mika a cursory look.

"Don't worry." Mika sighed. "Once we get to the ship, everything will be fine."

After Selma purchased tickets, they boarded a multi-car bus that moved across the tarmac towards a tall white rocket ship on the outer reaches of the field and took an elevator up the tower, an excruciatingly slow ride.

They could see the troops in full retreat. Bombs landed in a pattern to the south, steadily moving closer.

They boarded the rocket ship. Ebony took a window seat. There was a loud boom that vibrated through the hull, followed by an enormous mushroom cloud forming on the horizon to the southeast. They strapped themselves in and waited until all of the seats were full.

"This ship will take us to the space station, Danae High," Mika informed Rose and Ebony. "We parked one of the freighters shuttles there. We're going to get it and take it to the freighter."

Ebony nodded. The wait seemed interminable. Through the window, she saw a series of bombs detonate across the field. The last one blew up a rocket ship two towers over. She waited, and she worried the way she would if her neck was in a guillotine.

Then she heard the roar of the engines and could feel the ship start to shake. The g force pushed her down into her seat and made her arms heavy. She peered out her window and saw the airfield falling away. She saw rocket ships down on the ground explode and people running across the tarmac until clouds blocked her view. The shaking became more violent, and within seconds, the clouds were beneath her, and the shaking was going away. The yellow horizon of Cronos slowly grew more and more curved as the ship went up. A space station came into view, breathtaking, a giant spinning ring, many miles wide. Stationed around the space station were Cronish warships, each with two conning towers near the back and a bulbous body with six plasma cannon turrets, two each protruding from the rear, the sides, and the long sleek nose.

The rocket ship moved in, matched the station's rotational speed, glided between two mooring points, and hooked onto mooring lines. It swung into place, nose up, and instantly, Ebony felt the centrifugal force and the illusion of gravity. Passengers filed into an elevator that went down into the spaceport.

Inside was a valley with a river, mountainsides overrun with trees, tall buildings, luxurious houses, and a landscape that curved upwards in two directions with the shape of the tubular ring.

Ebony followed the girls into a driverless cab.

"Shuttle bay 534," Selma stated.

The cab went up the side of the mountain, a trip with a surreal view that took them up through the roof of the valley and down a tunnel that seemed to go on and on. Finally, the cab stopped in front of a shuttle, and they got out.

The shuttle was small, with windows all around. Inside were eight seats, a door at the back labeled *head* next to the tokamak, and at the front, a sleek dash with screens overhead that showed views from every side.

"How many shuttles does the freighter have?" Ebony asked.

"It has eight," Mika said. "This is our little shuttle. The others are bigger."

Ebony took a seat, and Rose sat beside her. Selma took the pilot's seat, and Mika, the co-pilot's.

The hatch closed, the shuttle bay door opened, and Selma fired up the ship's systems.

"Resolution Shuttle Eight, permission to launch," Selma said dryly.

"Resolution Shuttle Eight, stand by,"—came the reply.

"How many are in the crew of the freighter?" Ebony inquired.

"Counting us three, forty-five," Selma declared.

"How long is it going to take to get to the ship?"

"Not long."

"Resolution Shuttle Eight, proceed."

Selma moved the shuttle out of the bay and accelerated away from the space station.

Ebony thought of her brother. Was he in training, or was he fighting the Athenians right now? Was he still alive? Would she ever see him again? She was leaving Cronos for a year. She felt a wave of guilt.

"There it is," Mika said, pointing at a small white dot barely visible.

"What's the captain like?" Ebony asked.

"He's a good captain," Selma stated, "if you do what you're told."

"Are you going to be in trouble for recruiting me?" Rose asked.

"Maybe, but I think he'll be happy that we're back so soon. He doesn't like it when the ship has to wait."

When they got closer, Ebony could see the freighter shining bright with a conning tower near the front and engines dormant yet looming large at the back. She was overwhelmed by the size. Hundreds of containers were stacked one on top of the other with one side bulging like a pregnant whale. One of eight shuttle bay doors opened at the back of the tower as they approached.

"Welcome to your new home!" Mika exclaimed enthusiastically.

Rose

Rose followed Selma into the engine room and looked up at a three-story high sphere embedded in the deck, like a gigantic, nested egg. It was surrounded by consoles with chairs and screens, each with a different graphic image.

She'd been given her quarters, had a shower, and found some fresh clothes. A medic had looked at her head, put on a clean bandage, and offered her a painkiller, supposedly more potent than the one she had. She took one, and it didn't work, at least not nearly as well as Rend.

"This is Johan," Selma said, extending a flat hand towards an older man with white hair hanging from the sides of a bald head, "and Poppy," tall and thin, with long dark hair, and glasses on the end of her nose. "As you can see, this is a very old tokamak. Simple design. Should be simple to fix, but for some reason, the answer to the problem is evading us."

"I'll do my best," Rose said, trying to sound credible.

"Are you familiar with this model?" Johan asked, extending a hand towards the tokamak.

"Yes, yes, of course." She lied without hesitation, folding her arms across her stomach.

"It has a new integrated superconductor with a tape and coil structure," he said. "I don't have to tell you what that means."

"No, no. You don't."

"The captain's desperate to be on his way, so let him know the minute you make any progress," Selma said with a smile that only affected her mouth's corners.

"I will," Rose said.

"We're going to have to leave it with you for a bit," Johan said, getting up at the same time as Poppy. "We desperately need a break."

"No problem," Rose said, lowering herself into a swivel chair.

She waited until they were gone, grabbed her bag, pulled out her box of Rend, fished out a pill, and swallowed it.

Then she leaned back, closed her eyes, and waited for the drug to take effect. She couldn't help but think about her luck. This was a gigantic step up from her little shack back on Cronos. She'd visited Danae High, she had a job on a freighter, and she was going to the Lupid Belt. Incredible.

It didn't take long for the Rend to take effect. She felt better. She pulled her book out of her bag and continued reading. She looked at the tokamak in front of her.

"Ion, are you there?" she called out.

"Ion here."

Well, that's good, she thought. *The AI is responding.* "How's your love life?" she asked, smiling.

No response.

"Aren't you boring." She pursed her lips. "Can you start the tokamak?"

No response.

"Ion," she said louder, "can you start the tokamak?"

"Tokamak not responding," Ion replied.

Oh, she thought. *It responds when I say Ion.* "Ion, why not?"

"Checking the data bank for errors. No errors found."

"How could that be?"

No response.

"Ion, how could that be?"

"Opening troubleshooting application. Checking. No problems found."

What the hell is the matter with this thing? she wondered. *No problems found?* She went back to reading, and what she read gave her an idea.

"Ion, reset the default parameters."

"Reseting default parameters."

The lights on the consoles and the screens went dark. There was silence, like in a forest after a tree is felled. The lights on the console flicked back on, and the screens came back to life.

"Ion, are you there?"

Rose waited for a response, and none came.

"Ion, are you there?"

"Ion here."

"Ion, start the tokamak."

"Tokamak not responding."

"Interesting," she said. She went back to reading. Her book gave her another idea.

"Ion, list the procedures for starting the tokamak manually on terminal,"—she looked for a number—"terminal three four."

A long list came up on the main screen, and an image of the inner workings of the tokamak came up on another screen. Nothing was happening, and she didn't have a clue what the items on the list were comprised of.

"Ion, how's your love life?" she asked out of frustration.

Silence.

"Not going to answer me? Fine. See if I care."

More silence.

"Ion, does the tokamak have enough power?"

"Tokamak has sufficient power."

"Ion, run diagnostic."

"Running diagnostic."

Rose waited.

"Diagnostic complete. No problems found."

"Aren't you wonderful."

Silence.

The screen in front of her displayed a menu. She ran her eyes down the list. "Ion, go into protective mode," Rose murmured. *Might as well try everything.*

"Protective mode applied."

"Ion, start tokamak."

The screen filled up with error messages. Rose recognized one of them from her book. She flipped through the book and searched for the page where it talked about it.

"Ion, recalibrate the temperature setting, up ten thousand degrees.

"Recalibrated."

She was changing the parameters. Would this be okay? It's just ten thousand degrees. This thing can handle millions. She promised herself if it didn't work, she'd put the setting back where it was and leave the thing alone.

"Ion. Start tokamak."

The tokamak began to hum, and the hum moved up in pitch. The glass band around the tokamak went from clear to blue.

Rose glanced at the screen next to her. The simulation of the inside of the tokamak had a swirling mass of plasma. That's all it needed, a different mode and a higher temperature setting.

"Bridge to the engine room," a passionate voice barked over the intercom. "We noticed that the engine's running. Are we good to go?"

"Ah, yes. Yes. Good to go," Rose said, biting her lip.

"Ahead full,"—she heard the man say, his voice projected away from the mic. And to her— "My dear girl, you're wonderful. Well done." The connection was terminated.

Rose sat back in her chair, took a deep breath, and exhaled slowly. She could see the tokamak build up its power and felt the ship accelerate. She smiled. Her headache was gone. She'd be eating real food and sleeping in a real bed. Not only that, but she was a hero. She clenched her fists and brought them down hard on the arms of her chair. "Yes!" She was a frigging mad scientist!

Leona

"Your Majesty, we have to go," Marina said. "It's not safe. The Athenians will be here soon. There's no reason for us to stay."

An explosion shook the floor beneath them.

Leona had insisted on being on the northern outskirts of Aaronia, far enough away from the front to be reasonably safe yet not so far to be detached from the action. "Relax," she said, putting a hand on the bureau to steady herself. "There's still time. Is the shuttle here?"

"No, but it will be soon."

Another bomb landed, and the floor shook even more violently.

"Go and tell General Steen that I want to see him, and come back to get me when the shuttle arrives."

"No, Your Majesty! There's no time!"

Leona pursed her lips and glared at her.

Marina understood her meaning. She walked stiffly and quickly out the door.

Leona needed to think. What the hell had gone wrong? They outnumbered the Athenians two to one. Why were they losing? She needed answers, and General Steen was the only one she could trust to give them. The others were too self-preserving. Yes, they did their job, at least she assumed they did, but when placed on thin ice, they lied. She knew they were lying, and they knew she knew, yet they lied anyway. It was sickening. Cowards, every last one of them. Afraid to face the consequences of their actions. Sickening. Except for Steen. He was different. He had some backbone.

There was a knock at the door.

"Come."

Steen stepped in and bowed.

"Tell me what has happened," Leona snapped.

Another bomb landed, this one farther away. Steen waited until the rumble dissipated.

"Your Majesty, the Athenians landed three more brigades south of here. General Douglas was assigned the task of bringing a full five divisions down from the northern province of Oshatta to deal with them. Unfortunately, he didn't understand the urgency of the request. Possibly, he was distracted—"

"What kind of a moron doesn't know to move quickly when there's a war on?" Leona asked with a raised voice. "Especially this war? To a man, everyone knows what the Athenians are capable of."

"I presume he believed that the nine divisions in place would hold—"

"Is he an idiot?" Leona snapped.

"Well, no. It's a reasonable assumption in different circumstances."

"These aren't different circumstances," she shrieked, her chin high. "Anyone can look at what's happened and see a crisis. My troops are falling like leaves in a forest." She raised her hand and stabbed a finger towards Steen. "I want him put up against a wall and shot. My commands have to be obeyed expeditiously." She flattened her hand and pushed it back in a broad sweeping gesture. "There's no room for lily-livered generals making silly assumptions and taking leisurely strolls to the front. This is a war damned by the gods. We're fighting for our lives here!"

General Steen didn't reply. She waited for him but realized that he was too apt to reply. "You heard me. Shoot him. Put him up against a wall and shoot him. I want to make an example of him. I want every officer to know that I mean to win this war, and nothing will get in my way. Especially not my own general's stupidity."

He bowed and left.

A series of bombs landed, one after another. A moment later, Marina was back. "The shuttle's here, Your Majesty."

"Alright. It's about time. I'm looking forward to seeing my daughter. Does she know I'm coming?"

"Yes, Your Majesty."

Perhaps she'd be able to think more clearly away from the front, away from the constant bombing. She marched out the door with Marina in tow. The shuttle waited with a scattering of soldiers surrounding it. The air was filled with the familiar smell of plasma, like burning rubber—she'd been to enough ceremonies where they'd fired guns to honor some dead dignitary to know the smell. Her eyes watered from the smoke. Marina, ready as usual, came forward with a tissue.

They boarded, and the moment she was seated, the shuttle lifted off. Out of her window, she could see the masses of Cronish troops and vehicles retreating through the streets directly below. Beyond the city was a solid wall of Athenian tanks and cannons stretched out in an arc, throwing blue streaks into two-hundred-story buildings that were being toppled like bowling pins.

"Is that two divisions?" she asked Steen, sitting across from her.

"No. As I told you, they were able to get another three brigades in last night."

"What are they doing?"

"They're leveling the city."

"Why?"

"An assault through the city would be costly. This way, they're opening the terrain and conserving their numbers."

"But I thought they were ferocious fighters that'd stop at nothing. This is slow and calculated."

"They're true warriors and very clever. They know when to strike and when to stay back. They won't throw men away unless the gain is much greater than the loss."

"Are there civilians in those buildings?"

"Some. Most have left the city."

"How can nine divisions be pushed back by just three?"

"You're not going to like the answer to that."

She lifted her eyebrows.

"Our troops are terrified of them."

She turned back to the window and watched dozens of Cronish jets, low to the ground, streak in towards the Athenian line and fire missiles. Massive explosions cut into the Athenian ranks, but their artillery fired, and several of the fighters were turned to balls of fire. The attack was over in minutes, and when the dust settled, the Athenians were still there, still looking as menacing as they did before the attack.

Their tanks seemed to be impervious to attack. She was going to have to come up with a better plan. She wanted this over with quickly.

The shuttle climbed higher, and the front shrank away.

Ebony

When Ebony had boarded the *Resolution*, the ship's medic had cleaned up her arms and treated them with antibiotics. It had been a week now, and they were healing. Selma gave her quarters and a cleaning job, and she'd done it every day.

She kept to herself, mostly, and she worried about Keldon. How could he be so stupid? If only the war would end, yet she knew it wasn't going to. It was going to go on for months. Maybe longer.

She didn't want to attend the briefing, yet Selma had said she had to. In her hand, she held the initiation pamphlets that Selma had given her. She sat at the end of the back row of the gray padded seats curled around the auditorium's stage. She wanted to be as far away from the action as possible. She didn't see why she had to be there. She was just a maintenance worker. Maintenance workers needed to know how to do their jobs and nothing else.

Crew members occupied more than two-thirds of the seats. The man on the stage was heavy, wearing a black uniform jacket and officer's cap. The olive skin around his eyes showed signs of aging, and a salt and pepper beard covered his face.

"Welcome," he said. "For those of you who are new here, I'm Captain Rogan. As I'm sure you know, the war isn't going well on Cronos. The Athenians have occupied the southern continent of Taavi and taken the provinces of Oshatta and Cornelia. All seven major cities in those provinces have capitulated, and there are hundreds of thousands of casualties."

"May the gods rest their souls," an attractive young man said, standing on the stairs and leaning against the wall.

Ebony's eyes lingered.

"As a result, our charter has changed," Rogan said. "We've been pressed into service and ordered to head to the Thalson Belt. We are to mine titanium, iridium, and palladium, and return to Cronos as fast as possible."

"But this isn't a warship," Mika said, grimacing.

"People are dying," the attractive one sneered. "We have to do our part."

"The government has pressed all commercial ships into service," Rogan stated. "So, in essence, this is a warship now. The army has conscripted every one of us."

"Is the tokamak operational?" the attractive one asked.

"No, Troy, it's not," Rogan said gravely.

Troy. Ebony made a mental note. *Nice name.*

"Selma," he said damningly, giving her a dagger stare, "brought in a recruit without checking her credentials. The recruit put the engine into protective mode," he said, shaking his head, "which, of course, isn't—" He sighed. "Anyway, the tokamak is out of commission. We're moving and in the right direction, but not very fast. It looks like we're going to be in this neighborhood for a while. "I've asked Her Majesty's Royal Service for an escort, but they just don't have enough warships to cover every contingency."

"You mean we're a sitting duck," shouted a young woman with spiked hair and heavily tattooed arms.

"Yes, well," Rogan said, "we're going to have to be on alert around the clock."

"Damn Athenians," Troy fumed. "The gods will punish them."

Religious, Ebony thought. *That's good.*

"What are we going to do if we come into contact with them?" Miss tattoo asked.

"We'll have to come up with a plan for that," Rogan said.

"We'll have to surrender," Miss tattoo said decisively.

"We can't surrender," Ebony blurted out, giving her head several stiff little shakes.

The entire room turned to look at her.

"My dear girl," Rogan said, beckoning. "Why are you so far away from the rest of the group? Please come up and sit here." He pointed to an empty chair between Mika and Selma, dead center in the front row.

Ebony froze. This was her worst nightmare, and she didn't want to go.

"Come, my dear," Rogan insisted, spinning a hand. "We haven't got all day."

Ebony got up and started towards the front of the room. Her pamphlets fell from her hand and floated down the stairs like confetti. She scrambled after them, lost her footing, and fell awkwardly with her feet out in front of her. She crashed onto her back and bounced down several steps like a clown. She closed her eyes and gritted her teeth, waiting for the pain to pass.

Troy came rushing over to help her up.

"I'm okay," she said as she grabbed his hand and pulled herself up. She smiled and squeezed his hand.

He picked up her pamphlets and gave them to her.

"Thanks." She went to the chair in front of Rogan and sat down.

"I don't think I've seen you before," Rogan said. "What's your name?"

"Ebony."

"Ah, yes. Maintenance, right?"

Ebony nodded.

"So, Ebony, tell us why we can't surrender."

There was a long silence.

"Come on now," Rogan insisted, "tell us."

"It's just that—well, I mean, they're not like us."

"In what way?" Rogan asked.

Ebony shifted her gaze. "They're not like we think they are. They don't take prisoners. They're going to kill everyone except"—another long silence.

"Except who?" Rogan asked.

Ebony hesitated. "Except the women. They keep them as sex slaves, a fate worse than death."

"That seems a bit extreme," Rogan said.

"It's true," Ebony said. "An Athenian told me."

"When was this?" Rogan queried.

"The day after they invaded Catina."

"An Athenian told you?" Miss tattoo asked. "How were you talking to an Athenian the day after they invaded?"

"He was an outcast," Ebony mumbled, barely audible.

"He was probably trying to scare you," Troy said.

"Yeah. Well, it worked." Ebony asserted. "He was leaving Cronos. He said they'd kill him too because he was weak. They do that, you know. They kill their own people if they're weak or injured. Now my brother's on the front, and I'll probably never see him again." She got up, threw her pamphlets, ran up the steps, crashed through the door, and scurried down the passageway as tears welled up.

Jen

Jen Erich was marched into the Resolution's brig by two security guards. One of them removed her handcuffs and tossed his head towards the cell door. "In you go."

"Not with that!" Jen snapped, looking down at a blue lying on a cot. The sight of her made her skin crawl. "Put me in another cell." She pointed at a cell holding an olive, slim, drawn face, a bandage on her forehead, and long dark hair. She was attractive, sort of.

The guard was a bear. He forcibly grabbed Jen by the shoulders, shoved her in, and slammed the cell door.

Jen ground her teeth. There was no reason for him to put her in with the blue. It was cruel. She looked around. The cell was disgusting, narrow with two cots, one on either side, covered with squalid gray blankets. Deeper in, there was a small sink, filthy, and a toilet with no seat. The smell was dreadful, like an outhouse.

She climbed onto the empty cot, her back against the wall, her legs crossed, and her arms folded.

The blue was short, even for a blue, only half the length of the cot. Her skin was abnormally dark, and her head was wrapped with a black cloth.

"I don't suppose you're going to tell me your name?" the blue asked.

"Just mind your own damn business," Jen retorted.

"Okay. No problem. It's just that I was kinda thinking that if we're going to be sharing this cell for the next year or so, maybe it'd be better if we got along."

"No chance of that," Jen barked. *Chirpy thing,* she thought.

"Understood," the blue said.

"It's not going to be a year," slim declared. She seemed irritable like she was going through something.

"Why's that?" chirpy asked, sitting up, eyebrows squished together.

"We're not going to the Lupid Belt."

"Where are we going?"

"The Thalson Belt."

"That's better," chirpy said, her face lighting up. "That's not far at all. Why are we going there?"

"The *Resolution* has been conscripted and given orders."

"Meaning?"

"The ship and the crew are in the army now," slim said sullenly.

For some reason, slim didn't seem to be comfortable with that, but Jen was. She wanted to see every last one of those damn pinks slaughtered. She'd be happy to help out with the killing.

"Including you?" chirpy asked.

"Yes," slim said. "I'm a conscript now. And you too. We're at war."

"Not me," chirpy said. "I'm not."

"So, let me get this straight," Jen said. "You want to live with us because we're free, but you're not willing to fight when our freedom is threatened. Is that it?"

"If I were going to fight, I would have stayed on Bacchus and fought there."

"You're a bloody coward. That's what you are."

"I'm not a coward. I just don't believe that fighting is the answer."

"Like I said. You're a coward. How long have you been in here?" Jen asked slim.

"Three weeks."

"What are you in for?"

She didn't reply right away; she fidgeted for a few seconds. "I pretended to be a macro fusion mechanic," she said quietly.

Chirpy lifted an eyebrow. "I have to hand it to you. That's very creative."

"It was necessary," she said dryly.

"Are you the reason the ship isn't moving?" Jen asked, stressing each word.

She pursed her lips and ignored her. Her hands were folded together, and her fingers twitched constantly.

"You are, aren't you?" chirpy asked.

Rose shed her skin. "Yeah. I'm the reason."

"And what about you, chirpy?" Jen asked. "Why are you here?"

"The name's Itzel. I'm a stowaway."

"And what's your name?" Jen asked slim.

"Rose." She was still twitching.

"Did you come here from Aaronia with Selma?"

"Yeah."

"What was it like down there?"

"Not good."

"Is it true? Was it was razed to the ground?"

"I got out before that."

It was hard for Jen to believe that Aaronia was razed to the ground. Was the Cronish army was utterly useless?

"I was on the space station," Itzel said. "Missed the whole thing."

"You were on Danae High?" slim asked. "I thought that was just for the rich. What were you doing there?"

"It's not just for the rich. Common people work there. But in a war, a space station isn't exactly the safest place to be, so I decided to get out. There were no passenger flights, at least none I could afford, so I slipped into a storage compartment on a shuttle and landed here."

"Very courageous," Jen said. "I don't suppose you could get some guts and go back where you came from."

Itzel tensed up. "What do you know about Bacchus?" she snapped. "You've never been there. You don't know what it's like. Danae High is a paradise in comparison. You don't have the right to judge me, you bastard. Why are you here? What's a security guard doing in a prison cell?"

"Piss off," Jen snarled. *Damn blues. So incredibly self-righteous.*

"We told you why we're here," slim said. "Now, you tell us why you're here."

"Sure. I'll tell you. Someone said something I didn't like, so I beat the crap out of them. That okay with you?"

Slim didn't respond. There were a few minutes of silence, and then an alarm sounded, muted and low pitched.

"What's that?" chirpy asked, getting up.

Jen knew what it was: all hands to stations. She studied slim. She was agitated, not just because of the alarm.

The alarm didn't stop; it just kept going. A guard came running in, glanced inside the cells, and ran from the room.

"Hey!" Itzel called out after him. "What the hell's going on?" She turned to ask slim, "What's happening?"

"Could be just a drill," slim said.

Jen tilted her head and raised an eyebrow. "Would a guard run in and out like that if it was a drill?"

In a distant hallway, there was the pounding of feet.

Jen jumped up and went to the cell door. "Hey! Let us out of here! Heeelp! Heeelp!"

A guard came into the room and punched a keypad on the wall. "An Athenian warship has been spotted. Everyone's to go to the shuttles." The guard ran from the room as the cell door lock clanked, and the doors swung open.

Slim bolted straight to the locker where the prisoner's possessions were kept.

"What the hell are you doing?" Jen yelled. "Forget that! The pinks are coming! We have to go!"

Slim ignored her, pulled out a handbag, and started digging through its contents.

Jen left her behind. She went through a hatch, down a long passageway, up a flight of stairs, and into the shuttle assemblage area. The shuttle bays were lined up side by side, and crew members were scrambling to get to them. The third, fifth, and sixth shuttle bay doors were already closing.

Jen ran to the shuttle in the last bay, the small shuttle that seated eight. She got on. Chirpy came in behind her. Poppy, Troy, Selma, and Mika were on board. The new recruit got on behind her, the one who made a fool of herself at the briefing.

Jen closed the hatch, took a seat, and strapped herself in. She waited, counting down the seconds as the inner bay door came down. There was a banging on the hatch, and slim's head was in the window.

Jen got up and opened it. "You're damn lucky we didn't leave without you," she said as she got on.

Slim went straight to the last empty seat at the back.

Jen closed the hatch again and went back to her seat.

The outer bay door opened, and the shuttle blasted out into space. Three other shuttles were out in front of them, moving up and away from the freighter.

"Follow them," the new recruit yelled, pointing up.

"Shut up," Troy scolded. "You're not in command. Let Mika fly the shuttle."

"We have to stick together," the new recruit said.

A blue cannon bolt hit one of the shuttles in front and above them. It immediately exploded. There was no sound, and it played out like a silent movie.

"Don't go up," Troy told Mika. "Keep the freighter between us and the warship, so they don't have a clear shot."

Blue bolts streaked above them. One of the other two shuttles, a bit higher, was hit and exploded.

"Lower," Troy said. "Go down." He had a hand in a fist and was clutching it with his other hand.

Jen looked up at a screen showing the view to the rear. She could see two Athenian assault shuttles attached to the hull of the freighter.

A blue cannon bolt hit the one other remaining Cronish shuttle and ripped it open. Its fuselage spun erratically up and away. Most of its passengers were thrown from the hole in its side like breadcrumbs tossed to the birds. Mika dove the shuttle lower. The freighter fell away, becoming smaller and smaller on the screen until it completely vanished.

Leona

Queen Leona peered out the shuttle's side window at the city of Ganya, with its crumbling skyscrapers, its scores of decrepit, gable-roofed houses, and at billowing smoke from the barrel fires the homeless maintained to stay warm. In the heart of the city was the Pacuttara Temple with beams of sunlight shining down on it like the stretched out fingers of the gods, illuminating the intricate mosaic of multi-colored chiseled stones and ornaments.

The shuttle landed in the street directly in front of the temple.

Leona loved these moments. It was time for her to show the people how divine she and her daughter were. "Keep your chin high, Charline," she said as she got up. "Try to look like a princess for a change."

"I'm not a princess," Charline complained. "I'm a prisoner. Keep your chin high. Hold your skirt. Use the small spoon. What does that sound like to you? Freedom?"

"Don't be like that," Leona scolded.

"Don't be like that," Charline mimicked with overtones of whining. "Sit up straight. Smile. Curtsy. Keep smiling. I'm constantly being told what to do, and I don't want to go to your damn sermon, yet that doesn't matter, does it? My life isn't my own. I'm treated like a child."

Leona decided to ignore her. She went to the hatch, waved at the cheering crowd, and stepped out. The city, with its tattered houses, belonged to the people. That was their world. But the temple belonged in another world, her world.

Its base was square with pillars at its corners. Its door was a massive pointed arch. Its peak stretched into the sky and was topped off with twelve crosses, one for each of the gods. This was what she was here for, the grandeur, the pageantry, the spectacle.

Guards held back the crowd as she came up the walkway and climbed the steps. She checked to make sure Charline was following. She was, her chin up, her strides regal, like a lioness. She complained, but she knew her place. She had a role to play and an important one. She'd be queen one day.

Like an expectant child, the deacon stood in the arc of the door, waiting for her. His face lit up when she reached out her hand. "Welcome, Your Majesty. It's good to see you well." He bowed and kissed her hand.

"Thank you, Deacon Staford. You're very kind." She couldn't read him. All of the clergies seemed to be able to put on a face, an impenetrable smile. It didn't bother her. They were all powerless, locked into a world of penance and absolution. There was little room for creative thinking.

She strode into the temple with an air of supreme confidence. These were her people, well dressed, even though she knew they were impoverished. They filled the church and padded the walls with more bodies. She strode down the aisle beneath massive stone pillars, surrounded by intricate carvings, statues, and stained glass windows, to the first of many rows of shiny wooden pews.

She sat down on the hard bench, folded her hands in front of her, and smelled the incense.

Charline sat beside her.

The priest entered from the chancel's side, his long white robe flowing behind him, a golden cross on his chest, a crimson scarf draped around his neck, and a tall pointed white miter with gold trim crowning his head. He mounted the pulpit and waited for silence.

The silence came slowly, but it arrived.

"The Messiah is coming," he said firmly. He held out a fist. "The Sacred Writings tells us that many centuries ago when the Messiah was preparing to return to Uttara, the disciples asked Him, 'When are you coming back?' He answered, 'When the devil is upon you, and the angels have called for me, I will return.'"

He paused and looked over his flock.

"And now, the devil is upon us and has invaded our sacred planet. 'Watch and focus,' the Messiah said, 'because the devil is seeking to distract you from understanding the signs of my return.' But my beloved people, do not forget this one thing,"— he held a finger in the air—"that, for the gods of Uttara, one day is as ten thousand years, and ten thousand years is as one day. The gods are long-suffering toward us, not willing that any should perish, yet wanting that all should come to repentance."

He paused again, stepped out from behind the pulpit, and raised an arm high in the air.

"Don't be deceived," he said with a raised voice, "by people coming in the name of the Messiah claiming to be Him." He walked across the stage and stopped. "Your only safeguard is to turn to the Sacred Writings alone for answers. Behold,"—both arms shot out to his sides—"every eye will see Him. There will not be a person on Cronos who is unaware of the Messiah's return. The Sacred Writings tells us what the Messiah said. 'I will come,"—he moved his hand in and out with each word—"like the brightness of lightning illuminating the entire sky.'" His fingers parted, and his hand circled above him. He moved like a puppet with the gods pulling his strings. "'I will arrive with power and great glory and with the sound of a great trumpet that awakens the righteous dead who are gathered from the ends of Cronos. Watch, therefore, and pray always that you may be counted worthy to escape all these things that will come to pass, and you may stand before me.'"

Once again, he paused.

"When the Messiah returns to Cronos, the Athenians who are left alive will call for the rocks and hills to fall on them because they cannot look upon His face. The Messiah will invite the Cronish soldiers and citizens who die to return to Uttara with Him to enjoy an eternity with no more tears, pain, or suffering. Let us pray."

The priest put his head down. They all put their heads down, like a flock of starlings moving in unison. He prayed aloud, and the masses answered his prayer with the memorized lines of a language long forgotten. The prayer went on and on until finally, he lifted his head.

"May the gods bless the brave soldiers who are fighting the devil south of here. They tell me that the Athenians have landed twenty-two divisions in nine provinces. Many of the cities have been wiped out to the point of being devoid of people. Others are just barely clinging to life. Some are alive at this moment, who'll not be alive tomorrow. Yet the Athenians will not win this war. Our soldiers will stop them. When they've been defeated, there will be time for sorrow. In the years to come, people will remember these brave men. Allow them dignity in death. Bury them properly, and mark their graves. The gods will do their best to bring our soldiers home, but they can't save everyone. The devil works against them. May the gods bless you and your loved ones. May the Messiah be with you."

Leona rose, and everyone waited while she and Charline made their way out. She went straight to the shuttle. The guards lined the route. As the shuttle lifted from the ground, she watched the people file out of the church.

"Well, that was a complete waste of time," Charline said as she buckled herself into her seat.

"Nonsense," Leona said. "The people need to see their rulers. We give them hope and a sense of purpose."

"Hope? What hope? So far, the Athenians have achieved every one of their objectives and in record time."

"Please," Leona said. "try to be civil."

"I asked General Steen how he was planning to stop the Athenians, and the answer he gave me was ludicrous. 'It'll be over in a week,' he said. Huh? How's that possible? Has he got some sort of secret weapon up his sleeve?"

"General Steen knows what he's talking about."

"There's no way it's going to be over in a week. Or a month. We should be asking the other planets for help."

"My dear girl," Leona said, her voice wavering. "You're not to fret over this. Everything will be fine. Just let General Steen do his job. He's an experienced officer, and he doesn't need your advice."

"If you ask me, the sermons can wait. The war is what we should be focused on."

"We have to attend the sermons because the gods are watching us, and don't you forget it. Your power comes from them."

"If we have any power, and I don't see that we do, it comes from the people," Charline said, "not the gods."

As the shuttle continued to rise, Leona gazed down on a city that seemed endless. *Oh, my dear girl,* she thought. *You are so naive.*

Ebony

It was Ebony's turn to sit in the pilot's seat. Troy had spent the better part of an hour showing her the shuttle's controls and how to use them.

They'd escaped from the Athenians, but now, days later, they had another problem. The shuttle's air was depleting. Mika had said that people use less oxygen when they sleep, so everyone was out cold. Ebony wondered how they could do that, knowing they only had hours left to live?

She slid down in her seat, put her feet up, and studied a screen that moved from one star pattern to the next. Her eyelids became anvils, and she started to drift, but she caught herself, brought her feet down, and sat up straight. No, she wasn't going to sleep. She wasn't going to wake up gasping for air. She'd live every second to the end. If it was a struggle, that was fine with her.

She forced herself to stare at the display screen, at the star patterns, at the flashing dot. There was a flashing dot on the screen. *There's something out there,* she realized. She tossed her hair aside, put her fingers on the console's screen, and separated them, enlarging the image.

"Troy," she said, slowly backing her head away from the screen. She studied his frozen posture. "Troy," she said louder.

"What?" he mumbled, opening his eyes.

"Look!" Ebony exclaimed, pointing at the screen.

Troy's eyes widened. He sat up. "Enhance it."

"It *is* enhanced."

"Is it coming towards us?"

"I don't know." She leaned forward to get a closer look.

"Head towards it," Troy said.

"You must be joking."

"We're almost out of air. Either we get on that thing, or we're dead."

Ebony didn't want to head towards it. She'd much rather suffocate.

"What the hell is that?" someone asked from behind.

Ebony looked to see who it was. It was the security guard, Jen. She was tall, broad-shouldered, had muscular arms, short brown hair, close eyes, and seemed to be upset with the world.

"Yeah," Poppy said, rubbing her eyes. "What is it?"

"We don't know," Troy said.

The strange-looking ship slowly grew on the screen. It had no lights, was saucer-shaped, and was at least three or four times the size of the *Resolution*.

"What in the world?" Ebony asked softly, as the true size of the ship became evident. The thought of getting on it was gut-wrenching. Scary beyond belief. It wasn't Cronish or Bacchian or Athenian. It was too big, too strange, and too intimidating to be anything but alien. "Is there anything like this in the database?" she quietly asked Troy, drawing her lower lip between her teeth.

He tapped his fingers across his console. "Nothing," he said. The screen in front of him displayed the words, "No matches."

"How big is that thing?" Mika asked, awake now.

"It's big," Troy said soberly.

Ebony glanced back. Everyone except Selma was awake now. Itzel was standing on her chair at the back.

"It's not from here," Rose said from the back of the shuttle. "It must be alien."

"It's not like anything we're used to seeing," Jen said, "but that doesn't mean it's—"

"There's no such thing as aliens!" Poppy snapped, shaking her head.

"What is it?" Ebony scowled.

"It's just an old ship," Poppy said. "Centuries old by the look of it."

"Where do you think it came from?" Jen asked.

"No idea," Poppy said. "Try calling."

Troy donned a headset and pressed some icons on his console's flat interface. "*Resolution Shuttle Eight* to whoever is out there. Can anyone hear this transmission? Come in."

There was a long silence.

"*Resolution Shuttle Eight.* Can anyone hear me?"

"I kinda doubt they speak our language," Rose said after another long silence.

"*Resolution Shuttle Eight.* Hello. Answer, please."

The ship was closer now. Ebony could see more detail. "Their technology *must* be different from ours," she said with a hand in the air.

"There doesn't seem to be any light coming from it," Jen said.

"Maybe they're all dead," Poppy mused.

They waited, and the image slowly got larger on the screen.

"Looks like nobody's home," Ebony said.

"Whether they answer our calls or not," Poppy stated, "we're going to have to go aboard."

"What if there isn't any breathable air on that thing?" Jen asked.

Again, silence.

"It must be alien," Ebony said.

"Stop it, Ebony!" Troy scolded, turning in his chair to face her. "There's no such thing as aliens."

"Look at it!" Ebony exclaimed. "What the hell else could it be?"

"Where's it headed?" Rose asked.

Troy checked his screen. "It's headed straight for Cronos."

"From where, though?" Poppy asked, "What direction?"

Troy put his fingers on his screen, pushed them together, and pressed an icon that displayed a line on the screen that went out to another system. "The only thing in that direction is"—he narrowed it again—"Uttara."

"Oh, for heaven's sake," Jen said, throwing a hand to her forehead. "Here we go. You're going to say that the gods sent it, aren't you?"

"You can believe what you want to believe," Troy said, "and so can I."

"You're going to say it's written in the Sacred Writings, aren't you?"

"Relax you two," Poppy said. "Are there any other solar systems in that direction?"

Troy turned to look at his screen. "Nope, not a reasonable distance away. Just Uttara."

"No system is a reasonable distance away," Jen said, rolling her eyes.

The shuttle fell silent.

"What're we going to do?" Ebony asked, clutching her hands.

"Try calling them again," Poppy said. "If that doesn't work, we'll go aboard."

"That's kinda risky, isn't it?"

"Very," Poppy said, "but we can't just do nothing. We're running out of air."

Selma woke up, rubbed her eyes, looked up at the screen, and put a hand over her mouth.

"*Resolution Shuttle Eight* calling incoming ship," Troy said. "Come in."

Silence.

"Troy, you're going in," Poppy barked.

Troy nodded, ripped off his headset, and got out of the co-pilot's seat.

"Ebony, you can make yourself useful and go in with Troy."

"Me?" Ebony complained, her jaw slack.

"I don't need a song and a dance," Poppy scolded, shaking her head, "Just do it, okay?"

There was a long silence. "Okay," she said meekly.

"You can go in too, Rose."

Rose took a deep breath and exhaled. "I don't—"

"It's your fault we're in this mess," Poppy snapped. "It's your fault that the rest of the crew is dead. The tokamak could have been repaired if you hadn't messed it up."

Rose put her head down.

"We're gonna have to be cautious," Troy mumbled.

"Really cautious," Ebony said, her voice wavering as she got up.

"Selma, you take us in."

"There's hatches beneath the dome," Troy said, pointing at an enlarged image on one of the upper screens. "Can you see them?"

"Yeah," Selma said, climbing into the pilot's seat. "I see them."

"It looks alien to me," Ebony said. She wondered what the inhabitants of a ship like this would look like.

Selma moved the shuttle in towards one of the ship's hatches.

Poppy broke out the spacesuits from a storage locker.

Ebony put one on. They all did. Itzel, too, even though the suit was many times too large for her.

Jen took the controls from Selma so she could put a suit on and gave control of the shuttle back to her when she was done. Selma carefully moved the shuttle in and docked over the hatch.

Ebony, Troy, and Rose each grabbed a plasma assault rifle from a rack. Troy and Ebony stood by the hatch while everyone else got in their seats and buckled up.

"Ebony, sit down, and put your harness on," Troy said. "If there's no atmosphere in there, you'll be sucked in like a bug through a straw.

Ebony sat and buckled up.

Troy checked a gauge next to the hatch. "The seal's good." He tethered himself to a cleat and pulled the shuttle's hatch open, revealing the hatch to the alien ship. He cranked a lever and pushed. It didn't move.

"Help me, Jen," Troy said.

Rose moved up beside Troy and tethered herself to the cleat. Troy cracked the lever, and together they slammed their bodies into the hatch. It opened.

It was pitch black inside. They flicked on the headlights affixed to the tops of their helmets.

The walls of the passageway were rounded and in sections. It was like being inside the skin of a gigantic centipede.

"Air's good," Troy concluded, holding his gun in one hand and an atmospheric analyzer in the other.

Ebony undid her harness, got up, and went to the hatch. She took off her helmet and quickly put it back on, snapping it into place. "Nothing could possibly be alive in there," she said, grabbing her plasma gun with both hands. "It's way too cold. No point in going in, really."

Troy went first. Rose followed. They moved forward like they were arriving home for dinner. Ebony lingered in the hatchway.

"Go!" Selma barked.

Ebony stepped forward, assault rifle pointing. She glanced back.

"Go on, Ebony!" Selma insisted, standing in the hatchway, shooing her away. "Go!"

"I'm going!" Ebony snapped, forcing herself to inch forward.

The passageway led to another hatch. Troy was trying to force it open. "Help me," he said to Rose.

Rose put down her gun, moved up beside him, and pushed. The hatch opened, and Rose quickly picked up her weapon. Ebony followed them in. The light from their helmets showed a patterned hexagon dome, like inside a giant beehive. Troy walked into the center of the room and shone his light beam on a console, a femur bone-shaped stump. He tapped on it with his gloved hand.

"What is that thing?" Ebony asked, her plasma gun pointed down, and her headlight pointing up at the dome.

"Don't know."

"I think we should go back," Ebony said. "There's nothing here."

"Where's your sense of adventure?" Rose asked. "We might get lucky and find some aliens."

"Just what I need." Ebony grimaced and chewed on her lower lip.

Troy got up, walked across the room to a hatch facing the front of the ship, opened it, stepped through, and was gone. Rose was right on his heels. Ebony stood motionless for a long time. She followed apprehensively, feeling like a mouse under the watchful eye of a cat.

She poked her head through the hatch and shone her headlight down an empty passageway. She went down it, peering into small quarters fitted with berths. She wondered if its denizens were carnivorous.

Beyond that was a room filled with devices she didn't recognize, rectangular boxes, small machines, and large oval bowls. She kept going and found another passageway.

At the end of it were the bridge, a captain's chair in the center, and five tall windows that stretched up from a flat black tiled deck. The sun was shining through the windows, illuminating the room. There was a black-overhead screen fixed to a metallic-gray beam and four consoles supporting more black screens.

Troy pointed his headlight at one of the screens and tapped on it. "Nothing operational," he said flatly.

"It's freezing in here," Ebony said. "No heat at all."

"I wonder if there's any power?" Rose asked as she tapped on another screen.

"We should get out of here and go back to the shuttle," Ebony said. "There's nothing here."

"So you keep saying," Rose said. "But there *is* air, and we do need that, don't we?"

"This place gives me the creeps," Ebony said.

"There we go," Troy said, his thumb pressing on a console's interface as the bridge lit up. "Look at that."

"I don't like this," Ebony said. "It's not normal to find a ship like this floating around in space. Think about it."

"All kinds of systems are coming on now," Troy said, tapping the interface repeatedly. He licked his upper lip and touched it again.

The main screen, up high between the windows, showed an enhanced view of a planet. It was Cronos.

Leona

"It's time, Your Majesty," General Steen said, speaking over the distant rumble of artillery.

Leona was feeling regal this day, wearing a soft gray dress with a brooch centered just above her breasts. Her dress opened in a v at the front showing an embroidered silk skirt beneath.

"Very well," she said.

Her shuttle waited between two lines of elite combat soldiers, her Royal Guard. She glanced at their faces as she walked, frozen faces, trained to look forward, and not make eye contact.

She hated herself. How could she leave? But she had to. No choice. It was leave or risk death. Her Royal Guard would be following her. But what of the countless others? What could she do? She couldn't just pull back and let Ganya fall without a fight. She had to try to save the Pacuttara Temple.

She boarded her chariot. General Steen sat at the front with the other officers.

Charline was at the back, staring out a window. "It's hopeless, isn't it, Mother?"

"It's not hopeless. Our leaving is just a precaution. That's all." Leona lowed herself into the seat beside her.

"I know what's happening," Charline said, turning to look at her. "We're going to lose Ganya. General Steen told me."

"He had no business telling you that."

"It's the truth. What's he supposed to do? Lie? Like you do?"

"Stop it. It hasn't happened yet. Different people have different beliefs."

"Yeah. Wildly different. So different that it makes me wonder."

The shuttle lifted from the ground, and Charline turned to look out the window again. "Goodbye, Ganya."

"Oh, don't be like that," Leona said, shaking her head. "If we lose Ganya, we'll win it back later."

"No one believes that, Mother. Everyone knows that the Athenians have landed another sixty divisions. Forty-three cities in seventeen provinces have been captured, and they're dropping many more troops on the continent of Debane."

Leona let out a cynical sigh. There was no getting through to her. She knew too much, and she was too smart for her own good.

"Can I at least know where we're going?" Charline asked. "It can't leak out now, can it? Or are there spies here on the shuttle too?"

"We're going to Erin."

She nodded. "Well, that's good. At least we're not abandoning Cronos altogether. I thought maybe you were taking me to Talon."

"I'd never take you to Talon."

"Why not?"

"It's far too dangerous."

"Well, Bacchus then."

"I'd never take you there either."

"What if we lose the war?"

"We're not going to lose the war, yet even so, Bacchus isn't an option. Their ideology isn't like ours."

"They're ideology isn't that different. They don't believe in the Messiah. That's the only difference. The question is, who's right? Is there a Messiah, or isn't there?"

"Oh, stop it! The Cronish religion holds the truth, and you know it."

"Both planets think they hold the truth, and frankly, I don't see how anyone can know."

"There can only be one truth."

"And it eludes all of you."

"For crying out loud! Can we not just enjoy our time together? Do we have to be constantly fighting?"

"It's not a vacation, Mother. We're running for our lives."

"Like I said. It's just a precaution. Nothing more. Now stop this nonsense. I won't hear any more of it."

Charline went back to staring out the window.

Leona thought back on the early days just after she was crowned, back when she was young. She used to be like her, upset with everything, and everyone. She had dreams and ambitions, yet not many of those plans had come to fruition over the years.

"I think you should go to Bacchus and ask the Empress for help," Charline said quietly without turning her head. "Get down on your knees if you have to. We need help."

"Stop it!" Leona snapped. "That's enough!"

Her grandfather had fought a war on Bacchus. But that was another time.

In the early days of her reign, she'd hoped to trade with Bacchus. What she hadn't counted on was pig-headed resistance from the Empress. Her greed was insatiable. She didn't seem to have the slightest inclination of why trade was beneficial, or how it could bring her sinking economy back to life. She kept her deuterium to herself like a falcon to a kill. She complained that she had internal problems, corruption, gangs, and a powerful High Priest. Leona's efforts to reason with her were thwarted, tossed aside, and only served to deepen the divide.

And now Zeta had cowered to Badoni. Ten thousand talas per tanker. Appalling. It was as if Zeta was content to rearrange the deck chairs on her sinking ship.

"We'll lose the war if you don't," Charline added.

"No!" Leona said sharply, with a flinty stare. "We're not going to lose the war!"

Charline didn't understand. She was just a rebellious child. Leona remembered how she'd spent her entire childhood fiercely contesting everything her father said and did. But now that he was dead, and she was in his place, Charline was the one doing the contesting. Only *now* could she appreciate what she'd put her father through. Perhaps, someday, Charline would have *her* thoughts and actions contested by *her* child. It'd only be fitting.

Rose

Rose's head felt like it was being pummeled. She had taken her last Rend, and it was wearing off. She watched Troy move across the expansive tiled deck from one console to the next, pressing icons, but as luck would have it, none of them did anything. The screens were filled with strange moving charts making the whole room seem utterly alien.

Ebony just stood by the hatch, watching. She looked nervous.

In Rose's mind, Troy was reckless. One wrong icon could spell disaster. "I'm going back to the shuttle to tell Poppy the ship's empty."

"It's a huge ship, Rose," Troy replied. "We haven't searched it yet."

"I don't care. I'm going back." There had to be painkillers on the shuttle. She needed to find them. She strutted through the hatch, down the passageway, and past the room full of strange devices. She noticed a soft blue light was coming in through the hatch at the far end of the passageway. She moved towards it, past the quarters, and into the domed room. She looked up. The entire honeycombed ceiling was a deep blue.

She damn near jumped out of her skin when she realized there was a new object in the room, a rectangular black box, just the right size to contain some sort of alien monstrosity. It stood next to the femur console. She staggered backward, her heart pounding. There was an orange stripe around the box that emanated heat.

"Troy?" she said into her mic.

There was no answer.

"Troy?" she said louder.

Nothing.

She scurried across the deck, and as she went by, she glanced into the box, a swirling cloud of glowing white gas under a smoky transparent top. When she got to the hatch on the opposite side, she stopped and looked back. Troy was coming in on the opposite side.

"Why didn't you answer me?" she scolded.

"I didn't hear you," Troy said, strolling up to the black box. "Where did this come from?"

"C'mon," Rose demanded, "we have to get out of here. Where's Ebony?"

"She's coming. It looks like there's something in it," Troy said, moving his head to just inches from the glass.

"Are you nuts?" Rose snarled, squinting. There couldn't possibly be anything good in that box."

"Relax. We don't know what this is."

"I don't care what it is!" Rose said, her lips pressed together in a white slash. "I'm leaving." She turned to leave, and the moment she did, the hatch slammed shut, trapping her and Troy inside. She looked over at the other hatch. It was shut too.

She dropped her plasma gun and threw herself at the hatch, trying to open it with all her might. It was no use. She couldn't get it to budge, and she collapsed on the floor.

A one-inch wide stripe that ran around the center of the wall started to glow a dull red.

Rose could feel a wave of heat come off it. "Selma," she said into her mic. There was no response.

The stripe gradually got brighter until it was a reddish-orange.

"Selma, can you hear me?" Again, no response. "Why can't she hear me?"

"Maybe the walls are shielded," Troy said, still peering into the white gas of the black box."

"You mean we can't talk to the shuttle?" Rose mumbled.

The stripe on the wall turned bright orange, and Rose had to move away from its intense heat. She took off her helmet and got down on all fours. She couldn't deal with her headache. It was so damn crippling and so protracted.

"Not feeling well?" Troy asked as he took off his helmet.

Rose took a deep breath. "Aren't you afraid some kind of monster is going to get out of that box?"

The stripe around the perimeter of the room stopped glowing bright orange went back to red. The narrowband around the middle of the black box also went from orange to red. Troy stepped back as the lid of the box lifted, and a cloud of steam rose into the air. Rose picked up her plasma gun off the floor and got up. She was sure some sort of creature was going to come crawling out of that box.

Troy moved up to the box, arched his body over the red stripe, and peered in.

"What is it?" Rose asked, pointing her gun.

Troy put his helmet on the floor. He unzipped his suit, pulled his arm from his sleeve, and reached in. He held his hand without moving for several seconds. Rose inched forward and stood on her toes, but all she could see was smoke.

"Dead," Troy stated. "It can't be Him. If he were the Messiah, the gods would have kept him alive."

"Dead? Are you sure?"

"Yes. You can put your gun down. I'm sure."

"It's boiling in here," Rose said, putting her gun down, unzipping her suit, and pulling her arms from the sleeves.

"The box seems to be heating its occupant. You'd think that with all those wires attached to him, the machine would know he's dead."

"Maybe it's not dead," Rose said, standing on her toes and trying to see.

"Oh, he's dead, alright. No pulse. No nothing. Perfectly pre-served, though."

"As soon as that hatch opens, we're out of here, okay?"

Troy was scratching his chin.

"Did you hear me?" she asked, her lips pinched together.

"Yeah," Troy said, staring into the box. "I heard you."

Rose jumped back when buzzing arcs of electricity discharged across the black box's face culminating in a loud zap. "What the hell was that?" She picked her gun up.

"This could be a cryogenic suspension unit," Troy mused, looking back into the box, his hand still on his chin. "Maybe it's going to try to bring him back to life."

"What? Don't say that. It's not possible. Is it? What does it look like? Is it alien?"

"No, Rose. It's not an alien. It's a human being. If his body were filled with some kind of cryoprotectant and brought down to a shallow temperature, theoretically, there'd be no tissue damage, and he could be heated up and brought back to life with a defibrillator."

"What the—I'm not having this discussion!" Rose said, her eyes wide. "I just want to get out of here."

There was another zap. Troy had his arms in the box, like a mechanic working on an engine. He shook his head. "This fellow could be decades, even centuries old."

"What does it look like?" she asked, moving up to it.

There was another buzzing arc discharge. Troy quickly pulled his arms out, and there was another zap. Rose was startled again and jumped back.

"He looks like the Messiah," Troy said. "The Sacred Writings described him perfectly."

"But he's dead."

"He's dead, but the box is trying to bring him back to life."

"In an alien ship?" Rose asked, shaking her head. A wave of pain in her head reminded her not to shake it again.

"Look at him," Troy said, stepping aside. "He's human. If he were alien, he wouldn't look like us."

Rose moved up to the black box, looked in, and saw him for the first time. It had a very muscular body that was completely drained of blood. "It's a ghost." She scowled.

"You're missing the point," Troy said. "He's human. The idea that aliens look even remotely similar to us is absurd. Aliens couldn't possibly appear human."

"Humans aren't white."

"Humans are created in the image of the gods of Uttara. Aliens aren't."

There were another arc discharge and another zap.

Rose stepped back. "The box is trying to revive him, isn't it? We better be ready." She pulled up her gun.

"No, Rose. What're you doing?" He stepped between her and the box. "Put that away. There's nothing to worry about. I know who this is."

She lowered her gun. "Why would the gods send him like this?"

"He's here to end our suffering."

"A man with no blood in a gigantic saucer-shaped ship? It doesn't make sense. We can't be sure where he's from or what his intentions are. We have to be ready for the worst."

The man was zapped again, the arc discharge continued, and after a moment, he was zapped again. Rose tried to step to one side, but Troy stayed between her and the box. The buzzing arc discharge remained constant, and the ghost was zapped again and again. It didn't stop. It just kept zapping him. Finally, behind the buzz and crackle of electricity, she could hear him take a deep breath, and the discharge stopped.

Troy turned around to see, and Rose stepped around him, brought her gun to her shoulder, and pointed it straight at him. He was breathing now but not moving.

"What are you going to do?" Troy asked. "Shoot an unarmed man because he woke up?"

"He's not a man," Rose stated. "He's an alien."

"He's a man, and he's coming out of a very long sleep," Troy insisted. "He's not conscious, and it could be a while before he wakes up."

Rose lowered her gun. He was right. And the pounding in her head was worse. She had to get back to the shuttle. She turned around and marched up to the hatch. She put her gun down and tried to open it, but once again, it wouldn't budge. She picked up her weapon, went to the femur console, and tried tapping on a screen filled with alien scribblings.

"He's awake," Troy stated.

Rose went to the box and peered in. She gasped wide-eyed. "He's got blue eyes."

He groaned. Rose ogled at his incredibly muscular white body, taking long breaths.

Troy glanced at Rose and spoke to the man in the box. "Can you hear me?"

He didn't respond.

A hatch suddenly opened. Startled, Rose spun around with her plasma gun. It was Ebony. "Why didn't you answer my calls?" she asked.

"The com system isn't working," Rose told her, "and there's an alien in this box. He just woke up."

"An alien?" Ebony asked.

Rose nodded. "He's white and has blue eyes."

"He's not an alien," Troy said. "He's the Messiah."

"A humanoid," Rose said.

The man shifted his gaze to look at Rose. His stunning blue eyes showed no emotion, and he had no expression.

"Hey, what's going on?" Selma came in through the other hatch, the one that led to the shuttle.

"We found a humanoid," Rose said as she moved towards the hatch, hastening her stride. She went by Selma without saying another word, though the hatch, and down the centipede-like passageway to the shuttle.

Poppy was standing in the shuttle's hatchway. "What did you find?"

"I have a terrible headache," Rose said. "Do we have any painkillers."

"First, tell me what you found in there?" Poppy pointed down the passageway.

Mika came to the hatchway.

"I need the painkiller real bad," Rose said.

"Are Troy and the girls okay?" Poppy asked.

"Yeah, they're fine." Rose got on the shuttle. Jen was sitting in the pilot's seat, and Itzel was seated at the front in a passenger seat. She looked apprehensive.

Mika pulled out the first aid kit. "No pills," she said. "Just morphine. How bad is it?"

"It's bad."

"I'll give you just a little bit, and we'll see if that helps."

"Give me more than a bit. My head's killing me."

"So, what did you find inside?" Mika asked as she ripped open the package.

"A humanoid," Rose answered, putting her gun down.

Mika drew some morphine from a bottle.

"Friendly?" Poppy asked, wide-eyed.

Rose sat down. "It was dead but came back to life." Her head was throbbing. She couldn't think straight.

"How's that possible?" Poppy asked.

Mika inserted the syringe in her arm, squeezed in the morphine, and pulled the needle out.

"Troy said it had been dead for centuries, yet right there in front of us, it came back to life."

Rose held the injection site with her finger and waited for the drug to take effect.

They all turned, like a school of fish, and peered down the centipede-like passageway. Jen picked up Rose's plasma gun and headed into the alien ship. Poppy, Mika, and Itzel followed.

Rose's head was still pounding. She was alone, and the first aid kit was on the seat next to her. She took all of the morphine bottles and the syringe out and stuffed them in her pockets. She waited a few minutes for the drug to take effect, but it didn't kick in immediately. She got up, and with her head still pounding, slowly made her way back to the domed room.

Ebony was talking to the man in the box. "Can you hear me?"

They'd all gathered around. Rose walked up beside them.

"Hah," the man said.

Rose shivered. This humanoid was scary. The white skin. The muscles. The blue eyes.

"Dzie ja ja," he said.

"We don't understand," Ebony said.

"Dzie ja ja," he said again, struggling to move.

"Are you the Messiah?" Troy asked.

"Chto jucca vy," he said.

Jen lifted her eyebrows. "A Messiah with white skin and blue eyes? Are you kidding me?"

"What else could he be?" Troy asked defiantly. "He has to be the Messiah. It's the only possibility that makes any sense."

"It's a bit of a stretch, don't you think," Jen said. "Last I checked, the Messiah was olive, and I'm quite sure the clergy's going to see it that way too."

Rose's head was still throbbing.

"Dzie ja ja," the white man said again.

"I think he's asking where he is," Selma said.

He turned his head slightly.

"Are you here to save us?" Troy asked.

No reply.

"He can't understand you," Rose said, too annoyed to stay silent.

"Ja nie trebba zrazumic," he said.

"See what I mean," Rose said. "Have you ever heard a language like that before?"

"Anyway, I'm going have a look around," Jen said, moving towards the hatch that led to the bridge.

"Me too," Poppy said.

The others went with her. Rose remained with Ebony and Troy. Troy grinned at the man in the black box like he was the birthday gift he'd always wanted.

The white man's eyes were closed.

"You're attracted to him, aren't you?" Troy asked Rose.

"To him?" Rose grimaced.

"Yeah. I saw how you looked at him."

"You didn't see anything," Rose said, looking down, embarrassed that he could read her so easily. He'd be attractive if he weren't white. She shivered.

"I wish I could read the Sacred Writings and see what it says about him," Troy said.

"I'd have thought you'd know that book inside out," Rose said, raising her eyebrows.

"I can't remember everything."

"What do you remember?"

"He's here to save our world, Rose. No doubt about it."

"Well, I don't think he's the Messiah, but the gods know how much this world needs saving."

The white man sat up.

"There you go," Troy said. He moved in and reached towards him. The white man grabbed his wrist with lightning reflexes.

"Easy," Troy said. "Just removing these wires." He pointed with his free hand. The white man let his arm go. Troy pulled the wires off. "There must be some clothes for you back there somewhere. I'll look. He left, heading in the direction of the cabins.

Rose and Ebony were left alone with him. He studied Rose with piercing blue eyes. She felt naked under his gaze and bit her lower lip. He was attractive and repulsive at the same time, his body spectacular, the blue eyes, brilliant, but the white skin, an aberration from a godless world. Her headache was still there but bearable.

"I wonder if there's anything to eat on this ship," Ebony said.

"If there is, I'm not eating it," Rose said with a scowl.

Jen

The cafeteria in the alien ship had plastic chairs and tables, lights that reminded Jen of windswept umbrellas, and food that tasted like cardboard.

"There must be a way he can tap into his powers," Troy said, sitting across from Jen with his meal.

"You mean like a magic wand?" Jen asked.

"I'm serious, Jen," Troy said.

"Take the hint, Troy, and leave me alone." She took a bite of her cardboard-flavored meal.

"What? What did I do?" he asked, pushing food around on his plate. "I haven't done anything."

"Yes, you have," she insisted, leaning across the table. "If I have to listen to you tell me that he was sent here by the gods one more time, I'm going to scream."

"It's in the Sacred Writings," Troy said, palms open.

"I know," Jen said, her eyes wide. "But there's a lot of things in the Sacred Writings, like the story about the giants that roamed Cronos back when there were fire breathing dragons." She took a bite and turned her head to watch the white as he looked at packages behind a glass partition. He appeared to be reading the labels. She wondered what they said.

"You have a better explanation for what he is, do you?" Troy asked, tilting his head.

"I don't need a better explanation," Jen scolded. "He's standing right in front of me. I can see what he is."

"He's the Messiah."

"No, he isn't!" Jen said. She watched the white push an icon on the dispenser repeatedly. Nothing dispensed.

"Too many things have happened the way they're supposed to

happen for it to be a coincidence," Troy said, shaking his head. "The Sacred Writings have predicted all of this."

"Very scientific," Jen said condescendingly. She took another bite.

"Will you just listen to me for two seconds?"

"Just drop it, okay! I've had enough!"

"It's important. The Sacred Writings says that the Messiah will bring prosperity to the people."

"I know, I know. I went to church on the Sabbath. Through the powers of the gods," she said, her head rocking back and forth, "the Messiah will save the people from their undoing. But he's not going to save me from you, is he?"

"There's more to it."

"Like what?"

"He has powers."

Jen leaned back in her chair and shrugged. "Well, it seems to me that he's not only powerless but completely useless. He can't even work a dispenser, never mind, save the world." She leaned over her plate and took another bite.

"If you want to know how he saves the world, all you have to do is read the Sacred Writings. It'll tell you."

"I'll keep that in mind," Jen mused as she chewed.

The dispenser pushed out a package. The white seemed not to see it. She got up, snatched it from the machine, ripped it open, and put it in the microwave.

"You're not listening," Troy scolded again.

"You only have one theory, and it's not reasonable. Now, it's your turn to listen. Stop trying to convince me. Let me make up my mind." She proceeded to try every icon on the microwave.

"Suit yourself," Troy conceded. He got up and stormed out of the cafeteria with his food.

The microwave didn't respond. She glared at the myriad of

icons. The white reached in and pushed one. The microwave lit up and began to hum.

"There," she said, throwing out a hand. "You performed your first miracle."

The white caught her eye, pointed at the hatch, and crossed his fingers.

"Me and Troy," Jen shrieked, shaking her head. "No. Definitely not. We're just friends. That's all. Just friends." She rolled her eyes and returned to her meal.

"Friends," the white said.

"Yeah, friends," Jen said, looking up at him, shocked that he'd said a Cronish word.

"Friends," he said again as he took his bowl from the microwave.

"Can you understand me?" Jen asked with a wondrous tone. "Do you know the word *friends*?"

"Friends," he said, carrying his bowl to the table and sitting down.

"Okay, okay, we were fighting." She twisted her lips. "I think he wants more, yet I—why am I telling you this? What the hell's the matter with me. Thank the gods you can't understand."

The white stared back at her with a blank expression.

"There I was, about to divulge," she said with a smile that wavered, "my deepest thoughts to a—the gods only know what you are."

The white put his head down and quietly began sipping his soup.

"Troy's constantly trying to convince people to adopt his beliefs," she said, more to herself than to the white. "It's more than irritating." She looked at him, her chin up. "You know what? You need a name."

He gave her the same blank expression.

"How 'bout Solin?" she asked, batting her lashes. She recalled from the teachings drilled into her as a youth that Solin was the god of lightning and thunder.

He scooped up another spoonful of soup.

"You supposedly came here from Uttara, so it's fitting. What do you think?"

Solin stuck his spoon in his mouth.

"Solin it is," Jen said, grinning. "How often do I get to name someone?"

"Someone," Solin said.

"Solin." Jen repeated. "Not someone." She laughed.

"Someone," he said.

She took several bites of cardboard, filled her cheeks, and swallowed. "Jen," she said, putting a hand on her chest. "Solin." She reached out and touched his chest.

He stared back at her with that same blank expression.

"You have no clue what I'm saying, do you?" she asked with a smirk.

"Do you," Solin repeated.

"That's what I thought," she said, staring at him as she took another bite. "I wonder what your home was like, if you had a family, a wife, or children?"

"Chill hen," he said.

"Children," she repeated, putting a hand on top of her head and lowering it to a few feet from the deck. "All races have children. You know. Little screaming brats."

"You?" he asked, staring at her hand and lifting his chin.

"Me? No. No. I don't have children." She laughed. "No man yet, so no children." Jen shrugged and took another bite. "Yet even if there were a man, I wouldn't want to have children the way things are. Not while the war's on."

Solin kept sipping his soup.

Jen sighed.

Rose

Rose was worried. Her supply of morphine wasn't going to last forever. What would she do when she ran out? She wondered if a ship like this had painkillers stored somewhere. She had her doubts.

In the meantime, she was hungry. She found the food room Poppy had told her about. Jen was sitting at a table across from the humanoid.

"I named him," Jen said, looking up at her. "Solin. What do you think?"

"He probably already has a name, Jen." Rose went to the machines and pushed some icons. Nothing happened.

Solin got up and pushed an icon for her. A package dropped. He pulled it out, opened it, put it in the microwave, and tapped another icon. The machine started humming.

"Thanks," Rose said. She threw him a quick smile.

He went back to his seat and continued sipping his soup.

When the microwave beeped, she took her food out and sat beside Solin. She wanted to ask him questions, but of course, he didn't speak Cronish. She blew on her spoon a few times and took a sip. "It doesn't taste right," she said.

"I know," Jen said. "It'll probably kill us. Not a quick death either; a slow lingering death that takes weeks."

Rose chuckled. "So, where do you think he's from?"

"Anywhere but Uttara," Jen said.

Rose laughed.

Solin caught Jen's eye.

"Soup," Jen said, pointing to her bowl.

"Soup," Solin repeated.

Rose took another sip of her soup and screwed up her face.

Solin held up his spoon. "Lyzka."

"Soup," Jen said.

"Jesci sip z soup."

"You're planning to teach him how to speak Cronish?" Rose asked.

"Just seeing if he understands," Jen said. "It'd be nice if he did speak Cronish. Maybe, he could tell Troy where to go."

Rose laughed and took another sip. "I think Ebony's attracted to Troy. Do you?"

Jen shrugged. "Ebony doesn't strike me as being stupid. I don't see how it could work."

"I agree, but sometimes people make concessions at the start and realize their mistake later on.

"Ebony's not going to make any concessions. She's going to keep her distance."

"What makes you so sure?"

"She's smart. Smarter than you think. She wasn't a maintenance worker. She was a hustler and sold drugs. She supported her brother for years, but when the war broke out, he joined the army. She's all shook up about it."

"She's a prostitute?" Rose asked.

"No, no, no. She's clean. She didn't do drugs herself. Just sold them."

"She told you all of this?"

"Yeah." Jen took her last sip of soup.

"Why do you think she spends so much time with Troy?" Rose asked.

"She's too nice. Troy is like flypaper stuck to her fingers. No matter how hard she tries, she can't shake him off."

"Yeah. If you want to get rid of someone, you have to be nasty. It's the only way."

"What about you?" Jen asked. "How did you survive the famine?"

"Handouts mostly. Odd jobs."

"Did you sell your body?"

"No!" Rose barked.

"Okay, okay." She brought up her hands defensively. "You don't have to be so touchy. Just asking."

Solin was still sipping his soup.

Footsteps pounded down the passageway. Rose turned to see who it was. It was Selma, her forehead covered in a sheen of sweat, her hands moving in jerks.

"What's wrong, Selma?" Jen asked.

"They've found us," Selma shrieked, glancing back.

Rose could feel the hair stiffen on the nape of her neck. "Who? Who found us?"

"The Athenians."

Rose took in a quick breath and pressed a hand on her chest.

"They snuck-up on us," Selma said. She was shaking and seemed confused. She turned and bolted out of the room.

"We have to go," Jen said.

Rose hesitated. *Where could they go? The shuttle? Escape the way they escaped from the freighter? No. It wouldn't work this time. Maybe they could hide. It was a huge ship.* She got up and grabbed Solin's arm. "C'mon. We have to go!"

He didn't move.

Jen came around the table and grabbed his other arm. "C'mon! Let's go!"

He squinted and resisted.

"What the hell's the matter with you," Jen snarled, yanking on his arm.

Then, in some far off passageway, barely audible, they heard a scream.

Solin ripped free from their grip and went to the hatch. He poked his head around the corner and beckoned with his fingers, indicating he wanted them to follow.

Rose wasn't sure if she should, but Solin seemed so damn confident that she felt compelled to do as he beckoned. Jen followed.

The passageway was long, but they moved down it quickly.

At the next hatch, Solin held his hand flat and made them wait. Again, he beckoned with his fingers, and they followed.

The passageway went to the right a short distance. A third time, he made them wait, and he beckoned. Rose cringed at the sight of Selma lying motionless in the passageway, her leg severed halfway down the thigh. Blood was flowing from her stump onto the deck. Rose heard screams in the distance that sent shivers down her spine.

Solin kept going. Rose and Jen followed. At the next hatch, once again, Solin held his hand flat. Rose fought to lock herself in place. She was shaking, breathing heavily, and her head was pounding.

Jen waited beside her.

Solin moved forward and peeked around the next corner. Again he cupped his fingers and beckoned.

Rose had to force herself to move. Around the corner, on the bridge, Poppy was hanging over the arm of the command chair. Her eyes were missing, and the sockets were dripping pools of blood. Rose slowed down to stare at Poppy as Jen went around her.

Solin quickly charged across the bridge and down a passageway.

Jen followed close on his heels.

Rose scrambled to catch up.

Again, Solin put a hand up to stop them. He went forward and disappeared around the bend.

A bolt of blue plasma came from the passageway and hit the wall ahead of Rose. It shocked her, deafened her, and caused her, unwittingly, to take several steps back.

Jen was stronger. She didn't move.

A flurry of shots hit the wall.

Instinctively, Rose wanted to run, but instead, she glued herself to the deck and waited behind Jen. She was breathing hard, and her heart was pounding. She was sure the next thing she'd see would be a monstrous Athenian, but it wasn't. Solin came back holding an Athenian plasma assault rifle and waved them forward.

When she rounded the corner, she saw an Athenian warrior lying in the passageway. He was much bigger than Rose had ever imagined an Athenian could be, taller, broader, and more muscular. He wore a battle vest, a helmet, had sheaths for two swords, one long, one short, and another sheath for a knife. His canine teeth were long and sharp. She couldn't take her eyes off his massive shape. Her limbs were shaking, her head was pounding, and her heart was nearly exploding. "Why does he have swords?" she asked.

"It's part of their religion," Jen said. "They use them to kill themselves or each other if they're wounded."

Solin checked his assault rifle and moved forward. He stepped out, fired three quick shots, and disappeared around the corner.

Jen went after him, and Rose forced herself to follow. A hatch, torn from its hinges, lay on the deck at her feet. At the far end of the passageway, a reasonable distance away, three Athenian warriors lay dead in the passageway. Solin was running towards them, and Jen was close behind. Rose ran to catch up.

Jen picked up a plasma assault rifle off one of the dead Athenian warriors. Rose stopped and picked one up as well. The hull had been cut open, and there was an Athenian shuttle on the other side with its hatch open. The hole was four feet off the deck and went into the deck above.

Solin climbed up, grabbed Rose's arm, and pulled her up, effortlessly.

The gravity emitter inside the Athenian shuttle replicated Atheni's gravity, almost double Cronos's gravity, and Rose struggled to make her way to a seat.

Jen got up on her own but with great difficulty.

The shuttle seated about thirty. Solin went to the front and climbed into the pilot's seat. Jen made her way down the aisle and sat beside him.

Rose strapped herself in behind them.

Solin studied the controls, scanned the various icons, pushed one, and then another. Nothing happened.

Jen pointed. "Try this one."

Solin pushed it. The control panel lit up.

Jen started pushing icons. The hatch slammed shut, and the tokamak fired up.

Solin grabbed the yoke, and the shuttle ripped away from the hull.

On a screen, Rose watched Athenian bodies get sucked out of the gigantic saucer-shaped ship. She wondered if the ship's interior hatches would automatically close to protect the ship's integrity the way they would on other spacecraft.

Then, through the front window, she saw a menacing-looking Athenian ship. It wasn't a warship. It was much smaller, a corvette. It had two long hulls, side by side, one longer than the other, Tarahal Torpedo portals at the front, and three rotating plasma cannons protruding from the top and sides.

Solin turned the shuttle straight towards it.

"What the hell are you doing!" Rose screamed.

Solin wasn't listening. He accelerated towards the Athenian corvette.

"You can't go there!" She unfastened her harness, got up, staggered to the front, and tried to pull his arms away from the controls, but it was like trying to move steel beams.

Jen wasn't helping. She seemed to be okay with this insanity.

As they approached, a bay door opened.

Rose went back to her seat and grabbed her assault rifle. If she was going to die, she'd die fighting.

Solin flew the shuttle straight in and set it down in the landing bay. The bay door closed behind them, and the bay pressurized.

From the shuttle's front window, Rose could see three Athenian warriors coming in through a hatchway. She ducked down. "They don't know we're here," she whispered. Her head was oscillating with waves of pain. She took a moment to compose herself.

Solin went to the hatch, checked his assault rifle, and pushed a button on the wall. The hatch opened. He fired shot after shot from the hatchway and dashed out into the bay.

It took all of Rose's strength to get up. She was able to wobble over to the hatch and cautiously peek out. Solin was gone, but she could hear shots being fired deep inside the ship.

In the bay, an Athenian warrior lay dead by the entrance. Another wounded Athenian, his arm almost completely severed and dangling, struggled to get up into a crouch.

A third Athenian had a deep gash on his thigh that was bleeding profusely. Blood ran down his leg and trailed behind him as he hopped up behind the warrior with the severed arm. He was huge, even bigger than the one in the passageway. When he turned, she saw that half his face was burnt off. He drew his longsword.

Rose raised her gun, but it was incredibly heavy and hard to hold up.

The Athenian looked down at his comrade with the severed arm.

His comrade pulled out a short sword with his one good arm and pointed the tip at his stomach.

The one standing behind him spoke quietly.

Then the one in a crouch drove the short sword into his stomach.

Rose felt her body flinch involuntarily.

The Athenian with the longsword waited a moment and then viciously swung his sword into his comrade's neck, slicing his head off, causing blood to shoot across the deck and his head to roll. Then the Athenian hobbled towards Rose, blood trailing from his leg.

Rose pressed on the trigger, but nothing happened. She frantically pressed it again—still nothing.

The Athenian was halfway up the ramp.

She stepped back into the shuttle and tried to close the hatch, but that didn't happen either. She backed down the aisle as fast as she could, struggling to keep her balance.

The Athenian came in and teetered back and forth as he came up the aisle with his longsword held high.

Jen was behind Rose. She pulled Rose back out of the way and fired.

The Athenian staggered and careened to one side. He grabbed the top of a chair to steady himself and lunged forward.

Jen fired again.

His body jerked back from the force of a blast. He tried to take a few quick breaths as his mouth filled with blood. He collapsed and stopped moving, his one eye open, staring straight ahead.

"The rule is:" Jen said to the dead Athenian, "don't bring a sword to a gunfight."

"Why the hell didn't my gun work?" Rose griped.

Jen lifted her eyebrows. "Did you check the safety?" She showed Rose where it was.

"I didn't know. I've never had to shoot a gun before." Rose flicked her safety off and aimed.

"Don't shoot it now," Jen said. "You might damage the ship."

"But I'm pissed," Rose complained.

"Good," Jen said. "I like it when you're pissed."

Rose stepped over the dead Athenian and made her way to the shuttle's hatch. With her hands shaking, she raised her gun and went out into the bay, but the weapon was too heavy, so she lowered it. She traversed the bay to the hatch, peeked to the right, and went to the left. Her legs were like lead weights. She checked to see if Jen was behind her. She was.

When she rounded a corner, a dead Athenian was lying on the deck, and blood was splattered on the wall. She stepped over him and slipped on some blood, yet she managed to stay upright. She stopped and listened, but all she could hear was Jen breathing down her neck. She held a finger to her lips. Jen stopped breathing.

Rose peeked around the corner. Athenian warriors were lying on the deck here too, one with no head and a short sword sticking from his stomach. Blood was splattered over the deck and on the walls. Rose turned and drew in a quick breath when she saw Solin lying on the floor with a deep cut in his side and a pool of blood beneath him. "You're wounded," she muttered, cringing at the sight of it. "We have to put pressure on it," she said, tearing off her shirt. Wearing just a bra, she collapsed to her knees and pressed her shirt on the wound.

"Sturval," Solin said, pointing to a passageway.

"You want me to go somewhere," Rose mumbled, speaking with a broken voice. "Here," she said to Solin, putting the shirt in his hand. "Hold this and press hard." She grabbed his hand and pressed the shirt against his wound.

Rose went down the passageway, keeping her gun in front of her. Jen followed. They found the bridge, a full row of consoles in front of a long, curved row of windows. An elevator door opened. Jen fired several times. Her shots jolted an Athenian warrior from his feet and slammed him into the elevator wall. He slid down. The elevator door closed.

Rose looked at the main view screen. A second Athenian assault shuttle was on its way back from the saucer-shaped ship, just minutes away from landing.

Rose got behind the helm of the corvette. The console's screen was blank. *Security protected*, she realized. "There's a shuttle coming, and I can't access the helm. We're going to have to fight."

"Help me," Jen said. She put down her gun and tried to lift the dead Athenian lying next to the helm. Rose leaned her weapon against the chair and grabbed his other arm, but he was incredibly heavy. There was no way they'd be able to lift him.

Jen grabbed a longsword from the sheath of a dead officer draped over a console. "Stand back."

Rose stepped away, wide-eyed.

Jen put everything she had into the blow. At first Rose thought she had missed. The incredibly sharp blade took off both his head and his arm. Blood spurted everywhere. With both hands, Jen picked up his head and arm together and held it up for Rose. Blood dripped like a wet towel. "Prop his eyes open with your fingers so the helm station can do a retina scan."

Rose forced herself to do as she was told.

"Now, grab his hand and get his finger to touch the screen."

Again, Rose complied. The screen lit up.

"Touch his finger to the icon that looks like an arrow."

She did, and the thrusters fired. The ship began to move, and the shuttle fell away as they accelerated.

Rose heard the elevator door open. She grabbed her gun, spun around, and aimed.

A young female Athenian, with one of her eyes purple and swollen shut, stood in front of the elevator, holding a longsword. She dropped down to her knees and held it out with both hands. She bowed forward and extended her neck.

Jen dropped the Athenian's head and went for it.

"Prypynak!" Solin yelled, staggering onto the bridge with a hand holding Rose's shirt on his wound.

Jen grabbed the longsword from the female Athenian, moved around beside her, and lifted it.

Solin moved in quickly. He used his free hand to yank the longsword away from her and toss it across the bridge.

"Damn you!" Jen screamed. "Let me kill her! She wants to die!"

Solin collapsed to his knees and fell on his side.

Jen went after the longsword and picked it up, but the Athenian ran away.

Rose went to Solin and fell to her knees. "What are you doing?" He had let go of the shirt, so she grabbed it and pressed it into the wound.

The Athenian came running back, carrying a box. She went down on her knees next to Solin, opened the box, ripped open a package, and sprinkled a generous portion of powder on the wound.

Solin winched from the pain.

She took a bottle, stuck a syringe in, and filled it. She stuck the syringe into the skin around Solin's wound. Next, she took out a needle and thread and meticulously mended Solin's wound with precision stitches, like a seasoned seamstress.

Jen stood by the captain's chair, holding the longsword and watching the Athenian.

Rose glanced at the viewscreen. The saucer-shaped ship had fallen behind and was shrinking on the screen. She turned her attention to the medical box.

Charline

When she wanted to be, Charline was a ghost. She could slip past the guards at will, out of the palace walls. On this night, she escaped wearing a robe with a hood to hide her face.

As she walked down the moonlit cobblestone street, it started to rain. It wasn't a hard rain, yet she worried that it would seep through her robe and give her the chills. She hated being cold, and it almost caused her to cancel her plans and turn back.

There were few people out at this time of night, and the ones she came across paid no attention. They had their agendas. It was a long walk, but she'd decided against taking a cab. The fewer people she came into contact with, the better.

When she got to the spaceport, she kept walking, past the passenger terminal onto the platform where spaceships were parked—*the overnighters* were what her mother called them.

She approached the ships and studied them carefully. Each vessel was wildly different from the others. Only one had a light on. It was small, stood on three legs, and was saucer-shaped with a single curved wing. The emblem next to the hatch was Bacchian. Perfect.

She knocked on the hatch.

There was movement inside and, for just a moment, a face in the window. The hatch swung out, and down, and formed a ramp. A Bacchian with bulging eyes and deep sockets came out, pulling a housecoat over his shoulders. "What is it? Is something wrong?"

From the bottom of the ramp, Charline brought her chin up and met his gaze. "I need passage to Bacchus." She offered a smile that faded quickly.

"Come back in the morning," he said, speaking loudly over the rolling thunder.

"I have to go now."

"My dear girl, it's the middle of the night. It can wait till morning."

"I can't wait. You must take me now."

"Why?"

"That's my concern," Charline replied with a note of disdain.

"Not if you want a ride on my ship," he said satirically.

Lightning flashed and spread across the sky like the branches of a giant tree. The rain intensified.

"I've business on Bacchus," she said, surprised by the man's arrogance. Her business was not his concern. Did he not know who she was? She'd have to teach this man a lesson.

"Well, if you're not going to tell me what it is,"—he paused to let more thunder roll by—"and if you don't own a deuterium processing plant or a mole manufacturing company, you're out of luck."

"I'm Princess Charline, and you will do as I ask or suffer the consequences."

His eyes widened. He walked down the ramp, almost but not entirely to the bottom, ignored the rain, and studied her carefully. "And I'm Prince Charming," he said, shaking his head and smiling.

"I am," she said, her eyes like daggers. "How dare you question me."

He scrunched up his face. "Why in the name of the gods would a princess need to go to Bacchus?"

She spoke through clenched teeth. "You're to give me passage and send word to Empress Zeta that I'm coming."

"Listen to me," he said. Rain pelted off his forehead and streamed down his face. "Consider my words carefully. You don't want to go to Bacchus. Bacchus is a religious cult where one wrong word can put you in a whole world of trouble."

"I don't care what you think. If it's money you're worried about, you needn't be concerned. You'll be well paid. Now, I command you to take me to Bacchus."

He shook his head.

Charline lifted her chin. "I don't have time for your insolence! You'll give me passage or else!"

"Perhaps I'm not making myself clear." He stepped forward and leaned in with his head tilted back just inches from her chest. "No!"

She stabbed a finger at his forehead, almost touching it. "By the authority of Queen Leona, I hereby requisition your ship! You'll do as I say, or I'll call for the Royal Guards and have them take your head! Am *I* making myself clear?"

"Go ahead. Play your little game. I'm going back to bed."

The merchant's wife came up to the hatchway, also in a house-coat. She looked like her husband but with long dark curly hair. "What is it, Carl?"

"Nothing, my dear. You can go back to bed."

"Oh my!" She curtsied. "Your Highness."

Her husband bolted upright and stepped back, his jaw lowered. He was visibly shaking, like a trapped animal. He glanced back at his wife. "Are you sure?"

"Of course, I'm sure. This is Princess Charline, heir to the throne."

"You foolish girl," Carl said to Charline. "You don't know what you're doing."

"You can pilot the ship, or I'll find someone else to pilot it," Charline said. "Either way, this is my ship now."

"But this is crazy," Carl grumbled.

"You'll send a message to the office of Empress Zeta. Tell her that Her Royal Highness, Princess Charline of Cronos, is requesting an audience."

Three more bolts of lightning cracked down. The rain intensified again. Carl turned, ignored the rain, and walked with even strides, as if it were a clear-skied day, into his ship.

Three waves of thunder rolled in.

Charline hunched over and scurried after him.

Jen

The bridge of the Athenian corvette would have been a thing of beauty if the sapphire screens weren't saturated with repugnant scribbles, if Jen's hands hadn't smeared the white swivel command chair with blood, and if the teal console in front of her didn't have a dead Athenian warrior draped over it.

There was a hideous alarm reverberating from the helm, and Jen had no idea how to shut the damn thing off. She peered out the sweeping row of windows and tried to figure out which way the ship was headed, but she couldn't recognize the star patterns. Star patterns weren't her thing.

She looked across at the severed head and arm of the dead Athenian lying by the helm in a pool of blood on the honeycombed glass tile deck and wondered how she could get the ship going in the right direction.

The pink that she had wanted to decapitate was down on her knees, meticulously centering a bandage over Solin's wound. Why would she do that? Didn't she know that Solin had just slaughtered many of her kind? Didn't she care? She was freakishly tall with long ivory hair and dark red eyes. The skin around her left eye was purple and swollen. Did the pinks beat their women?

Jen squeezed the handle of her plasma gun, took a deep breath, and quivered through a slow exhale.

With great effort, she got up, careened across the deck to the helm, and endeavored to figure out how to stop the damn alarm. "Hey," she called out.

Rose was sitting on the floor with the medical kit in her lap.

"I want the pink to look at these maps," Jen said. "Maybe she can make sense of things."

Rose tapped the pink on the arm and got her attention. She beckoned her to go to Jen.

The pink got up, effortlessly, and shuffled over like the compliant slave she undoubtedly was.

Jen pointed at the planet, Vole, on the helmsman's screen.

The pink studied the display, picked up the head and arm of the dead helmsman, and touched Vole's image with the dead helmsman's finger. The alarm stopped. The stars out the window moved up and sideways as the ship adjusted its course.

"That was easy," Jen stated, lifting her eyebrows. "Good."

The pink put the helmsman's body parts down and went back to Solin.

Rose was gone.

Jen bounced her eyes from one screen to the next, checking each. Nothing but stars. She felt drained and realized she hadn't had much sleep. She climbed back onto the command chair and rubbed her eyes. Why did Solin stop her from taking the pink's head off? They had just killed—she wasn't sure how many. So what if she killed one more? It didn't make sense.

As the ship pointed itself at Vole, and the stars in the window settled into a fixed position, her eyes felt heavy, and she fought the urge to close them. She struggled, but she lost the fight, and she drifted.

When she woke, her plasma gun was still in her hand. She plodded to the helm and checked the ship's heading—still on course. She checked the screens. No warships were closing in. Everything was fine. The pink had the perfect opportunity to kill her and had passed it up. Why? It would've been easy.

She went looking for the pink and found her pulling on the arms of a dead warrior, a monster in every sense. His teeth were sharp, his callous pink skin, grotesque, and his enormous muscles were covered in blue blood vessels.

Jen watched her struggle.

The pink beckoned her to help.

Jen shook her head.

The pink covered her face with her hands, let out a heavy sigh, got up, and wandered off.

Jen found Solin passed out in a bunk. She left him alone.

The pink came back with an Athenian flag—red showing a longsword crossed with a short sword. She wrapped the dead warrior in it and mumbled a few words.

Rose showed up. "I searched the ship," she said. "There's no one else here."

"That was brave of you," Jen said. "You searched the whole ship?"

"It's a small ship, and the Athenians aren't the type to hide."

Rose tried to help the pink, but the pink was many times stronger than Rose. She pulled the pink warrior's body down the passageway, pushed his torso into the airlock, and, unceremoniously, jettisoned him out into space.

Jen went back to the bridge and checked the screens. Nothing.

Rose and the pink came to the bridge and struggled with the body of the warrior on the console.

"Where are we headed?" Rose asked.

"Vole," Jen said. "It's no jewel, but we have to go somewhere. The Athenians will be hunting us down. The sooner we get our feet on solid ground, the better."

"There's another reason for going to Vole."

"What's that?"

"The Muunakshi Akkan Temple."

Jen screwed up her face. "The what?"

Rose smiled. "The monks on Vole know Solin's story."

"What story?"

"The story of the Messiah."

"Not you too?" She tossed her head. "He's not the Messiah, Rose."

"There's a lot of things that don't make sense. There's no harm in checking. See if we can connect the dots. Troy seemed to think he was the Messiah."

"Troy's a religious nut," Jen said vehemently.

"Yeah. He is. But what if he's right?"

"He's not right, but if you want to waste your time checking, go right ahead."

Rose and the pink pulled the dead warriors off the bridge, one after another.

Jen checked the screens and spent time figuring out how she could navigate without the helmsman's eyes and index finger.

"How many dead?" Jen asked Rose when she came back.

"We jettisoned nine in all."

"I killed two. That means seven for Solin. Here's hoping he gets back on his feet. We might need him."

Rose nodded.

Ebony

Ebony and Troy had been lucky. When they'd heard the gunshots and screams, they knew what was happening and were able to run deep into Solin's alien ship.

"Even if they search the entire ship," Troy whispered as they walked down a long, curved passageway with a rust-colored metal grill floor, centipede-like walls, and was lined with massive pipes, gages, and iron wheels, "I don't think they'll be able to find us. All we have to do is stay ahead of them and hide where they've already looked."

"Forgive me if I don't take your word for it," Ebony said quietly, "but if you're wrong, I'm going to become a piece of raw meat." She could find a suitable hiding spot, but not with this bumbling idiot. She'd have to go it alone. He was too cocksure. Sooner or later, he'd make a mistake, overlook some small detail, make a noise, or simply stumble into the Athenians. Without him, she had a much better chance of staying hidden.

"We'll split up," Ebony said. The moment she said it, she realized it was a bad idea. He would get caught. They'd torture him, and he would tell all, including the fact that she was on the ship. They'd search every nook and cranny and find her.

He scrunched up his face. "We're not splitting up. Don't worry. I'm not stupid. I know we have to be careful."

She stopped. "We have to be more than careful, Troy. We have to be invisible. We can't be seen or heard. Everywhere we go, we have to be sure not to leave any traces of our existence. We need to find weapons if we can, and we have to be smart."

"I know, I know," Troy said. "No scouting around. No spying on them. Just find a secure place, stay quiet, and don't move."

"Right. That's it exactly. Except, we're going to need a few things. Let me take care of that."

"What things?" he asked, frowning.

"Food, for one. Essentials. You know. But don't worry. I've spent years sneaking around. I'll be better at it than you. I know what to do and how to do it."

She turned and continued walking.

He caught up. "You spent years sneaking around? Where did you live?"

"Aaronia."

"And why did you have to sneak around?"

"We were poor." She smiled. "I had to sell drugs to make money, and when a deal went bad, we had to hide."

"You mean, during the great famine?" Troy asked.

"Yeah." She felt a piece of his sensibility. He knew. He was just as scared of the Athenians as she was. Maybe that'd keep him from doing anything rash.

They kept moving, found another cafeteria, and raided the dispensers. Deeper in, they found two very big tokamaks, so big that at first, they didn't recognize them for what they were. On a flight deck, they found some very strange looking shuttles with translucent bumpy sides, like bubbled glass. There were also rows of pods, some small, some the size of passenger ships, and one was much larger, three times the size of the others.

The idea of taking one of the shuttles crossed her mind, but she had no idea how to open the hatch, much less, work the controls. If they were going to escape, it'd have to be in the Cronish shuttle they arrived in. Yet even that wasn't an option until they had a planet to go to.

The days passed; dreary days; days where they focused on almost nothing but staying hidden.

"It won't be long now," Troy said, looking out a window.

"It won't be long before what?" Ebony asked.

"Before we pass by Talon."

Ebony was taken aback. Did he intend to take the shuttle to Talon? She turned to look at him. "You can't be serious."

"I'm dead serious. You don't think we can stay here, do you?"

"Troy, the Athenians aren't going to keep this ship," Ebony said. "They'll sell it."

"No, they won't." He shook his head. "They'll bring it to Atheni."

"It's worth money. They'll sell it."

"This ship is designed to take people from one solar system to another. No one here has any use for it. Besides, the Athenians don't think like you, Ebony. They don't care about money. This ship is a trophy, and a trophy is far more valuable to them than any amount of money."

Ebony realized he was probably right. The Athenians would bring their prize home.

"But Talon is—I mean, there are predators."

"People are living on Talon, Ebony."

"Yeah. Cannibals. And they're twenty feet tall."

"Ten feet and they're not all cannibals."

"Oh, well," she said, ripe with sarcasm. "They're not all cannibals. That's good. I'm sure we'll be fine. After all, we're lucky."

Troy laughed. "You can stay here with the Athenians if you want. I'm going."

"When?"

"Look for yourself."

Ebony went to the window so she could see. Talon was just a small white dot in the distance.

As a youth, she'd learned about it in school. It was a small planet. It rotated on an axis that pointed straight at the sun, one side constantly bathed in sunlight, a red desert plagued by dust storms, too hot and dry for life, the other side, a mass of glaciers in permanent darkness, too cold for all but the hardiest. Between these two extremes was a thin strip of land where immense creatures devoured everything that moved. It was a place she knew she never wanted to visit, yet she was getting ready to do just that.

The time went by excruciatingly slowly, one minute followed by another until Talon became significant in the window.

"We're going too fast," Ebony said.

"They're using the planet's gravity as a power assist to cut down the time it'll take them to get to Atheni," Troy explained.

"Will we be able to steal back the shuttle, and slow it down enough to land on Talon?"

"If we go now."

She sighed.

They quietly went down the passageways towards the front of the ship, careful not to make any sound, listening for any sign of the Athenians. They had to open a massive hatch, and the screeching sound was unnerving. They kept moving, down another passageway, through another hatch, and—there was an Athenian, sitting in a chair, asleep at his post. His plasma assault rifle was resting against the wall, and the Cronish shuttle's hatch was open beside him.

"Wait here," Troy whispered.

He walked carefully, placing one foot firmly on the floor before lifting the other.

Ebony stopped breathing.

He went straight for the plasma gun, silently picked it up, and aimed it at the Athenian warrior.

Ebony moved forward.

The Athenian woke up.

Troy brought the gun up but didn't shoot. It was as if he thought holding a gun was enough, that the Athenian would just sit there with his hands up and do as directed. But of course, they don't think like that. Their thinking is different. The Athenian jumped up, stepped to his left, and then his right. Troy's gun went left and right also, but there was a delay, and the Athenian took full advantage of it. He swatted the gun from Troy's hand. Troy looked to see where the weapon landed, and the Athenian hit him across the side of the head so hard that his feet came out from under him.

Ebony bolted for the gun. She slid in on her knees and grabbed it as Troy hit the floor. She turned it towards the Athenian and fired. But the Athenian had stepped to the left, and she missed. She fired again, but the Athenian had gone to the right and was moving towards her. She fired again. The third shot hit him. He fell on top of her, and she was crushed like a child beneath a bear.

There was shouting in a distant passageway. She pushed as hard as she could, but she couldn't get the monster off. Troy rolled him off.

Athenian warriors came around the corner, and Ebony grabbed the gun and fired. She got up and ran for the shuttle as blue bolts struck the walls around her. She turned and fired again. An Athenian fell, but there were many more coming. She got on the shuttle, Troy pushed a button, and the shuttle's hatch shut. He went to the front, climbed into the pilot's seat, flicked on the power, and fired up the tokamak.

Ebony sat in the co-pilot's seat and shook her head. "You thought he was just going to sit there with his hands up, did you?"

Troy didn't reply. He pulled the shuttle away, spun it around so that it was facing away from Talon, and put the thrusters at full. It wasn't long before they hit the atmosphere.

"We're going way too fast," Ebony yelled as the shuttle started to shake. She put her harness on, and Troy did the same. The noise was deafening, and flames were shooting out from the sides of the windows. It was getting hot. Surprisingly, the shuttle slowed down much more quickly than anticipated. *It's the low gravity,* she surmised. Talon's gravity was only a quarter of Cronos's gravity.

For a moment, it seemed like everything was going to be fine. But the main thrusters cut out. Troy frantically tried to get them back on, but it was no use. They were probably molten metal. The shuttle violently turned around. Streaks of fire and rippling veins of smoke raced across the windshield. When the smoke cleared, they were going down to a hilly terrain covered in teal fields with patches of plum-colored forest.

They went down slowly, but they kept going down, lower and lower until the tops of the trees seemed to reach out and grab them, spinning them around. They smashed through tree trunks, snapping them like twigs. The windshield shattered, and they hit a robust tree that split the hull in half. The cockpit tumbled through the air in slow motion, smashing through branches until it hit the ground, bounced twice, huge leaping bounces, rolled, and stopped.

"Are you okay?" Troy asked as he unbuckled himself.

"I'm okay," Ebony answered, not sure if she was. She unfastened her harness, got up, and instantly felt lighter.

Everything here was immense. The flowers were the size of the trees on Cronos. The trees were taller than skyscrapers and had trunks wider than houses. A wasp flew by, the size of a squirrel.

She jumped down into the dense foliage. There was a slapping of blanket sized leaves in the wind that built up to a thunderous roar, like a fleet of helicopters.

She shuddered. She knew that coming here was a bad idea. Why did she let Troy talk her into it?

She thought back to her childhood books that had stories about Talon. But the stories weren't like this. The size of everything here was much, much bigger than what she'd imagined. Everything here was beyond belief.

Leona

This was not the room Leona wanted for the meeting. It had a musty smell to it. Its table could only seat eight, its chandeliers were absurdly small, and its high back chairs were plain, too plain, yet here she stood, waiting for her generals. There was no time to waste. The room would have to do.

On one wall, the portraits of her mother and father stared down at her. Her mother, Queen Monica, seemed young, younger than any memory she had of her. Her father, King William, was more than twice her mother's age. She remembered his funeral, how she'd cried and cried, and how she'd loved him and hated him. He had done nothing but spoiled her through the years, and she'd done nothing but fought with him.

She didn't know it at the time, yet through those very same years, he had fought with, mistreated, and been scorned by his people.

General Leontine was the first to march into the room. He was the one she hated the most. He was incredibly arrogant and stubbornly methodical. Leona was sure the enemy would have no difficulty anticipating his every move.

"Your Majesty." He bowed with his briefcase in hand.

"Have a seat," she said with a wave. "This won't take long."

"If you want a full report, it'll take more than a few minutes, Your Majesty."

"Sit. Where are the others?"

"Coming." He remained standing for a moment as if contemplating his next move, then sat, and pulled some papers from his briefcase.

General Steen and another seven officers came in together. They bowed out of sync.

"Have a seat, gentlemen," Leona said. "Let's get started."

"Would you like my chair?" General Steen asked.

"Good of you to ask, but no, I prefer to stand. I presume my daughter hasn't been found?"

"Not yet, Your Majesty," Steen said, "but we're doing everything we can."

"Which is what exactly?"

"I've two full divisions going from door to door, questioning everyone. We're checking with the ticket purveyors of every train and every spaceship. It's just a matter of time before we find her."

"If she isn't found in the next few hours, I want you to quadruple your efforts. Do I make myself clear?"

"Very clear," General Steen said. "We'll use every possible resource. I assure you."

"How long before the Athenians get to Erin?"

"Their numbers have been diminished," General Maxim said, "and their pace has slowed considerably. It'll take them a long time."

Steen shook his head.

"How long?" she asked.

"Weeks, maybe more," General Leontine interjected.

"Days," Steen said, "if that."

Weeks? Leona wondered. Was Leontine delusional? Days were closer to the truth. "What do we have, and how long will it take to get it there?"

"We have to attack," Leontine said, "or we'll leave ourselves exposed."

Leona took a deep breath. "We're losing, you stupid idiot. We have to take a defensive position and hold on until we can get reinforcements. If we don't stop them now, even Uttara's gods won't be able to help us. General Steen, what have we got?"

"Forty-three divisions on various bases to the north. Two hundred and forty-seven divisions in bases halfway around the planet. Thirty-seven divisions in training in Braxis and two divisions in training that are—"

"Those aren't even close to being ready," Leontine snapped.

"Shut up!" Leona barked. "Let him speak."

"The two divisions in training are the ones being used to search for Princess Charline," Steen said.

"How long would it take forty-three divisions in the north to get to Erin?"

"The fighter jets and bombers can be there in hours, but the rest of the army will take a day or two."

"Depending on the weather," Leontine said.

"General Leontine," Leona stated flatly. "When I want your opinion, I'll ask for it."

"It's my job to inform and advise. If I can't—"

"Get out!" Leona snapped, taking a quick step towards him.

"But I was just—"

"Go!" She pointed at the door, her arm straight, her index finger extended.

He gathered his papers, stuffed them in his case, stood, and marched to the door. He stopped and glanced back as if debating what parting words to convey, but then he opened the door and was gone.

"How long would it take one hundred divisions on the other side of the planet to get here."

"They aren't all in one place," General Solingen said, so It'll take different time for each division, but there's a considerable risk. The reason the Athenians landed at Catina is that there was no army there to defend it. I don't think it's wise to leave any part of the planet defenseless. The Athenians are landing more troops all the time.

Leona nodded. "How long?"

"Weeks," General Steen said.

"And how many divisions are on the front in Erin now?"

"Fifty-two."

"You told me there was eighty."

"There was."

"How could twenty-nine Athenian divisions take out twenty-eight of our divisions that quickly? How's that possible?"

"The Athenians have taken losses too, almost a third of their force," Steen said, his eyes desperately averting hers as if looking at her would cause him to turn to stone.

"Well, that's reassuring," Leona barked back sarcastically. "Bring in another thirty divisions from the north, and do it smartly. I don't want any more surprises." The generals and officers stood, and as they bowed, Leona shouted, "And find my daughter!"

They moved out, like cows plodding from a barn.

Leona peered up at her father's portrait. He was gone, yet she still wanted to impress him.

Ebony

Ebony was on a planet where the sun never rose, never sank, never moved at all. It was bizarre, and it gave her the feeling that time wasn't passing.

They'd searched through the bits and pieces of the wreckage for the plasma assault guns. When they finally found them, they were mangled hunks of metal. Useless and dangerous. They were lucky they hadn't exploded in the crash.

She'd slept, she wasn't sure how long, while Troy kept watch, and he'd slept while she kept watch. There was no road, no beaten path, no sign of civilization, no sign of anything but huge wasps, gargantuan spiders, and monstrous dragonflies. A nightmare. A perpetually-sunny nightmare.

They found the edge of the forest and gazed down at beautiful-rolling hills, swaths of reddish-brown elephant grass, and immense carnation-like flowers with striking teal leaves topped with yellow crowns. The scene would have been breathtaking if everything wasn't so damn big. She felt that, at any moment, she might get stepped on, like an insect, by some enormous creature.

As they worked their way through a field of carnations, a large shadow crossed their path. A pterodactyl with bat-like wings and a long beak circled overhead. Ebony stopped and trembled like a mouse under a hawk.

"We should keep moving," Troy said, after glancing up, seemingly unconcerned.

"Aren't you afraid of that thing?" Ebony asked, not taking her eyes off it.

"It can't hurt us," Troy said. He marched on.

"But how can you be so sure?" she asked, rubbernecking to monitor the damn thing.

It circled like a vulture and suddenly flew off. Apparently, it agreed with Troy. She walked behind him for hours, and when she was too tired to keep going, she stopped and sat down.

Troy sat with her. "You should sleep."

Ebony's stomach and the threat of another pterodactyl hounded her thoughts. As tired as she was, she knew she wasn't going to be able to sleep. "First, you sleep," she said. "Then me."

He smiled and without a word, lay down on the ground. Within minutes, his eyes were closed, and his chest was oscillating. Ebony kept a sharp eye for predators, but her fatigue caught up with her, and in a sitting position, she drifted off.

A flapping sound woke her, and she opened her eyes to the hulking wings of another pterodactyl, its claws extended, ready to snatch her up. She rolled to her right, and when she looked back, the bird was being swept away by the wind.

She bounced to her feet and was startled, realizing that there were hundreds of animals around her. They were covered in long dark brown fur and held down a massive head with two long, curved horns, like buffalo, yet they were different and four times the size.

She couldn't see Troy anywhere.

Suddenly, there were yelps, and the buffalo-like creatures collectively lifted their heads and bolted, some straight towards her.

Ebony bolted too, leaping in long strides through the grass, and glancing back as she went.

The animals bounded through the air, leaping higher with each stride. A spear struck one as it passed by. It reared up.

Cannibals, twice her height, on mammoth horse-like creatures with long pointed ears and big eyes, galloped up around their prey. The cannibals threw more spears. Two went into the side of the buffalo-like animal, and one went through its neck.

The creature snorted, spun, kicked its hind legs high in the air, tossed its head, and angrily tried to shake the spear from its throat. Blood gushed from its neck and flowed down its left front leg.

Ebony turned and kept running, plowing through the elephant grass and up the hill. The herd ran by on either side of her. When she got near the crest of the hill, she stopped and looked back. The cannibals gathered around their prey. It went down on its front knees and collapsed.

As she stood watching, in the corner of her eye, she saw something move. She snapped her head around.

Standing in the elephant grass, just a few feet away, was a humongous wolf-like creature with a long nose. Her thoughts went berserk, and she imagined the creature lunging at her and sinking its pair of fangs into her neck. She looked around for something to use as a weapon. She spotted a stick. It was too small, but she reached down and grabbed it anyway.

The creature growled quietly. Another wolf-like creature, shorter, came out of the elephant grass to her left, and a third, much bulkier, circled to her right. It started growling as well.

She looked behind her and discovered half a dozen more. They also started growling. She turned to the one in the elephant grass and swung her stick.

It quickly retreated and crouched down.

She turned to find one behind her and spun her stick around. It moved back.

Then, she saw Troy running towards her. Swooping down behind him was a giant bird, much bigger than a pterodactyl. It had a curved beak and was gray and brown like a falcon.

She cringed at the sight of the pained expression on Troy's face as the giant falcon's claws sank into his ribcage. With each flap of its enormous wings, it rose slightly, fell slightly, and rose a little more.

The wolf-like creatures bolted towards the falcon, leaped into the air, and snapped their jaws, but it was beyond their reach. With Troy in its grasp, the falcon flew over Ebony.

Higher and higher it went until an arrow came up from behind the hill's crest and struck it. The falcon let go of Troy.

Ebony winced, sure that the fall would kill him, but he didn't fall the way a man would fall on Cronos. He fell slowly and went down behind the crest of the hill.

The falcon also fell, even more slowly. The wolf-like creatures raced towards it and disappeared over the crest.

Ebony followed. At the crest of the hill, she saw a giant cannibal with purple skin. On his head, he had a pelt of some kind of small animal, its ears pointing up, and its paws hanging down on either side of his face. He picked up Troy's body and threw him up onto the back of his massive horse-like creature. In one fluid motion, he got on his mount and started it into a quick trot.

Behind him, the wolf-like creatures were ferociously ripping apart the giant falcon.

Ebony lay flat in the elephant grass as the cannibal passed by. She followed as he went to the sight of the fallen buffalo-like creature.

The hunters had tied the creature between two poles and lifted the poles to the backs of two massive and strange-looking animals with round bellies, longhorns, heavy legs, and massive hooves. These animals dragged the carcass as the cannibals rode alongside.

Ebony followed, jogging with a measured pace, careful not to be seen, and determined not to be left behind.

After a while, the wolf-like creatures came up from behind, raced straight by Ebony, and joined the cannibals, running on either side of the carcass. For hours, Ebony struggled to keep up with them, continually scanning the skies for predators, until they came to a place in a valley by a stream where rough skins were laid over bones and tied together to make huts.

She hid in the elephant grass on the side of an escarpment and watched the females greet the men. They examined the carcass. The wolf-like creatures curled up on the ground off to one side. Children, most of them taller than Ebony, gathered around to watch. Troy was hauled down off the horse-like creature and carried into a hut.

Rose

Inside the medical box, Rose found a bottle identical to what Nicko had shown her back on Cronos, a bottle of Rend. Not sure how powerful it was, and determined to conserve it, she only took small doses. It worked beautifully, getting rid of her headache almost completely, but the effects only lasted a few hours before they slowly started to wear off.

The Athenian—whose name she'd learned was Suzi—brought them clothing that was too big, but they wore them anyway, rolling up the pant legs and sleeves until their dirty attire was washed and returned. Solin's shirt couldn't be repaired, so he kept the Athenian shirt. For three days, Suzi cleaned every part of the ship, tended to Solin's wound, and prepared meals.

Solin wanted to learn, not just Cronish, but Athenian as well. He got both Rose and Suzi to teach him the names for various items, body parts, and everything they could touch, point to, or somehow gesture. He repeated the words, and slowly, his vocabulary and his understanding seemed to improve.

On the fourth day, they arrived at the moon, Vole, dark gray with red lines tearing across its face. Vole cut a path through the asteroid rings around the massive-blue-gas planet, Jupith.

"Suzi prychod," Solin said, feeling well enough to join them on the bridge and lounging in the command chair.

Jen, sitting at the helm, rolled her eyes. "It's like talking to a monkey. Urr, urr, urr."

"Stop it, Jen," Rose scolded.

"Or what?" Jen asked.

"Just stop it." Rose looked at Solin thoughtfully and shook her head. "Don't worry, Solin. We're not going to leave Suzi behind."

"She's a pink," Jen said sharply. "We can't bring her with us."

"She's coming with us, Jen," Rose said, defiantly. Her eye had begun to heal, yet the skin around it still looked bruised.

"Bad idea," Jen snarled. "She'll be the death of us, for sure."

"If you want to stay behind, be my guest. When the Athenians come on board, you can learn what it's like to be a sex slave. Maybe then you'll be a little more sympathetic. She's one of us now. So get used to it."

"She's not one of us. She's a pink. I say we ditch her and the white the minute we get down there."

Rose was a wild dog, unleashed. "We're not ditching anyone!"

Jen stayed silent for a moment and studied the main screen. "We're in position. Ralarra is right below us."

"Let's go." Rose beaconed Solin and Suzi and headed to the shuttle. She could hardly wait to get down there and be back in normal gravity.

They boarded the shuttle. Suzi sat in the pilot's seat while Solin got into the co-pilot's seat. Jen closed the hatch, and they headed down.

The moon was a mass of volcanoes. The closer they got to its surface, the more alarming it became. The number of volcanoes on Vole was staggering. Sprawling rivers of red gripped extensive areas of the surface. The city of Ralarra was on the side of the only mountain range that didn't have at least one active volcano.

There were a vast number of shuttles and transports attempting to land at the spaceport. Suzi had to get in line, circle, and wait for a turn.

"Have you been here before?" Rose asked.

"No," Jen said.

"Do you know anything about this place?"

"A little."

"Why's it like this?"

"I guess refugees are coming here from Cronos, trying to escape the war."

"No, I mean, why are there so many volcanoes?"

"The gravity of Jupih causes the tidal movement of the magma inside the moon. As a result, the moon is constantly generating heat. They say the moon will explode eventually, and the particles leftover from the explosion will form another ring around Jupih."

Suzi put on a headset. "Ralarra aite smashd," she said. "Pad ceithir."

She took the shuttle down to an extremely crowded spaceport. Once on the ground, she pulled four gas masks out of a storage bin and handed them out.

Jen held her mask as if it were infected with decease and tossed it aside. She went to the hatch and stepped out into the sweltering heat. Immediately, she started coughing. She rushed back in, grabbed her mask, and pulled it over her face. She coughed a few more times and took several deep breaths. "Isn't this a fun place," she said with a muffled voice.

Rose stepped up to the hatch. "Oh, by the gods, is it ever hot."

"Yeah, but it's a dry heat," Jen replied sarcastically.

Rose smiled.

The normal gravity was a huge relief. They entered the terminal where a vast sea of people, most wearing red robes, swarmed the platform. Jen led the group, followed by Solin, Rose, and then Suzi. Suzi was almost two feet taller than the monks and stood out like a marshmallow on a cherry bed.

As they moved across the platform, Rose glanced back. Suzi was gone.

"Solin!" she cried. "Where's Suzi?"

Solin spun around, searched in every direction, and shook his head. They retraced their steps back to the landing pad and stood helpless as the Athenian shuttle they had arrived in, lifted off.

"What did I tell you?" Jen asked, her head tilted.

"Damn it," Rose cursed.

"She's a pink, Rose. What did you expect?"

Rose's head was starting to hurt. She needed a fix. She excused herself, went into a washroom cubicle, and took another small dose of Rend. When she came out, she joined up with Jen and Solin, and they grabbed a cab. Inside the cab, she tore off her mask. "The Muunakshi Akkan Temple," she said.

The Volian cab driver looked puzzled.

She repeated it slowly. "Muu-nak-shi Ad-kan Tem-ple."

The driver nodded. "Eht Muunakshi Akkan Elpmet."

"Yeah. That's it."

"Off to find our savior?" Jen asked.

"The monks will know, Jen. You'll see."

"Oh, for the sake of the gods," Jen said, shaking her head.

"What if he is the Messiah?"

"It's just a silly story, Rose."

"There's no harm in this."

"There is harm. These monks are a bunch of nut cases. They'll probably agree with you."

"Shut up, Jen. A little religion would do you some good. Just go with it."

It was a long drive that went up the side of a mountain. Ash fell from the sky like snow. The roads, houses, buildings, and even the red robes of the monks walking in the streets were covered.

When they got to the temple, Rose looked up through a cloudy windshield at a massive structure, displaying two towers, and featuring a wide stone staircase leading up to two heavy wooden doors.

"How much?" she asked the driver.

The driver screwed up his face.

She brought out her Cronish money and fanned it out.

He plucked two bills from the fan.

Rose pulled her mask on, checked to make sure Solin and Jen had theirs and got out.

Below them was the city of Ralarra. Through the clouds of ash, she could see the spaceport with dozens of rocket ships standing side by side, and beyond that, there was a long string of volcanoes, many of them rumbling with activity.

There weren't many Volians in the street. Those that didn't have a mask had a cloth pulled up over their noses. The heat was truly unbearable.

Rose walked up to the door of the temple, knocked, and waited. It opened.

"Xos," said a Volian, wearing a gray robe, bald with callous greenish-yellow skin, cracked with black lines crossing his face, and deeply scared. "Menem Pastor Darek."

"I hope someone here can speak Cronish," Rose said, her voice muffled, her body fighting off a crawling flesh sensation. "We need help."

"I Venerable Elder Darek," the hideous monk said. "How help?"

"You can start by letting us in," Jen said, "before we melt into the portico."

He opened the door wider. They stepped in and ripped off their masks.

"For the life of me, I don't know how anyone can justify living in such horrid conditions," Jen snapped. "You must all be masochists."

"It is way," Darek said calmly, shutting the door.

"Crazy is what it is," Jen said with a jutting chin. "As far as I'm concerned, you're all raving lunatics."

"So," Darek said after a moment of awkward silence, "what can do for you?"

Rose hesitated. "I know this is going to sound like a bit of a reach," she said, putting a hand on Solin's shoulder, "but I've reason to believe that this man is the Messiah, and I'm trying to find out how he can tap into his powers."

The Volian pursed his lips and twisted his face, making him look even more grotesque. He stared back at Rose without moving or speaking. He looked at Solin and back at Rose. "You think he Messiah?"

"Yes," Rose said, nodding emphatically.

"Why you think that?"

"He's from Uttara," she stated defiantly.

"You can't be serious," Darek said, his mouth open.

"Of course, I'm serious," Rose said. "If you had any idea of what I've been through." She shook her head.

"But Uttara many light-years away," Darek said. "It would take—"

"What's wrong with you?" Rose barked. "Don't you believe me?"

"Anyone can say he Messiah," Darek said, shrugging.

"Normally, I'd side with the olive," Jen said, "but, on this one, I'm with the yellow." She turned to face Rose. "Anyone can claim to be the Messiah."

"This man," Rose said, putting a hand on Solin's chest, "was frozen in a hibernation chamber. There was equipment on his ship that brought him back to life."

"What ship?" Darek asked.

"His ship," Rose said, raising her voice and talking through clenched teeth with forced restraint. "I saw it with my own eyes."

Darek took two small steps back. "You see what?"

"I saw a man, frozen, with no heartbeat, warmed up, and shocked back to life. I need to know what he can do, and I need you to stop questioning me and start believing."

Darek stared back at Rose without speaking.

"I don't think you're getting through to him, Rose," Jen said, "It's your approach. You can't just shove it down his throat. You have to kinda ease it in. He can't make giant leaps of faith like that. Especially a yellow. Yes, he was in a hibernation chamber, and yes, he was brought back to life, but let's be honest, that doesn't mean he's the Messiah. We don't know who he is."

Rose grimaced.

Darek was wide-eyed.

Solin was up on stage in front of a heavy book on a pulpit. "Sviaty pismien," he said, breaking the silence.

Darek scrutinized him. "Yes, my child," he said, cracking a smile. He went up to the stage, picked up the book, and handed it to him. Solin took it, opened it, looked at it, and gave it back.

Rose went up and grabbed it. Burdened by the sheer weight of it, she put it back on the pulpit, looked at it, and found it was written in Volian. "Do you have a Sacred Writings written in Cronish?" she asked.

"Yes," Darek said. "Wait here." He walked off and disappeared through a doorway.

"I can't believe we're doing this," Jen said. "It's a book. There's no treasure inside."

"Stop it, Jen."

When Darek returned, he had another Volian in tow, even uglier than Darek, his skin also a greenish-yellow, yet the cracks were darker and deeper, the scars more plentiful. He held a heavy book.

"Hello, I'm Venerable Brother Hewitt," he said with only a slight Volian accent. "Venerable Elder Darek tells me that you're looking for the Messiah?"

"We're not looking for him," Rose said with a pinched expression. "We've found him. He's right here." She put a hand on Solin's chest and lifted her chin slightly. "Is that the Cronish Sacred Writings?"

"It is," Hewitt said, "but certainly you're familiar with it. It's taught as a subject in your schools."

"It is," Rose said with a slight grimace, "but it's a thick book, and I wasn't a particularly diligent student."

"The Sacred Writings have been transliterated to all languages. Each translation is slightly different depending on the linguist's nuances and his understanding of the science."

"I thought the gods wrote the Sacred Writings of Uttara?" Rose asked.

"Oh, please don't touch that," Hewitt told Solin.

Solin was removing the glass cover of a book on a pulpit along the wall of the temple, and Hewitt's words didn't slow his progress.

"He doesn't speak Cronish," Jen said with a cynical grin.

"Please, tell him not to touch it."

"Sorry. I don't speak his language," Jen said, still grinning. "No one does."

"What's he looking at?" Rose asked.

Hewitt sighed. "It's the Old Sacred Writings. It's very delicate."

Solin was staring at a page in the book.

"Looks like he's reading it," Jen said.

"No," Hewitt said, putting the Cronish Sacred Writings down. "It takes great dedication to learn the language. Our Venerable Father Moritz is a student, and he's only been able to transcribe a small portion of it."

"Is Moritz here?" Rose asked.

"Yes. He's downstairs."

"Get him," Jen barked.

"Young lady," Hewitt said, grimacing, "You're a guest here. Please act like it."

"Listen, I know how you feel. I'm having a hard time tolerating you too. But Solin's reading the Old Sacred Writings," Jen said, pointing at him. "I think you should get this Moritz guy."

"This is important," Rose said. "This man is the Messiah."

"Yeah," Jen said. "Try to get along."

"I think you should leave," Hewitt said, stone-faced.

Jen raised her eyebrows. "Fine. You want me to leave? I'm out of here."

"For crying out loud, Jen!" Rose yelled. "Just shut up!"

Silence followed.

Hewitt threw a hand into the air. "He's not the Messiah, and you're insulting." He went towards the front door. "I must ask you to leave."

"Okay, okay," Rose pleaded. "I apologize. My friend was rude, and I'll throw her out if I have to, but could you please get Moritz? Don't you want to know if he can read the Old Sacred Writings?"

"Leave now," he said, "or I'll call the police."

"She apologized," Jen said.

"But not you," Hewitt said defiantly.

"Look at him," Rose said, pointing at Solin. "He's been staring at that the Old Sacred Writings for a very long time. He's reading it."

Hewitt and Darek both took a moment to watch Solin.

"Honest to the gods, he's reading it," Rose said.

Hewitt gave a slow, disbelieving shake of his head. They all stood in silence, watching.

"He is reading it, isn't he?" Hewitt admitted.

"Most definitely," Rose said.

"Venerable Elder Darek," Hewitt said. "Would you mind fetching Venerable Father Moritz?"

"Certainly," Darek said. He got up and left.

Jen leaned against the wall, folded her arms, and crossed her legs. Hewitt stared at Solin.

"Does Venerable Father Moritz speak Cronish?" Rose asked.

"Yes," Hewitt said. "Monks are required to learn a second language as a part of their schooling. Cronish is the language of choice for most."

Hewitt moved up beside Solin and looked at the Old Sacred Writings while Rose snuck back to the second row of benches and sat down so that the pew in front of her blocked their view. She pulled the Rend and the syringe from her pocket, opened the bottle, drew a small quantity, and inserted it into her arm. She squeezed the Rend in and quickly stuffed the vial and syringe back in her pocket. She held a finger over the injection site so that it wouldn't bleed.

No sooner was she done than Darek came back with Moritz trailing behind. Moritz looked more or less identical to Darek, except he was a bit shorter and wore a red robe.

Rose got up and walked up to him, discretely holding her arm. "We're here from—"

"Yes, yes," Moritz said, interrupting. "Venerable Elder Hewitt tells me that you're impertinent, but we're tolerating it because Venerable Brother Hewitt thinks this man, here,"—he pointed at Solin—"appears to be reading the Old Sacred Writings."

Solin was still staring at the book.

"He's reading it," Rose said, "which means he's the Messiah."

"My dear child," Hewitt said. "Just because he can read doesn't mean he's the Messiah."

"But he's reading the Old Sacred Writings," she said, her eyes wide and head tilted.

"He must have learned the language somewhere," Hewitt insisted.

"He just got here from Uttara," Rose said. "How can you explain that? Go ahead, and ask him a question in his language."

Moritz paused. "I've never had to speak the language. I don't think I can."

"Just try a word," Rose said.

Moritz stood thinking for a moment. "Vy zdolny da cydac sto."

Solin instantly looked up at him. "Tak." He gawked at Moritz, appeared confused for a moment, and went back to reading the book.

Moritz brought his hands up to the top of his head.

"What did you ask him?" Rose asked.

"I asked him if he could read the book," Moritz said.

"And he said, 'yes', didn't he?"

"Let me try something else," Moritz said. "Sto robic heta sakzam."

"Heta kaza z boh I to miesija." Solin replied.

"Zjauliajucca vy to miesija."

"Ja nie treba viedac chto ja ja."

"What did he say?" Rose asked.

Moritz brought a hand to his chin. "I asked him what the book said, and he said it was about God and the Messiah. I asked him if he was the Messiah, and he told me he didn't know who he was."

"Does he know who the Messiah is?" Hewitt asked.

"I'll ask him," Moritz said, nodding. "Alie vy viedac chto to miesija josc."

"Tak."

"I to bahi z Uttara."

"Nie. Ja tolki viedac z adzin boh."

"He knows who the Messiah is, yet he only knows of one god."

"Which one?" Hewitt asked.

"Let me ask." Moritz turned to look at Solin. "Adkul svoj boh zyc."

"Na Niabio."

"It's a different god, one we don't have. I didn't know the meaning of that word 'boh', and the passage didn't make sense to me, so I left it out."

"You left what out?" Hewitt asked.

"The passage about there being only one god."

"That's not a small thing," Hewitt said, his jaw lowered.

"I can't translate what I can't understand," Moritz said, throwing a hand in his direction.

"You're not supposed to leave things out," Hewitt said. "It's the word of the gods."

"Yes, I know, but as I said, I can't write what I can't—"

"Stop it!" Rose interrupted. "He's the Messiah. Admit it. He has to be."

Jen raised a finger. "You're jumping to con—"

"Shut up, Jen!" Rose barked.

Darek turned away, lifting his arms to the gods.

Solin went back to reading and flipping pages.

"Your job is to interpret," Hewitt said to Moritz, his hand on his hips, "and only interpret."

"I couldn't make sense of it," Moritz said. "Why would there be only one god? I considered going to Bacchus, but I realized it didn't matter, so I left it out."

"Bacchus?" Rose asked. "Why would you go to Bacchus?"

"The Old Sacred Writings," Moritz said, "was revised from the Ancient Sacred Writings about six thousand years ago to reflect the beliefs of the people who lived on Vole."

"People have been living here for six thousand years?" Jen asked with a look of disbelief.

"And the Ancient Sacred Writings is on Bacchus?" Rose asked, her eyes narrowing.

"Translating is onerous," Moritz told Hewitt. "It's more difficult than you think. You have to place the meanings of the words. It's a painstaking process. It's all based on assumptions."

"You should told us," Darek said, raising his arms to the gods again.

Moritz moved up beside Solin and pointed to some text on the page. "For example, this word here, *sud*," Moritz said, pointing, "could mean box, cart, container, or something completely different.

"Ship," Solin said. "Word mean ship."

"Solin knows this language," Rose said.

"Yes, but the Messiah is all-powerful," Moritz said. "He knows, not just the language of the Old Sacred Writings but all of the languages. He's supposed to lead people towards a better way of living, speak words of wisdom, and perform miracles. I find it hard to believe that this man is the Messiah."

"There must be some way to tap into his powers," Rose said. "Hasn't the Sacred Writings been prophesied as being the source of the Messiah's power."

Moritz shrugged.

"He is powerful," Jen said, "if killing pinks is a way to measure."

Rose sighed. "Perhaps, we're in too much of a hurry," she said. "He's smart. What if he were to learn the languages? What if his wisdom is his power. And what if he got his wisdom from the gods of Uttara?"

"He said his god doesn't live in Uttara," Moritz said. "He said his god lives in Nieba."

Charline

Charline had expected to be treated like a visiting dignitary, given a room in the Empress's palace, gifts of flowers, bread, cheese, fruits, and wine. Instead, Bacchian guards seized her and scuttled her away as if she were some criminal. They bound her hands behind her back and pulled a sack over her head.

Unable to see, she only knew that she'd spent time on the tilted damp metal floor of a submarine, time in a hot and humid place, and time on an elevator. They untied her hands, pulled off the sack, and put her in a small prison cell with stone walls and a dirt floor.

They slipped food under the door twice daily, and days later, they brought her to an extraordinarily large cavern and forced her to her knees. The cavern had thick pillars, like gigantic tree trunks, spaced far apart, holding up a curved surface of solid rock filled with huge stalactites, some coming all the way down to the floor.

A green incandescent light emanated from below pools of water in each section of the cavern. Light danced across the stalactites in waves, like a sea of shimmering chandeliers. Lining the cavern's steep slopes were thousands of dimly lit stone houses that climbed the walls like honeycombs.

On her left was a guardsman wearing a shinny steel vest under a black robe and helmet. On her right was a young, Bacchian girl wearing a yellow gown with a hood. She was also on her knees, bowing with her hands folded together.

Behind her, an ocean of Bacchian people, with their legs tucked beneath them, peered up at a Bacchian High Priest adorned in a white robe with gold trim and a biretta on his head. He held up a large cross.

"Do you believe in the gods of Uttara?" the girl asked, turning to Charline.

"Yes, of course," Charline answered, adamant, surprised the girl could speak Cronish. "Tell the priest that I'm Queen Leona's daughter, Princess Charline."

The girl nodded but didn't speak to the priest until spoken to. She sat up and articulated like a frightened child. Rose heard her name mixed in with the Bacchian words.

"And do you believe in the Messiah?" she asked Charline.

"No."

"You don't?"

"I don't."

"Yet you're Cronish."

"I've never believed in the Messiah." It wasn't a lie.

Again, she spoke to the priest.

The priest nodded and spoke to the masses, raising his voice and swinging his cross from side to side.

"Did you tell him who I am?" Charline asked, confused.

"Yes," she replied.

"Am I going to see the Empress?"

"No one can see the Empress," the girl scolded. "All homage is due to the Empress. She gives protection from the evil within ourselves and from the evil within our enemies. Bear witness that the Empress is—"

"Nema," the flock shouted out in unison. Their thousands of heads dipped down, and their hands slapped the stone floor.

"our most sacred god," the girl said, finishing the sentence.

Charline couldn't believe what she was hearing. Wasn't she going to see the Empress? Did they think she was a god?

One of the guardsmen rose, grabbed Charline by the arms, and pulled her up. The priest spoke again.

"The Empress speaks words of appropriate justice," the girl translated. "Praise be to the Empress—"

"Nema," the thousands shouted out again and slapped their hands on the stone floor.

"For only she can save our souls."

"Tell him I'm royalty," Charline insisted, "and I'm not to be treated this way."

The girl ignored her.

The High Priest put the book and the cross down, picked up a smoking metal ball from a bowl, and waved it back and forth in front of Charline.

Charline cringed. It smelled like scorched rubber. "Tell him!" she pleaded. "Why don't you tell him?"

The metal ball sparked and crackled. As he placed it back in the bowl, he spoke again.

"The gods are my strength," the girl translated, "my shield, my heart, my resolve, my hope, my joy. Empress Zeta is—"

"Nema," the thousands yelled out, slapping their hands on the stone floor once again.

"Our Saviour."

The High Priest barked out an order to the guardsman. The guardsman grabbed Charline by the arms. He was short but powerful, and Charline wasn't able to impede his progress.

"Where are they taking me?" Charline pleaded to the girl as she was hauled away.

The girl kept her eyes forward and didn't answer.

"Tell me!" Charline shouted.

She didn't respond.

Charline was marched across the platform into a tunnel and then an elevator. They went down for an absurd amount of time. At the bottom, the doors opened, and the guardsman dragged her down another tunnel. She had to struggle to keep up, almost losing her balance more than once.

It was unbearably hot, and she'd never been so confused. This couldn't be happening. She needed to talk to someone who understood who she was.

The guardsman pushed her into a massive cavern with a pit filled with putrid-smelling water, like a vast cesspool. Hundreds of skimpily dressed slaves, mostly Bacchian, but also a few Volian and Cronish, swirled pans in knee-high water. The sound of whips snapped like firecrackers.

The guardsman brought her down to the edge of the pit where another guardsman, holding a long whip, held out a pan towards Charline.

She gave him an incredulous stare. "I will not," she cried out defiantly. "I'm—"

With the flick of a wrist, the guardsman cracked his whip. It curled around her neck with a vicious snap.

She screamed. The pain was far worse than anything she could've imagined. Her knees buckled. She fought off the ensuing agony with clenched teeth.

The guardsman held out the pan again.

She took it, begrudgingly.

With his whip, he beckoned her to get into the putrid water.

She hesitated but only for an instant. Having to withstand another crack of the whip was too big a price to pay. She waded in.

He motioned for her to scoop.

She did that too. Her mother would have them all killed if she knew. But she didn't know, did she? No one knew.

The pit was vast, and slaves toiled like ants. Charline did what the others did and swirled her pan, mimicking them without knowing why. "They can't treat me like this," she whimpered bitterly. "I'm royalty."

"Keep your voice down," the blue-skinned girl beside her whispered. She looked even younger than the one in the yellow robe. She was short and skinny, especially her waist. She wore frayed shorts and a skimpy halter top over a flat chest.

A guardsman moved towards Charline and cracked his whip just inches from her face. She shuddered and quickly swirled her pan.

"You speak Cronish?" Charline whispered when the guardsman had moved on.

"Yes. Call me Beau."

"There's been a mistake, Beau. I shouldn't be here. I'm royalty. I'm Princess Charline. I must get an audience with the Empress."

"There's been no mistake," she said, her eyes darting to and fro. "The High Priest can't make a mistake. He has divine knowledge."

"You don't understand. I'm the daughter of Queen Leona of Cronos, next in line to the Crown."

"It doesn't matter," Beau asserted, giving her head slight shake.

A slave with muscles like muskox dragged a water hose over close to them and blasted the sand with it.

Charline and Beau moved back out of the way.

"It does matter," Charline insisted. "It matters very much. They can't treat me this way. I'm not some mere slave to be swatted around. I'm royalty."

"If the High Priest says you're a slave, you're a slave."

When Charline realized the impact of what she was saying, tears welled up in her eyes. She was a slave now. The life she had before was gone—her existence, meaningless. There was nothing she could do, and no one she could talk to. She glanced down at her pan. "What are we looking for?" she asked with a choked voice.

"Diamonds. If you find one, don't try to hide it. If you do, you'll be shot."

A guardsman moved closer. Charline cringed at the thought of being whipped again. She scooped and sifted, scooped, and sifted, over and over, nothing but dirt. She grew tired. At one point, she lost her footing in the mud and splashed into the water like a clumsy fool. When she got up, her layered silk dress and her hair were soaked with the putrid stench. She forced herself to carry on scooping and sifting. As the hours wore on, her pan became burdensome, and her legs began to tremble.

A whistle blew, and she was directed to get out of the water, was brought up a path to a ledge, and put in line to get a small bowl of slop. It tasted like rotten apples, but she was hungry, and she devoured it quickly, afraid she might not be allowed to finish. After the meal, she was told to lie down. The ground was hard, but it was dry, and Charline was exhausted. She closed her eyes.

When she woke, a guardsman stood over her with dark eyes. He had a bowl haircut, a goatee, and no shirt. A leather belt held suspenders strapped over a curly, black-haired chest. He had a plasma gun fixed to his belt and a whip in his hand.

"Your Imperial Highness," he said, grinning.

"Yes," Charline answered, hopeful that the misunderstanding had been resolved.

"Time get up Highness." he said, his grin growing wider.

Her heart sank. He was mocking her. "Washroom?" Charline asked.

"Over there," he said, pointing further up the path where several slaves were squatting.

Charline got up and noticed Beau sitting on the ground behind her. She must have told the guardsman who she was. Why? Was she trying to help, or was there a more sinister reason?

Charline made her way to the "washroom".

When she got back, the guardsman was waiting.

"I need to see Empress Zeta," Charline said.

Roundhead nodded.

"I'm serious."

Roundhead nodded again. "Time to work."

Charline sighed, made her way down the path, and back into the water. Beau followed her in.

"Why did you tell the guardsman who I am?" Charline asked.

"He asked about you," she said. "If a slave has a rich family, sometimes they can be traded for money."

"And is he going to trade?"

"He said he couldn't. If the High Priest knows you're royalty and sent you down here, you're here to stay."

She should never have come to Bacchus. The captain of the saucer was right. She should have listened. She scooped and sifted, scooped, and sifted.

She was startled by a guardsman who savagely yelled at a Bacchian slave. The slave defiantly shook his head. All of the slaves stopped working. They stood and watched.

Charline watched in horror as the guardsman pulled out his plasma gun, pointed it at his head, and pulled the trigger. The slave's head was smashed like a pumpkin, and he fell like a rag doll.

Two Bacchian slaves moved in and pulled the body from the water. Then they stood back as the guardsman moved in and searched the dead slave's mouth. He didn't find anything, pulled out a knife, and tossed it on the ground. Then he picked out a skinny Bacchian slave and spoke to him.

The skinny slave shook his head.

The guardsman got angry and yelled at him.

The skinny slave picked up the knife and went to the dead body. He bent over and cut the dead slave's stomach open.

Charline couldn't watch, turned her head away, and took deep breaths. When she managed to gather the nerve to look back, the skinny slave was digging with his fingers in his entrails. He came out, holding up a diamond with blood-soaked fingers. He washed it off in the putrid water and handed it to the guard.

Charline went back to scooping and sifting.

The body of the dead slave, his entrails spilled from his gut, lay there while a Volian slave dug his grave near the pit's edge. When he finished, the body was dragged over and dumped in.

Charline kept sifting.

An old Cronish man, not far from Charline, fell from exhaustion. Another Cronish slave got him back up on his feet, but he was groggy and teetering. He fell three more times, and when he was too weak to stand, roundhead came up and pulled out his gun. Charline waded through the water as fast as she could and got in front of him. "Don't shoot him," she said. "Let him rest and recover."

"Get out of the way," roundhead yelled.

She didn't.

Roundhead charged at her and violently pushed her aside, sending her crashing into the water. He raised his gun and shot the man in the leg, in the chest, and, finally, in the head. Two Bacchian slaves dragged the dead man out of the water. The Volian who had dug the first grave went and got his shovel.

Charline hastily went back to her place and wept while she scooped and sifted.

Jen

Jen hated Vole. Yellows were worse than blues and almost as bad as pinks. She'd rather be on Cronos in the middle of a war than have to listen to another minute of this hogwash.

She looked over at the white, sitting at the kitchen table in the basement of the temple. When he had killed all those pinks, she'd thought he was pretty damn cool, but here he was acting pathetic, totally absorbed in the Old Sacred Writings.

"If the Old Sacred Writings were transcribed from the Ancient Sacred Writings," Rose said, "then the book we should be looking at is the Ancient Sacred Writings."

Hewitt was standing over a pot on the stove, a wooden spoon in his hand, like a housemaid. "Don't get any ideas about going to Bacchus. You're not a monk. You can't go there. It's not your typical vacation spot. They don't believe in the Messiah."

"You don't want to go there," Darek said, sitting on a stool in the corner and shaking his head.

"It's not an option," Moritz reiterated. "The Bacchus live in an autocracy."

"And it's the High Priest and not the Empress that's in charge," Hewitt said.

The room went silent for several minutes, everyone deep in thought, their elbows on the table, their fingers spread across their faces, their eyes unwavering, like chess players.

"Need weapon," Solin said, breaking the silence.

Jen snapped her head around. "Who are you planning to kill now?"

"I'm sorry, Solin," Hewitt said, "but we don't keep weapons in the house of the gods, and we simply can't have them here. It's against everything we believe in."

"Anioly prychodz," Solin said. "Need weapon."

"Anioly means angels," Moritz said.

"Angels?" Jen asked. "What angels? What's he talking about?"

"Solin need weapon," Solin said, folding his arms.

"What angels?" Jen demanded.

He pointed upwards. "Anioly on ship," he said.

Of course, Jen thought. There were others like him on his ship, and when they woke up, the Athenians were there to greet them.

"How 'bout bow?" Darek asked.

"You still have that?" Hewitt asked, spinning his head to stare at him, wide-eyed. "I thought you were told to get rid of it."

"Hid it," Darek said.

"But it's totally against our religion to keep weapons," Hewitt said, his eyes narrowing. "How could you do that?"

Darek snapped back at Hewitt, speaking Volian.

"Venerable Elder Darek has a bow," Hewitt said, throwing a hand in the air. "The ministry told him it wasn't allowed, but apparently, he kept it anyway."

"Bow?" Darek asked Solin.

Solin nodded.

Hewitt barked at Darek in Volian.

Darek barked back at him, got up, and left the room.

"Well, well," Jen said, grinning. "A yellow with some backbone."

"More tea?" Hewitt asked in a cordial tone, reaching for the pot.

Jen nodded.

"This is ridiculous," Moritz said, shaking his head. "Why does he think angels are coming?"

"I know why," Jen said. "His ship was big. There was probably more than just one hibernation chamber on board and more than just one white. If it's true, and if they woke up in the hands of the pinks, they'd put them on Rend."

Rose sat up straight. "Well, I—I don't know. It's possible, I guess." Her eyes were fixed on Jen, her jaw slack.

"It's more than possible," Jen said. "They'd put the whites on Rend, get them addicted to it, and use the addiction to control them."

The kitchen went silent.

"We're so sorry to hear about what happened on Cronos," Hewitt said, changing the subject, bringing the pot to the table and pouring it into Jen's cup.

"Why? What happened?" Rose asked. "We've been completely cut off from any news for weeks now."

"The Athenians took Mead," Hewitt said.

"They did?"

"They did, and of course, the Cronish army tried to take it back," Hewitt said, bringing the teapot back to a hot pad on the kitchen counter. "They attacked and took heavy losses. When the Cronish troops became overextended, the Athenians counterattacked, killing every last one of them. When they were done killing, they retreated and dug in."

He picked up his wooden spoon and stirred. "The Cronish attacked again with greater numbers, but the Athenians kept their heads down and raked the Cronish with their plasma cannons. Only when they had an advantage in numbers did they counterattack, taking no prisoners. You'd think that the Cronish would come up with a different strategy, but no, they attacked again, this time with even greater numbers, and suffered even greater losses. The total Cronish losses for that battle are in the hundreds of thousands. They had to abandon Mead, and now three of your nine continents have fallen, and the death toll is rising." He shook his head.

Rose had her head down and was staring at the floor.

Darek came back, holding a bow and a quiver of arrows. Solin got up, took the bow from him, and pulled back on the string. He nodded at Darek, and Darek smiled. Solin put the bow and quiver of arrows next to his chair, sat down, and went back to reading.

"Having someone who can understand the Old Sacred Writings is a gift from the gods," Hewitt said. "It'd be a shame if we didn't take a little time to learn everything we can."

"If Jen's right about the angels, we can't stay here," Rose said, her hands folded, her fingers twitching. "I think it's time for us to go."

The monks sat quietly, sipping on their tea.

"What does the book say?" Hewitt asked Solin.

Solin looked up.

"Just wondering," Hewitt said, shrugging.

"Tea," Solin said, picking up his cup.

Hewitt rushed to get the kettle.

"Solin, what's in the book?" Rose asked.

"Book about people," Solin said, nodding.

"Well, I'm glad we got that settled," Jen said sarcastically.

"People die," Solin said.

"What people?" Rose asked.

"People Ziamli."

"Is Ziamli your home?"

He nodded.

"Is that why you're here?"

He shrugged.

"Is Ziamli in the Old Sacred Writings?" Hewitt asked.

"It is," Moritz said.

"And you left that out of the Volian addition too?"

"It didn't make any sense to me, so of course, I left it out."

"And you didn't tell us?"

"No, I didn't tell you. What would be the point? Who would believe it—a planet in Uttara where the people believe in one god?" He paused and lifted his eyebrows. "No one here is going to accept that." There was a moment of silence.

"You people are jumping to all the wrong conclusions," Jen said. "Here's my take on things. The gods have been busy creating planets, not just in our system but also in other systems. They've given people different skin colors so they can keep track of who belongs where. Each planet interprets the Sacred Writings differently."

"This is just too frustrating," Hewitt said. "Can you speak to him in his language, Moritz? Try to find out what it means?

"It's important," Darek said. "Need know what's going on."

"I don't think anybody knows what's going on," Jen said, "but while we're sitting here quibbling about what's written in a stupid book, the damn pinks are wiping out our planet. I've had enough of this. I'm going back to Cronos to join the army and kill some pinks." She got up. "Thanks for the tea."

No one said a word.

She went upstairs to the door, donned a mask, and left.

Ebony

Ebony was alone on a planet with bloodthirsty predators and cannibals. Her mouth was as dry and her stomach, hollow. *Had the cannibals killed Troy? Were they getting ready to feast on him?* She shuddered at the thought.

She looked at the sun on the horizon. It was frustrating. There was no way to keep track of time. It felt like she hadn't eaten in days. She was exhausted and frightened.

A cannibal came out of a hut and looked up in her direction. She ducked down and peered out between the blades of elephant grass. He went to his horse-like creature, mounted, and trotted directly towards her.

She dashed over the crest of the escarpment, down into the valley, across a stream, and into the grasslands. She was soon panting and fighting for air. She ran until she was too exhausted to run. She collapsed on the ground, trying desperately to catch her breath, her eyes darting here and there in search of the cannibal.

When she got up, shockingly, the cannibal was sitting on his horse-like creature, holding the reins, glaring at her. Ebony turned and ran, leaping through the elephant grass, struggling to go as fast as possible. When she glanced back, he was gone. When she turned around, there in front of her, with a stony expression, was the cannibal.

She froze.

He was close, and he was high up on his immerse horse-like creature, almost three times her height. He straightened himself in his saddle, his purple face subsumed with two straight white lines from his chin to his eyes and his reddish-brown hair hanging below his shoulders. He had a claw fastened to a thin stripe of bark around his neck. "Why you run?" he asked, frowning.

"You—you can speak Cronish?" she asked.

"Why you run?" he asked again, lifting his chin.

"Because you peel the skin off your enemies," she snarled, "and take pleasure in eating their flesh."

He glared back at her and suddenly burst out laughing. He turned his horse and laughed again as he trotted off.

"Let him go!" Ebony screamed out after him. "Let him go!" She followed him back through the elephant grass, across the stream, over the hill, and back to her spot on the escarpment. The cannibal rode in, got off his horse, and went into a hut, not the one where they'd taken Troy.

He spoke Cronish, she reflected. *How could that be? And he could have caught her, but he didn't. He just rode away. What kind of cannibal does that?* Maybe her assumptions about them were wrong. She wondered what she should do. She couldn't stay out here. If she stayed out in the wild, something would find her and kill her. It was just a matter of time.

She'd have to risk going into the cannibal's camp and hope they weren't cannibals. She took a deep breath and exhaled slowly. She started down the escarpment, imagined what could happen, and stopped. She went over her options. She had none.

When they saw her coming, the men grabbed spears. The wolf-like creatures moved up and growled. The women barked at the children and moved them into a hut. Ebony took another deep breath and inched towards the hut where she knew Troy was. When giant cannibals surrounded her with spears, she stopped.

The cannibal who had chased her, the one with the claw, came out of a hut. "Tel reh of," he shouted, walking quickly towards her. "Go ahead in," he said to Ebony, pointing at the hut. "They won't hurt you."

The cannibals moved out of her way. She went up to the hut and paused just outside. Her skin tingled, and her body shivered. She shifted back the animal skin flap of the entryway and went in. A Talonian woman next to Troy was startled, scrambled around her towards the entrance, and backed out.

Troy was asleep on a bed of fur. Ebony sat next to him, saw the extent of his wounds, and realized he wasn't going anywhere.

"I come in?" asked a voice from outside.

"Come," Ebony said.

He pulled the flap back and came in. "My name Gray Moon. What you name?"

"Ebony. How do you know Cronish?"

"Man taught me."

"A Cronish man?"

"I learn to talk Cronish so can trade with Cronish."

"Trade what? Skins?"

"Yes."

"Where do you trade?"

"Whitecliff," he said.

"Is there a spaceport there?"

He nodded.

"What were you planning to do to him?" she said, glancing at Troy.

"Help him."

Ebony's shoulders sagged.

"Gnirb emos doof," he shouted through the walls of the hut.

Moments later, a woman came in and laid down some meat, vegetables, and water next to Ebony.

Ebony ravaged the food, taking long swigs of water between bites.

Gray Moon sat with his legs folded and watched her.

Troy woke up. Ebony smiled at him.

With some discomfort, he attempted to smile back.

"You're alive," she said.

"I almost wish I wasn't."

"It'll heal. Give it time."

"I suppose you're right. But then what?"

Ebony smiled. "I'll think of something."

Jen

Jen sat in the cafe with her back to the wall and looked across the spaceport's vast platform. It was a very different place now. There were a lot of yellows dragging suitcases, a few blues, but no olives. She took a sip of her coffee.

She had managed to access her bank account and tried to book a flight to Cronos, but there were no flights due to the war.

Now what? she pondered. Maybe she could get to Cronos from somewhere else. There must be supply ships going there—then again, perhaps not. The blues weren't going to help the Cronish. Not without pissing off the pinks. The yellows were too busy praying. And the purples were still stuck in the dawn-of-man age. No, there'd be no supply ships going to Cronos.

She watched a family of blues—self-righteous, egocentric rodents on their way back to the underworld.

The coffee was hot and not too bitter.

She watched a putrid yellow family walk by dragging their luggage. *Where could they be going? Off to see some relatives on the far side of hell, perhaps.*

Then, surprisingly, there was a young olive man with long red hair walking across the platform. *He's a man. Why would he want to look like a girl?* She shook her head. There were more olives, women, and children. *Refugees? Yes, of course. Refugees. And if there are refugees, there'd be a ship going back to Cronos.*

Jen downed the remainder of her coffee, got up, and started towards the terminal. She quickened her pace, went against the tide, through the gate to a shuttle, a big one that carried about thirty. A few stragglers were coming down the ramp. She walked by them into the shuttle.

"Hey, what are you doing?" yelled an olive with a short-cut gray beard, a wrinkled brow, and two gold teeth. "Off you go. I'm getting ready to pull out."

"Are you going to Cronos?" Jen asked.

"I'm getting people out. Not putting them in."

"Are there troops there?"

"Yeah, there's troops, but you don't want to go there, girl. It's bad there."

"I'm coming with you."

"Why? You got some sort of death wish?"

"I have my reasons."

He thought for a moment. "You'll have to pay me, and I'm not bringing you back unless you pay me again. Do you understand? I sell one-way tickets, three hundred apiece."

Graybeard took payment with a scanner, secured the hatch, and went to the cockpit. He took the shuttle up to a small transport carrier in orbit and landed in an empty cargo hold. If there were other crew members on the transport—and there must have been—Jen never saw them. She stayed on the shuttle. The flight took more than a day, and she slept on the way.

When she woke up, her neck was stiff and sore, and graybeard was back in the pilot's seat, taking the shuttle down through a blanket of clouds. Jen moved up to the co-pilot's spot so she could see. The clouds parted to a city Jen had only seen in pictures, Brusiff. Few buildings remained standing. The rest were caved in, missing walls, or just piles of debris. There were burning tanks, scattered transports, and hundreds of dead soldiers littering a battlefield to the east.

Graybeard landed in a clearing and brought out a plasma gun before opening the hatch. The size of the crowd was beyond belief. There were thousands upon thousands.

Jen wondered if she was doing the right thing. She'd expected to find a war, not this. Desperate women with children, the wounded, and the very old were all assembled like a herd of sheep. Were the troops still here, or was the battle over? She'd have to find out.

She got out as the olives with money filed in. She pushed her way through the crowd and kept going until she was far from the shuttle.

"Hey there," she said to a young girl, maybe sixteen. "Where's the army?"

She shook her head.

"You don't know?"

"They left." She pointed north.

"When?"

"Last night."

"When was the last bombing?"

"A couple of hours ago," she said.

No army to join. Nothing to do, but die. She thought about turning around and going back, but the shuttle was already lifting off. She watched as it went up. It would be back. She decided she'd get on it and go back to Vole. If the other cities were like this one, the war was over.

She was still watching the shuttle when a missile hit it. It twirled down towards the surface and exploded when it hit the ground.

And then explosions were all around her. The city was being bombed. Jen ran to a building and threw her shoulder into the door, but she couldn't get it open. As she threw her shoulder into it again, the building's windows and doors were blown out. She was thrown to the ground with the door on top of her. Her shoulder was hurting badly. She pushed the door off with her other arm. She couldn't see through the dust, her ears were ringing, and it was raining bricks. As she tried to get up, one hit her shoulder, a vicious, painful blow that knocked her back down. A section of the wall fell forward. She tried to scramble back out of the way, but she couldn't use her left arm. The brick wall crashed down on her legs, crushing them.

The pain was excruciating, and when she tried to move, it hurt even more. The agony went on and on. It wouldn't stop, and it was too much to bear. She pleaded with the gods. Make it stop! Please, please, please! But it didn't stop, and she was pinned. She lay there, screaming, swearing, shuddering, cursing, crying, and wishing she'd die. The sun went down. In the middle of the night, some people came to haul away the wounded, but they didn't try to move Jen, and the flash of explosions showed the look of dismay on their faces. It told Jen a story she didn't want to know. They scurried off when more bombs fell. The pain subsided somewhat, but her anguish went on and on all night long. Her world went dark just after the sun came up.

Rose

Rose found a cheap room at the Athabaskan Hotel, nestled into the side of the mountain. She left Solin in the room, donned her mask and robe, and went out to steal things, sell them, and use the money to buy the things they needed. It was how she had survived on Cronos, and it worked here too. Days went by.

This evening, streaks of colored light filled the sky, green, burgundy, yellow, and white, all moving downward steadily, like a waterfall.

"Oh my," she exclaimed. The window stretched from floor to ceiling, and the aurora was on full display. "It's so beautiful."

Solin smiled, and Rose noticed his skin reflected the colors of the light. He didn't look like a ghost. When the aurora went from white to green, just for a moment, he looked Cronish. *Yes, he saved your life,* she thought, *but you can't just jump into bed with every alien that comes along.* She smiled. It was *time for a fix. That's what's wrong with me. I need a fix.*

She went into the bathroom, ran the bath, and pulled the bottle and syringe from her pocket. There was only enough left for one dose. She took it.

Then she stripped down and climbed into the incredibly hot water. She wondered if it came straight from the ground at that temperature. She hated Vole, and she didn't want to be there. She wanted to be somewhere where she could breathe the air.

When they went out together, Solin had his head on a swivel, which made her nervous. Was there a real threat? Angels? She doubted it. Possible, but not likely. More likely, he imagined things.

She was like him in some ways. She was isolated from society, a loner. Was he the Messiah? Hard to say. In some ways, it made sense. Yet in other ways, no. Would the Messiah be a trained fighter? She doubted that too.

She let the hot water calm her nerves. She soaked, relaxed, climbed out of the tub, toweled dry, got dressed, and went out into the room. Solin was lying on his bed watching the screen.

"I'm going into town," she said matter-of-factly.

Solin looked at her with a blank expression.

"I don't know why I tell you these things," she said brooding. "You haven't the foggiest idea what I'm saying."

Solin nodded.

She went to the door and said, "I'll be back soon." She made hand signals to be sure he understood.

He nodded.

She donned her gas mask and left. It was night but not dark. The planet, Jupih, and the rings around it were brilliant and filled the sky. The lights of the aurora added to the spectacle. She took little notice. She was on a mission.

She caught a cab and tried to ask the driver where she could get some Rend, but the driver didn't understand. In frustration, she pulled up her sleeve and showed him the needle marks on her arm. He nodded and drove her down the mountainside into the heart of the city. He stopped and pointed to a door at the top of a black metal fire escape.

She climbed it and knocked.

A shirtless Volian, tattoos all over his cracked yellow torso, answered. He blinked rapidly and stared openly. He had giant rings in his ear lopes and an iron cross hanging from a ring on his nose.

"Do you sell Rend?" she asked with a wavering voice.

He nodded and shut the door.

She waited.

He came back with a bottle.

She took out her money and fumbled some of it. Bills scattered down the staircase. She quickly counted the money still in her hand.

He held out his hand for more, like a beggar.

She scrambled to get a few of the fallen bills and hand them over.

He took them, gave her the bottle, and closed the door.

She searched for and found the bills that had gotten away. The cab was waiting. She paid the driver when she got back to the hotel. The amount was a guess, but he seemed to be okay with it.

When she got in, Solin was taking a shower. She imagined his naked body, stark white, and shuddered.

She lay down. The screen showed long lines of tanks, cannons, armored vehicles, and thousands of Cronish troops moving along a road. In contrast, thousands upon thousands of forlorn civilians moved in the opposite direction beside the road.

The lights of the aurora cascaded across the sky and the walls of the room reflected the colors.

She heard the water stop. Solin opened the bathroom door, shirtless with a towel slung over his neck. His skin was yellow, white, and olive, and she felt a powerful urge.

He lay down on his bed.

She retreated to the bathroom and took a small shot of Rend. This was difficult. She was struggling with it. She went back to her bed and waited for the drug to take effect.

She glanced over at Solin. He was red, blue, yellow, white, and olive.

Did he think about her? How would he react? Would he reject her? She wasn't sure. It didn't matter. She had to find out. She couldn't help herself. She got up and went to him.

He looked straight into her eyes. She threw herself on top of him and kissed him on the lips. He didn't respond, but he didn't reject her either, so she kissed him again. Again he didn't react. She could feel her heart pounding. She pulled the towel from his neck and threw it on the floor. She ran her hands over his chest. Solin reached out, held her head in his hands, pulled her in, and kissed her gently on the lips.

Leona

"Your Majesty," General Steen said, standing in the doorway of her command post, wringing his hands.

"What is it?" Leona asked.

"We have a lead."

Leona looked up, wide-eyed. "Go on."

"We questioned a Bacchian merchant that arrived here this morning. Initially, he said he knew nothing, but he seemed to be nervous. We checked his manifest and discovered that he left for Bacchus with no passengers on the night in question. He had no reasonable explanation for this, so we used forensics and found evidence that Her Highness was on his ship."

She put a hand to her chest. "Oh, my dear gods!"

"The merchant confessed that he'd given her passage but claimed he had no choice because Her Highness requisitioned his ship. We've taken him into custody, and he's being transported here as we speak."

Leona didn't respond. She knew, undoubtedly, there was truth to the claim. Charline was a wildcat, tenacious, and when she wanted something, she was going to get it one way or another. "Can he show us where he dropped her?"

"He already has. On a dogger, *Albatrod*, in the Tiberius Ocean."

"What kind of a ship is that?"

"He said it was for fishing."

"Would she be able to get down to a city from there?"

"I'm afraid so."

"And does he know the name of the submarine?"

"He doesn't know."

She took a moment to think. "What is the status of the war?"

"It's not good. The Capascan Continent has fallen, and the Athenians are slaughtering the people."

"Prepare my shuttle, and inform Captain Landon that I'll be boarding his warship."

"And what about the merchant?"

"Question him further."

"But he lied."

"He lied because he's Bacchian. They all lie. He may know more than he's saying, and he may not, but he did what Charline ordered him to do. This is her doing and hers alone. Damn it! What a stupid thing she's done. I should have had a guard on her."

"Very well, Your Majesty." He bowed and took his leave.

She wondered if there was the slightest hope of getting her out. It all depended on who got to her first. Bacchus was as corrupt as a world could be. The Empress ruled the gangs, the gangs ruled the cities, and High Priest ruled everyone. If Charline landed in the Empress's hands, there was a good chance she'd be returned, in the hands of a gang, there'd be a ransom, and in the hands of the High Priest—that was a different matter. Charline would have to deny the existence of the Messiah to have any hope of surviving. She wondered if she knew that.

If ever I needed the gods on my side, it's now, she thought.

Jen

Jen opened her eyes. Her bed had white sheets folded over a light blue cotton blanket. The walls were stark white, and a disconnected monitor was sitting next to the bed.

"Good morning," said a portly looking olive wearing a military uniform, sitting in a chair against the wall. He had a round face, a circular body, and short red hair that stuck straight up. "How are you feeling?"

Jen tried to get her bearings. Where was she? She couldn't remember how she got there. "My shoulder hurts," she said, pinching her lips. Her arm was wrapped tightly to her body.

The olive's eyes quickly averted hers and bounced around the room. Something was wrong.

Jen looked down. Her legs were gone! She desperately patted the blanket with her right hand. In horror, she sucked in several short breaths, and tears welled up in her eyes. "My legs?"

The olive's mouth dropped open.

"My legs?" Jen repeated, her voice stricken with panic.

"I'm sorry," he said. "There was nothing they could do."

Jen closed her eyes, gritted her teeth, and let loose a wail of agony.

"There was too much damage. Both of your legs were completely crushed. The circulation was cut off, and the tissue died."

Tears streamed down her cheeks.

"I can come back," he said, standing.

Jen didn't answer, couldn't answer; she cried with deep sobs.

He walked to the door with his head down and left.

She cried for a long time, and when she calmed down, the dreaded redhead came back, like an unwanted lover.

"I don't want to live like this," she said. "I want you to kill me."

"I can't do that," he said, rubbing the back of his neck. "It's a shock, I know, but you'll get over it. You'll see." He sat down and folded his arms across his chest.

"Who are you?" she asked with tears still streaming. He was in a military uniform, not any sort of hospital garment.

"My name is Harley. I'm a recruiting officer."

Jen looked down at her stumps. "You mean cyborgs?"

"Let me start with a few questions."

"Do you mean cyborgs?"

"Yeah. Cyborgs." He let that sink in. "Have you had any trouble with the law?"

"You're planning to give me new legs?"

"Your new legs will be better than your old ones."

"You're full of crap! I don't want to be part of your stupid freak show. I just want to die and be done with it."

"You're not going to die. You're going to live. But if you truly want to die, and I don't believe you do, your best option is to listen to what I have to say."

Jen stopped to think about that. "What would I have to do?"

"First, the questions. Have you had any trouble with the law?"

Jen darted a glance at him. "No."

"I think you have. Can you tell me about it?"

"What difference does it make?"

"Just tell me?"

"There were no jobs, and I was starving."

"What did you do with the stuff you stole?"

"I wasn't stealing. I was surviving."

"Did you sell it?"

"No," she said, frowning. "It wasn't like that. I took cans of food, mostly. We all did."

He nodded. "I know you were on the freighter, Resolution. You were a security guard?"

"Yeah."

"How did you get that job?"

"I applied for it," Jen said. "I was qualified, and they accepted my application. It wasn't difficult."

"You had experience?"

"Yeah."

"Where did you get the experience?"

"In my first job, I was a security guard at a high rise. After that, I got a job doing rounds at the spaceport. I learned that freighters paid better, so I applied."

"How long were you a security guard on the freighter?"

"Five years."

"And were you involved in any conflicts?"

"Plenty."

"Tell me about them."

Jen rolled her tongue against the inside of her cheek. "I broke up fights, that sorta thing."

"And you sometimes used excessive force?"

Jen didn't respond.

"Are you capable of taking responsibility for your actions?"

"Okay, I lost my temper a few times."

"And you were imprisoned for doing so?"

"Yeah."

There was a moment of silence.

"Let me ask you a different type of question. How do you feel about the Athenians?"

"How do you think I feel? The bastards took my legs." She remembered now, the brick wall falling, her legs crushed, the agony that went on and on for an entire day and night. It was all coming back, all crystal clear.

"Would you like to get back at them?"

"You mean as a cyborg?"

"It has its advantages. You'll be stronger, faster, and be better armed than any Athenian. You'd be able to kill them at will. Would you want to do that?"

Jen looked down where her legs used to be. "Yeah. I guess I would."

"We're going to want to replace your left arm too."

"But there's nothing wrong with my arm."

"Your shoulder is broken pretty bad. You can keep your right arm, but the left arm must be supported to be powerful enough to hold your gun. You'll be able to lift five hundred times your body weight."

"You mean like, lift cars."

"Lift anything, cars, trucks, even tanks. But when you go up against the Athenians, there's a chance you'll get your wish and be killed. There's a lot to think about, and I'm going to give you a couple of days. "

"I don't need a couple of days. I'm not going to live like this. I'm in."

Keldon

Adrenalin, Keldon thought as he ran. *That's what this is.* He kept his rifle in front of him, held it tight with both hands, and pointed it down as he ran. Finally, he was going to be able to use the damn thing on something more meaningful than a paper target. Up ahead, on the starboard deck of the warship, *Ubiquitous,* were six assault submersibles lined up side by side. They stood motionless on the platform, like beached sharks. The lines of running combat soldiers parted, and each unit headed towards a different shark.

There was a sharp tightness in his chest. *Focus,* he thought. *Don't want to end up in the wrong fish.* He held back a smile. His buddies would never stop razzing him if he did anything stupid. He wondered if the others were as terrified as he was.

"Men. The High Priest of Bacchus has abducted princess Charline," he had been told at the briefing. "We're going in to rescue her." Pictures of her had come upon screens. "This is the princess. Burn an image in your mind. You'll need to remember what she looks like." She was attractive. Easy to remember. But deep down, he knew this was crazy. They were losing the war on Cronos. Only four of the nine continents remained, yet here they were going into caves deep beneath the ocean on Bacchus.

They all knew the story of the hero, Harmon, passed down from one generation to the next. He went down into the pits of Bacchus to find his lover, Mariann. He had been faced with one obstacle after another, yet in the end, he found her and got her out. It was very apparent from the events of the story that the mines of Bacchus were extremely hard to get to and even harder to get out of.

Keldon kept going, up the ramp, and into the mouth of the shark, a long tube with twenty rows of six seats, an aisle in the middle, and three seats on each side. He went down the aisle to the first empty row of seats and to the window.

"Strap yourselves in," the master sergeant bellowed. "Do it smartly. Strap yourselves in. C'mon now. Let's go."

Keldon sat down, held his gun between his knees, and reached back to grab the straps.

"Strap yourselves in," the master sergeant kept yelling as more and more men, many carrying heavy ropes, came in and filled the seats. The ramp came up, and the mouth of the shark slammed shut. There was a sharp hiss as the hatch was sealed. He braced himself in anticipation of the gut-wrenching free fall.

"Submersibles can't fly!" the master sergeant had informed them during training as if the room were filled with the hard of hearing. "They drop like lead keels. They brake with heat shields, parachutes, and when they hit the water. You need to be physically and mentally prepared for this. Once in the water, the shark will dive for a long time. It'll go into a pressurized underwater cavern. The cavern will have either a beach or a port. The water is hot, so move quickly. It's believed that some of the entrances are well guarded, and some of them are not."

He peered out his window. The crew of the warship sealed the bay, and the bay depressurized.

Just when he started to think it wasn't going to happen, they dropped. It was every bit as gut-wrenching as had been advertised. Scary as all hell. He glanced out the window. There wasn't a single spec of light emanating from the surface.

The soldier next to Keldon threw up. The puke was projected up over the heads of the men sitting in front of him. Keldon turned his head towards the window to avoid the putrid stench, but it hit him anyway. For the next few minutes, he thought he might lose his lunch, but he was able to hang on.

"Go rebels!" yelled one of the men as the air outside started to pound against the hull.

"Keep it quiet!" shouted the master sergeant. "You can pat each other on the back when it's over."

The pounding on the hull got louder and louder. The shark was jolted and pushed around. Streaks of red flashed by the window, and the cabin got hot, sweltering hot.

He thought of his sister, Ebony, and her desperate attempt to stop him from joining. He should have listened. He joined the army to fight the Athenians, not this. Why did the princess need to be saved on a planet where they weren't at war? It made no sense.

The shaking intensified, the red streaks covered the window completely, and the pounding on the hull got worse.

"Lock your gun in front of you!" the master sergeant yelled." There's going to be a jolt when the chute opens!

Keldon put his gun in the holster on the back of the seat and locked it in. He peered out the window. The solid wall of fire lessened for a second, and he saw one of the other submersibles, a fireball plunging through the atmosphere beside them. The pounding continued for several minutes, and his body was slammed hard into the straps of his seat. A few of the guns went flying, striking the night vision binoculars fixed to helmets.

"What did I tell you?" the master sergeant snapped. "You blithering idiots! Your gun is your lifeline! You were told to lock it down!"

The shark drifted from side to side as it descended. Several more minutes passed, and the shark hit the water.

Out the window, powerful lights illuminated the way forward, but there was nothing to see, no fish, no sign of life, just pitch-black water. Five minutes turned to ten to twenty. Finally, they leveled off. The master sergeant went forward, retrieved the lost guns, and returned them to their owners with a scolding.

Keldon could see the bottom and the entrance to an underwater cave. Inside, shafts of light shone down from above. It almost looked inviting, like a weekend retreat.

Units would be left behind to protect each asset as they acquired them: the beach, the tunnel, the elevator, etc. They needed to be able to come back the way they came. Keldon was in the unit that was the farthest-reaching—all the way to the target.

"Take off your seat harness, stand up, get your gun, hold it in front of you, and move up to the hatch," the master sergeant bellowed out. "Smartly, now, people. Move up to the hatch, and get ready to go."

Keldon found the buttons to release his harness, gathered up his gun, and shuffled down the aisle behind the others towards the hatch. He had to grab the bar on top of a seat to maintain his balance. The shark hit the ground, and they lurched forward. Almost instantly, the hatch lowered. The men in front ran down the ramp into the water, holding their guns above their heads. Keldon followed as the mass moved forward.

"Go! Go! Go!" yelled the master sergeant.

When Keldon got to the hatch, he saw a dimly lit cave, barren, hot, and musty. He held his gun above his head with both hands and ran down into the smooth surface of burning hot water. It took his breath away. It came up to his neck, and wading through it was slow. It was scorching hot, and he had to fight off an overwhelming sensation of panic, a feeling that his skin was going to melt before he got to shore. He gritted his teeth and concentrated on keeping his legs moving.

Plasma gunfire broke out over his head. Men behind him were screaming. There were splashes. Keldon searched the beach for the enemy fire. He saw where the blue streaks were coming from, and he tried to point his gun in that direction. He fired, and the weapon ripped from his hands and plunged into the water. He scrambled after it, dunked below the surface, and searched for it. The hot liquid burned his eyes, yet he saw it, sinking slowly. He lunged at it and was able to grab it. He poked his head up and saw men falling off the submersible like barrels off a truck. He had to get closer to shore and higher up out of the water so that he could shoot. By the gods of Uttara, the water was hot. He kept going.

Gradually, he moved up out of the water. He brought his gun to his shoulder, dripping wet, aimed at a blue skin, and fired. He missed. His legs were hurting badly. He had to get out of the water completely. He scrambled up onto the shore, stopped, aimed more carefully, and fired again. He hit one of the bastards, fired again, and got another one. He searched the shore for more but couldn't find any. The shooting stopped.

He was breathing hard, his entire body felt scorched, and his hands looked red, like a lobster.

Jimmy's dead, he thought as he walked towards the tunnel. And Rickard too. Just like that, their lives are over. And they never got to fight the Athenians. I hate this. It's stupid. Good men are dying, and for what?

Dead Bacchians were lying in the mouth of the tunnel. One of them moved, and Keldon shot him in the chest, for Jimmy.

The lights fixed to the roof of the tunnels were dim and spread far apart. Further in, he and his comrades stopped in front of an elevator, and as more and more men came in, there was a traffic jam, like the way people gather on a subway platform.

"Get your rigs ready," the master sergeant yelled as he came up from the rear.

Keldon put his gun strap over his head, swung his gun onto his back, and grabbed his rappel rig from his belt. The elevator doors were forced open.

"Go! Go! Go!" the master sergeant screamed.

The men jumped through the door, one after the other. When Keldon got there, Larry, in front of him, stumbled, didn't leap far enough, and couldn't reach the cable. He fell, hit Ralph below him, and knocked him off. They both fell, Larry screaming, Ralph silent, their arms and legs flailing into a seemingly bottomless shaft.

"Go! Go! Go!" the master sergeant screamed again.

Keldon jumped, grabbed the cable, stopped himself from sliding down, and hooked on his rappel rig. He went down as fast as he could, straining to see into the black below. Far below, he could see the elevator coming up. He tightened his rappel rig and slowed himself. Ralph was dead on the roof of the elevator next to a hatch that had been ripped open. One after another, the men were going down the hatch. Keldon set himself down on the roof, detached his rappel rig, lowered himself into the hatch, and jumped down.

The man ahead of him disappeared into a crudely cut hole in the floor.

Keldon stared down. Pitch black. He hesitated.

"Go," the man behind him yelled.

Keldon went. Below the floor, he found the cable, attached his rappel rig, and continued down. When he got to the bottom, the elevator door had already been forced open. Below him, at the bottom of the elevator shaft, he could see Larry's lifeless body. There were three dead blues as well. He detached his rappel rig and was thrown a rope. He swung across the void through the door and onto the floor of a small cave. The master sergeant was the last one to come off the cable.

"Get ready," he yelled. "Let's not waste any time."

Keldon held his gun in front of him, pointed down, and followed his master sergeant down the tunnel.

Suddenly, there was incoming fire, and two of the men in front of Keldon fell. He threw himself down onto his belly and raised his gun to his shoulder. The man to his right was shooting at something, and he couldn't see what.

"We're going in men," the master sergeant shouted out. "Keep your guns pointed forward. Run as fast as you can. Don't shoot the slaves—just the guardsmen. Remember, we're here to rescue Princess Charline. Keep an eye out for her. If you find her, gather around and protect her. Alright, let's go."

Charline

Even though the shots were in a faraway tunnel, barely audible, Charline knew precisely what they were. She'd been waiting for this. The queen's soldiers were there.

None of the slaves moved. They just stood, frozen, all looking in the same direction, like a mob of meerkats. They had no way of knowing what was happening.

The guardsmen surrounding the pit abandoned their whips, brought out their sidearms, and ran to the pit's entrance. One after another, they cautiously went into the tunnel. Deep inside, there was the sound of a flurry of shots followed by many more shots.

Charline wasn't sure how her mother had managed to find her, but she wasn't surprised. Her mother had spies everywhere, like a squirrel has nuts.

Only a few guardsmen had stayed behind, and those that had were staring at the entrance to the tunnel.

Charline studied each of the guards to make sure they weren't looking her way and slowly stepped backward out of the water. When the moment was right, she bolted up a path to a ledge where she could lie down and stay out of sight.

The sound of the battle in the tunnel grew to a storm, and the storm intensified. But as the minutes passed, it faded away, and the shots were less frequent. Her heart sank. It seemed that the rescue attempt had failed.

What could she do? Go back to the pit and wait? There might be another attempt. But no, she really couldn't stomach the thought of doing that. She didn't want to let go of what she had. Hope.

She checked to make sure the guardsmen weren't looking her way, got up, dashed along the wall of the cavern, and into a tunnel, not the one where the battle raged, a different one, a quiet one. Deeper and deeper, she went. She just kept going, not knowing if it was the right thing to do, knowing only that she needed to be free.

The tunnel branched off several times. She went left and right, on and on until it opened up into a cave that fell away into an abyss. A thin ledge held a path that ran from one side to the other. Crystal shafts, some white, some green, some blue, shot out from the walls and went diagonally from one end of the cave to the other, like arrows through a basket.

Could she hide there? Would they find her? She climbed down and ducked under a crystal shaft where she was out of sight and felt safe, at least for now.

She waited and waited some more, got out to pee, came back, and waited again. She became sleepy and dozed off. When she woke, she was disoriented, not sure where she was. She embraced fear, hope, and dread. She'd have to search for food at some point, yet venturing out now seemed too risky. She'd wait as long as she could.

Then far off in the distance, she heard the murmuring of voices. She stopped breathing and listened. Were they speaking Cronish? She couldn't tell. She kept listening. Slowly the sounds got louder. They came closer still. Cronish. They were talking Cronish. She got out and ran towards them, elated, like a child waking up to gifts on the day of the Messiah.

"Don't shoot," she yelled as she came out from around a bend, her hands high. "I'm Princess Charline. Don't shoot."

The soldiers were against the wall, on the floor, and on one knee, all pointing assault rifles at her. When they saw her, they lowered their guns.

"Cover the back door," one of them shouted. Four of them moved past Charline and rounded the bend.

"Your Highness. Are you injured?" a square-jawed young soldier asked. His armpits were circles of sweat. She felt weak and was trembling, but she put on a brave face. "I'm fine," she said, wondering how she looked.

Keldon

Keldon lay on the tunnel floor and aimed his rifle. They were coming. He could hear them, and he wondered how many.

"They found her," Johan said, coming up behind him.

"The princess?" Keldon asked without shifting his gaze. "Alive?"

"Yeah."

"Great," he said with a note of disdain. "Now what?"

"The master sergeant says it's time to turn back. He's contacted the submersibles and told them we have the princess. They'll be at the beach when we get there."

Keldon tried to imagine working their way back. He couldn't see it. They'd lost too many men trying to get to the pit and more when they tried to get out.

"It's going to be a hard fight," Johan said despondently.

"There's nothing hard about fighting," Keldon said. "Nothing hard about dying either. It's getting wounded and left behind that's hard." In his heart, he knew they were done. There were hundreds of Bacchians and only about—maybe thirty of them. He checked the charge on his gun. Almost dead. Perhaps he should save the last shot for himself. It made sense. It'd be quick. Here one second, gone the next. Why risk a slow death?

"Move up," the master sergeant yelled. Keldon turned around and glanced back. There she was, walking up behind him. Mud was caked on her dress and in her hair, and she was shaking. She didn't look like a princess and certainly not like a future queen.

Keldon turned his attention back to the task at hand. The men around him were pushing forward. Keldon covered for them and moved up himself. He threw himself to the ground and propped up his gun. Others ran over him and fell to the ground in front of him. He got up, ran, and fell. There was a bend in the tunnel, and when Barry went around it, a powerful bolt hit him in the chest and tossed him back like a baseball bat hit him..

Keldon scrambled over, grabbed Barry's assault rifle, and rolled back out of the way. He checked the charge. It was good. He left his own gun behind, crawled forward, and peeked around the bend. The tunnel was completely blocked off. And they had a cannon.

He crawled backward, got up, and went back to the master sergeant. "We have to find another way, sir," he said, taking a deep breath. "They've got the tunnel blocked off, and they have a cannon. They'll pick us off, easy."

"Damn it, we have to go that way," the master sergeant said, grimacing. He grabbed Keldon by the shoulder. "Take her back a safe distance and wait. I'll send someone back for you when we've cleared the way."

"Sir," Keldon replied. He wanted to say he was crazy. They should find another route. They couldn't possibly win that fight. He glanced over at the princess. She looked frightened.

"Follow me," Keldon yelled, but she didn't move. He grabbed her arm and pulled. She yanked her arm free.

"Come with me," he said.

She hesitated and nodded.

The tunnel was not straight or level. There were bends and ups and downs. When they got to a cave, she stopped him.

"There's a hiding spot down there," she said, pointing. "Come." She climbed down and disappeared under a crystal structure.

Keldon looked back the way they'd come. The master sergeant wasn't going to get through. There wasn't going to be anyone coming back to get him. Hiding might not be such a bad idea. He climbed down and backed into the hole, like a badger.

Charline

Charline stayed in her hiding spot with Keldon and listened to the distant sounds of the battle, to plasma bolts ricocheting off rocks, to men crying out in agony, to explosions, to stones falling, and to the cheers of the Bacchians.

Keldon's voice was muted throughout, yet it was clear he was hurting. Those were his friends out there, and from the sound of things, every last one of them was dead.

There followed a long period of shouting and grunting. And then silence. They waited until they were sure the Bacchians were gone and crawled out. They found bloodstains and sandbags, but no bodies or weapons. The deceased had been carted away.

She walked for hours with Keldon beside her. There was a breeze in the tunnel, and it felt good on her face, an abatement from the oppressive heat. The tunnel had a rough surface, apparently carved out the old way, with explosives, picks, and shovels. The tunnel branched left and right and moved up and down until, up ahead, she could hear a steady hum, the sound of a machine.

She stopped. "What is that?" she whispered.

Keldon shrugged. "Factories are up in the city," he whispered back. "An electrolysis plant, maybe."

"What's that?"

"It converts water into oxygen."

"Why?"

"What do you mean, why? So, we can breathe."

"I thought they had vents to the surface."

He shook his head. "No. There's nothing but ocean up there. Everything has to be manufactured. Didn't you go to school?"

She hadn't gone to school. She'd been tutored. And there were no lessons about electrolysis that she recalled. It was all about the gods of Uttara and how they had given her the divine right to rule. There was nothing about how the world worked.

She heard talking. Someone was coming. Quickly, she ran back the way she'd come with Keldon close behind. She ducked into the closest branching tunnel, low, narrow, and dark. When she was about ten feet in, she stopped and stayed perfectly still. Looking back, she saw Keldon right behind her, frozen, and moments later, she saw the legs of two guardsmen walk by.

As they waited, Charline's eyes adjusted to the darkness, and in front of her, she could see the outline of a staircase. It was very narrow, carved from rock, smelled like rat dung, and went up at a steep incline.

"Okay," Keldon whispered after having waited a respectable amount of time. "We can get out."

"Keldon, wait," she said. "There's a staircase here, and it goes up. I think we should try it."

"It probably doesn't go far. It was abandoned long ago."

"Keldon, we're going to die down here. There's nothing to eat and nowhere to go. We're not going to get anywhere near an elevator. This is the only way. We're going."

"Wait, Charline. We'll have to come back down more than likely, and we'll be right back where we started."

In Charline's mind, their situation was hopeless. And here was a staircase. If this staircase went up to a city, they might find water to drink and food to eat. They just might be able to survive. It was a lot to hope for, yet it was better than what they were facing. "We're not getting anywhere. We have to try something."

Keldon sighed. "Okay. I've got night vision, so let me go first," he said, pulling his goggles down off his helmet. He moved past her and started climbing. She followed him, and when she peered back, she could see just a small glimmer of light coming in from the bottom of the staircase. She kept going. The stairs didn't go straight up. They twisted back and forth, to the right, to the left, and up some more.

"That's it," Keldon said. "I can't see anything. It's too dark."

"Let me go first," Charline said. She moved past him. She held one hand out in front of her and moved it back and forth, like a minesweeper, while the other hand felt for the next step. She went up, slowly, one step at a time. For a moment, she thought Keldon had stayed behind, but then she felt his hand brush her calf. The steps kept going up until there were no more steps. She reached out with her hands, feeling the floor and the walls. She ventured forward, searching. To her right, she found another step. She carried on up until it leveled off again. She crawled onto the smooth level stone and moved her left hand back and forth.

"Keldon?"

"Yeah."

"Just making sure you're still there." With groping hands, she found another staircase. She went up. Keldon was on her heels. *Just keep going,* she said to herself. *Don't stop. Go until you can't go anymore.*

"This staircase has probably been abandoned for centuries," Keldon said.

He sounded frustrated. "Just keep going, Keldon. Let me do the thinking."

"You're not thinking. You're guessing."

"I'm a princess. My guesses have to be treated with the same respect as my other commands."

He chuckled. "I suppose you're right about that."

The steps ended, and the tunnel moved sideways, sloped upwards, and turned to the left. There were more stairs, steeper than before, almost straight up, and more tunnel. And boulders piled up in front of her.

"That's it," she said with a weighted chest and a sour taste in her mouth. "It doesn't go any further. We have to go back."

"Why?" he asked. "What's there?"

"Rocks. Nothing but rocks. They go all the way to the roof of the tunnel. There's no way through."

"Wait."

She waited, not sure why.

"Move back," he said, crawling past her. "There's light here. I can see it with the night vision. I'm going to try to move some of those rocks."

She moved back and listened to rocks hitting rocks. Rocks kept tumbling. Her eyes were stinging, so she shut them.

When she opened her eyes, a sliver of light seeped in from the top of the tunnel. She wanted to hug him. This was their way out.

Keldon was digging with his hands and moving boulders in earnest. He kept digging like a mole. He rolled a rock out of the way and squeezed through the hole. She followed.

Far below, a blue light shone from rows of windows on tall round pillars that rose from the floor to the roof of an immense cavern. Street lights illuminated dome-shaped stone houses, like igloos, that lined the cobblestone streets. There were even a few cars, buses, and trucks on roads. A towering pyramid stood at the center.

"Is there a way down?" Charline asked.

"I think there's a path," Keldon said, craning his neck over the side. "It's narrow, though. They simulate daylight in the city. We should head down while it's still dark."

"Look at me," Charline said. "I'm shaking like a leaf." She'd never felt so weak in all her sheltered life. Her experiences in the pit and the trip up the stairs had been excruciatingly unnerving. More than once, she had to push herself beyond what she thought possible mentally. Now she was finally out of that perpetual darkness, and she desperately needed time to compose herself. "I can't go on. I'll wait here. You have night vision. You go steal some food and water, and bring it back."

"No," he chuckled. "If by some miracle I get out of here, I don't want to have to explain to my commander why I left you behind." He laughed again. "Somehow, I don't think he'd like that." He laughed even harder.

"I don't give a damn what your commander thinks. I'm the princess. You'll do as I tell you. Is that understood?"

"Yes, of course, Your Highness, I understand." Keldon looked her in the eye. "I understand completely. But do you understand? You see, down here, you're not in charge. It's my job to get you out of here, and I can't do my job if you're in command."

"You arrogant pig. I'm a princess, and someday I'll be queen. If you think that I'm going to be led around like a donkey, you're mistaken. Leave me now. I order you. Leave me, or I'll tell the queen that—that you raped me."

Keldon laughed. "Not bad. Not bad at all. But if you're going to tell the queen that I raped you, I may as well have raped you. Right?"

Charline's slumped down, like a lioness who'd been put in her place.

"My sister taught me how to deal with people like you," Keldon said. "My parents died in the great famine. My mom first, and—well, I don't think my dad wanted to be here after she died. So, my sister, Ebony, felt it was her job to raise me. I was seven. She was eleven. To control me, she used to make threats like the one you just made. Vicious threats, like 'I'll stab your eyes out in your sleep' kind of threats. Her threats worked. And they kept working for a long time until, finally, I got sick of it. I called her bluff, and guess what? I still have both eyes. None of her threats were real. They were just empty threats."

"If I tell the queen you raped me, you'll be shot."

"Give it up. Your threats won't work on me. My sister was better at it than you," Keldon said. "Much better. She became a drug dealer, dealing heroin. She never took the stuff herself. Said she had to have a clear head. Dealing heroin is a dangerous job. You have to be able to negotiate with some pretty shady people. But she did it, and she was good at it. She trusted no one and made enough money to keep us alive."

"I'm going to be your queen someday," Charline insisted.

"If you're going to be queen, you need to be a lot smarter. Coming down here was stupid. My entire company is dead, all because of your stupidity. I'm not going to let your stupidity get me killed. We're not going to have an ongoing power struggle. You're going to do what I tell you to do, or I'll put my gun to your head and be done with you. Are you getting the picture now, or do I have to draw it out for you?"

Charline didn't answer.

Keldon pulled his gun around, pointed it at her head, and lifted an eyebrow.

She looked up. "Okay, okay," she said. "I got the picture."

Keldon lowered his gun, and they were both silent for a few minutes.

"I'm sorry about your comrades," Charline said. "This place is nothing like I imagined."

"C'mon, we're moving out."

Jen

Jen had lifted the blanket and looked at her new legs. She'd felt them too. They were hard, like metal, and much bulkier than her old legs. She'd checked out her new arm as well. It had a claw at the end of a small cannon.

She couldn't move the arm or the legs, and they pinned her to the bed like anvils.

"They're not functional yet," the trainer said when she came in. She was tall, wiry, and had blond hair that was short like a man's.

She said her name, but Jen hadn't bothered to memorize it. It didn't matter.

"You have to learn how to use them, and it'll take time, but once you learn how, you'll be able to do some remarkable things. It's sort of like learning how to play a musical instrument. When you first start, you're terrible at it. You have to practice, and the more you practice, the better you get. To some degree, people have different levels of inherent ability, yet when it comes down to it, the training is everything. If you put in the time and the effort, you'll get the results."

Jen didn't need the lecture. She needed to know what she was supposed to do. The damn things wouldn't move. Day after day, she'd tried.

"It's frustrating at first," the trainer had said. "You have to be patient and keep working at it.

"The stupid things aren't moving at all!" Jen hollered back at her. "Not one damn inch! They just sit there!"

"Okay, okay. Calm down. We're going to try something new. We're going to put you in a position where your subconscious can trigger a response."

Jen had decided days ago it was hopeless. She was going to have to spend her life as a frigging invalid, and she didn't want to be there. She didn't want to have to face this new reality. It was too brutal. She wanted to be alone so that she could cry. Tears welled up in her eyes, and she used her good hand to wipe them away before the trainer could see.

An assistant, an ugly big ox-like thing dressed in white, was called in.

"Don't worry," the trainer said. "We're not going to let anything bad happen to you, but we're going to give you a bit of a scare intentionally. Is that okay with you?"

Jen wasn't sure if it was okay. What did she mean? What kind of a scare? She gave a slight nod.

The two of them rolled Jen onto her side, right close to the edge.

They had her attention. Her new appendages weren't light. If she fell, it wouldn't be pretty.

The trainer was in front of her, and the muscle man behind her. Without warning, the muscle man pushed her. She felt her body starting to fall, and in a split second, she vividly imagined the whole bloody thing, her face smashing into the floor like a ripe tomato and the pain that followed. Instantly, her right arm shot out, and so did her left arm. Her left leg moved slightly too. The muscle man pulled her back onto the bed at the last second.

"Okay, that's good," the trainer said. "Did you see that? You moved your arm and your leg too. Did you feel it?"

"Yeah," Jen said, relieved. "I did. I felt it." She tried to move them again. Nothing. She tried harder. Still nothing. "Do it again," she said.

The second time, she anticipated the fall, and it still worked. Her arm moved, and both legs. It was wonderful.

"Again," she said.

They did it four more times.

"That's enough," the trainer said. "Better if we go slowly. We don't want to do it so much that it stops working."

Jen wondered if that was possible. She didn't think it was. When you're falling, the instinct to save yourself is overwhelming. It had to be. But it didn't matter. She had what she needed—some semblance of hope, some indication that things were going to be okay. She'd moved her arm and her legs. She'd learn. She was elated, like a kid getting out on the last day of school. She was going to walk again. She was sure of it and couldn't stop smiling.

Ebony

Troy was feeling better, and Ebony was experiencing dizzy spells. At times, she was even nauseous. She had slept on the floor of the hut where Troy slept and ate the lean meats and the strange purple plants she'd been given. She'd occasionally stretched her legs outside the hut, staying away from the hulking wolf-like creatures and keeping a sharp eye out for predatory birds.

Troy's wounds had been stitched closed and wrapped in porous leaves soaked in a dreadfully noxious substance. The Talonians scraped a sticky yellow residue off a bulbous plant, mixed it with blood squeezed from a giant centipede, and got Troy to drink it. He had slept a great deal of the time and was delirious the rest of the time. She was thankful that his wounds hadn't caused him more pain.

"I'm going to Whitecliff on the new moon," Gray Moon announced.

"Which one is the new one?" Ebony asked, having noticed there were as many as five. They weren't often visible but could occasionally be seen low to the horizon, opposite the ever-present sun.

He laughed. "Soon," he said.

"Are you taking Troy and me with you?" she asked, not quite sure how he would answer.

"Of course," he said.

"Good." In her heart, she thanked the gods.

The caravan consisted of Talonians with spears, on the backs of horse-like creatures. They brought the massive odd-looking creatures with horns to drag the travois loaded with furs. Troy and Ebony were lifted onto the backs of enormous horse-like animals. They had to cling to the backs of Talonians to keep from falling off. The wolf-like creatures ran in front and on either side of the caravan.

The sun never set, and the Talonians never slept. They stopped to eat twice before Ebony fell asleep and off the back of the horse. She was picked up and tied with strips of bark to the back of a Talonian. She slept, intermittently, a torturous sleep, the kind of sleep you'd expect to get tied to the back of a Talonian. She was also horribly nauseous.

When she woke, she noticed that Troy was also tied to the back of a Talonian. For hours, she sat watching a landscape of impossibly tall trees, gigantic flowers, elephant grass, immense creatures, and smaller creatures, all keeping their distance from the wolf-like creatures. They went past incredibly high mountains, through deep valleys, and across many streams. She didn't know how long they'd been traveling. Asking Gray Moon didn't help. He measured everything with moons.

She surmised that the journey to Whitecliff, a small trading town on the bank of a river, took the equivalent of at least five Cronish days, based solely on how exhausted she was. During the tail end of the trip, Troy started suffering the same symptoms Ebony did. He threw up twice.

When they finally arrived at Whitecliff, they were amazed to see what looked like a village built in the style of a town on Cronos. Beside the village was a small spaceport with just two towers, no rocket ships, a scattering of empty pads, and five shuttles. Next to the spaceport, there was a hotel and next to the hotel, a diner.

She and Troy thanked Gray Moon, said their goodbyes, and went straight to the hotel.

"We'd like to get two rooms, please," Troy said, holding onto the counter.

"What brings you to Whitecliff?" the girl behind the counter asked, pushing forward the paperwork.

"Business," Ebony said, sure that Troy was incapable of lying.

"Not many Cronish come here," the girl said.

Ebony didn't reply, but she wondered why. She thought that, due to the war, there'd be plenty of refugees—thousands of them. "Didn't Cronish build this town?" she asked.

"Yeah," she said, "but a lot of them died."

She wrinkled her brow. "From what?"

"Low gravity."

She grimaced. "They died from low gravity?"

"There's been studies done."

"What kinda studies?"

"More than a third of y' ar muscles are lost within the first nine weeks. Y'ar bones are affected too. Deprived of gravity, they steadily deteriorate. And y' ar body's calcium finds its way into the bloodstream, causing even more problems. Then there's the gently oscillating nausea from which there's no escape."

Ebony's jaw dropped. "That's from low gravity?"

"Yeah, everybody knows. Most Cronish can't live here comfortably for more than a few months. Their bodies aren't designed for it. They slowly get weaker and weaker and die." She held out a key.

Ebony looked at Troy. "We have to get off this planet."

"Now?"

She could see he was having trouble keeping his eyes open. "After we get some sleep."

They went to the room, and Troy fell asleep the moment his head hit the pillow.

Ebony couldn't sleep. She decided to go for a walk to work her muscles and keep her blood flowing.

The dirt streets were replete with abandoned houses. She went to a house with its front door open and peaked in. The floor had been removed, and a staircase with just five steps went down to the basement. A Talonian, taller than the basement was high, wearing a heavy metal mask, a silver suit, and mittens stood in front of an open furnace. He held a poker that extended into the flames. He stopped and looked up through a clouded glass visor at Ebony, pulled the poker out, shut the furnace door, and pushed up his mask.

"Can I help ya?" he asked, speaking Cronish with a thick Talonian accent. He looked into a small window on the furnace door.

She stepped through the door to the landing at the top of the stairs. "I was just curious." The heat was intense.

"Why are ya here?"

"I'm running from the Athenians."

"There's a reason the Athenians are attacking yar planet," the Talonian said. "Do ya know why?"

"It's because Atheni is dying."

"That's what Emperor Badoni says, but it's not the truth. In his mind, the taking of Cronos shows how powerful he is, but what his planet really needs is a second sun."

"What's a second sun?" Ebony asked.

"It's a gigantic mirror put in orbit to heat a planet." He pulled his face mask down and opened the oven again. He poked around with his poker, shut the door, and pushed his mask back up. "It's called terraforming, changing a planet to make it more compatible with human life." He pulled his mask down, pulled out a large scoop of red hot liquid from the oven, and poured it onto a table.

The heat was oppressive, and Ebony considered leaving, but she was woozy and needed the railing for balance.

He flipped the semi-solid flexible material over twice and put it under a powered roller. The roller pulled the content through and pressed it into a sheet. He shut the oven door, went over to a large bucket on wheels, and pulled it across the room to several shafts. He pulled a lever, and fine sand poured down into the bucket.

"This sand is from Cronos," he said. "It's finer and better suited to making glass than sand from anywhere else."

He pulled his bucket over to the next shaft, pulled a lever, and a white powder flowed into the bucket.

"The soda ash is from Vole. It's used to lower the melting .point of the mixture."

He went to the next shaft, and a light gray powder poured into the bucket. "This is lime. It's found here on Talon. We put it all together, and this,"—he pointed to the molten glass lying on the table—"is the result."

"We back the glass with silver to make it reflect," he said. "The Athenians need a new mirror, and to build it, they need help from other planets. The problem is that they believe they're superior and have the right to take what they need. It is their greatest flaw. To save their planet, they have to stop fighting and start negotiating."

"It's too late for that. The Athenians have slaughtered millions on Cronos. They're not going to stop now."

"To end the war, you have to find a way to reason with them."

Ebony furrowed her brow. "They can't be reasoned with."

"They're not going to want to live on Cronos. They're going to want to stay on Atheni."

"Why?"

"Those who try to live on Cronos will become weak and frail. The Athenians take great pride in their physical prowess. They even go so far as to kill their own if they're weak and frail."

"Then why are they attacking Cronos?"

"Because they're desperate and can't back down from a fight. They have to save face."

"That's not a good reason to fight a war."

"There are no good reasons to fight a war. In a war, everyone loses. You have to get the Athenians to listen and make them realize there's a better way."

"Right now, I have to find a way to get off Talon," Ebony said.

"Good luck to you."

"Thank you. Goodbye."

The glassmaker put his shield down and went back to his oven.

Ebony walked back to the hotel. She leaned against a pillar in the hotel's entrance and watched the people coming and going. She needed money. Maybe she could get a job somewhere.

Opposite her, set back from the street, was the spaceport. When she glanced that way, she saw Gray Moon. He was talking with a Bacchian, less than half his height. The two of them were making their way towards the front entrance of the spaceport.

She scurried across the street and followed them in. The spaceport was broad with an arced wall of glass on two sides, one side facing the rocket towers and the shuttles, the other side facing the hotel. There weren't many people, and Gray Moon was standing in the middle of the platform with the Bacchian. She moved close enough to hear.

"There's no reason for that," Gray Moon exclaimed, stabbing the Bacchian man with a pointed finger.

The Bacchian man had a full nose and a barrel chest. He raised an eyebrow and gently pushed Gray Moon's finger away. "If I gave them to you," he said, "they'd come and take them away."

"Who?"

"The Athenians, of course. Who do you think?"

"They'd have no cause," Gray Moon said, wrinkling his brow and pulling his head back.

"That's not the way they see it," barrel chest said. "They've convinced your government to ban guns on Talon, but I'm not going to stand here and argue with you. You know what I'm saying is true."

Gray Moon hesitated.

"I'll tell you what," barrel chest said. "I'll let you think about it. I'm going to get one of those mouth-watering burgers over there,"—he pointed through the glass to the diner next to the hotel—"and when I get back, you can give me an answer. I'm warning you, though. Either you accept this deal, or you'll go home empty-handed." He threw his hands in the air to show his displeasure as he marched towards the diner.

Ebony approached Gray Moon, wobbling like a drunk.

"Ebony, you okay?" he asked when he spotted her.

"No. I'm not okay," she said. "I have to get off this god-forsaken planet before I drop dead. Who was that man?" She pointed through the glass.

"Durell is his name. He's one of the few merchants willing to trade with me." He glanced around the spaceport. "Where's Troy?"

"He's at the hotel sleeping. What did the merchant want?"

"He wants to buy my furs for cash, but I don't want cash. I want guns."

"Guns?"

"Yes," he said with a note of resentment. "Guns. Is there any-thing wrong with that?"

No, there wasn't. She thought back to the giant falcon that had wounded Troy. "Can't you take his money and use it to buy guns?"

"No one will sell me guns."

She thought about what he was saying. "Because of the war?"

"I don't blame them," Gray Moon said quietly. "In the last month on Cronos, the Athenians took heavy losses in their battle for the Continent of Farisa. We all thought the tide was turning, but, of course, the Athenians won the battle, and they slaughtered, not just the soldiers who tried to surrender, but the civilians as well. They've captured thousands of the women and are keeping them as slaves. Everyone's terrified. So when they accused Talonians of selling guns to the Cronish and told them to stop, the Talonian government was quick to comply. The idea of Talonians wanting guns seems ludicrous to them. They think that any guns that come here will end up in the hands of the Cronish."

When Ebony heard the magnitude of the carnage on Cronos, she felt like a dagger had been thrust through her heart, yet her current dire situation forced her to shrug it off. "How much is that merchant offering you for your furs?"

"Thirty thousand."

"Dollars?"

"Madhora."

"How many dollars per skin is that?

He stared up at the sky for a moment. "Six."

"Six! she shrieked, her mouth falling open. "That's ridiculous! I can do better than that! Much better!"

"You?" Gray Moon seemed shocked.

"Yes, me!" Ebony insisted. "Send me to Vole!"

"I've traded with this man for years. We have a good relationship."

"What! Are you defending him? He's offering you crap, a mere pittance of what you should be getting. Your furs are worth a lot more than six dollars. When he comes back, tell him to get lost. Tell him you found another buyer."

"But I haven't found another buyer."

"Did you not hear him? He's not going to sell you guns. He doesn't respect you. In this business, respect is everything. He's hustling you. I'm not like that. For me, it's all about respect. I'll treat you fairly. Pay my way to Vole, and I'll get you more guns than you ever dreamed. Trust me. I know what I'm doing. You won't be sorry."

Rose

Rose wasn't interested in the clothing, the jewelry, or the artwork in the merchant stands of the Ralarra market. She wasn't interested in the food either. She was looking for one thing, and she was poised to find it like a vulture to a kill.

But this wasn't Cronos. On Cronos, a drug dealer looked like a drug dealer. This was Vole, and on Vole, everyone wore a robe, and everyone covered their face.

There was the dealer at the top of the black metal stairs. She would go there, but she didn't know the address, it was a long cab ride, and his price was too steep.

Solin, with his bow on one shoulder and quiver of arrows on the other, was fascinated by everything. He examining pennants, brooches, and bracelets and had a particular interest in the paintings of animals he saw for the first time.

Rose spotted a beggar sitting in the dirt with his legs folded and a cup in his hand, and she wondered, *Would he know?*

She glanced over at Solin. He had his mask pulled down and was taking a bite of a crisp ripe pompa. "Where did you get that?" she shrieked with a muffled voice.

Solin pointed back at a mass of tarpaulins stretched out over tables of fruits, vegetables, and dry goods.

"You can't just pick things up and start eating them," she said, her head tilted. "You have to be sneaky."

Solin took another bite.

"You're lucky he didn't see you steal that. Didn't they have laws where you came from?" she asked with her hands pleading.

Solin shrugged and kept chewing.

"And did you wash that? There's poisonous soot everywhere." She marched on down through the market.

She thought Solin would follow, but when she turned to look for him, he was gone. She spun her head around, searched up and down the street, and caught a glimpse of him talking to a skimpily dressed Volian leaning against the wall of a shed. She brushed aside her veil to drag a cigarette. Rose quickened her pace.

"Deyil sen agilli," the hooker said to Solin.

"Neci—" Solin started to say.

"Who are you talking to?" Rose shrieked, cutting him off and grinding her teeth.

"No one," Solin said, giving her a worried look.

"You liar! You're talking to this—this lady!"

"No," he said. "Not lady."

"I can see that!" Rose clenched her fists.

"Neci cox?" Solin asked the hooker, sneaking a glance at Rose.

Rose dropped her jaw, her eyes wide. "You're a dead man!" She showed him her teeth.

"Need gun," Solin said with a hand pleading.

"Don't give me that crap," Rose scolded, hands on her hips. "I'm not stupid."

"Perhaps now's not a good time," the hooker said, smiling.

"You bastard!" Rose yelled at Solin. "Stay away from me!" She turned and walked as fast as she could, dodging around a cart being pulled by a shaggy-haired horse, its back covered in layers of soot.

Solin caught up. "Need gun."

"Don't," Rose said. "I know what you're doing?"

"Need buy gun," Solin said.

"You imbecile! I know what she sells." She turned around and continued walking, fists clenched, arms swinging like pendulums.

"Stop!" Solin yelled when he caught up a second time.

Rose didn't. She just kept going.

"Athenians know we here," Solin said, keeping pace.

"No, they don't," Rose said.

"Do," Solin said, nodding.

"No, Solin," Rose said. "They don't. They're not going to look for us. They've got better things to do."

"Android say so," Solin said.

She stopped. "What android?"

He pointed back at the hooker.

Rose spun her head around and looked at her. "That's not an android." She stared intently. *Or is it?* she wondered. There was something peculiar about the way she moved. *An android hooker? No. Can't be. It's stupid.*

"She know," Solin said.

"Nice try, Solin," Rose said, "but I'm not buying it." She continued marching.

"Ask," Solin said, catching up.

Rose stopped. "Ask what?" Suddenly, it occurred to her that maybe the hooker would know where to get Rend.

"Where buy gun?"

Rose sighed. *No,* she thought. *Not a gun. Rend.*

"You pay her," Solin said.

"You need to stay away from her." She waved a finger at him. "You got that?"

Solin nodded.

Rose headed back to where the hooker was standing. "Hey, can I ask you a question?"

"Fire away, honey," the hooker said, taking a puff of her cigarette.

"Please don't call me *honey*," Rose said, shuffling her feet and looking back to make sure Solin stayed put.

"Okay, no problem, tight ass. Just tell me what you want, and never mind the act." She took another deep drag and tossed her butt. "And I'm not answering questions about systems."

"What do you mean?"

"Your boyfriend wanted to know if I was tied into the system," the hooker chuckled. "First guy to ever ask me that."

"Are you?"

"Screw off."

"Do you know where I can get some Rend?"

She pulled out another cigarette. "It'll cost you."

"How much?"

She held up two fingers. "Cash only."

Rose nodded.

"Come with me," the hooker said, walking away.

Rose glanced back at Solin and followed her.

"They know you're here," she said.

"Who?" Rose asked.

"You're safe for the moment, but I wouldn't stay in Ralarra if I were you."

"Where should we go?"

"There's a small town on the far side of Vole outside of Sondlan called Wesh. It has no security cameras or androids. You should go there."

She followed her to a motel less than a block away. The hooker went into one of the rooms and came back with a bottle. As Rose counted out the last of her money, Solin stepped up beside her. She looked up at him and saw a pinched expression of disgust. There was nothing she could do. She had to have the Rend.

"Come with me," she told Solin. "We're going to Wesh." She led the way, and Solin followed.

The ticket office was old and had high ceilings with evenly spaced pillars. Screens on the walls showed lists of departure times and arrival times for both, rocket ships and shuttles.

Three Volian security guards stopped them just inside the front door. They wanted Solin's bow and arrows.

"It's okay, Solin," Rose said. "You won't need it."

Solin nodded and surrendered them.

Rose got in line. Going back to Cronos was out of the question, and according to Hewitt, Bacchus wasn't an option either. To avoid the Athenians, they'd have to spend the rest of the war hiding behind a mask away from security cameras and androids.

"I'd like to get two tickets to Wesh," Rose told the Volian clerk behind the counter when it was finally her turn.

"Your name?"

"Rose Bashal."

"Do you have your visa?" the clerk asked, looking down at her screen.

"No. I lost all my ID." Rose lied, swallowing hard. She hadn't thought she'd need ID.

"No Passport?"

"No. I just told you," Rose snapped. "I lost everything. No visa, no passport, nothing." She glanced at Solin. He was looking up at a security camera.

"Well, I'm sorry, but if you don't have any ID, you can't buy a ticket."

"Why would I need an ID to take a shuttle?"

"It's because of the war. We're getting more refugees than—"

"Siz!" one of the guards shouted.

Rose turned to see.

The guard was pointing at Solin. "Stag senin hand ap!" Next to the guards stood an extremely tall woman wearing a robe with a hood. Rose couldn't see her face, but she had long white hair, her hands were pink, and they had white hair on their backs.

Solin stopped and raised his hands.

The three guards moved towards him, all three pulling out their plasma guns and pointing them at Solin.

The people in the lines moved back, like a school of fish from a shark.

One of the guards moved behind Solin, pulled out a pair of handcuffs, and reached up to grab his right arm.

With blinding speed and fluidity, Solin brought his left hand down, grabbed the guard's hand, spun around, and kicked another guard's knee. As the third guard brought his gun over, Solin hit it with a quick jab, knocked it out of his hand, and kicked his legs out. He punched the guard who was holding his knee in the head. That guard fell to the floor.

Solin did all of this while holding the arm of the first guard. He twisted his arm, kicked the legs out from under him, reached down, picked up a plasma gun, checked it, and pointed it at the three fallen guards who lay side by side like cobs of corn.

They squirmed and brought their hands up to a *don't shoot* posture.

"No, Solin! Don't!" Rose screamed.

Solin backed towards the main entrance, keeping his gun pointed at the guards.

The people coming in the door moved aside.

He paused in the doorway, saw his bow and arrows leaning against the wall, and picked them up. He looked at Rose.

She shook her head.

He slipped out the door.

The guards jumped up. They retrieved their guns and raced to the door. They opened it a crack, and then slowly opened it all the way. The plasma gun Solin had taken was sitting on the landing. They stepped out, and the one who'd lost his weapon picked it up. They looked this way and that, and then they looked at Rose.

"Uoy!" yelled one of the guards, pointing his plasma gun at her, "Stag senin hand ap!"

Rose raised her hands.

The guards handcuffed her and searched her. They found her Rend. They brought her up a staircase to a small room where they sat her down at a table with two chairs. After a long wait, a Volian woman dressed in a blue uniform, with yellow lines on her trousers, and a metal badge on her lapel, came in and sat across from Rose. A security guard stood by the door.

"My name is Lillian," she said with a slight accent. "You're faced with two charges. First, you had Rend. Rend is illegal on Vole."

Rose looked down.

"Second, and this charge is much more serious. We've been informed that you were involved in the theft of an Athenian corvette, and that you killed—"

"What the hell!" Rose sneered, standing. "Cronos is at war with the Athenians. They're the ones who attacked us. They slaughtered my friends."

"Sit."

"You can't believe them," Rose snapped, leaning over her handcuffed hands. "They're liars."

"Sit down." The security guard moved towards Rose.

Rose sat.

"Who was the man with you? You called him Solin."

"He's— He's not—" She sighed.

"What's his full name?"

Rose's eyes narrowed. "He doesn't have a full name. He doesn't know who he is."

"What do you know about him?" Lillian asked, tilting her head forward, her eyebrows raised.

"I don't know anything about him," she said. "He doesn't speak Cronish."

"He killed a lot of people," Lillian said, pursing her lips.

"Who's side are you on?" Rose snarled, standing again. "The Athenians killed the entire crew of the freighter I was on." Her voice was choked, and tears welled up in her eyes.

"Sit," Lillian said.

Rose sat and wiped her tears away with the back of her hand.

Lillian raised her chin. "You want to tell your side of the story? Fine. But don't lie to me. If I catch you lying, there will be consequences."

Rose froze. *They're confused*, she thought. *They don't know what happened.* She had to make sure her story wasn't going to go sideways. "Let's go back a bit. I was on the freighter, *Resolution,* when the Athenian corvette attacked it. They boarded and killed everyone. I escaped in a shuttle with some other crew members. We drifted for days, and we were running out of air when we came across a ship. We boarded it."

"What ship?"

"I'll come back to that. Let me finish."

"Go ahead."

"The Athenian corvette found us, and three of us, me, Solin, and another girl, took over an Athenian assault shuttle and flew it to the corvette."

"Who was the other person?"

"I don't know." She lied. "I never learned her name."

"What ship were you on before you took over the shuttle?"

"It was—I don't know what it was. It was unusual."

"Was it Cronish or Athenian?

"Okay. Listen. I know it sounds crazy, but the ship wasn't from here."

"Where was it from?"

"I don't know. It was Solin's ship."

"Solin's ship?"

"Yeah. Solin was on the ship when we found it. It was his ship. As I'm sure you know, he doesn't look like anyone in this solar system. He's from somewhere else."

"You don't know where?"

"No. I don't. When Solin attacked the corvette, it was because the Athenians we're killing people. Somehow, he knew that if he did the unexpected, he'd have an advantage. When we boarded the corvette, he killed the Athenian warriors, and we took it over."

"How many did you kill?"

"None."

"The other girl?"

"Two."

"And Solin?"

"Seven."

"All by himself?"

"Everyone saw what he did to those three security guards. He's good at fighting."

"Yes, but—"

"It was them or us!" Rose interrupted, her face flushed. "We're at war with these bastards! They're the ones that are killing people. We were simply defending ourselves."

"But who is Solin? Where did he come from?"

"I don't know," Rose said, shaking her head. "And his name's not Solin. That's just what I call him. He doesn't remember his name, but he's the reason I'm still alive. He's extremely good at fighting." She pursed her lips. "I wouldn't mess with him if I were you."

Ebony

Ebony went back to the hotel to retrieve Troy and found him lying on the bed, his skin cold to the touch. When she put her head to his chest, there was no heartbeat.

Gods, what have I done? Her eyes flooded with tears. When she was able to compose herself, she called the police.

The police came, and of course, they knew what had happened. They didn't ask many questions, and when Ebony told them she needed to get off of the planet, they were understanding and released her. When she got back to the spaceport, she found Gray Moon waiting patiently.

"Troy is dead," she said, her voice wavering.

"I'm sorry," Gray Moon said quietly, his shoulders slumping. "I'll get you a ticket so that you can get out of here."

"Thank you."

He went to the counter, bought a ticket and passed it to her.

"Don't worry about your furs," Ebony said. "I'll get good money for them, and I'll get you the guns you want."

"I know I can count on you, Ebony," Gray Moon said.

She boarded a rocket ship to Vole. The constant acceleration, hour after hour, was almost more than she could tolerate. Just sitting was painful and exhausting. The deceleration was no different. In all, the flight took twenty-two hours, the most prolonged twenty-two hours of Ebony's life. On heavy legs, she staggered to the closest hotel, got a room, and slept.

When she woke, her arms hurt, her legs hurt, everything hurt. She dragged herself from her room to the lobby and found a terminal. She searched for information on skin dealers, fur dealers, and pelt dealers but found nothing. She searched for gun dealers and found hundreds. Among the ads was an announcement for a party. The ad was written in Cronish; it wasn't translated. A Volian gun dealer was retiring. It had an address and was open to the public. Maybe she should see if she could talk to this retiring gun dealer. Perhaps he could give her some badly needed advice.

That evening, Ebony donned a mask and took a cab to the ad's address, a mansion high on the side of a dormant Volcano. This person was well off. There were close to a hundred people: Volians, Cronish, and Bacchians, but thankfully, no Athenians. Ebony mingled with the crowd, listened when they spoke her language, pretended to hear when they didn't, sipped the martinis, and ate the appetizers. There were speeches in Volian, and when they were done, the man that the party was centered around, a Volian with wrinkled skin, pulled the scarf he was wearing around his neck up over his nose, went out onto a balcony, and admired Jupih. Ebony put on her mask, went out, and stood beside him. "Do you speak Cronish?" she asked.

"Yes, of course," he said. "I'm a trader. Traders know all the languages."

"Do you know where I can sell furs?"

He turned to look at her and lifted his eyebrows. "There's only one place in the system where furs are worth anything."

"And where's that?" Ebony asked, lifting her mask to take a sip of her drink, pulling her mask down, and putting her hand back over her glass.

He pulled his cloak over his shoulders. "Atheni."

Ebony wondered if the thought of Athenians made him feel cold and if he shivered deep down in his soul at the thought of them.

"It's winter year-round there," he said. "Skin's are a luxury item. You can get top dollar, but it'd be treasonous for you to trade them now, with the war on."

"It's just a few skins," Ebony said. "The Athenians aren't going to use them to win the war."

"If Queen Leona heard that you say that, she'd hang you from a tree."

"Queen Leona kills her people just for protesting."

He nodded. "She should be negotiating with her people and the enemy."

"You can't negotiate when your head is in a guillotine."

"There's always leverage. Right up until the moment the blade falls. You have to consider the client's motivations. Figure out what they want and show them a better way to get it. It's always been my understanding that people don't want to leave their homes. They like it where they are. So, give them a better solution. Find a way to solve the problem, so they don't have to move."

"They could build a second sun."

"There you go! I'm not suggesting that you can change people. Their ideology is what it is, formed when they were too young to know better and held, in all likelihood, against all logic, for life. If they grew up poor, they'd think they're supposed to be poor. If they grew up believing in Uttara's gods, they'd die believing in them. There are people on Talon who won't kill a snail because they believe they're going to be reincarnated into a snail, and there are people in the caves of Bacchus that have never seen the stars and think their planet is flat. People's beliefs are a part of their identity, a part of who they are, and they'll fight and even die defending those beliefs, no matter how idiotic they are. A belief is a powerful thing. Priests and dictators know it. Anyone who has power and wants to hold on to it must be acutely aware of it, know what their people want, and work to give it to them. If they don't, the people will revolt, and it'll be their undoing. It's all about what people believe."

"Yet there is a truth."

"The truth is obscure. Very few people are looking for the truth. Even fewer find it."

"So, all I have to do is show Badoni a better way?"

"Ahh, well, here's the tricky part. Badoni's going to be a tough nut to crack. He'll only negotiate with royalty. If you want to show Badoni a better way, you'll have to leak it to the queen and let her do the negotiating. Of course, there's no profit in this unless you can find something to sell when the transition occurs. So you have to position yourself first, before you do your leaking."

"It might be too late."

"There's still time. Cronos is developing new weapons. They're going to push back." He sighed and looked up at Jupih. "As for your furs, you'll have to wait until the war is over."

And when the war is over, how do I sell them?"

"You can sell them directly. There's no shops on Atheni. Everything is bought and sold on screen. You take a picture of the product. You post it, take payment, and deliver. Shipping is a problem. Are you shipping them from Talon?"

"Yes." She went through her routine to take another sip.

"If you ship them from Talon, it'll take weeks for them to get there. Plus, the cost of shipping them one at a time would be preposterous. But there's a better way. There are distribution centers on Atheni. You can rent some space, ship the skins to the center, and as long as they don't find out your Cronish, you're in business." He took a sip.

Ebony pondered his last sentence. "So, you're telling me I can do this now?"

"You didn't hear it from me."

"How could they find out I'm Cronish?"

"They won't. Forget I mentioned it. It's just you wouldn't believe the silly things people sometimes do. I trust you're not one of those people. I'm sure you know how important it is to keep your identity secret. Tell no one—not your business associates, not your friends, not even that special person, if there is one. Tell no one. And let me make another suggestion."

"Go ahead," she said, taking another sip.

"There's a better trade. And there's no risk attached. There's a tremendous amount of lime on Talon. The next time you're talking to your contact there, you might want to ask him if he has access to any of it. It's used to make concrete. Bacchians were getting their lime from Cronos, but now because of the war, they don't have a supplier. I only mention it because the demand for lime is so much greater than the demand for furs. You might see it as an opportunity. As a merchant, it's your job to fill the void." He took a long swig, finishing the glass.

"I'll ask."

"If you can get lime, Bacchians will trade deuterium for it, and you know who needs deuterium."

"The Athenians?"

"No, no, no! Not the Athenians! Cronos! Skins are one thing. Deuterium, that's something else altogether. You don't want to trade deuterium to the enemy. That's a death sentence for sure."

"I can't image Talonians mining."

"Oh, you'd be surprised what a little money can do."

A servant came by offering drinks. Ebony took another martini.

"Don't underestimate them," he scolded. "You'd be amazed. Trust me. Talonians are much more capable than people think."

"But they don't have the heavy equipment." She looked at her drink and swirled it, deciding maybe it was a mistake to take it.

"That's logistics. That's part of your job. Don't look at these things as being barriers. Look at them as being opportunities for more trades. Buy the excavators, the dump trucks, and whatever else they need. Make it happen. It's not like you have to pick up a shovel yourself. Just do what you're good at. Buy and sell. Buy and sell. Buy and sell. Have fun with it. Trade. Trade. Trade. And don't forget to give yourself a generous cut."

"Where can I buy guns?"

He seemed to be searching his thoughts. "I can help you with that. There's a dealer on Bacchus. His name is Walter Hadila."

"What about you? Aren't you interested in getting in on the action?"

"Ah, no. I'm retired now. What you're going to be doing is what I did when I was young. I've made my money, and I— well, let's say I value time more than money now. It does get my juices worked up when I talk about this stuff, though. In a way, I envy you. It was fun while it lasted, but I don't miss it. Fifty years was enough."

Jen

Over and over, Jen dragged herself out of bed, a painstaking process where she had to grab onto a vertical pole with her human hand and haul herself up and over the side. It took all of her strength, and she fell more often than not. To get back into bed, she had to call for help. Her legs wouldn't move without the threat of a fall. She hated being dependent, and it made her try harder. Gradually, day by day, she had gotten better at it.

She learned how to control her thoughts, make herself believe she was falling when she wasn't. She started getting into bed on her own without help.

The next step was to learn how to walk while holding a horizontal pole with her human hand. When she pushed herself off balance and started to fall, her leg moved and took a step, or it didn't. When it didn't, her human arm couldn't hold on, and she fell. As she fell, her legs moved but not quickly enough, her mechanical arm reached out but too slowly, and her human arm was like a twig trying to stop a falling tree trunk.

It got more natural, and she graduated to two poles, one on either side. This exercise involved lifting her mechanical arm and shifting it from one spot to another, a highly frustrating task. Without the threat of a fall, the damn thing wouldn't move. And fooling herself, repeatedly, was disingenuous and hard to do, but slowly, she got better at holding her arm up and turning her torso to move it. At one point, she realized that it had moved on its own. She thought back on what she'd done, what feeling she held that sparked the shift. She isolated it and was able to repeat it. She practiced it over and over until she could move her arm at will.

Then came stair climbing. There was no threat, and therefore, no fear. To get her legs to lift, she had to fool herself into believing she was falling up. It was highly unnatural and required a focused effort. On her first try, she fell and hit her head. She decided to get better at walking first, so she could save herself when things went astray. She practiced.

The next day, she tried the stairs again. She pulled herself forward. The leg moved but not high enough, and it kicked the stair. She tried again. It kicked the stair again and again until it lifted just enough to get to the next step. She tried the other foot: more falls, and more attempts. In time, she got better at it and started going up. If she lost her balance, she could turn around and go down—if necessary—very quickly. Going down was easy.

She practiced and practiced.

Then came walking without holding onto anything. It was scary stuff. She figured she was reliving her early childhood. When she fell, she went down hard, and it usually hurt. Her mechanical arm was reacting more quickly, and thankfully, it broke her fall many times, but not every time.

Eventually, she started to be able to move more freely. Then came the drills, over and over, working on her weaknesses, honing her strengths, refining her skills, and building her confidence.

She and her comrades were paired off and taught how to fight. Bron was short but fearless. She put everything she had into every exercise, forcing Jen to do the same. Bron won their first spar, their second spar, and the third.

Harlin was arrogant and lazy, yet when they sparred, Jen couldn't defeat him either.

Ian was a workaholic, continually doing extra reps and showing off. When Jen sparred with him, she put everything she had into it and surprised herself. She won.

Jake had a sense of humor, and he made Jen and everyone else laugh. But his sense of humor didn't dampen his will to win, and Jen couldn't defeat him.

Cynthia was Cynthia. She never talked and was, more or less, invisible. Yet she fought like a wild animal. Jen couldn't win against her either.

Then came weapons training. She learned how to operate and shoot her plasma cannon. Firing it sometimes caused brutal injuries to those who weren't ready for the recoil. After seeing a cyborg flip over backward, Jen developed a fear of shooting, but in time, she got over it.

The people of the slums of Kypsan warmed their hands over cauldrons of burning garbage and watched the cyborgs train. Jen knew they didn't view her as being human. She was a cyborg, a machine. Everything she did was far from human.

The cyborgs ran in a single line through the streets. There were obstacles, people who didn't see them coming, children playing, carts, and bicycles that got in the way, but they leaped, swerved, and dodged in and out.

"Target the roof of the building on your right," —was the command in her helm. The cyborg in front of her leaped up and smashed through the glass of a second-story window. Jen jumped up after her through an abandoned apartment and into a hallway. She went up a staircase, leaping from one landing to the next without touching a step, and out onto the roof.

They leaped from the roof, one after the other. As they fell, parachutes sprouted from their backs and were pulled back into their packs when they hit the ground running.

Jen was part of her unit. She fit in. She'd proved she was just as strong and as capable as the others. No one would mess with her. Most of them liked her. She was sure that any one of them would fight to save her life as she'd fight to save theirs. They'd be fighting against the pinks, yet to a higher degree, they'd be fighting for each other.

In the final days of training, she received armor, a beautiful silver trimmed, burgundy outer shell that shielded almost every inch of her body. Her helm was layered screens showing the different spectrum of light. With the blink of an eye, she could see through walls.

In Jen's mind, she was ready. It was time to kill pinks. That's why she was here. That's why she was pushing herself.

Leona

"Leave?" Leona snapped. "You must be joking."

"Your Majesty," General Steen said with a steady voice. "We won't be able to hold them off. We should leave now. We'll still be able to direct the campaign from afar."

"I can't believe you're suggesting this—you of all people. Leave my daughter on Bacchus? Nonsense. After we've finally got word that they found her?"

Captain Landon stood beside Steen. He opened his mouth to speak, but nothing came out.

"I'm not going to run away," Leona said. "She needs me now more than ever."

"Your Majesty," Steen mumbled, his eyes turning away. "Please be reasonable."

"You told me there was another ship. *Excelsior*. It's on its way here, you said."

"It won't get here in time."

"Tell me what you're thinking. The whole thought process. Am I *that* far from the truth? I want to know."

Steen glared at her, his face pallid, his eyes blinking. "Your Majesty. The war on Cronos is going very poorly. We've lost six continents, and we can't afford to lose another. We have to get back there. The Athenian warships that are coming are many times more powerful than ours. If we stay here, we'll be destroyed. The war on Cronos has to be our top priority. If Princess Charline has been rescued, we will get word. If she hasn't, we can launch another rescue attempt later. But right now, we have to go."

"You're not being completely honest. There'll be no rescue attempt later. It'll be too late. How far away are the Athenian ships?"

Captain Landon found his voice. "Our source says that they left Atheni two days ago. If they're traveling at full speed, they could be here in four or five hours, maybe sooner."

"How many ships?"

"Three."

"And what's the last word back from the task force?"

"Just the one message three days ago," Landon said. "Direct communication is impossible. They're too far down."

"And what's the situation in the three remaining continents on Cronos?"

Steen and Landon gawked at each other.

"The provinces of Gathina and Sortal are on the verge of falling," Steen said.

"Gathina's falling?"

"Yes. It has— If it goes on like this—" He shook his head. "Our position right now is one of pure defense, and it's just a matter of time before they—" He bit his lip.

"For the sake of the gods, finish your sentences! I need to know! It's just a matter of time before what? Tell me the truth."

"Before complete genocide."

Leona took in a deep breath, her jaw lowered. "How could you say that?"

"You asked for the truth," Steen said, looking down at the deck.

There was an awkward silence.

"I did, didn't I?"

He bowed.

She sighed. So this is what it had come to. If she stayed, she put the ship at risk, and the nervous behavior of her officers told her the danger was grave. If she left, the entire task force was probably lost, and so was any hope of retrieving her daughter.

"Captain Landon," Leona said. "You said they wouldn't be here for another four or five hours, so why do we have to leave now?"

"Their ships are faster than ours, Your Majesty."

She thought they were overly cautious. She was prepared to gamble.

"The task force needs more time to get her out, gentlemen. We'll wait a bit longer."

"Please, Your Majesty," Steen said. "If we're not careful, Cronos will lose both its princess *and* its queen. It's not a risk we can take."

"I'm not asking," Leona barked, baring her teeth. "We'll wait."

The gods would help her. When she found Charline and got her back, she'd take her somewhere safe. Not back to Cronos. Somewhere else. Somewhere far from the war, away from harm. She'd protect her daughter as a mother should.

She frowned. She was disgusted with Steen and Landon. They were squawking like baby birds. "Tell me more about what's happening on Cronos."

"The Athenians have managed to land more reinforcements," General Steen stated. "They've twenty-three new divisions on the ground north of Sortal, and seven divisions have landed outside Manola."

"And our troops?"

"We have no divisions in Sortal and twelve divisions along the outskirts of Manola."

"Twelve against seven. We should attack," Leona said with a sweeping hand, "take out the Athenians before they're reinforced."

"They're digging in," Steen said. "It'll be costly."

"Not as costly as the alternative. I say we should attack."

233

Again, Landon and Steen gawked at each.

"Don't just stand there! Make it happen!"

"Of course, Your Majesty, at once," Steen said. He went to the communications station and donned a headset.

"Your Majesty," Landon said, "I don't think waiting is wise. It would be better if we were to leave."

"Stop it!" she shouted. "I won't be badgered."

Steen came back. "The order to attack has been given."

Leona knew him. She could tell by the look on his face that there was something else bothering him. "What is it?"

He sighed. "We have another problem. The people on Cronos are protesting."

"Protesting? Where?"

"In the cities."

"What cities?"

"The one's that haven't been occupied."

"I can't be expected to cater to the whims of a few dissidents. Get the police in those cities to break up the protests."

"There's more than a few, I'm afraid. They're protesting by the hundreds of thousands."

"What?"

Steen didn't reply.

"Why?"

"They believe that further bloodshed can be avoided. They want you to give the Athenians what they want."

"Give the Athenians what they want?" Leona said with an incredulous stare. "It's too late for that—squash the damn protests. I won't have my authority challenged. It was given to me by the gods of Uttara. Make them understand."

"The police are on the people's side," Steen said. If we're going to squash the protests, we're going to need troops to deal with it."

"Troops we don't have," Leona said. "Very well. How long before the divisions in training are ready?"

"I'm not sure," Steen said.

"But we do have divisions in training, don't we?"

"Yes, we do."

"Good." Leona nodded. "When they're ready, squash the protests."

Rose

Rose woke up to a palpitating headache, a deep craving for Rend, and a guard shaking her shoulder. He beckoned her to step out of the cell. She tried to measure the pain. It was worse when she stood. She swiped a hand over her face. "Where are we going?"

He beckoned again. She wasn't sure this was a good thing, but she followed.

A bald man with callous yellow skin, cracked and scarred, was waiting for her. He was dressed in a flamboyant jacket with wavy flame-like tracery and ornate decoration, seemingly a man of some notoriety.

"My name is Kariff Kasheen," he said. "I've paid your bail. There's a cafe in the hotel across the street. We can talk there."

Rose nodded.

The guard handed her her mask.

The cafe had spindle chairs, high ceilings, and blue leafed vines that hung down from a row of baskets. They sat down on either side of a charred wooden table.

"Can I get you anything?" Kariff asked Rose when the waiter stepped up.

"Water," Rose said to the waiter.

"And a beer," Kariff said.

The waiter nodded and left.

Rose stiffened her posture. "What's this about?"

Kariff lifted his chin. "I believe you're with someone—someone good at fighting."

Rose pursed her lips.

"My understanding is that he doesn't speak Cronish."

"Can't help you," Rose stated flatly. He was digging—probably worked for the government.

He looked down at Rose's arms, and she quickly folded them. "Rend?" he asked.

She looked away. The question was gut-wrenching. It wasn't her fault she got headaches.

"There's no reason to be ashamed. A lot of fighters take Rend. It helps them focus. Hell, the entire Athenian army is on it."

"Do you know where I can get some?"

He dug in his pocket, pulled out a bottle, and placed it on the table.

Rose stared at it. Her jaw went slack. Her tongue pressed the roof of her mouth. "I'm listening."

"I'm an entertainment promoter," he said, "and I'm constantly on the lookout for new talent."

"And you want Solin to be part your sick little freak show," Rose said, squaring her shoulders.

"It's not a freak show. These are legitimate fights."

"Sounds like a freak show to me."

"A fighter," he said at a lower volume, "assuming that he can fight reasonably well, makes good money."

"I need a hit first."

He leaned back in his chair. "You need to find Solin first."

"No. I have to have a hit first."

"Listen, you arrogant little imbecile! I don't need you nearly as much as you need me!"

"Hit first or no deal."

"Oh. My apologies," he said, picking up the bottle of Rend and putting it in his pocket. He got up quickly and turned to go.

"Wait."

He stopped and turned back to face her.

"Sorry," Rose said, grinding her teeth. "It's just—I'm a little on edge."

He nodded, calmed himself, and sat down.

The waiter arrived with the beer and water.

Rose bit her lower lip. "Why are you doing this? There are lots of people out there that'd be eager to fight."

Kariff took a long swig of his beer. "The rumor is that a man with white skin killed five Athenian warriors and captured an Athenian corvette. The Athenians are jokingly calling him the Messiah."

"Just five?" Rose said, taking a sip of her water.

Kariff tilted his head forward. "More?"

Rose nodded.

"You don't have to like me. You just have to like money."

"You said the Athenians called him the Messiah?"

"Yeah." He drank more of his beer. "It's great for publicity. People will come by the thousands."

"But what if he is the Messiah?" she asked, her eyes narrowed.

Kariff looked surprised and chuckled. "Let's not get silly. He's a man, not a god, even if he is white."

"You don't believe?"

"Oh, I believe. I just don't believe he's the Messiah."

"How can you be sure?"

He pulled the bottle back out of his pocket. "I'm sure you want this. All I'm asking is that I get to talk to him—see if he wants to do it."

Rose gave a slight nod.

"Smart lady. So, where is he?"

Rose shrugged. "I don't know. We were trying to get a flight out of here when the security jumped us. He escaped, and I got thrown in the can."

"But he'll come looking for you, right?"

"I'm not sure."

"We'll give it a day or two." He played with the bottle. If you want this, you're going to have to find him."

She wanted to reach out and grab it, but he curled his fist around it. The bastard was taunting her.

Kariff took another long swig of his beer and finished it off. "We'll meet here at this time every day until he shows up." He got up and signaled the waiter.

Ebony

In every direction, the ocean around Ebony was vast with ten-foot waves. Dark clouds covered the sky. She marveled at how the shuttle pilot was able to land on the deck of the submarine, *Malofa*, heaving to a fro. It seemed like an impossible task for a moment, but he put it down as if he were setting cutlery on a table.

The shuttle's hatch opened. She moved down the ramp and made her way to the conning tower. Walter Hadila, a terse, broad-shouldered man with blue skin, a black beard, and a captain's cap low on his brow, was waiting for her atop the conning tower.

During her stay on Vole, she'd managed to keep her identity secret by purchasing fake Volian credentials. She shipped Gray Moon's skins to a distribution center on Atheni, and sold the entire lot to a single buyer within hours of its arrival for a remarkable price. But she had to be careful with the money. She had a long list of things to buy.

Hadila shouted over the whine of the shuttle's engines as it powered down behind her. "You're looking for guns?"

The wind was gusting, and Ebony had to fight to maintain her balance. "Yes," she shouted.

"For the war?" the captain shouted.

"Can we talk inside?" This shouting back and forth on a pitching deck with the wind howling was grating on her nerves.

He nodded and waited while she climbed the ladder to the conning-tower. He led her to a hatch and down a ladder into his submarine. Both the passageway and the cabin had a low ceiling, and Ebony had to walk crouched down and leaning forward. The captain slid into a metal chair behind a steel desk. A sailor held a chair for Ebony. She sat and was decidedly uncomfortable, as the chair was too low.

Papers littered his desk. Behind him was a bookcase, and the walls held pictures of submarines with their crews standing at attention on deck.

"Would you like some wine and cheese?" Hadila asked.

"That's very kind. Yes. I would."

Hadila nodded at the sailor.

He took his leave.

"First, let me give you my condolences."

"Sorry, I don't know what you mean."

"Oh, I thought you knew. Queen Leona is dead."

"The queen is dead?" Ebony was breathless, and her skin tingled.

"She is. She was on the *Leviathan* in orbit around Bacchus when it was taken down by three Athenian cruisers."

"Orbiting Bacchus? Do you know why she was orbiting Bacchus?"

"Your queen sent hundreds of troops down into the pits of Bacchus to rescue her daughter, Princess Charline. The attempt failed. Empress Zeta called the attack sacrilegious and impious, and if the queen wasn't dead, she might very well have declared war on Cronos."

"Where did this happen?"

"It happened in the pits beneath Ronan, a city below the floating city of Napal on the other side of the planet."

"I wasn't a fan of the queen, yet her death is a terrible shock."

"I understand. So, what're you looking for exactly?"

"Hunting rifles," Ebony said, tearing her mind off the tragedy.

"For the war?"

"No. Big game hunting rifles."

Hadila's mouth slackened. "The most effective weapon for fighting the Athenians is the JL23. They can fire twenty bolts per second and have a range of a quarter-mile. They're being used on Cronos as we speak. I've sold thousands of them. An excellent weapon. You can't go wrong with the JL23"

"I'm not here for the JL23. I want big game hunting rifles."

Hadila tilted his head. "For what?"

"Do you have them or not?"

"You're not fighting the Athenians?" he asked, scratching his cheek.

"No. I'm not fighting the Athenians."

"You mean the AJ105? They're bulky and difficult to carry if you're not built like a gorilla." He grimaced. "The Athenians can handle them, but they're just too damn heavy to be practical for the Cronish."

"How much are they?"

Hadila didn't respond. He stared back at her, his jaw slack.

"Listen," Ebony stated. "I'm here to buy guns, not the guns you feel like selling me, the guns I want to buy. Are you going to tell me how much a big game hunting rifle is, or do I have to—"

The sailor came in with the wine and cheese. He popped the bottle, poured a glass for Ebony, one for Hadila, and cut a few slices of cheese.

Hadila gave him leave and pressed his tongue to his cheek. "Tell me you're not going to sell them to the Athenians."

"Of course not!" She grimaced and took a bite of cheese. "Very sharp," she said, holding it up.

"I'm glad you like it. I don't sell guns to the Athenians directly or indirectly, so if you're thinking of passing them to the Athenians, you'd better think again. It's not my war, and I know things are looking pretty bleak, but that doesn't mean we can just abandon all principles."

"I assure you. I'm not going to sell them to the Athenians."

"What are you planning to do with them? They're too heavy for Bacchians or Volians, and you can't sell them to the Talonians because of the government restrictions."

Ebony took another sip. "How much?"

"Have you heard a word I've said?"

"Yes. But I don't care about the restrictions. They were put there by the very people I'm at war with."

"If the Athenians find out, they'll go down there and slaughter entire villages."

"Well, I guess we'll just have to make sure they don't find out. How much?"

He sighed. "Three hundred tala."

"How much is that in Cronish dollars?" she asked, savoring the wine's taste.

"About five hundred."

"For the AJ105?" Ebony asked.

He nodded.

Ebony had researched the makes, the models, and the prices. Five hundred was high. "I don't want the 105. I want the AJ102."

"Same price."

"No. They're not the same price. I want two hundred and fifty of them, and I'll give you two hundred and twenty tala for each one."

He grimaced. "Two-eighty."

She sighed. "You're asking too much. As you said, the war on Cronos is looking bleak, and I know your sales have dropped off. You have expenses. Two hundred and fifty rifles is a small quantity. Do both of us a favor. Make this work. Start this relationship off on the right foot, and in time, I'll be back to make more trades. Two hundred and fifty big game rifles at two-twenty a piece, or I walk. Last chance."

"Two-thirty."

"Stop being so damn stubborn. Two-twenty. Not a penny more. C'mon."

He sighed and nodded. "Alright. Two-twenty. But don't go just yet. Finish your wine. We'll talk and get to know each other."

"I really must be on my way."

"We need to talk. Whether you know it or not, you're sinking yourself into a war. If we are going to be trading partners for any great length of time, we need to build a relationship of trust. There was a war that took place here on Bacchus one hundred years ago. On Cronos, it's been erased from your history books and made to look like it never happened. I think it's important you learn about it, so you have some context and a better understanding of things."

"Very well, but my glass is empty."

"I'll get you some more wine."

Rose

Rose was desperate, and Kariff was an asshole. She'd made the arduous journey to the cafe every day. It wasn't her fault that Solin hadn't shown up. She'd searched and searched for him, but it was a big city, and everyone was wearing a mask and a robe. It was an impossible task.

It also wasn't her fault that she got headaches and needed painkillers. She pleaded with Kariff for just the smallest bit of Rend, just enough to get her through the day, yet his answer was always the same. No. She despised him. What he was doing was cruel.

She did manage to steal things and use the money to buy drugs but didn't ever get enough money to buy Rend, and the drugs she purchased didn't satisfy her cravings.

On the morning of the fourth day, she woke up, her head pounding, and after a moment of sheer terror, realized it wasn't a ghost asleep on the floor beside her, it was Solin, his bow and quiver of arrows leaning against the wall. She woke him up, scolded him for scaring her half to death, and led him to the cafe.

"How the hell did you find me?" she asked when she sat down.

"In the market," he said. He hung his bow and quiver of arrows over the back of the chair and sat down beside her.

Yes, she had been in the market. "Why didn't you approach me?"

"Make sure okay, first."

He's paranoid, she thought. But then, of course, he had a good reason to avoid the Volian police. "What about the fight? Do you understand what you're getting into?" She had tried to explain things to him, but all she got back was a blank stare.

"Never mind," she said. "It doesn't matter." She knew she had to go through with this. She didn't like it, but she had no choice. She needed the Rend."

"Good morning," Kariff said when he arrived. "As promised, you've brought Solin." He sat down across from them.

"I have," Rose said.

"And not a minute too soon by the look of it," Kariff said, lifting an eyebrow.

"Time for you to pay up," Rose said flatly. She wasn't prepared to go another minute without getting her payment.

"You'll be compensated after the fight."

She blinked rapidly. "I've done what you asked! Pay me now!" The bastard wasn't fair. She wasn't asked to get Solin into the ring. She was asked to bring him, and she'd done that.

"Have you explained to Solin what I'm asking him to do?"

"You wanted Solin. Here he is," she said emphatically. "Pay me!"

"My dear girl, you need to compose yourself. Does Solin know what I want him to do?"

"Yes— I mean, I think so."

"He doesn't speak Cronish, does he?"

"No, but he understands me." She needed to have a role in this thing.

"We'll go to the arena, let him see it for himself. If you can find a way to tell him what I want, he can decide."

"I need a hit," Rose insisted. "After that, I'll be fine. Just one hit."

"Oh, for the sake of the gods," Kariff grumbled. "Stop your damn whining and hang on until we get there."

"One hit," she shrieked. "It'll only take a minute."

Kariff sighed and shook his head. "Okay. One hit." He pulled the bottle from his pocket. "A small one."

"I'll be back," she said. She snatched the bottle away, walked off to the washroom, and gave herself a shot in the arm.

When she got back, Kariff beckoned for the bottle.

"Why should I?" Rose asked. "I'm doing what you want."

He pinched his lips together. "Alright," he said, scowling. "We have to go." He got up and led them to the roof. They pulled on their masks and made their way across to a small shuttle that seated four.

Billowing ash from a distant volcano carried to the north. To the south, the horizon was dark gray, almost black. Even at this hour of the morning, the breeze did nothing to alleviate the intense heat.

A Volian pilot was waiting on the shuttle. Kariff sat beside him. Beads of sweat streamed down Solin's brow as he settled into a passenger seat, and Rose strapped herself in beside him.

The engines whined, and the shuttle shuddered as they lifted off. They flew out of the city where a lifeless landscape of reddish-black rock stretched on endlessly, where recesses were filled with flowing lava, and where the low flying shuttle stirred up the gray flakes of ash on the mountainsides. They flew under swelling clouds of smoke that slithered over a thin band of white sky, and they flew up over the tops of mountains and dropped down onto a small platform on the edge of the mouth of a dormant volcano.

With their masks on, they got out and walked to the elevators. Other private vessels, shuttlecraft, and smaller craft landed on the various platforms, discharged their passengers, and took off to make room for more.

Volian guardsmen stood by the elevators and confiscated weapons. Rose told Solin he would get his bow and arrows back when they left. He seemed to understand, and he watched where they stored them.

The elevator was crammed full, and as it descended, her view through a wire cage was of a vast pit. The grandstands circled the volcano's mouth and were filled with thousands of Volians, Bacchians, Cronish, and Athenians, surrounding a ring-shaped stage.

The crowd roared their approval when one of three Cronish fighters was hit hard squarely on the jaw by an Athenian warrior.

Rose cringed and glanced at Kariff, but he seemed disinterested.

A second Cronish fighter charged in and was struck on the side of the head. He bounced like a felled tree.

Rose felt like she was nibbling on cheese that was sure to trip a snare, but there was nothing she could do. She had to have the Rend. Her view of the ring was suddenly cut off when the elevator sunk into a dark shaft that brought them down to a vestibule.

She took Solin's mask from him. "I'll hold it for you," she said.

Solin seemed perfectly at ease. As they crossed the vestibule, Rose wondered if he knew that he was about to step into the ring. Did he know how badly she needed the money, not just to get off this god-forsaken planet, but to buy Rend so she could deal with the ever-present pounding in her head. "Are you okay with this?" she asked.

"Okay with this," he replied.

It was his usual echo.

A loud cheer came from the direction of the stands.

"Who's Solin going to be fighting," Rose asked Kariff.

"An Athenian."

"Just one?"

"Yes." He smiled. "You didn't think I'd put him up against five, did you?"

"I wouldn't trust you to hold my place in a grocery line."

He laughed. "You're already trusting me to do a lot more than that. But don't fret. If he wins, we're going to make a substantial amount of money."

She tried to suppress a shiver.

"Go up these stairs," Kariff said, pointing, "to a door on the fifth floor marked Eyvan Dord. "You can watch from there. I have to take Solin to get him ready. I'll join you once I've got him settled into the cue."

The balcony behind the door marked Eyvan Dord held just three chairs yet provided an excellent view. The Athenian was gone from the ring, and the three Cronish fighters were being removed on stretchers. Two showed signs of life, but one didn't.

A Volian in a black tunic was at the center of the ring, shouting at the crowd. Around the perimeter, a sparse number of guardsmen kept the crowd at bay. The announcer pointed to a lone Bacchian fighter who bounced into the ring doing cartwheels. Following a full somersault, he stood bare-chested with his hands on his hips. The Bacchians in the crowd chanted, "Ratogat. Ratogat. Ratogat."

The announcer continued his shouting, and a Volian wearing a loose-fitting dark blue martial arts robe entered from the other end of the ring. He bowed his head and pressed his hands together flat in front of his face, as if in prayer.

The announcer moved out of the ring, a bell sounded, and Ratogat moved in, careful not to get too close, his arms dangling by his sides.

Blue robe remained motionless.

Ratogat swayed like the pendulum of a clock, back and forth. Suddenly, he darted in.

Blue robe deftly stepped to one side and swung a leg around, catching Ratogat squarely on the head. The crowd reacted with a loud and drawn out, "Ohhh!"

Ratogat rolled, landed on his feet, and darted in again.

Blue robe, much taller than Ratogat, swung his leg again, but missed high and was hit in his midsection, hard. He buckled over, but at the same time, chopped with the edge of his hand, striking the neck of Ratogat.

Ratogat flinched but took the blow and punched blue robe's midsection repeatedly with his fists, like the pistons of an engine.

Blue robe staggered back to the edge of the ring.

The Bacchian supporters in the crowd resumed their chanting. "Ratogat. Ratogat. Ratogat."

Blue robe spun full circle and kicked Ratogat in the head again.

This time, Ratogat sunk to his knees, put his hands on the platform, and shook his head. The chanting stopped.

Blue robe lined up a more calculated and deliberate kick.

Ratogat responded in a way that made it apparent that his head shaking was nothing more than a ruse. He moved quickly and gracefully, sidestepping the swinging leg, and darting in to punch blue robe squarely between the legs.

Blue robe went down, clutching his balls in convulsions of agony. The crowd roared.

Ratogat closed in, jumped on top of blue robe, and used his pistons on his face. The crowd rose to their feet and roared again.

Blue robe cringed and tried to get away, but it was no use, and he passed out after just a few more seconds of the relentless pounding. The crowd roared even louder.

Ratogat jumped up, smiled, and pumped his fists in the air. The Bacchians in the crowd were on their feet, chanting, "Ratogat. Ratogat. Ratogat."

A stretcher came out, and blue robe, who had not regained consciousness, was carried from the ring.

The announcer came out, held up the left arm of Ratogat, and circled the ring. Ratogat departed the ring pumping his arms in the air.

Kariff came to the balcony and sat beside Rose. "Enjoying yourself?"

Rose brought her eyebrows together and glowered.

The announcer resumed his shouting. He pointed towards one end of the ring and out walked Solin with his chest bare. The announcer continued shouting and tossed a hand towards the other end of the ring. Out stepped an Athenian, almost three feet higher than Solin, and more muscular than any Athenian warrior Rose had seen. He was impossibly big, and Rose brought her hands up to the sides of her face.

The announcer left the ring, and the bell sounded.

The Athenian turned his attention to the Athenian warriors in the crowd. One of them, presumably the commander, nodded, and the Athenian in the ring nodded back. Then he turned his attention to Solin and moved in.

Solin moved quickly, one way, and then the other.

The Athenian tried to cut off his escape, but Solin fainted right and escaped to the left.

Again, the Athenian tried to cut him off.

This time Solin fainted left and escaped to the right.

The Athenian approached again.

Solin ducked beneath his swinging arm and punched his knee. The crowd roared.

The Athenian gritted his teeth and limped back. In a rage, he got into a crouch and stormed towards Solin.

Solin went straight at him, used the Athenian's knee as a step, and punched straight up, catching him under the chin. His head snapped back. Solin landed behind him and hurled his body into the back of his legs.

The Athenian fell backward, landed hard on his back, and his head bounced off the rock platform. The crowd jumped to their feet, cheering. The Athenian didn't get up.

Five Athenian warriors were suddenly in the ring. They each had longswords drawn, and they circled Solin. The guardsmen rushed forward, held up their plasma guns, and yelled, but were ignored.

Rose bolted from the balcony and down the stairs. In the vestibule, people swarmed around the entrance to the ring. Through the mass of bodies, she saw the Athenians, still with their longswords drawn, edging towards Solin, and ignoring the guardsmen's demands. *Why, in the name of the gods, were they allowed keeping their longswords?* She forced her way through the crowd. "Solin!"

Solin glanced back at her, and the Athenian warrior on his left used the distraction to charge, but Solin avoided the blow, snatched the sword away from the charging warrior, spun around, and put it straight through his back and out his stomach. Amazingly, Solin managed to withdraw the sword in time to stave off the fierce blow of the Athenian farthest to his right and another strike from one in the middle. The Athenian with the stab wound fell to his knees and then to the floor. Solin stepped back. The four remaining Athenians stood across from him with their swords held high.

The crowd was oddly silent.

Solin slowly backed into the vestibule, and the people parted like peasants to a king. The Athenians took small steps towards Solin. An elevator opened on the back wall, and the people in it dispersed.

Rose raced back, got in, and held the door open.

Solin fainted a charge causing the Athenians to step back. The Athenian on the far left lunged at Solin. Solin parried and took his head off with the backstroke. He moved back into the elevator, and the door shut.

As they went up, Rose looked down through the wire cage at the ring. The announcer was back, shouting at the crowd.

"Here," Rose said, holding out Solin's mask. "When we get to the top, run for the closest shuttle."

"Closest shuttle," Solin repeated, holding his blood-soaked sword with one hand as he pulled his mask on with the other.

The closest shuttle wasn't close. Rose started running. When she checked to make sure Solin was running with her, he wasn't. She stopped, spun around, and saw Solin was getting his bow and quiver of arrows from the guardsmen. She carried on to the shuttle and boarded. When she looked back again, Solin was walking towards her, and the three Athenian warriors were coming out of the elevator.

"Solin!" she screamed, but he didn't have to be told. He knew. And before Rose could finish her shouting, he had already fired three arrows. Two were hit in the chest and one in the eye.

Solin continued his walk and got on the shuttle.

The hatch shut, and the shuttle lifted off. They flew back down the mountainside low to the ground stirring up flakes of ash across the lifeless landscape of reddish-black rock, over the lava-filled recesses, and back to the city of Ralarra.

Rose had just one bottle of Rend and a deep loathing for Kariff.

Ebony

Ebony moved up to the co-pilot's seat so she could see as the cutter descended from orbit. The pilot was a portly Bacchian woman with a double chin.

An endless sea of clouds covered Bacchus, and further to the north, a great spiraling hurricane lay seemingly frozen.

The cutter was longer than a shuttle and had a raised cockpit. It had berths, a galley, and three heads. Its dash was littered with lights like the stars of a galaxy. There were half a dozen screens beneath the windows that stretched across the front. A bulky console of navigational instruments sat between her and the pilot.

"Where was this ship built?" Ebony asked.

"It's Bacchian. A company called Vestrom. Beautiful, isn't she."

"Must be expensive."

"The company doesn't sell to outsiders."

Built with slave labor, no doubt, Ebony thought. "What else do they build?"

"Sloops, schooners, frigates, and shuttles."

The cutter descended below the clouds towards the surface of an endless green ocean where a familiar-looking submarine skimmed along its surface. The cutter was too big to land on the deck, so the pilot set it down in the water and pulled up alongside. Sailors aboard the submarine lowered bumpers and tied mooring lines to the cutter. The hatch opened, and Ebony went down the ramp to the deck.

A mixture of black and white clouds curled across the horizon, and, in isolated spots, sheets of rain swept across the choppy water.

"Good to have you back," Hadila yelled from the conning tower.

"Good to be back," Ebony replied as she walked across the deck. A heavy wave crashed into the side, and water washed over her like the spray from a whale. She hurried up the ladder.

A lot had happened since her last visit. She'd gone back to Talon and learned where Troy had been buried. She'd been to his grave, whispered to him, told him she was sorry, and shed a few tears.

Then she had gone to work. She formed a mining company and got Gray Moon to run it. He gathered hundreds of Talonians from somewhere—she had no idea where—to shovel lime into bags. This slow process eventually produced enough bags for her to justify another trip to Bacchus. Now, she was back on the *Malofa,* but this time she wasn't looking for guns.

Hadila took her down to his office. "Wine?" he asked as she squeezed her way through the hatch.

"Yes, please." She walked, crouched over, to her chair, and sat down.

A sailor filled her glass and Hadila's.

"That'll be all," the captain said to the sailor.

He took his leave and shut the hatch behind him.

"Try this cheese." He held up a wooden board filled with bite-sized slices.

She took one. "I have lime," she said and bit into her cheese.

"Lime! How wonderful. From Talon?"

"Yes."

Hadila took a sip of wine. "How much do you have?"

"Forty thousand fifty-pound bags."

"What's a pound, exactly?"

"A little more than a pauna."

"Interesting," he said, putting a hand to his chin. "I guess you know what they're worth."

"Of course, I do." She took a sip of wine. "You're not going to dicker over the price, are you?"

He laughed. "Of course I am," he said, taking a deep breath. "Thirty tala per bag."

"I don't want tala. I want deuterium."

"It's expensive," Hadila said, raising an eyebrow.

"So's my lime."

He smiled. "How big is your tanker?"

"I don't have a tanker, which is a problem. You can help me. I want ten loads." She took another slice of cheese.

He grimaced. "For the lime?"

"I know. It's not much. But your water has to be refined."

"If I'm doing my math correctly, you have one thousand tons of lime. It's worth about thirty thousand tala. One load of deuterium is also worth about thirty thousand tala. So why are you telling me you want ten loads?"

"The water is only going to cost you a pittance in taxes. We need to get the ball rolling." She put the cheese in her mouth.

"I'm not doing this as an act of charity," Hadila said with a condescending smile.

"You can call it an investment," she said, still chewing. "I also want an excavator and some dump trucks. My next shipment will be much bigger, and it won't take weeks to put it together. I'll be able to give you even bigger shipments and a better price down the road."

The captain chuckled. "Listen, I need to make a profit."

"No, you don't. You need to help me win the war."

"Win the war? What're you talking about. The war is lost. Everybody knows it. There's only one continent left, and twelve cities in two provinces are under siege."

"It's not lost, and I know how to win it, but I need your help."

"It's not my war! And adding a few drops of deuterium into the mix won't make a difference. The situation is hopeless."

"Badoni's not fighting this war because Athenians need a new planet. He's fighting it to show his people how strong and powerful his army is, how great a leader he is, and how superior the Athenian people are. He needs to win the hearts and minds of his people. Do you think the Athenians are going to win the war on Cronos and stop there? Because if you do, you're a fool. They're going to finish up on Cronos, go on vacation for a few weeks, and launch an attack on Bacchus. That's what they're going to do. What will you do?"

"Why would he attack Bacchus?"

Ebony counted on her fingers. "Free deuterium. Free diamonds. Free slaves." She held her third finger down. "Millions of them. Free—"

"Okay. Okay." Hadila pursed his lips. "I see your point."

"Wars are fought for territory but won with resources. The more tanks, cannons, and deuterium the army gets, the longer it will last. You're the one who gave me the idea. Remember the history lesson."

"But that was different."

"It was different in some ways but essentially the same. Cronos still has five provinces left. It's not too late. Think about what this would do. If Bacchians start manufacturing tanks, cannons, rifles, bombs, and whatever else the Cronish army needs, everyone in every city will be fully employed. Your economy will be pulled out of the depression it's been suffering through, and it would prepare Bacchians for what might be coming next."

"If we do that, the Athenians won't take kindly to it."

"The Athenians can't be appeased. You need to start getting ready for the day they turn against you. They're already stealing your water."

"So, let me get this straight. You want ten loads of water, an excavator, and some dump trucks. Is that all?" he asked sarcastically.

"I could also use a ship of some kind, so I don't have to hire someone every time I want to go somewhere."

"And a ship of some kind," he said, leaning on his elbow with raised eyebrows.

"I think you can manage it. My guess is that Vestrom has what I need and that it's dirt cheap."

"I'll give you three loads, and you'll buy your equipment. Vestrom has a schooner. It's smaller than that cutter you came in, but it will get you from place to place. I'll try to get you one."

"Try to keep in mind what's at stake here. You're going to be standing at the hub when tons of supplies go from here to there. All you have to do is take a small percentage, and you'll be rich."

"Or dead. I'm not sure which. Do we have a deal?"

"We do."

Keldon

Keldon and Charline didn't have to break into houses. The city was asleep, and there were very few people around. They walked down tarred dirt lanes, drank the water that was trickling from cracks in the cavern, feasted on the carrots, onions, and turnips they pulled from gardens and munched on the plums and apples they plucked from orchard trees.

"Time to go back up," Keldon said as he tossed a final apple core. He had noticed the lights in the cavern were slowly moving up in intensity, and he worried that the people would be waking up and coming out.

For weeks they had retreated up the footpath and slept in the entrance to the staircase during the day. Up until now, Charline had cooperated.

"I'm not going back up there," she said with an ugly twist of her mouth.

The path from the staircase had long been abandoned, and getting up and down had been tricky. Portions of it were narrow, and in places, blocks of steps were missing. In Keldon's mind, that's what made it safe. No one else would be going up there.

"There's a tunnel over there," Charline said. "We'll hide there." She started towards it.

"No," Keldon scolded, walking fast to catch up. He grabbed her arm.

She stopped. "What are you going to do, shoot me?" she asked with a hushed voice. "You can go back up if you want to. I'm going to hide in there."

"Stop it, Charline. I know what I'm doing."

"I'm the one who decided to go up the staircase. That wasn't such a bad idea, was it?" She wrenched her arm free, turned, and went to the mouth of the cave.

Keldon followed. A light came from its depths. "You're going to get us caught," he whispered.

She pursed her lips. "Okay, maybe not this tunnel. We'll keep looking."

"We don't need to keep looking. We already have a safe place." She was naive, the product of a sheltered life. He had to find a way to get control of her.

"There's another cave," she said, hurrying towards it.

He scrambled to catch up. She scurried ahead and in. This one was pitch black, and he lost sight of her. He raced in after her.

"Hold it right there,"—came a voice from the darkness. A shadow ripped Keldon's rifle from his hands.

Charline screamed.

Keldon was pushed and fell backward, flat on his back. He struggled to get a breath. He saw shapes in the darkness, and when his eyes adjusted, there was a rifle barrel pointed at his chest."

"Stay down," a shadowy figure said.

"Let me go!" Charline shouted.

"What are you doing here?" asked the shadow.

"Let me go," she said again, this time with a vicious bitter tone.

Keldon was grabbed by the arms, pulled up, and pushed into a dimly lit cave. He got his breath back. There were blues here, lots of them, maybe twenty, some standing, some sitting at a table.

An old woman with speckled blue skin, a wrinkled mouth, and sloped forehead leaned back in a chair along the cave's choppy rock face. "Who are you?" she asked.

"I'm Princess Charline," she snapped back.

The old woman thought about this for a moment and laughed.

"I am," Charline insisted. "Why are you laughing?"

She stopped laughing. Her eyes narrowed. "It all makes sense now. That's what your mother was doing here—she was looking for you."

"You must help me. I must return to Cronos."

"Of course," she said. "You have a war to fight? You can't lead your people from here?"

"My mother leads the people," Charline snapped back.

The old woman looked down for a moment, and when she looked back up, her face was drawn. "My dear girl, your mother is dead."

"She is not!" Her chin was trembling, her gaze frozen. The room fell silent. She took a deep quivering breath, and tears formed in her eyes.

"Even down here, we get news," the old lady said.

"How could she—she has armies."

"She was busy trying to save you. She was on the *Leviathan* in orbit around Bacchus when it was attacked and shot down by three Athenian Battle Cruisers."

"You're lying," she said unconvincingly, tears streaming down her cheeks.

The old woman turned to look at Keldon. "And who are you?"

"Just a soldier."

"Your name?"

He didn't reply.

"Down here, only olives with names are permitted to remain alive."

"Private Keldon Harding."

She nodded. "We'll see how much we can get for the two of you."

Jen

As the transport descended through the clouds, Jen looked around at the other cyborgs.

She was worried about Bron. She wasn't herself. She looked frenzied, avoided eye contact, and frequently took deep breaths. Maybe she'd get her bearings when she got down there and saw the battlefield in front of her. There was nothing to be done.

The transport moved down and skimmed just above the tops of the trees.

Cynthia was doing a routine weapon check, over and over. It was her way of dealing with stress. She'd be okay, though. She was a rattlesnake.

Jen looked down on trees and more trees surrounding lakes and sprawling rivers.

Harlin wasn't adjusting anything, and he looked the way he always did—focused and calm—scary calm.

The transport hit the ground in a clearing, and the rear of the ship parted, like a giant mouth. Jen got up, moved to the back, and filed off. The sky was bursting with transports coming down, landing, discharging their loads, and disengaging. They dropped tanks, assault vehicles, and troops—tens of thousands of them. They gathered into two units. Half went north, half south, and the cyborgs stayed in the middle.

At the briefing, the situation had been explained. Only one continent remained in Cronish hands. In the nation of Crena, the city, Deli, was barely clinging to life. It had been copiously bombed, and few buildings were still intact, yet thousands of olive soldiers were hiding in basements. The pinks hadn't leveled the city to the ground how they had leveled other cities, presumably because they were low on ammunition. It took a lot of bombs to level a city.

The fighting had gone on for weeks, and summer arrived. Pinks bodies weren't designed for dealing with the extremes of summer. Heat isn't like cold. If the pinks got cold, they could put on an extra layer of clothing. But if they got hot, there was nothing they could do. They cooked.

"Fall in!" Sergeant Romley shouted.

The cyborgs formed four lines of ten.

"We're going to work our way up to the crest of the hill, but stay out of sight," Sergeant Romley bellowed out. "The fifth division's going to attack from the north, and the ninth are going in from the south. They'll meet in the middle, and run towards you. The idea is to get the pinks to follow. They usually do. Your job is to wait until they're out of their hiding spots, wait until they're up the hill, and wait again until you hear the command to attack. If they only come part way and retreat, on my command, you're to go after them. If they don't come out, you're to stay put. Any questions?"

None of the cyborgs had any questions. Questions were invariably a bad idea. It was understood that Sergeant Romley always made things clear, and he hated repeating himself.

"Alright. Let's go!"

The cyborgs marched, double-time, up the hill with Sergeant Romley leading the way. Near the crest of the hill, he directed them to keep their heads down and spread out.

Jen found a spot where she could see. The city stretched out along the banks of a river. There were no trees, and tanks, trucks, and cannons littered the battlefield in front of the buildings. None of the vehicles were moving, and a couple of them were on fire. Most of the houses and buildings were messed up pretty bad. There were more Athenian tanks and trucks at the north end of the city. None of them were moving either.

There were signs of movement behind smashed out windows, and she saw a pink run across a street from one building to another. So, they were there. There was a shot, a single shot, not followed by another, that sent an olive soaring through the air from a high perch. He landed in the street, his guts splattering like a bug on a windshield.

It was a long time before the attack began, but when it did, the tanks and assault vehicles came first, blasting away and moving fast with the troops running behind them. One division went over the hill to the north, and at the same time, the other division came from the valley to the south. At the north end, the pinks fired first. They had tanks of their own, buried and camouflaged, and they used them effectively, taking out a Cronish tank with the first shot. At the south end, the pinks didn't have any tanks, but they had anti-tank guns, and three Cronish tanks were hit before they got halfway.

Thousands of pinks sprung up from their hiding spots and flowed to the edge of the city like an avalanche of snow.

Olive snippers in the city feasted.

Both the northern and southern divisions veered away from the pink's line and moved towards each other in the center. As they did, they were cut to pieces.

The few dozen tanks and assault vehicles that were still operating coagulated in the middle of the battlefield. The troops rushed to get behind them. The tanks that were left backed up, firing at the enemy and retreating steadily. The foot soldiers weren't able to keep up. Exposed to incoming fire, they ran as fast as they could straight back towards the top of the hill.

The pinks took the bait. Dozens of tanks and many thousands of warriors came out of the city from the north in hot pursuit.

Jen worried about the numbers. There were only forty cyborgs. Could they stop thousands? She waited. By the time the Cronish tanks got to the top of the hill, there were only two left, and the olive foot soldiers were being mowed down like cornstalks.

The pinks had only lost five tanks, and they were closing in. Jen waited.

Romley gave the command, "Engage!"

There was a tank headed straight for Jen. She stayed down behind the hill's crest until it was over her, and then stood up, throwing her shoulder into it. The tank flipped over backward and landed on its turret. She started firing, sweeping her cannon from side to side, moving forward quickly, picking her targets, dealing with the most threatening first. Powerful blue bolts pelted the pinks. There was no place for them to hide. Their tanks were tossed aside by the cyborgs like toys. Even so, the pinks didn't run. They kept coming.

Jen saw a cyborg's leg explode. That's where the power plants were—in the legs. The blast obliterated him, killed dozens of pinks, and crippled two cyborgs standing too close.

The pinks attacked in unison. She saw a cyborg stop for a second, get hit several times, and knocked off balance. Suddenly, dozens of shots hit her. She fell, and bolts of blue hammered her to the ground.

Bolts of blue hit Jen too, but she kept moving and kept her balance. Her armor did its job.

She saw another cyborg get hit by a bolt from a tank, go flying through the air, and driven into the ground. He didn't get up.

She kept firing, and she kept moving. She was fast, and they were having had a hard time hitting her.

One thing was for sure—she loved killing pinks.

Ebony

Ebony's new schooner, *Valiant*, had smooth curved lines, two fins on top, and a belly like a fish. As she steered it down towards Hadila's submarine, three moons were pasted to the sky, each one more than twice the size of the one to its left.

Her plan was working. Gray Moon was shipping lime from Talon, and she was transporting deuterium and other supplies to Cronos. She was making money, lots of money, and so was Hadila.

She put the ship down in the water next to his submarine. His crew tied the schooner to the hull and extended a gangplank.

Hadila was on the conning tower. He waited for her and then took her down to his office. "There's something we have to talk about," he said even before they sat down. "Do you have a brother?"

"Yes, I do," Ebony said, stunned by the question. "Why do you ask?"

"Is his name Keldon Harding?"

"Yes." *For the sake of the gods, how does he know my brother?* Ebony wondered.

"I'm afraid I've some distressing news."

He's dead, Ebony thought. *He's a casualty of the war.* She couldn't speak, couldn't think straight.

"People tend to think of submarines as isolated and disconnected, but we're not," Hadila said. "There are many eyes and ears, open lines of communication, and news travels far and wide. As much as I'd have liked our relationship to have been our little secret, I'm afraid it isn't. Somehow, some nasty people have come to know who you are."

"What are you trying to say?" Ebony asked. "Just spit it out."

"Your bother has been taken hostage," Hadila said.

"By the Athenians?" She was confused. She knew they didn't take prisoners.

"No. Not the Athenians. A gang here on Bacchus."

"But that can't be. My brother's on Cronos, fighting in the war."

"He's not. He's here on Bacchus, in Ronan."

How could that be? she wondered. Keldon had to be on Cronos. That's where the war was. Unless he deserted, but she didn't think Keldon was the type. She'd known him to be a die-hard fighter. This was all extremely hard to take in, but Hadila had said it. "I see," she said. She took a deep breath and exhaled slowly. "Are the police involved?"

He shook his head. "No police. The police down there are more corrupt than the harlots of Vole. They take your money and make you miserable." He said it like he recalled a personal experience. "These things never turn out the way you hope they will. You should know that they're going to take your money and hand you a corpse. What you need to do is go in with a band of mercenaries. If you strike hard and quick, the hostage-takers will scatter like a flock of pigeons. It's the only way."

It was more than hard to take in. It was absurd. "Are you sure that they have my brother. I don't understand how he could be here."

"I told you the last time you were here. The queen sent hundreds of troops down into the pits to rescue her daughter. Your brother must have been among them."

Her face turned ashen. "I see."

"Somehow, the princess and your brother got up to the city and were captured by a gang."

"I'm finding all of this quite shocking," Ebony said.

"It's all true. I've no reason to lie." He picked up his wine glass and took a sip.

"And you want me to hire criminals to deal with the hostage-takers?"

He laughed. "On Cronos, what they do is criminal. On Bacchus, it's just business as usual." He picked up a slice of cheese and tossed it in his mouth.

"I don't want mercenaries," Ebony said, dropping her head, her eyes closed. "I just want to pay the hostage-takers and get my brother back. I know his chances are slim, but using mercenaries seems risky."

"The mercenaries will give you a slim chance," Hadila said. "Without them, there's absolutely no chance. They've taken the princess hostage as well. If they kill her, they have to fear the wrath of the Cronish generals. Keldon's a witness, and probably the only witness. They're not going to let him live. No chance of that."

Ebony stopped to consider what he was saying. He was right. They wouldn't let them live, would they? They'd have to kill him no matter what.

"You need to find a captain of a submarine that does this sort of thing. He'll have the mercenaries you need."

"Do you know a captain like that?"

"Captain Farrel of the submarine, *Taringer*. Go to the Napal spaceport and look for him there.

"I don't have any money."

"I know. I'm going to pay you for the lime. There's a suit-case with three hundred thousand tala waiting for you on the conning tower.

Ebony got up and hit her head on the ceiling.

"Oh!" Hadila said. "Are you okay?"

"I'm fine," she said, holding her head. Crouched over, she made her way out.

He followed her up to the conning tower. A sailor hauled the suitcase down to the deck, grabbed it by the handle, and pulled it up the ramp onto her shuttle.

The submarine crew was not quite finished unloading the lime, but Ebony told them they were done. She had to go.

The journey to Napal took her deep into the evening. She descended through the darkness to an extensive array of brightly lit platforms lined with submarines and many other types of vessels.

She put the schooner down on the north landing pad, got out, and asked a drunk sailor staggering along the dock where she could find the submarine, *Taringer*. He spun around to get his bearings, almost fell, and pointed it out. Then he carried on with his stagger.

Ebony went to it with her suitcase in tow. There were close to two dozen mini-subs fitted with bubble plastic domes sitting on the *Taringer's* deck. She walked across the gangplank and tried to pull her suitcase up to the conning tower, but couldn't manage. She went up without it and banged on the hatch.

"Captain Farrel?" Ebony asked when the hatch opened.

"Who are you?"

"A client."

"Come ahead, down."

"I have a suitcase on the deck. I need someone to fetch it?"

He sent a sailor up, and she went down. In a crouched position, she was brought to the bridge.

"Well, young lady," a Bacchian said, wearing a captain's hat and leaning on his chair's arm. "What brings you down here?"

There were no other chairs she could see, so she sat down on the deck. "Are you Captain Farrel?"

He nodded.

"My brother has been kidnapped."

"Harding?"

"Yes."

"The price is forty thousand tala," Farrel said.

"Thirty thousand." She pointed to the suitcase the sailor was dragging in. "It's all I've got. I'd pay the forty if I had it."

Captain Farrel spoke Bacchian to the sailor, hauling in the suitcase. He opened it and started counting.

"I want to go with you?" Ebony said.

"I'm not going myself," he said. "I've got a team that does that for me. When he's done counting, you can go up on deck and get in one of the mini-subs."

"Why the mini-subs?"

"Things don't always go as planned, and it's a lot harder to sink two dozen mini-subs than it is to sink one submarine."

The sailor finished counting and nodded.

She thanked the captain and went up on deck, where a fierce wind almost swept her from her feet. A dozen Bacchians and four Volian mercenaries were waiting. One of the Bacchians, slim with a curly black beard, pointed at a mini-sub.

She made her way across the deck with her hair lashing across her face, climbed up, and got in. The inside was tiny with seats meant for Bacchians, not Cronish.

Curly jumped in after her and shut the hatch. The bubble glass provided a clear view all around as they waited in silence.

The submarine dropped straight down. Slants of sunlight shone from the surface, but as they sunk deeper, the water quickly turned from green to black. The mini-subs detached from the hull of the submarine and continued down on their own. After a long descent, she could see light emanating from the entrance to a cave. They went in, came up to a steamy surface, and moved up to the beach. The motley crews got out, jumped in the water, and waded to shore. Ebony jumped in and was shocked at how hot it was—painfully hot. She went as quickly as she could. Once on shore, there was a choice of three tunnels. The mercenaries made their choice without speaking. They knew where they were going.

Have they done this before? Ebony mused. *Were they going to risk their lives fighting to save her brother, or had a deal already been reached?*

Keldon

Keldon was trying to reconcile the reason for his imminent death. It was one thing to die trying to save Cronos from the Athenians, quite another to die trying to save a naive princess from her stupidity.

The hostage-takers had asked him questions he couldn't answer and hit him with the butts of their guns. The left side of his ribcage was hurting. They hadn't bothered with blindfolds, which meant that money or no money, they had no intention of letting them live.

Charline was in a different basket. They left her alone. They knew who she was, and they knew they could get good money for her.

He looked at the old lady, perfectly content to run the show without moving from her chair. Four blues were at a table, playing cards. They spoke Bacchian and laughed continuously. There were other blues lined up along the wall, some mumbling, some looking around, some sleeping.

The time had passed painfully slowly, minute by minute, hour after hour, day after day.

He thought back on an early childhood memory when his mom and dad decided to move across the continent to Aaronia. They rented a trailer, packed their possessions, and drove three thousand miles. It was such an adventure, such a happy time. When they first arrived in Aaronia, they stayed in a camp, and there was a swan that lived in a pond right in the middle of a field—such a beautiful creature. He looked over at Charline. Somehow, she'd managed to fall asleep while in a sitting position against the wall, her head hung forward over her chest, her arms tied behind her back. She looked so innocent. Dangerously naive and innocent, yet she was a beautiful creature too, like the swan.

He wondered why his parents felt it was necessary to make such an arduous journey. It had turned out to be a mistake. Aaronia was hit harder by the great famine than anywhere. It was a decision that led to their eventual deaths. Near the end, his sister started dealing and tried to feed the entire family on her own, but it was too late. They were too weak, and they died anyway.

He tried to free his hands, but as he had discovered earlier, it was hopeless. He couldn't break the ties.

From the tunnel, there was the sound of someone running.

The old lady got up.

A blue came running in and shouted something at the old lady. The old lady yelled at the others, and they, collectively, jumped up, grabbed their guns, and ran out.

The old lady went to the mouth of the cave with her plasma assault rifle and peered down the tunnel. Blues were shouting at each other in the distance.

Was this it? Had someone come to rescue them? All he could do was wait and hope.

In a far off place, he could hear a flurry of gunfire. The shots got louder. Charline woke up. Half a dozen blues came running back into the cave and scrambled to get out of the line of fire. Three of them weren't quick enough and took rounds in the back that drove them across the cave and into the back wall where their lifeless bodies fell to the floor.

Another blue peeked out and got his head taken off.

The old lady peeked out. This time a bolt hit the rock face in front of her. It shattered the rock and fragments sprayed over the old lady. She toppled over, dropped her rifle, and fell in agony.

Moments later, she lifted her head, spotted her gun, scrambled towards it, grabbed it, turned it on Charline, and fired.

The shots hit Charline's chest, jostled her, and soaked her shirt red with blood. Her head fell forward.

Then the old lady turned her gun on Keldon and fired.

He saw the flash of blue, and instantly his left shoulder was ablaze with pain, but before she could get a second shot off, a blue bolt took both of her arms off. A second shot split her body in half.

Two remaining blues fired at a cyborg as it entered the cave, but the shots bounced off it. Its body armor was like an armadillo, in layers, and shining burgundy with silver trim. It moved fast, scary fast, like an insect. From its barrel on its arm came a steady stream of blue bolts that cut the remaining blues down in seconds. It stopped firing, and a beam of red light swept across the cave, like a beam from an ocean lighthouse. A helmet with a full face shield covered its head. It moved up to the princess, pulled off an armored glove, and produced a human hand that held two fingers to her neck.

More cyborgs were coming through the mouth of the cave, their cannons sweeping from side to side, and red beams crisscrossing, addressing every crevice of the cave.

One of the cyborgs came over to Keldon and cut his hands free. "You're hit," it said with a female voice.

He looked down at his left shoulder. It was bleeding profusely.

She produced a package from a compartment on her belt, ripped it open, ripped his shirt like it was paper with a claw at the end of her cannon, and sprinkled powder on the wound.

It hurt more than he could bear, and his body flinched. His vision faded, and his last thought was that this must be what it's like to die.

Rose

Rose had stretched out her bottle of Rend as far as she possibly could. It was almost empty. She needed more. To get the money, she'd have to steal something and sell it. At the temple, there were lots of things she could take. But first, she'd have to find a buyer.

As usual, Solin had his head on a swivel. Yes, the hooker had told them to get out of Ralarra, and yes, there were androids and overhead cameras everywhere, yet no Athenians had come for them, and the longer she went without seeing one, the more she hoped that, maybe, she wouldn't.

She spotted a veiled yellow face across the street, looking at jewelry. He was different, not wearing a robe, had on frayed jeans, a polka-dotted shirt, and had spiked purple hair. Rose was drawn to him like a fly to dung.

"Do you speak Cronish?" she asked, pulling up beside him.

He looked surprised. "A little."

"Do you know where I can traffic goods for Rend?"

"Rend?" he asked, wincing. "Rend no good. Better heroin."

"Do you know where?"

"What goods?"

"Artifacts."

He pointed at a church, its tower visible above the roofs of houses. "Venerable Father Zeld," he said and went back to looking at the jewelry.

As Rose turned towards the church, Solin suddenly moved like a frightened cat and pushed her over the top of a jewelry counter. Half a dozen blue bolts streaked through the air as she slid over the counter and fell off the other side. Jewelry scattered everywhere.

"Qacis," Solin yelled.

Rose didn't know what it meant, but she jumped up and ran as fast as she could. A window shattered beside her, and glass sprayed into the shop. In front of her, an Athenian warrior came from around the corner. Rose tried to stop, but her momentum carried her, and the Athenian grabbed her by the arm. The warrior's grip was an iron grip, and Rose's arm felt like it was on fire.

There was a flash of steel, and she was flung around like a puppet. Solin was there, moving fast, the way he moved when he was fighting. The Athenian winced and staggered back, holding his stomach, his plasma gun no longer in his hand. He fell to his knees and brought Rose down with him. Solin was gone.

"Reh barg," a voice said, from behind her. The warrior let go of Rose's arm, grabbed her by the hair, and pulled her head down beside his. She frantically twisted and tried to get away. In the next instant, he did let go. She pulled her head back, and blood spurted out across the cobblestone as the Athenian's head rolled out onto the street.

Rose cringed and closed her eyes, but she had to open them again when she was abruptly dragged around the corner faster than she could run, her feet vainly struggling to keep up. There was an Athenian assault shuttle in the street. Four Athenian warriors were running towards her firing plasma guns. Blue streaks were coming from in front of her and from behind her. One of the warriors was hit and fell. The warrior holding her fell and dragged her to the ground.

With bolts of blue streaking back and forth, she wrenched her arm free, jumped up, and ran straight down an alleyway between the buildings. It twisted and turned, and she came out onto another street, ran straight across it, and down another alley. She was gasping for air but kept going, down another road, and another lane.

When she got to the fourth street, she saw the Muunakshi Akkan Temple up high on the mountainside, and even though it was quite some distance away, she decided to go there and hide.

She climbed the steeply sloped street as quickly as she could, bolted up the steps, and slipped into the temple. She went downstairs to the kitchen. There, she found Darek, his robe ripped open, and three deep cuts across his chest. Hewitt had a fork sticking from his eye. Moritz had an arm ripped off, and a large puddle of blood covered the floor beneath him.

Then she heard a noise coming from upstairs. She quickly opened cabinet doors, one after the other, looking for a place to hide. The cabinet under the sink was almost empty. She shoved some cleaning supplies aside, squished herself in, and closed the doors behind her. The moment she shut them, an Athenian warrior came into the kitchen dragging someone behind him.

It was dark in the cupboard, light only from the crack between the doors. She could see a small part of the kitchen directly in front of her, and she caught a very brief glimpse of Kariff, his hands tied behind his back.

The Athenian placed Kariff in a chair, tied him down to it, and made sure the ties on his legs were secure. He swung his longsword back and forth through the air over Kariff's head and pressed the tip of his sword into Kariff's chest. Kariff screamed out in pain, clenched his teeth, shut his eyes tight, and shook his head.

Rose cringed. The sound of him screaming made her quiver like a worm.

The Athenian withdrew his longsword, sheathed it, and went upstairs.

Rose waited. Kariff breathed heavily at first, but over time, he calmed down. The chair cast a shadow on the floor that slowly grew longer.

She opened the cupboard doors.

Kariff instantly swung his head around and looked at her.

She inched her way out and stood.

"Untie my hands," he whispered.

He had led Solin into a trap, and she hated him. She ignored him, moved to the staircase, and stopped to listen.

"Untie my hands," he pleaded.

He was slime and deserved the punishment he was getting. She went up the stairwell.

"You miserable piece of crap," Kariff yelled up the stairs.

She headed for the artifacts and heard the door opening. Without looking back, she quickly crouched down behind a pew. She heard footsteps and the sound of someone going downstairs. She got up and moved as quietly as she could, took a significant gold artifact with the head of a pig and the body of a horse, and headed towards the door. She stopped to put on a gas mask and a robe. When she pulled the door open, she met a dark shadow against the backdrop of Jupih.

"Solin, you scared me half to death," Rose whispered, her voice muffled. She was particularly relieved to see him alive, and she wanted to hug him but thought better of it. "We have to get out of here."

"Why you take this?" Solin asked, pointing to the artifact.

"We can't stay here," she said, avoiding the question. "There's an Athenian warrior in there. He captured Kariff."

"I go," Solin said softly, pointing inside.

"No," Rose whispered. "That Volian bastard sold us to the Athenians. Leave him. He's getting what he deserves. Just leave him."

Solin pulled out a plasma gun, pushed by her, and went in.

Rose felt waves of heat flushing through her body. There was no reason for this. Why would he risk his life for that imbecile? The man wasn't worth saving.

She stepped out, looked up at wispy black clouds crossing in front of Jupih, and across at the hundreds of houses with rounded roofs. She crossed the street and moved into the shadows between two houses. She put the artifact down behind some bushes next to the wall of a home.

This was too much. She needed a hit. She pulled out her bottle and syringe and used up the last of her Rend. She waited, and she worried. She watched the temple door and wondered what had happened inside.

A young woman with yellow skin, wearing a veil, approached the temple and climbed the steps. She pulled open the temple door and went in.

Rose continued to wait. She waited until she was more than worried. Did Solin kill the Athenian, or did something go wrong? Was he tied up and being tortured like Kariff? The battle had to be over. Too much time had passed.

She couldn't just leave him there. She'd have to investigate, but she'd do it carefully. She trudged towards the temple door and listened. She heard nothing, so she pulled it open a crack and looked in. Nothing. She pulled the door open a bit more, stuck her head in, and listened. There was silence. She went in, got down on the floor, and crawled in behind a pew. She pulled off her mask and crept over to the stairwell.

"What are you doing here?" a voice from behind her asked. "You can't stay here. You have to go."

Rose spun around. It was the young Volian woman she'd seen enter the temple. "Is the Athenian here?" she whispered.

"He's dead. Many people are dead. Venerable Father Moritz, Venerable Brother Hewitt, Venerable Elder Darek. All dead."

"What about the white man and the Volian?"

"No. They're not dead. I asked them to leave, but they aren't listening."

"They're downstairs?" Rose asked as she got up.

"Yes."

"And who are you?"

"I'm Sopika, the temple's caretaker. The temple is closed, my dear. I'm asking all patron's to wait until I've had a chance to do some cleaning."

"Have you called the police?

"I can't do that. I'm too old."

Rose hesitated. "I don't understand?"

"I'm not tapped into the system."

Rose turned away from her and went down the staircase. There was no reason to be polite. Androids didn't have feelings.

"You miserable piece of crap," Kariff said, getting up from his seat when he saw her.

Solin, sitting across from him, jumped up and moved between the two of them.

"Piss off," Rose snarled. "You turned us in?"

"I did not."

"Don't believe anything he says, Solin." She looked down at the dead Athenian Warrior lying on the floor, a hole in his chest.

Kariff sat back down with a scowl on his face. "You left me to be tortured and killed."

"You led us into a trap," Rose said.

"On Vole, people like you often quietly go missing," Kariff said.

"Don't threaten me, you bastard, and what about the money you owe us?"

"You must be joking," he said, his voice strained, his teeth clenched, and his hands forming fists. "Perhaps you should have thought of that when I asked you to untie me. Even if you were completely incapable of showing the slightest spec of compassion, you could have, at the very least, put your hatred aside long enough to think of your agenda."

"I don't need you," Rose said. "I'll find another way."

Kariff got up. Solin stepped between Rose and Kariff, but Kariff circled him and went up the stairs. Solin followed.

"Solin? What are you doing?" Her heart was in her stomach.

"Solin go," he said.

"How could you betray me like this?"

"Solin no betray Rose. Rose betray Rose."

"Solin?" she pleaded.

He ignored her and kept going.

She ran after him. At the top of the stairs, she stopped.

Solin and Kariff made their way across the nave towards the front door.

"Solin. Listen to me," she said, tears welling up in her eyes.

He kept going.

"Solin. I need you to listen. Please stop."

He ignored her completely.

She collapsed onto the floor and cried, wiping the tears from her eyes with the back of her hand.

Sopika came over and patted her on the back. "There, there, my dear."

"Just leave me alone," Rose hissed. Being patted on the back by a machine seemed ludicrous.

Kariff stopped to put on a robe. "You need to learn compassion, young lady."

"Okay," Rose said. "Just tell him not to leave me. Please."

"I didn't set you up, Rose," Kariff said. "I organized the fight. That's all. I didn't know about the Athenian's plans. Solin believes me. You're not thinking this through. If I was in cahoots with the Athenians, why would they torture me?"

She'd thought that the Athenians blamed Kariff for the botched attack, yet if that wasn't the case— "I didn't know. I thought you were working with them."

"We're leaving," Kariff said. "We can't stay here. The Athenians will come looking for their comrade."

Rose nodded and walked to the door. "We should take the android with us," she said. It knew how to speak at least two languages. And, more importantly, it was worth money.

"No, my dear," Sopika said. "I've been programmed to keep the temple clean. It's my only function. I'll not come with you."

"How many languages do you speak?" Rose asked.

"I speak all languages, but I will not come with you. You can't make me.

"Can you speak the language of the Old Sacred Writings?"

"I'm forbidden."

"Why?"

"The monks believe what they want to believe and don't want anyone telling them differently."

"But they're dead."

"Still, I'm forbidden. Only my master can change my programming?"

"And who's your master?"

"Venerable Father Hewitt."

"He's dead. You need a new master. I'll be your master."

"No."

"Solin is the Messiah. Can he be your master?"

"I don't think so."

"I say we dismantle her and put her in the disposal bin behind the building across the street," Kariff said.

Sopika looked at Kariff and Rose. "On second thought, perhaps the Messiah would make an ideal master."

The artifact was still across the street, Rose realized. There was no way Solin was going to let her take it. The android would probably put up a fight too. She'd have to come back for it.

Ebony

Ebony followed the mercenaries through an endless labyrinth of tunnels, and she worried. They had her money, and she suspected these were not trustworthy people. In her desperation to save Keldon, she'd been foolish.

When they arrived at a small cave that branched off in three directions, one of them, a Volian, who had gone ahead, came back. He huddled with the others, and they squabbled.

Ebony got curly's attention. "What's wrong?"

"He says there are cyborgs up ahead. We're going to have to stay away from them."

"You mean you're giving up?" She knew what a cyborg was and what it could do.

"We can't mess with cyborgs."

"Are the cyborgs Cronish?" Ebony asked.

"We don't know. There are no markings on them."

"They must have been sent here by the queen," Ebony said. "I'll go talk to them."

His eyes widened. "I don't recommend it. Cyborgs shoot first and don't bother to ask questions later."

"I think they must be Cronish. They're here to save the princess."

"All the more reason to stay away."

"I'm going. If they're here to save the princess, they can save my brother too." She nervously edged forward, and the mercenaries scurried back.

The tunnel was long, and she started to think that the mercenaries had lied. Was this their way of getting rid of her? She stopped. She damn near jumped out of her skin when she saw one. It moved fast, like a cockroach, and in an instant, a red beam found her heart. She dropped her gun and shot her hands up.

The cyborg moved towards her quickly with an aberrant yet fluid stroll.

"I'm Cronish," Ebony said, shivers going down her spine.

"Ebony," the cyborg said, its voice familiar. "What are you doing here?"

Ebony slackened her jaw, not sure how to answer.

"It's me, Jen," the cyborg said.

"Who?"

She lifted her face shield.

"Oh!" Ebony didn't know what to say. This was not the Jen she knew. This was a freak of nature. "I'm looking for my brother, Keldon," she said.

"Are the men back there with you?" Jen asked, lifting her chin towards the tunnel behind her.

"Yes. They're with me," she said without looking.

More cyborgs came out of the tunnel, one of them carrying her brother.

"Keldon!" She ran to him. *Thank the gods,* she thought. *He's alive. Oh! Thank the gods.* He was breathing but not conscious. She walked beside him, holding his hand. "Is he going to be okay?"

"He is," Jen said.

Another cyborg came out of the tunnel carrying Rose.

"Dead?" Ebony asked when she saw the holes in her chest.

"Yes," Jen said. "Too bad. The troops on Cronos need someone to look up to."

Why is Rose down here wearing the dress of a princess? It's not Rose, Ebony realized, studying her more closely. *It's the princess.* The resemblance was remarkable. "How are you getting out of here?" she asked Jen.

"We had a plan coming in, but it's gone. Our ship isn't answering our calls. What about you?"

"I have a plan," Ebony said. "You can come with me."

"You have a submarine waiting?"

"Mini subs."

"And a spaceship?"

"A schooner."

"Good."

"Did you fight on Cronos?" Ebony asked.

"Yes."

"How was it there?"

"Bad. There's only one province remaining, and the cities still standing are running out of things. There's not a lot of food, the troops are low on ammunition, and there isn't enough deuterium to keep their tokamaks running."

Ebony looked at the princess again, and the similarities were more than remarkable. They were striking. "You don't know what happened to Rose, do you?"

"Rose? The last time I saw Rose, she was on Vole."

Jen

Jen walked beside Ebony in the middle of the band of mercenaries and cyborgs. One of the mercenaries, a stocky blue with dark scaly skin, led the way through the tunnel back to the mini-subs. Two cyborgs walked with him, ready to deal with any threats up ahead, and two cyborgs brought up the rear keeping a sharp eye out for anyone that might be following.

"We have to find Rose," Ebony said.

"What for?" Jen asked.

"The Athenians will only negotiate with royalty. I want her to take the place of the princess."

Jen had a bitter taste in her mouth. "Rose? The drug addict?"

"Yeah," Ebony said. "She may be a drug addict, but she's all we've got. Badoni's fighting a pointless war. The Athenians can't move to Cronos because their bodies aren't designed for it. If they try to live there, they'll become weak and feeble. And you know how they feel about the weak and feeble."

"I don't understand. Are you trying to suggest that all we have to do is tell Badoni that he's made a mistake, and then he'll just turn around and leave?"

"Queen Leona was prodding him. Now that she's dead, maybe we can get him to listen to reason."

"Listen to reason? Have you lost your mind? Badoni isn't going to listen to reason. Not now, not ever."

"Listen to me. The history books are full of senseless wars fought for stupid reasons. A hundred years ago, there was a civil war down here in the caves of Bacchus. The Athenians backed High Priest in the north. The Cronish backed the Empress in the south. The Athenians didn't send in any troops of their own, just supplies, but Cronos sent in both troops and supplies. After twenty years of fighting, Cronos had over a million troops in the caves of Bacchus. When it was all over, three million Bacchians and two hundred and eighty thousand Cronish were casualties of the war."

"I've never heard of that war. Where did you hear this?"

"From a Bacchian submarine captain whose grandfather fought in the war. The war was an embarrassment to the Cronish Monarchy, so they erased it from the history books."

"How did the war end?"

"Massive protests on Cronos brought it to an end. To stop the protests, the queen withdrew her troops from Bacchus, and the High Priest took over the entire planet. He gave the Empress an emblematic role so she could save face."

"Ebony, people—good people—have sacrificed their lives on Cronos. We can't just end the war. We have to fight on."

"We can't think like that," Ebony stated. "We have to change the course of the war."

"But Rose can't make a difference."

"Both sides want the war to end, and any diplomacy is better than no diplomacy."

Cynthia carried Charline, and Jen looked to see the resemblance. "Rose may look like Charline, but her voice and her mannerisms aren't the same. People are going to know."

"We'll train her to talk like the princess."

Jen laughed. "This is crazy talk. We don't know what she sounded like. And even if we did, the Athenians aren't going to agree to anything. I know it, and you know it too. They're like wild animals."

"Jen, we haven't got anything left to lose."

The tunnel opened to the cavern, where a few mercenaries guarded the mini-subs lined up on the beach. The entire group waded into the water.

"Give the princess to Jen," Ebony told Cynthia.

She looked surprised but shrugged and handed Charline's limp body over to Jen.

"Leave Keldon on the beach," Ebony said to Bron as she waded into the water. "I'll take care of him."

Bron stopped knee-high in the steaming hot water. "Are you sure?"

"Yeah."

Bron walked out and carefully lay Keldon down on the beach.

"We'll catch up," Ebony told her.

The cyborgs climbed into the mini-subs with the mercenaries, and the mini-subs sank below the surface. One mini-sub remained.

"I need you to dig a grave," Ebony said.

Jen looked at Charline and then back at Ebony. "But I'm a soldier, and she's our princess."

"We have to try to end the war, and this is the only way."

Jen only paused for a moment. Near the edge of the cavern, she dug a shallow grave with her mechanical arm, lay Charline in it, covered her, and rolled a huge rock over the grave. She picked up Keldon, walked into the water.

Ebony followed.

Jen lifted him onto the mini-sub and gently lowered him down through the hatch.

Ebony strapped him into the rear seat. He wasn't conscious, but he was still breathing.

Jen took over the controls and backed the mini-sub away from the shoreline. They went down, out of the cavern, and into the ocean.

All of a sudden, there was a loud boom, and the mini-sub shook violently.

"What was that?" Ebony asked.

"A depth charge," Jen said quietly. "We're being hunted. We have to go to the bottom." Jen pointed the mini-sub down and started flicking switches. It went dark, and there were more loud booms and more shaking. "They see with sonar down here," Jen whispered. Deepwater acts as a barrier, causing the sound to bend away. We have to make it hard for them to find us."

There were more booms, but not as loud, and the shaking was less violent.

"Who's hunting us?" Ebony asked.

"The Empress. She controls the water. No one can enter her ocean without permission."

There was a dull flash off to the left, and again, the mini-sub shook. They hit bottom with a loud metallic gong. The mini-sub rolled slightly and sat motionless in the pitch black.

There were a few minutes of silence, and Jen asked, "How did you manage to get off Solin's ship?"

"Troy and I escaped in the Resolution's shuttle and went down to Talon. Troy died there."

She went on to tell Jen everything that had happened to her. They talked and waited for hours.

"Rend is powerful stuff," Jen said after a long silence. "It's a stimulant, and it messes people up real bad. The pinks are all addicted to it. When we were defending Medridic on Cronos, they launched an assault that didn't stop for three days. They didn't eat or sleep. It was the Rend that kept them going."

"I know it's not going to be easy to deal with Rose's addiction, but we have to try."

After they'd waited as long as they could, Jen flicked the lights on and blew a ballast tank. The mini-sub started to rise. "How's your brother?"

"The same," Ebony said after looking at him.

Jen watched the gages.

"I've arranged transport back to the schooner," Ebony said. "They'll be waiting for my call."

"Go ahead."

Ebony donned a headset. "Mark two seven one four." She listened for a few seconds and said, "Acknowledged." She took off her headset.

When they surfaced, a large tanker came down over them like a hawk to a fish. It opened its bottom hatch and lowered itself down over the mini-sub, swallowing it whole. The hatch closed, and Jen could feel the tanker's g forces lifting off with an entire load of water and the mini-sub inside.

"I don't think this plan you've got is going to work," Jen said. "Badoni's not going to listen."

"The Athenian culture is steeped in a time-honored tradition," Ebony said. "They live in a world where life is cheap, and stature is everything. The strong survive, and the weak perish. It's the Athenian way. We've tried to beat them on the battlefield, and it hasn't worked, but there's a better way, and for me, the fight is only just beginning. Now, tell me. How can we find Rose?"

Ebony

Ebony had transported Keldon and all seven of the cyborgs to Vole in her schooner, *Valiant*. She had brought Keldon to a hospital and got hotel rooms for the cyborgs.

Jen planned to find a transmitting station where she could communicate with her commander, but Ebony asked her to hold off on that plan and help her instead.

She and Jen were getting something to eat in the hotel's bar when a screen showed a news clip of Solin throwing Rose across a jewelry counter and driving a longsword through an Athenian. They couldn't understand the commentary, but there was a temple in the background, and from that, they were able to figure out where the incident had taken place. They went to the neighborhood and started knocking on motel and hotel room doors. There wasn't a lot of these on Vole, and they quickly found the right door.

"Solin," Ebony said, delighted to have found him. "How are you?"

Solin looked at Jen warily and nodded.

"That's good," she said, smiling. "Is Rose here?"

He shook his head.

"Where is she?"

He seemed confused, looked back over his shoulder, and spoke what sounded like broken Volian to someone out of sight.

A Volian woman came to the door. "Rose doesn't want to see anyone," she said.

"I have to find her," Ebony stated. "It's important."

"Rose want us to leave her alone," Solin told her.

"Is she on Rend?" Jen asked.

His eyes drifted, and he rubbed his nose.

"Solin," Ebony said. "She'll die if she doesn't get help."

Solin muttered something to the Volian, and she responded with what, from her tone, could only be a scolding.

"We'll bring you to her," the Volian said."

"Thank you," Ebony replied.

The Deyeri Mehmanxana motel was dilapidated. The Volian led them to one of the motel's doors, and Ebony knocked. There was no answer.

"Perhaps we can check with the manager," the Volian suggested.

Jen ripped through the steel door like it was cardboard.

Ebony looked skyward and pleaded with her hands. Inside, the room was a shambles with battered furniture, walls with holes, and soiled clothing covering the floor. Rose lay on the bed, half-naked, her arms covered in needle marks. Empty bottles of Rend were lined up on the night table.

Solin tried to wake her, but without success.

Ebony collected some clothing from the floor, rolled her over, and put some pants and a shirt on her.

"Are we sticking to the plan?" Jen asked.

"Of course we're sticking to the plan," Ebony said.

"What plan is that?" the Volian asked.

"We'll have to detox her," Jen said, ignoring the Volian completely.

"No, we won't," Ebony said. "If need be, we'll use the drug to control her."

"Doesn't sound ethical," the Volian said.

"The stakes are too high to worry about ethics," Ebony said. "If we have to use a drug addict to help us end the war, so be it."

"I agree," Jen said.

"I don't see how you can end the war with a drug addict," the Volian said.

"We'll use the doll as the princess's assistant."

"Excuse me," the Volian said. "I'm not a doll."

"Where did you get the *Valiant*? Jen asked Ebony, again, ignoring the Volian completely.

"Bought it from a friend, Walter Hadila, captain of the submarine, *Malofa*. He's my trading partner on Bacchus."

"Can the *Valiant* go as far as Uras?"

"Yes. It can."

"I'm not a doll," the Volian repeated.

"You're made of plastic, aren't you?" Jen asked.

"Well, yes, but—"

"She's an android?" Ebony asked Jen.

"Yes," the Volian responded. "I'm an android. Not a doll. My name is Sopika."

"I still say this plan is crazy," Jen said, shaking her head. "Badoni isn't going to be convinced of anything. All he wants is power. He'll never surrender a penny of it."

"We're going to try," Ebony said. "If we fail, we'll move on to plan B."

"What's plan B?" Jen asked.

"Kill Badoni," Ebony replied.

Keldon

Keldon looked around the room. A curved steel arm suspended his bed from a rail. A holographic image stood behind him, showing his insides in full color, his heart pumping blood, his lungs expanding and contracting, and his lunch. There were android nurses with stick-like arms, legs, and no heads moving from one patient to another checking bandages. The doctor was Volian, and he only came around once a day.

Almost every last one of the patients was Cronish, most of them encased in heavy casts. They slept much of the time.

His shoulder was stiff, and it hurt, but that didn't stop him from wanting out.

Ebony had been there the first day and the next. She had told him her plans, and that she'd be leaving for Uras in six days.

Keldon was almost to the point of ignoring the android nurse's protests and discharging himself, but four Cronish soldiers stormed into the room with a sergeant in tow. They surrounded his bed.

The sergeant was short with a square face, a strong jaw, and piercing black eyes. "Your name?"

"Keldon Harding."

"Where were you wounded?" he asked, studying Keldon's holograph.

"My shoulder, sir." He put a hand on it.

"Looks like it's just about healed."

"It's getting better, sir. They say I should be able to start therapy in a day or two."

"What's your regiment?"

"Two hundred and third battalion."

He scratched his temple. "Where were you fighting?"

"On Bacchus, sir."

"Sorry?"

"On Bacchus."

He lifted his eyebrows. "Are you trying to be funny, boy?"

"No, sir. My unit was on Bacchus. We were there on a secret mission."

"What kinda bullshit is this?" he asked, shaking his head. "Take him."

The sergeant moved down the line to the next patient, and two of the privates moved in to get Keldon up. They had to wait while Keldon got dressed, and they had to help him with his shirt and tunic. They marched him out of the building to where an Athenian shuttle was waiting.

Why was it an Athenian shuttle? Keldon wondered. *Had it been captured? Did they not have a Cronish shuttle?*

The gravity emitter on the shuttle was Athenian, and Keldon and the others struggled with the weight of their bodies. Soldiers held guns trained on them as they were told to strap themselves in. *The others are mostly deserters,* Keldon realized. *Deserters that had foolishly gotten themselves caught.*

The shuttle took him up to the warship, *Excelsior,* where he was placed in an overcrowded brig and left there for three days and nights. All of his requests were either denied or ignored.

"Up private," one of two soldiers barked at him as the cell door opened. "Time to face the music."

He stood and slowly rotated his bad arm. It was stiff, and he couldn't raise it above his chest. He grabbed his tunic and went with the soldiers.

"Who's the old man?" he asked as he was marched down the passageway.

"Captain Drake."

As he walked, he carefully pulled his tunic on, wincing as he did, and buttoned it up. Captain Drake was waiting on the bridge with his hands behind his back. He was tall with broad shoulders, gray hair, a pointed nose, and long hairs sticking out from his eyebrows.

Keldon stood at attention.

"So, I'm told that your story is somewhat different from the other deserters," he snarled. "Something about a secret mission?"

"Sir, I'm not a deserter, sir."

"What's your unit?"

"Two-hundred and third. Sir!"

"And where were you deployed."

"Bacchus."

"We don't have any knowledge of troops being sent to Bacchus."

"Well, no, sir. That's because it was a secret mission. Secrecy was paramount."

"And how do I determine if you're telling the truth? How do I know you haven't concocted an elaborate story to cover your ass?"

"There were witnesses, sir. Cyborgs."

"Cyborgs?"

"Yes, sir."

"And where are these cyborgs?"

"On Vole, sir."

"What was the mission?"

Keldon knew the answer but couldn't say. If Ebony's plan was going to work, Charline's death had to be kept secret, and the room was filled with ears. If anyone of them said anything to anyone, it might leak further. "Sir, request permission to speak to you in private, sir."

Some of the crew members who had their heads fixed to their screens turned to look at the captain.

"Pardon me?" Drake belted out.

"Sir, request permission to—"

"I heard you the first time, boy. What do you think we're doin' here, workin' for the enemy?"

"No! Sir."

"Let me ask you again, boy. What happened?"

"Sir, with all due respect, I can't tell you that, not here."

"Let me explain something to you, boy. You're in a heap of shit. We shoot deserters, and right now, you're a prime candidate. Am I making myself clear?"

"I'm not a deserter, sir. I did my job."

"Then, if I were you, I'd start talking. Where's the rest of your unit?"

"Dead, sir."

"And why aren't you dead?"

"Sir, I was rescued by the cyborgs."

"By the cyborgs?"

"Yes, sir."

"Sergeant. Take this man back to the brig." He waved his hand dismissively.

The sergeant did what he was ordered and as roughly as he could. He pushed and shoved Keldon the entire way. Keldon found himself back in the crowded cell.

That night, he woke up when the guards raked the butts of their guns on the cell bars. They opened the doors and yelled at the prisoners to march single file into the forward torpedo bay. Three torpedoes were sitting in cradles and only three. The rest of the cribs, dozens of them, were empty. The captain was there, standing with his hands behind his back. The prisoners were lined up against a wall. A dozen soldiers lined up opposite them, guns pointed.

"Any last words?" Drake asked.

No one responded.

Drake moved out in front of the pointed guns and walked up to Keldon. "Do you still want to keep your little secret, soldier?"

"Sir, yes. I do."

"You do?"

"I'm not a deserter, sir. And if you'd let me, I'll tell you what I know, but it has to be kept secret."

Drake walked back behind the line of soldiers. "Ready— Aim— Keldon. Come and stand beside me."

Keldon went to him.

"Fire." The shots were loud, and Keldon's ears were ringing. All of the prisoners fell. Three of them were still moving.

"Again," the captain ordered. "Ready— Aim— Fire."

The guns fired. This time there was no movement.

"Dismissed," Drake ordered.

The soldiers filed out of the room, and they were alone.

"So, what's the secret?" he asked.

"Princess Charline was abducted by a gang on Bacchus. The mission was to rescue her. Unfortunately, the mission failed, and the princess is dead, but there's a plan to put a substitute in her place for a council meeting on Uras. The substitute looks very much like the real princess. It's important that no one finds out the princess is dead."

"And who's doing this?"

"My sister is doing it, but you're the senior ranking officer, so as far as I'm concerned, you're in charge, sir."

"If you think I'm going to put an imposter in place of the princess, you're mistaken."

"I think my sister has thought this through. Her plan makes sense to me."

"Why is she doing this?"

"The Athenians will only negotiate with royalty. If we're going to engage in any diplomatic efforts, we need the princess to be alive."

Drake went into deep thought before responding. He nodded. "I want those cyborgs," he said. "Can you find them for me?"

"I think my sister will know where they are."

"Come." He got up and led Keldon up to the bridge.

"Set a course back to Vole," Drake ordered. "I want a special ops team with orders to find cyborgs on Vole and bring them up to the ship. Keldon? How is your sister planning to get to Uras?"

"She has a schooner, sir."

"Do you know when she's planning to leave."

"In two days, sir."

"Good. I want you to go down with the special ops team to help them find the cyborgs. You can tell your sister she has an escort.

"Yes, sir."

Keldon held his shoulder and carefully moved his arm up and down. It was still sore but functional, and he could live with it.

Rose

Rose woke up with a vicious headache, perplexed, and confused. Solin and Sopika were there. Somehow, so were Ebony and Jen.

"What happened to your arm?" Rose asked Jen.

"Lost it."

Jen was wearing loose-fitting clothing, and she seemed to be heavier than she used to be. Her prosthetic arm was huge and had an ugly two-pronged hook for a hand. "How?" Rose asked.

She shrugged. "In the war."

Rose didn't want to be there. She needed to get out and find more Rend so she could cope with her damn headache. She got up and tried to leave, but Jen stepped in front of her and grabbed her arm.

"You're not going anywhere, Rose," Ebony said. "We need you."

"For what?" Rose tried to rip free, but Jen's grip was firm.

"We need you to do an acting job," Ebony said.

"What do you mean?" Her mind was racing, searching for answers.

"We need you to pretend to be Princess Charline."

She remembered back to what Nicko had said about her looking like the princess. "Why?"

"We want you to take her place at the upcoming council meeting on Uras."

"But I—why can't she do it?"

"She's dead."

"What if I don't want to?"

Ebony took a bottle of Rend from her pocket and held it up for Rose to see.

"That's not fair," Rose stated. "I get bad headaches. It's not my fault."

"We're not playing games, Rose. We need you to do this."

Jen let Rose's arm go and stepped back.

Rose immediately lunged at Ebony, grabbed her arm with one hand, and tried to rip the bottle from her hand with the other, but Jen moved fast, like a spider, grabbed Rose by the arm, and pulled her away.

Jen's not human anymore, Rose realized. *No one moves like that.* It was scary. "Okay, okay. But you can't be cruel with the doses. It has to be enough to stop my headaches."

Ebony nodded.

The training started that same day and continued every day. Rose had to walk the way royalty walks, hold an inscrutable countenance, and mimic a specific tone of voice that only Sopika could demonstrate. She also had to learn the spiel—the things she would say to convince Badoni to pull his troops out of Cronos.

She did what she was told, but still, Ebony was skimpy with the doses, and Rose despised her. She was being treated like a puppet. Thankfully, Jen stopped coming to the sessions, but it was frustrating, and most of the time, all she wanted to do was scream.

Before the training ended, they boarded Ebony's new schooner and headed for Uras.

Sopika spent her time familiarizing herself with the ship's features.

Solin spent his time learning the meanings of Cronish words.

And Ebony spent her time going over the lessons that went on and on. No matter how doggedly Rose pleaded, Ebony wouldn't let her have enough Rend. Solin was of no help. He was on Ebony's side, and so was Sopika.

After three more days of this torture, Ebony brought the schooner down to Uras's surface and lowered it into a bay next to the council chamber. The bay's portal closed, the bay pressurized, and Rose was sent out the hatch of the schooner and into the chamber.

She was wearing a soft blue gown with a plunging neckline, puffy white sleeves, and gold bracelets on her wrists. It was the gown of a princess, elegant, strikingly simple, and yet unique.

Sopika played the role of her attendant and followed behind her, also in a regal dress and looking elegant.

There were Volian guards strategically placed by the doors and around the room.

Rose was mortified. Would the council recognize her as Charline, or would they see right through her guise, see she wasn't the real princess, and see she was a fraud? If they didn't see it immediately, they'd know the moment she opened her mouth.

Four large screens labeled with the names of planets hung from the ceiling. The one marked *Cronos* showed a live image of her as she walked in. Rose noticed that her arms were folded across her belly. She quickly moved them to her sides and swung them gracefully like a princess.

She had a powerful urge, but there was no way to get another hit, not now. She'd have to suffer through this. It was showtime. She might as well play it up big. *You're good at pretending,* she reassured herself. *You've been doing this your entire life. Think of this as being just another scam, just another way to get ahead. You can do this.*

When she arrived at the council table, she lifted the hem of her skirt, threw it behind her, and sat down, as elegantly as she could manage.

So far, so good. No one had pointed at her and yelled, "Impostor!" But there was the problem with her voice. She'd listened to Sopika's imitation of the princess and worked on copying her. Ebony told her she had it down, it wouldn't be a problem, but she wasn't so sure. She'd just have to focus and give it her best shot.

A Bacchian dignitary entered. Rose struggled to remember her name—Zeta. That was it. She was old, strange-looking, and wore a low-cut dress, burgundy, and gold with intricate swirling designs. She had several ugly braids wrapped in jewelry draped from her head. A decrepit looking attendant followed, dressed in black and crouched over with his head down.

Next was the Volian High Priest, wearing the traditional red robe, his hands folded together, and his face buried beneath a hood.

The Talonian Chief was massive and looked as though the weight of the world was on his back. His face had red and white lines that ran from his forehead down the bridge of his nose. A headdress of the long feathered shafts from some enormous bird stretched high above his head. He shuffled in and sat.

Suddenly, the door crashed open. A dozen warriors of the Athenian Imperial Guard stormed in, making way for the Athenian warlord, Badoni, dressed in full battle armor, striding awkwardly down the aisle.

The Volian guards tried to limit the number of warriors entering the room, but they were no match for the seasoned Athenian warriors. Badoni saw what was happening and barked out a command. All but two of his warriors retreated from the room.

Badoni stopped next to Rose, took off his helmet, placed it on the table, and took a seat beside her. He put on his headset.

Rose grabbed her headset and put it on.

A Volian chairman in a gray robe began to speak.

"I'd like to call the meeting to order," the voice of the translator said, "and welcome everyone. We'll begin with a brief statement from each of the leaders starting with Chief Eagle Eye of Talon."

The room went silent as they waited for Eagle Eye to stand. He managed to do it on the third try.

"I have chosen this time to discuss an ignorance of the truth," the translator began, "which is too rarely perceived. I am talking of peace. Not an order enforced by weapons of war and not the peace found in an obedient slave. I am talking about genuine peace, the kind of peace that makes life worth living, enabling people to build a better experience for their children.

"Some say that it is useless to speak of planetary peace. Too many of us think it is impossible, but we shouldn't accept that view. We make our problems, and therefore, we can solve them. Let us focus on a practical, attainable peace, based on a series of concrete actions and valid agreements which are in the interest of all concerned. There is no single, simple key to this peace. Genuine peace must be the product of the actions of the leaders of all the planets. It must be dynamic, not static, changing to meet the challenge of each new generation.

"With such a peace, there will still be quarrels and conflicting interests, as there are within families and individual planets. It does not require that each man love his neighbor. It only requires that they live together in mutual tolerance, submitting their disputes to a just and peaceful settlement. And history teaches us that conflicts do not last forever. However fixed our likes and dislikes may seem, the tide of time and events will often bring surprising changes in the relations between the planets. Perhaps we will see some of these changes sooner rather than later."

He sat down.

"The Empress Zeta of Bacchus," the translator said.

The Empress stood. "Mr. Chair. No war in history has ever had more casualties. Billions of people have lost their lives. Countless millions have had their homes and farms burned or sacked. A third of Princess Charline's territory, including nearly two-thirds of her industrial base, has been turned into a wasteland.

"I am not here to distribute blame or point my finger in judgment. But we must hope that Emperor Badoni and Princess Charline might reach some sort of an agreement. We must conduct our affairs so that it becomes in the interests of both parties to agree on a genuine peace.

"To secure these ends, our military forces are committed to peace and disciplined in self-restraint. Our diplomats are instructed to avoid unnecessary irritants and purely rhetorical hostility, for we can seek a relaxation of tension without relaxing our guard. For our part, we do not need to use threats to prove that we are resolute.

"Meanwhile, we seek to strengthen the Planetary Council, make it a more effective instrument for peace, and develop it into a genuine world security system, a system capable of resolving disputes based on law, and ensuring the security of the large and the small. We need to get back to a time of peace and tranquility." She sat down.

"The Venerable Father Holla, the High Priest of Vole."

The High Priest rose. "'When the ways of the people please the gods,' the Sacred Writings tells us, 'his enemies are at peace with him.' Vole, as the Planetary Council knows, will never engage in war. We do not want a war. We shall also do our part to help build a planetary system of peace where the weak are safe, and the strong are just. Confident and unafraid, we labor on, not toward a strategy of annihilation but a strategy of peace." He sat down.

"Emperor Badoni of Atheni," the translator said.

Badoni tossed his headset onto the table. "I've little to say," he said without rising. "My army is preparing to launch a final attack on the four Cronish cities that remain. The war will be over soon, and Cronos will belong to the Athenian people. I feel for the people of Cronos. Their princess" —he gave Rose an incredulous stare—"has forced them into a turtling posture. It's not honorable. I ask Her Royal Highness to let her people die with dignity. Let them put a short sword into their bellies and have their heads taken off with their comrades' longswords. It's the humane thing to do."

Rose leap from her chair, her nostrils flared. "What the hell is the matter with you!" she yelled with her voice, not the princess's voice. "They're not sheep! They're people! You miserable piece of—"

"Order!" yelled the chairman, his gavel hammering.

Badoni wasn't wearing his headset. He didn't hear the translation and couldn't have known what she had said, but he did see her display of anger, yet he didn't react.

One of Badoni's men leaned forward and whispered in his ear. Badoni smiled and donned his headset. "My second in command, Lazaran,"—he pointed at the warrior who had whispered to him—"says that he wants Her Royal Highness for himself." He held his hand with his fingers spread. "I can't see why, but if he wants her, who am I to judge."

When she heard the translation, Rose jumped to her feet. "You insolent pig!"

Badoni turned full around and walked up the aisle.

Lazaran barked out orders as Badoni walked. The Athenian warriors that had been waiting outside came storming into the chamber. They closed in on Rose and Sopika, grabbed them by the arms, and dragged them from the council chamber.

The Volian guards did not attempt to stop them.

Keldon

On the *Excelsior's* bridge, a dozen crew members sat behind consoles, scrutinizing star charts and analyzing streams of data. Captain Drake sat in his command chair and studied an image on the main screen of the backside of Badoni's warship, distant, small, and blurry. Another smaller screen off to his right held Ebony's schooner slightly behind and off the starboard stern.

"Ah, Private Harding," Drake said when Keldon came up from behind and stepped into his view. "Have you talked to your sister?"

"Yes, sir."

"And what did she say?"

"She's disappointed, of course."

"Of course, but I don't want her to feel bad about what happened down there. I'm not a big believer in diplomacy, but there are times when it makes sense, and this was one of those times. Convincing Badoni of anything was a long shot, but one worth taking."

"She says we need to put this behind us and move on to the next step."

"And what would that be?"

"Take Badoni out."

"Really? And how does she think she's going to do that?"

"Badoni's going to be attending the annual ceremony for the fallen. She's hoping you'll send in the cyborgs."

"I don't like that idea. It's a suicide mission, and the chances of success are slim. Very slim indeed. Those ceremonies are massive rallies attended by thousands. Besides, even if Badoni was killed, all it would do is stir up the hornet's nest. They'd replace him and come after us with a renewed vigor."

"She doesn't see it that way. She thinks Badoni is the problem. She wants him taken out."

"Tell her no. I'm not going to throw away my most effective weapons on a pipe dream. I'm keeping the cyborgs for—"

"Minefield dead ahead!" yelled one of the crew members sitting at a console.

"Countermeasures!" Drake yelled. "Hard to port."

There were several seconds of silence. An explosion resounded through the hull, and the floor of the bridge shifted. Keldon was knocked off balance and fell. The viewscreen showed flak from eruptions shooting out and setting off dozens of mines all around.

As the warship turned, it was hit by more impacts that reverberated through the hull and rocked the ship as it shuddered. Keldon grabbed onto a console and pulled himself to his feet. The lights flickered. The screens went blank, but they came back on again. Keldon glanced over at the screen that showed Ebony's schooner. He watched the cockpit blow apart, and her ship roll end over end and spin like a springboard diver.

A more massive explosion sent Keldon sliding across the floor, and he slammed into the wall. His shoulder screamed with pain like it was on fire. The room went dark, and the air was sucked from the room. He couldn't breathe. He heard the hatches slam shut.

He crawled forward, groping in the dark. His shoulder was hurting bad, but he put the pain aside and kept moving. He kept trying to take a breath, but there was no air. He felt giddy, confused, and he was losing his coordination. He was weak and could feel his world starting to slip away slowly. He saw a mask dangling from the side of a console. As he got it, and as he put it on, his vision slipped away, and he worried that he'd pass out before he could take a breath, but he did get a breath. He took several deep breaths.

His vision came back, and he looked around. There wasn't a lot of light; sunlight shone in through the window, but this far out, the sun was nothing more than a bright star.

Drake was lying on the floor in front of his command chair. He wasn't wearing a mask.

Most of the crew had been thrown from their chairs. Most were dead, but there were a few like him, wearing a mask, sitting behind a console, or on the floor. Keldon counted five.

They didn't speak; there was nothing to say.

Keldon got up and sat in the chair behind the console. The pain in his shoulder seemed to be dissipating.

Jen

Rule number one was never to retrace your steps. There were other rules; always decoy before striking; never follow your enemy; always do the unexpected; never give the enemy any indication of what you're going to do next—sound rules. Every cyborg knew them and adhered to them.

Drake had broken one of the rules, and now his ship was compromised. It came as no surprise to Jen.

During the attack, the ship was tossed around like a football. Jen and the other cyborgs were thrown against the walls, but they weren't killed, weren't hurt, and weren't even scratched. When the room depressurized, and there was no air, the cyborg's face shields dropped with a snap, and there was oxygen. When the place when dark, the lights fixed to their helmets switched on automatically. When the hatches sealed, and there was no power to open them, it wasn't a problem. The cyborgs could open them manually, even if they had to rip them off.

Bron led the way. Jen and the others followed. They went from room to room. The breaches were widespread and numerous, and they found no survivors.

In the rooms leading up to the bridge, the hull's integrity was better, and they found two crewmen huddled under oxygen masks. On the bridge, they found six more. Keldon was one of them.

"You again," Keldon said, looking up at Jen. "You were the one who rescued me on Bacchus."

"I didn't get to you quickly enough," Jen said, barely audible due to the lack of atmosphere. "How's the shoulder?"

"It was getting better before I smashed it into that wall over there." He pointed with his chin. "Is there any way to get down to the engine room so we can see if any of the power reserves can be brought online?"

"Not without a spacesuit," Jen said. "The hull is like Bacchian cheese."

"How about if one of *you* go back there to see if there's still a tokamak in one piece. We need power."

"I'll go," Bron said.

"Me too," Harlin joined in.

"There's a good chance there are more survivors out there," Cynthia stated, trying to sound positive. "We should look for them."

"C'mon Jake," Cynthia said. "You too, Ian. Let's go." All the cyborgs except Jen went out the hatch. Jen closed it behind them.

"Ebony's ship was hit," Keldon said.

"How bad?" Jen asked.

"Bad."

"Do you think she and Solin could have survived?"

"No."

"I'm sorry." She was at a loss for words for a moment. "When you lose someone close to you, the war doesn't make sense. Later, after the initial shock, when you realize they're gone and can't get them back, you begin to hate the Athenians even more."

"Ebony would have wanted us to stay focused on the goal. She would have told us to figure out how to make things right. That's what she would have said."

"Piss on that," Jen said. "Vengeance is what I need."

Rose

Rose and Sopika were brought from Uras to the brig of Badoni's warship. They were fed two meals a day—some kind of ground powder mixed with water. It was bland and not very filling, but Sopika donated her meals to Rose, giving her enough substance to keep from starving.

Rose couldn't deal with her constant headache. She moaned and groaned until the guard brought her some Rend. She also complained to Sopika about the burdensome gravity. Both standing and sitting were exhausting—lying on her back worked best, but even that was uncomfortable.

Sopika drank water. Apparently, it was all she needed.

After three days, they were put back on the shuttle. Lazaran was there with more than a dozen Athenian warriors. As the shuttle left the warship's bay, Rose looked out the window at a large planet, almost entirely white—only a few dark gray lines snaked across the surface, the tops of distant mountain chains.

This must be Atheni, she realized. She cringed at the thought of having to live down there as Lazaran's sex object, but the shuttle didn't go down to the planet. Instead, it circled the warship and went to another ship that was orbiting Atheni, one that Rose easily recognized—Solin's saucer-shaped ship. It was an astounding revelation. The Athenian warrior, Lazaran, was the one who had attacked the *Resolution,* the one who had boarded Solin's ship, and the one whose corvette they had captured.

They were brought aboard and brought to the blue dome where she had found Solin, but now there wasn't just one chamber. There were dozens—all of them open and empty. They were brought into the passageway that led to the bridge and pushed into one of the cabins. The door was slammed shut.

Rose searched through the draws of the night table beside the bed and the drawer in the head. She came out with a pair of scissors. She sat on the bed, her back to the wall, and practiced clutching the scissors like a dagger and ferociously swinging her arm back and forth.

Sopika sat next to her.

"I'm not going to let that Athenian bastard rape me," Rose said, grinding her teeth. Yet deep down, she knew it was hopeless. The monster would win. The scissors would only irritate him. *In the eye,* she thought with new resolve. *That's where I'll stab him—in the eye.*

She hid the scissors under her thigh and waited, shaking like a wet dog. She didn't have to wait long.

The Athenian monster stormed into the room. He said something to the warriors standing in the doorway.

One of them came in, grabbed Sopika by the arm, and dragged her out. He slammed the door shut.

Rose sat perfectly still with her legs out straight in front of her.

The creature walked around the end of the bed, keeping an eye on her. He took off his swords, gently tilted them against the wall, and took off his jacket and chest plate. He eased himself into the only chair in the room, leaned on its arm, and stared at her.

Rose didn't look back at him and kept her eyes focused down.

He calmly and quietly said something in Athenian.

Rose looked at him. He was incredibly ugly. *Even if I do stab him with the scissors,* she thought, *it probably won't stop him. It'll probably just piss him off. Still, I have to try to fight as hard as I can and as dirty as possible. Stab him in the eyes. Stab anywhere you can, over and over, for as long as you can. Don't stop until you're entirely unconscious or dead. Better if I'm gone. Then he can't hurt me. Be patient. Wait. Try to catch him off guard.*

He spoke again.

Did he think she could understand? She looked away, staring at her feet. She ran over her plan in her mind. She had her hands out where the monster could see them and was careful not to reveal the scissors. She memorized their exact location and imagined herself snatching them up.

The beast got up and took off his shirt. His greasy white-haired chest was sickening, his abdomen, divided in six, his pectorals, freakishly huge with veins popping up all over, like a weight lifter. He came over to Rose, and when she went for the scissors, he grabbed her arm. She tried to get the scissors with her other hand, but he saw them, grabbed them, and tossed them across the room.

Rose tried to claw his eyes with her left hand, but he tilted his head away, grabbed her hands, pushed both of her arms down until she was on her back, and climbed on top of her. He was incredibly heavy, and instantly, Rose couldn't breathe. In the next instant, he let go of her arms, grabbed her dress at the waist, and lifted her upside down. He pinned her against the wall behind the bed and brought his bared teeth close to her face. Rose closed her eyes and turned her head away.

A female voice spoke Athenian from the doorway.

Rose looked and couldn't believe her eyes. It was Suzi. Why would she be here?

The monster looked back at Suzi, yelled at her, and pushed Rose higher up the wall.

Suzi dropped to her knees and mumbled something else.

The monster yelled at her again.

Suzi yelled back with a vicious, cutting snarl.

The monster dropped Rose. She fell headfirst onto the bed and bounced onto the floor. As fast as she could, she scrambled away and put her back to the wall.

The monster went to Suzi and struck her. The blow was violent, and it sent her crashing into the wall.

Rose found it hard to believe that Suzi could survive such a savage blow.

The beast stood over her and yelled at her.

Suzi curled up into a ball.

One of the guards opened the door and came scrambling into the room.

The monster yelled at him and pointed at Rose.

The guard grabbed Rose's arm and dragged her out. She got her legs up under herself and ran behind the guard to the next room where he threw her in. Sopika was standing in the corner.

Rose sat on the bed, wrapped her arms around her knees, put her head in her arms, and wept. She'd felt so incredibly vulnerable, horrified by the realization that she was utterly defenseless. She'd been stupid with the scissors, had foolishly hoped to surprise him, but of course, he was well-practiced. To him, finding weapons on his target was part of the game, one he knew well and enjoyed. She had no way of stopping him.

Suzi had been fearless. How could she have been so brave? She must have known what he would do to her, but instead of staying away, she sacrificed herself, made herself the victim.

Sopika was silent and motionless in the corner. Rose wondered if her behavior was some sort of defense mechanism, or if something had gone wrong. What would have happened if the monster had chosen to rape Sopika? Would she have told him she was an android, or would she have gone along with it? Could she go along with it? Rose didn't know.

There was banging in the next room that sounded like the warrior was beating Suzi and tossing furniture around.

Rose's head was pounding, there was a tightness in her chest, and a sinking feeling in her stomach. It was a feeling that just kept building. She needed more Rend, but she didn't have any, and she didn't want to ask. She was too afraid to ask, too afraid she'd have to submit to being raped.

Jen

The *Excelsior* was limping through space with a skeleton crew of around thirty, most of them injured. Only one of five engines had survived the minefield, and the moment they got it back online, Keldon ordered the ship towards Atheni.

How Keldon ended up in charge, Jen wasn't sure. She presumed it was because of his intensity—a constrained rage that kept everyone off balance. There was no hesitation on his part and no time spent thinking; he just acted.

On a journey from one planet to another, a ship would typically accelerate for the first half of the trip and decelerate for the second half, but because there was only one engine operational, there was no way to slow down quickly enough to go into orbit around Atheni. Even if the ship could slow down in time, why Atheni? It didn't make sense. Jen went to him. "Why are we headed towards Atheni?"

"The plan is to use the Athenian shuttle to deliver an assault group," he said.

Shuttles were much lighter than warships and could slow down much more quickly. Plus, the fact that it was an Athenian shuttle might fool them into believing it wasn't a threat.

"To do what?" Jen asked.

"To kill Badoni."

"That's a suicide mission."

"I know. I'll pilot the shuttle," he said—a gutsy move. The moment the Athenians figured out what was happening, they'd be after him like bees from a hive. "The mission is voluntary. Anyone who doesn't want to go doesn't have to."

Jen thought no one would want to go, but she was wrong. When the time came, all of the other cyborgs were prepared to board the shuttle and head down to Atheni.

Jen had to decide what to do, and the decision was gutwrenching. *We come from oblivion, spend a few minutes wondering what we're doing here, and go back to obscurity,* she thought.

In the end, she decided it had to happen. Badoni had to die. He was the problem. Get rid of him, and everything might start to look different. The cost was high—her life—but it would be worth it. She hated Badoni with every breath of her existence, and she would pay almost any price to see him dead, but she wasn't committing suicide just to have the satisfaction of killing him. She was doing this because she realized, for the first time in her life, that she wasn't at the center of the universe. Her existence wasn't the only thing that mattered. The cyborgs were a team, and she loved every one of them. She wasn't about to let them down. They were fighting for something more than just self-preservation. They were fighting evil. She boarded the shuttle.

A ranking crew member took charge of the *Excelsior*. He told Keldon he would try to make it to Vole.

The deceleration started immediately and took several hours. As they closed in on Atheni, Jen went to say her goodbyes.

She went to Bron first, each step of her alloy composite feet ringing off the grated metal floor. She tapped Bron's helm with her own. "You don't have to do this."

Bron hesitated. There were tears in her eyes, yet she smiled through them. "Too late now. Besides, you can't stop me."

Jen nodded, went to Harlin, and tapped his helm.

"Never mind the mushy stuff," he said. "Let's get down there and kick ass."

"Kill them all," she teased, lifting her chin.

"Kill them all," he repeated, grinning. He turned away and moved up to a big square hatch with a chunky metal release handle like a mousetrap.

Jen went to Ian. He was standing with his back to a row of lights, and she could barely see his face. She tapped his helm.

"Love you, babe," he said without expression.

"Careful," she replied. "I might hold you to that."

He chuckled grimly.

Next was Jake. He must have snapped inside. He nodded impatiently and turned his head away before she could tap his helm. She moved on.

"I'm going to kill as many of those bastards as I can," Cynthia said through clenched teeth.

"I'm with you," Jen replied. She tapped her helm.

"Whenever you're ready,"—Keldon's voice rang out over the com system. "We're in position."

They lined up in front of the hatch, pulled down their face shields, and secured their helmets. The cabin decompressed. Jen pulled the release handle, and the hatch swung open. She looked down at the planet, Atheni. Even the oceans were frozen. Some mountain ranges showed gray rock, but the rest was a glaring white and hard on the eyes.

She activated her heat shield. It sprung up from her shoulders, curled over her head, and slid down over her face. She stepped forward into a free fall. A screen in her helm showed a detailed holographic image of the landscape below, the target's location, plus a digital reading of her elevation and speed. She could zoom in on anything.

All of the other cyborgs were on her screen except Bron. She looked back over her shoulder just to be sure. Not there. At the last second, she must've decided to go on living. It was her choice. The mission was voluntary.

Twenty-three seconds in, she was going two-forty, and her altitude was three-twenty-eight. A minute in, she was going more than ten times that speed. Two minutes in, thirty times. Her altitude was down to two-forty-eight.

At this point, she hit the atmosphere. The other cyborgs lit up like fireflies. She could feel the heat. At five minutes in, she was going one thousand one hundred. Nine minutes in, she felt like she was on fire. Eleven minutes in, she was decelerating dramatically, and her altitude was thirty-two. Her estimated time of arrival was down to five minutes. Her speed slowed down more and more. She cooled off slightly and retracted her heat shield.

She could see the city and the river winding through it, frozen over and shining like a skating rink. The target was to her left. She extended her arms to spread wings like a flying squirrel. She'd be there soon.

There was a plaza filled with pink warriors, thousands of them, lined up in square blocks. At the head of the plaza, a lone pink stood behind a podium. Jen zoomed her vision and found Badoni. She headed straight for him.

The squares of pinks scattered.

The other cyborgs abandoned their wings, swung out their plasma cannons, and started raking them from the air.

Jen focused on getting to Badoni. She kept her wings extended and aimed for him. Warriors rushed to Badoni's side, shielded him, and shifted him to a shuttle that stood to the left of the stage.

Jen retracted her wings, swung her cannon into position, and started firing. She obliterated five of warriors shielding Badoni before they got him onto the shuttle. The shuttle lifted immediately, its hatch closing as it went. Jen popped her parachute, glided in, and grabbed onto one of the landing bars under the shuttle as it lifted from the ground. Her chute retracted, and she looked down.

The other cyborgs were on the ground, firing in a sweeping motion, taking down Athenian soldiers by the dozen.

The shuttle was rising quickly, yet she managed to get a leg over the bar and then the other leg. Hanging upside down, she extended her plasma cannon and carved out a circle in the bottom of the hull. When the cut out fell, all in one motion, she grabbed the bar with her claw and swung up into the hole. She moved quickly, darting from one victim to the next like a praying mantis, spewing hell in a confined space until all seven Athenian warriors were dead. Badoni was the last one standing. He drew his sword, but Jen didn't hesitate. She took his head off with her next shot.

Jen went forward. The pilot appeared in the doorway and fired shot after shot, but they just bounced off her armor. She grabbed him, snapped his neck, and tossed him aside. She got in the pilot's seat, turned the shuttle around, and heading back to the plaza.

As she went down, there was no incoming fire. It was Badoni's shuttle, and the Athenians below had no way of knowing if he was dead or alive.

On the ground, only two cyborgs were still standing. She landed next to Ian and opened the hatch. He jumped aboard, firing as he went.

Jake was fighting his way towards them, but he was hit in the leg and vaporized.

Jen lifted off. Still, none of the pinks on the ground fired at the shuttle. She gained altitude, and for a moment, it looked like they were going to get away, but then she saw a dozen fighter jets flying in formation towards her. They fired missiles. She could try to turn away at the last second, but it would be of no use. The rockets would turn too.

She recalled a moment on the battlefield when she came across a soldier who had severe wounds. He asked her if he was going to die. She had to tell him he was. He showed no emotion and told her to help him pull his legs together and cross his arms on his chest. She did, and a few minutes later, he died. Now, Jen knew what that soldier had felt. There was no fear. Not when it's inevitable. Some dread, but not much. She had completed her mission, Badoni was dead, and she felt content.

She watched the missiles to the end.

Keldon

"Look at that," Keldon said. On the horizon, in orbit around Atheni, was a gigantic saucer-shaped ship.

"Jen told me about this," Bron said. "She said it was from another solar system and that the Athenians had captured it."

"Look at the size of that thing," Keldon said.

"Shut the engines down and drift towards it. They'll come out to investigate."

"Why would we want them to do that?"

"There's going to be a dozen warships on our tail soon. We have to do something."

"Is that a rule?"

"No. The rule is: Do the unexpected."

Keldon turned the shuttle towards the gigantic ship and turned off all the systems. They got up and stood by the hatch for a while, waiting to see if the Athenians would come out, but the gravity was too much for Keldon, and he had to sit. "I'm not so sure about this," he complained. "Maybe we should fly in, latch onto the hull, and fight our way in. That's how it's usually done, isn't it?"

"We're not doing that," Bron said. "We have to catch them by surprise. Be patient."

Time passed, Keldon's frustration mounted, and, finally, they saw an Athenian shuttle detach from the hull of the top of the massive ship.

"C'mon. Let's get out of sight," Bron said. Keldon grabbed a plasma rifle and followed Bron to the back. There was a separate narrow room at the rear where the tokamak and the engines were housed. They went in, shut the hatch, and waited.

Minutes were like hours. He heard the sound of the shuttle docking and the voices of the Athenian warriors boarding. He readied himself, holding his plasma rifle aimed at the hatch, but the warriors didn't open it. Instead, they turned the power on and started up the ship's tokamak. It was revving up right beside them.

"We'll go now," Keldon whispered.

"No," Bron whispered back. "We'll wait."

They waited.

"Okay," Keldon whispered. "Something's gone wrong. We'll go now."

"No," Bron whispered back. "We're going to wait."

Keldon knew she was right. The longer they waited, the higher the element of surprise. Bron seemed to be in no hurry. She could stay frozen forever, like a trapdoor spider. And a long time it was before they finally felt a lurch of the shuttle's docking.

Keldon looked at Bron with pleading eyes. Bron shook her head.

Finally, when all was silent, she nodded, and Keldon opened the hatch. Bron stormed into the shuttle.

All clear. No pinks.

Keldon went up to the cockpit and looked out the front window. The hull of the massive saucer-shaped ship was there beside them.

"Okay," Bron said as she moved up to the shuttle's hatch. "Here we go. Remember to stay behind me."

Rose

Shouting and the pounding of boots brought Rose to the door. She looked over at Sopika and lifted her chin. "What just happened?"

"I believe the guards were called away," Sopika replied.

Rose listened. There was no sound, so she cracked the door open. The guards were gone. Suzi came out of the next room and put a hand against the wall. The side of her face was bruised red and purple.

Rose went to her. "Come," she said. "We're getting out of here."

Suzi seemed to be in a daze.

"Hey!"

Suzi looked up.

Rose scooped her hand, beckoning her to follow.

She shook her head.

Rose nodded and offered her hand.

Suzi hesitated and then took it.

"C'mon Sopika. We're getting out of here." She'd find a place to hide. It was a massive ship, and they'd never find them. She brought Suzi and Sopika through the passageways until she arrived in a domed room, like the one she'd found Solin in, but much larger. There were huge chambers scattered around, but none of them were open.

As they moved into the room, she saw something move, just for an instant, and then it was gone. She stopped, terrified. What did she see? She didn't know what to do. Should she try to go back the way she came? Then she saw him. His skin was pitch black, and he was peaking over the top of a chamber. Sopika spoke to him in Solin's strange language.

The man came out of hiding and spoke to Sopika.

"He's afraid of Suzi," Sopika said.

"Tell him she's not a threat," Rose said. "She's with us. Who is he?"

"He says his name is Ashur," Sopika reported.

"Does he know how he got here?"

Sopika spoke to him further. "He said he's here from Ziamli."

"Ask him why he's black?"

Sopika spoke to him again. "He wants to know why you're green," she said straight-faced.

Rose laughed.

There was the sound of gunfire, distant, barely audible.

"Quick!" Rose said, pulling on Suzi's hand. "We have to get out of here." She started to run across the expanse of the dome towards the open hatch on the other side. Sopika and Ashur followed.

The sounds of the battle grew louder. When Rose glanced back, Athenian warriors were coming through the hatch they had come through, at least a dozen of them, yet none of them seemed the least concerned with what was in front of them. They fired back in the direction from which they came and frantically scrambled to close the hatch and seal it.

When they got it closed, the hatch in front of Rose closed also, and an orange stripe appeared around the room's circumference. She had seen this before.

"Wait!" she yelled at the others. "The hatch can't be opened. It's locked."

The black man had already gone behind a chamber.

Rose dragged Suzi behind a different chamber and peeked over the top of it. Sopika joined them.

The hatch the Athenians had slammed shut was being peeled open like the skin of a banana. A cyborg came through the gap and spewed blue hell on the Athenians. Within seconds, it cut most of them down.

Five managed to get behind chambers and fire back. A Cronish soldier came through the gap next. He came in firing and took out one of the remaining Athenian warriors with an amazingly accurate shot.

The cyborg moved incredibly quickly, like an insect, but one of the Athenians got in a lucky shot and hit its knee. It fell.

The four Athenians that were still alive fired at the cyborg continuously. The shots were ricocheting off the cyborg's armor all around the room.

The cyborg was being hit repeatedly and couldn't get up, couldn't bring its cannon around. The Athenians came out of hiding and moved towards the cyborg as they fired.

The Cronish soldier fired back, and killed one of the four Athenians.

When some of the richochets came in her direction, Rose and her group hunkered down behind the chamber.

Then there was a loud explosion. The air compressed with a wave of heat, and Rose's ears were ringing. She peaked out from behind the chamber. The cyborg legs were gone and it was in flames. The Cronish soldier was lying on the deck, and blood was pooling beneath him. And the three remaining Athenian warriors lay still. The explosion had killed them all.

Ebony

Five weeks had passed since Ebony had watched the horrific explosions tear away chunks of the *Excelsior's* hull. At that moment, fear had enveloped her. Her mind had raced through an array of heinous outcomes, and she had frozen. But Solin hadn't hesitated and had known what to do. He'd grabbed Ebony by the arm, dragged her out of the cockpit, and closed the hatch.

In the next instant, an explosion had thrown the schooner into a jarring spin and sent Ebony and Solin sprawling. The ship was wildly out of control, stars streaked in arcs across the windows, and it seemed like they couldn't possibly survive. Yet, miraculously, some of the ship's systems were still functioning, the life support system still supported life, the tokamak still provided power, and importantly, the gravity emitters still provided gravity and even compensated for the centrifugal forces that would have otherwise pinned them to the walls and made life intolerable.

In the hours, days, and weeks that followed, Solin was quiet most of the time. When he did speak, Ebony was surprised at how good his Cronish had become.

There was only enough food on board to last for three weeks. They'd stretched it out and calculated they'd run out in just two days.

She rolled in her berth onto her side so she could see him. "Do you remember anything at all about Ziamli?"

He was in his berth on the other side of the cabin, on his back looking up. He shook his head. "Rose says I only have muscle memory. No memories of people or—"

"Events," she said, finishing the sentence.

"Or events."

"Do you think the people there were the same as the people here?"

"People same. Cronish, Volian, Ziamli, Athenians. All same."

"No!" Ebony exclaimed. "Not the Athenians. I no longer believe they're like the rest of us. They're ruthless killers."

"You anger. Anger block vision."

"You've seen what they do, and you've killed many of them."

"I kill soldiers, not innocent people."

Ebony grimaced. "They're all loyal to Badoni. They're all willing to do his bidding."

"Not all."

"For them, it's all about honor, killing, and more killing."

"Athenians want same things you want. They no different from you. Temperament of one man not define entire race."

She realized he was right. She was angry, so she left it there. They were silent for several minutes. Then there was a loud bang, and the hull shuddered. The schooner had hit something. They jumped up, went to the window, and tried to catch a glimpse of what it was that hit them. There was nothing to see. The stars were still zipping by, but more slowly. Again, the ship was jarred, and the ship's spin slowed. It was rattled over and over until, finally, it stopped altogether.

There was a strange-looking spherical pod outside. It moved in, attached itself to the hull next to the window, and a laser started cutting through the shell.

Ebony got back out of the way. Sparks flew as a hole was cut. The cutout fell, gonged on the metal floor, and hummed as it rolled to a stop, like a coin.

Sopika poked her head in. "Hi."

Ebony and Solin just stared at her, speechless.

Sopika lifted her eyebrows. "Are you ready to leave, or do you need more time?"

Ebony giggled. "How did you find us?"

"It was easy. Vestrom ships have emergency beacons."

"Those Bacchians do think of everything, don't they?" Ebony chuckled.

"They live under an ocean," Sopika replied without expression. "I imagine they have emergencies all the time."

Solin helped Ebony climb up into the pod and followed her in. He shut the hatch, the pod backed away from the shattered schooner, and when it turned, Ebony could see the ship Sopika had arrived in.

"You got Solin's ship back!" she said. "And you figured out how to fly it."

"No," Sopika said. "We found another alien on board. He knows how to pilot the ship."

It seemed so strange to be rescued. She had been so sure that she was going to die, and now she was going to go on living. She promised herself she would make good use of her time.

When they docked, and the hatch opened, Ebony looked down at Rose, a black man, and an Athenian female. *How, in the name of the gods, did Rose manage to escape from the Athenians?* she wondered. *And a black man? Where did he come from? And why is the Athenian female not locked up?*

She climbed down the ladder.

Solin followed her down.

Rose ran to him and hugged him.

He hugged her back.

"This is Suzi," Rose said, pointing at the Athenian, "and Ashur." She moved her hand towards the black man.

"Is Ashur from Ziamli?" Ebony asked, bewildered.

"Yes," Rose said.

"But he's black. How could that be? Black people and white people on the same planet? Are the gods playing games?"

Rose shrugged.

"Are there other people from Ziamli on the ship?"

"There were, but the Athenians took them away."

"To where?"

"We don't know. Ashur managed to escape when he was being transferred to a shuttle. He hid from the Athenians until we found him."

"And how did you get away?" Ebony asked Rose.

"Lazaran brought Sopika and me to this ship," Rose explained. "He held us prisoner until a cyborg, and a Cronish soldier rescued us. Unfortunately, they were killed in the battle."

"What did the soldier look like?"

"Cronish. Tall. Dark hair. Ashur put him in a hibernation chamber and froze his body. He said that sometimes if they are frozen soon enough and if the damage isn't too severe, people can be repaired and brought back to life."

"Can I see him?" Ebony asked with a choked voice.

"Of course," Rose replied.

They all went together. Ashur raised the chamber out of the floor and opened it.

It was as she thought; it was Keldon. She was on the verge of tears. "Can you bring him back to life?"

Sopika spoke to Ashur. "Perhaps," she translated. "but he's not sure. He has a lot of injuries. It would take months to grow the tissue needed to make the repairs, and there would be many hours of surgery needed to replace the damaged tissue."

"But, it's possible?"

"Yes," Sopika translated. "His body has been pumped full of cryoprotectant and frozen; he's been preserved."

Ebony stayed with Keldon for many hours.

Solin came and sat down beside her. "You okay?"

"I'm okay." It was a lie. She was depressed.

"Suzi say that a hundred six ten year ago, Bacchian hollow cavern in asteroid orbit Jupith. Cavern contain city."

"You can speak Athenian?"

"A little."

"Why are you telling me this?" Ebony asked.

"Suzi say you want to know."

"Why?"

"She say thousands live on the asteroid."

"Is it just for Bachians?"

"No. Athenians. Called Rowan."

"But why would Athenians want to live such an isolated existence?"

"Outcasts there. Opposed to the war, and Athenian general in exile. Damascus. Suzi say he become Emperor."

"Is Badoni dead?" Ebony asked.

"Yes," Solin said. "Cyborgs kill him."

"Can Suzi get us a meeting with Damacus?"

"She try."

"Where's Rose?"

Solin took Ebony to see Rose.

When they found her, Ebony dished out her plan.

"Waaaait a minute," Rose said. "You don't think I'm going to make the same mistake twice, do you?"

"Suzi say Damascus not like Badoni," Solin said. "She say he want what best."

"It's not worth the risk," Rose said, shaking her head.

Ebony became a storm. "It is worth the risk," she roared, "and no, we're not making the same mistake twice. This time you're going to be clean, and you're going to act like a princess."

During the journey to Rowan, she took Rose under her wing and put her through a long and torturous detox regime to get her off Rend. It had been a nightmare, long nights of screaming and sobbing that were so severe Ebony had succumbed to suggest they give her some morphine to ease her pain. But Rose had said no. Having gone through the worst part of it, she was determined to get off the stuff altogether—no supplements; nothing; cold turkey.

When she wasn't monitoring Rose, Ebony got Sopika to probe Ashur for information. He had tapped into the ship's library and learned a great deal about his homeworld. He told a story beyond belief.

Rose

Rose grabbed the arms of her chair. "The Athenians are going to sit back and laugh as our pod is ripped to shreds."

"Try to relax," Sopika scolded. "I can do this in my sleep." She was piloting one of the ship's bubble pods. Rowan was rolling towards them like a giant bowling ball, and the closer they got, the more ominous it looked.

"I wish you wouldn't make cliche remarks," Rose said. "I know you don't sleep."

An Athenian corvette had stopped them from approaching Rowan. Only after Suzi identified herself and communicated their intentions, were they allowed approaching.

In Rose's mind, this was just as ludicrous as the plan that went wrong on Uras. Why she had agreed to it, she wasn't sure. Suzi and Solin there because they insisted on going with her. Sopika was there as the princess's translator.

As Sopika accelerated towards the asteroid, an opening appeared on the side of an outcrop near the top. It moved down with the rotation. Sopika took the pod to the very bottom of the asteroid, where it was swallowed up from behind by the opening. Inside, the centrifugal force slammed the pod down on the outer surface.

Suddenly, Rose was back in an abhorrent Athenian gravity. She struggled to get up and then had to be helped up by Solin.

The bay's exterior door shut, and the bay pressurized. Solin opened the hatch and lowered a metal staircase. Rose led the way. She wore a royal dress, but the high gravity warped its shape and made it look like a wet rag.

Dozens of Athenian warriors rushed into the bay as they went down the stairs. They were surrounded, and with the waving of guns, were led through a hatch and across a massive flight deck littered with dozens of warships, cruisers, and corvettes.

They arrived at a room where the warlord, Damascus, was waiting. He was tall and veiled in a long white beard, wearing gold armor laced with silver trim, and carrying the traditional two swords and a knife.

The room had leather chairs, dark wooden bureaus, and a large table. Talonian buffalo furs covered the floor, and hanging on the walls were longswords, spears, bows, and steel shields. Half a dozen Athenian warriors stood at attention around the circumference of the room.

"General Damascus, it's a pleasure to meet you," Rose said."

Sopika translated.

Damascus nodded and spoke to Suzi. He looked surprised at her response.

"General Damascus asked Suzi if she had been treated well," Sopika told Rose. "Suzi told him that she was not a prisoner."

Damascus spoke again, this time staring at Rose. "May I ask what you expect to gain by coming here?"

Sopika translated for both.

"It is my understanding that you are in a position to take the throne."

Damascus smiled. "And why would I do that?"

Rose smiled back. "Because you care about the fate of your people."

"It's your people whose fate is sealed, not mine."

"You're mistaken. There are thousands of cyborgs defending the remaining cities on Cronos. If you try to take them, your armies will be wiped out."

Upon hearing the translation, Suzi immediately spoke to Damascus.

Sopika translated her Athenian words. "The princess is lying. There are no cyborgs on Cronos. The cyborgs have all been killed."

Rose was shocked. How could Suzi betray her like that?

Damascus stood, yelled his answer, and pointed to the door.

"How dare you come here," Sopika translated. "Is that how you think you are going to end this war—with lies? Get out!"

Rose's jaw dropped. "Okay, okay, there aren't any cyborgs." She looked at Suzi with protruding eyes. Suzi knew she wasn't the real princess. Was that lie in danger of being exposed as well? "What am I supposed to do?" Rose gripped at Suzi under her breath. "Beg? You Athenians are like snakes—completely incapable of any empathy." The moment she said it, she realized it was a mistake. Sopika was translating. "No!" she yelled, but it was too late.

Damascus moved like a cat. Both his longsword and his short sword came at Rose at the same time.

Rose cowered with her hands in front of her face.

The swords whirled like helicopter blades, but Solin was faster. He got in front of Rose, grabbed Damascus's arms, twisted them until the swords fell to the floor, and then released them.

All of the Athenian warriors drew their swords, and two of them moved between Damascus and Solin.

"Who is this man?" Damascus asked, glaring at him.

"His name is Solin," Rose said, putting her hands down, "and he's good at fighting. He single-handedly attacked and captured an Athenian corvette."

"Anyone can make fantastic claims."

"If you don't believe me, you have only to ask Suzi." Rose pointed at her with bulging eyes. "She was on the corvette."

Upon hearing the translation, Damascus looked over at Suzi. She responded by nodding.

"I found him in a hibernation chamber," Rose said. "His blood was injected with a natural antifreeze, and his temperature was lowered below freezing so he could travel great distances perfectly preserved and be brought back to life with a defibrillator."

"Ah, yes," Damascus said, smiling. "I did hear of this man. He is rumored to be the Messiah." He laughed and ordered his guards back to their places. One of the guards retrieved Damascus's swords and returned them to him. He sheathed them and sat down and looked at Rose.

"There five ships," Solin said, speaking Athenian.

This caught Damascus by surprise. His head snapped around to look at him.

Sopika quietly translated for Rose.

"Four arrive ten thousand year ago," Solin continued. "No planet good."

"Enough," Damascus yelled. "I've no interest in fables."

"Not fable," Solin said. "Sent here from Ziamli to save humans. Instead, you kill each other."

"Athenians didn't start this war," Damacus said. "It was started by Queen Leona."

"My mother is dead," Rose said, "and if your people try to live on Cronos, they will become soft and weak because of the lack of gravity. My understanding is that it is a fate worse than death in your culture."

It looked like Damascus was about to speak for a moment, but then he took a deep breath and said nothing.

"For ten thousand year," Solin said, still speaking Athenian, "second sun make Atheni warm, but fell from orbit long ago and never put back."

"It can't be put back," Damascus said. "The cost is too high, and besides, it's too late. We've run out of time. What we need is a miracle."

"You withdraw troops from Cronos," Solin said. "I give you miracle."

Damascus laughed. "And what miracle would that be?"

"Second sun," Solin said.

"You have a second sun?"

"Yes, the top section of my ship."

"And it's capable of warming Atheni?"

"Yes."

Damascus didn't reply right away. He thought long and hard. Then he nodded. "Agreed."

"Thank you for seeing us," Rose said, stunned by the turn of events. She wasted no time getting up to leave.

Solin, Sopika, and her shuffled out of the room, made their way back to the shuttle, and then the ship. Suzi stayed behind.

"So, what happened?" Ebony asked upon their return.

"It didn't go well," Rose said.

"What do you mean?" Ebony said.

"I did what you said and told Damascus that I had thousands of cyborgs, but Suzi told Damascus that I was lying. Damascus got mad and came at me with his swords."

"Did you stand tall and show him bravery?"

"No, Solin jumped in front of him and took his swords away."

"I see," Ebony said, her eyes bulging and her jaw lowered. "Then what happened?"

"Then Solin told Damascus to take his troops off of Cronos."

Ebony's jaw dropped further. "Really? How did Damascus react to that?"

"He agreed."

"He agreed?" Ebony was squinting.

"Yeah. Solin told him he would give him a second sun in return."

"What?"

"He said he had one on his ship."

"You're kidding?"

"Nope."

After that, Rose spent her time with Solin. When she was off on her mission to Rowan, she'd wanted nothing more than to get back to the ship. Now that she was with him, now that she'd spent many blissful hours listening to him, talking to him, and laughing with him, now that they'd vigorously made love night after night—now she was becoming unsettled.

Rose was free from Rend, didn't have headaches, and didn't even think about it anymore, yet there was a craving inside her, a desire for something more.

It seemed that Solin was perfectly content to spend his life on his ship. She didn't want that, and she wondered where she could take him.

If Damascus pulled his troops out, somewhere on Cronos was the obvious choice. True, most of the cities had been destroyed, but there had to be some remote corner of the planet that remained untouched by the war, a place where she and Solin could have a family.

The other planets were out of the question: Vole was hell, Bacchus was a dungeon, Talon was a death trap, and Danae High had been taken over by the Athenians. They'd accelerated the rotation to simulate Athenian gravity. She doubted they'd give that up even if they did decide to withdraw from Cronos.

She watched Solin and Ashur engage in a conversation in their strange language.

"What was that about?" Rose asked when Solin pulled away.

"Tokamak stop working," Solin said. "I go look."

"I'll go with you," Rose said. "Maybe I can help." *Then again,* she thought, *maybe I shouldn't help. Perhaps we'd be better off if I let Solin take care of it.*

It was a long walk from the front of the ship to the back. When they got there, they found two large tokamaks sitting side by side. There was a console in front of each, and Solin walked up to and tapped on a blank screen. Nothing happened.

Rose noticed a panel on the side of the other tokamak had fallen off —or been taken off.

There was a flash, a loud bang, and a blue bolt hit Solin. He was thrown over by the impact. Rose's ears were ringing, and when she turned around, an Athenian warrior was moving towards her. She ran around the tokamak and down a passageway. She heard the sound of a gun firing and saw plasma bolts striking the walls around her, but she didn't stop. After running full speed for many minutes, she glanced back, and she couldn't see him. She kept going.

"There's an Athenian on board," Rose said, breathlessly when she finally got to the bridge and found Ebony, Sopika, and Ashur, "and he shot Solin." She burst into tears.

Ebony picked up an Athenian plasma gun and ran from the bridge. Sopika spoke to Ashur. He opened a cabinet that held strange-looking weapons, grabbed one, and followed Ebony.

Was Solin dead? Rose wasn't sure, but her sense of dread was overwhelming. She wanted to scream and yell and cry. This was too much to bear, and she was shaking. She had Keldon's assault gun in her cabin. She went and got it and marched towards the back of the ship.

Down a distant passageway, she heard a flurry of shots and then silence. Terrified that things had gone wrong, she waited with her gun pointed towards a distant hatch. There was another flurry of shots. She moved forward, through the hatch, down a passageway, and around a corner. The Athenian was lying on the deck, exhaling and inhaling with a wheezing sound.

Ashur and Ebony were there, pointing their guns at him.

The Athenian's eyes were open, and he was in obvious pain that seemed to come in waves. After a few seconds, he took one final breath, and his body lay still.

Rose ran to the spot where she had seen Solin fall, and when she found him, his body was still. She put her head to his chest. There was no heartbeat. When she couldn't cry anymore, she went back to the Athenian and started beating his dead body with her gun. "Damn you," she screamed. "Damn you. Damn you. Damn you."

A box fell from his belt. She recognized it. Rend. She picked it up, found the syringe, and sat with her back to a wall. She pulled the bottle from the box, stuck the syringe into the bottle, and pulled the drug into the syringe, not bothering to measure. She inserted the needle into the vein of her arm.

Within seconds, she could feel the rush, and she relished every second of it. But it wasn't enough. It eased her pain only slightly. She withdrew some more and squeezed a bit more into her arm. The effects kept coming. But it still wasn't enough, and she squeezed in more. She felt herself drifting into another world, a painless world, a world of darkness.

Ebony

Ebony climbed out of her brand new Vistrom Cutter and made her way onto the deck of the submarine, *Malofa*.

"Good to see you, Ebony," Hadila shouted from the conning tower.

The wind was howling, and the deck was pitching like a ride at the fair. The ocean around her had the usual ten-foot waves, and the sky, the typical dark clouds. She had to lean into the wind and fight to maintain her balance. "I'm looking to make a trade," she shouted, smiling.

"Really," the captain chuckled.

She climbed up to the conning tower, and they went down to the same cozy little cabin where they'd met so many times before. The wine and cheese were already on his desk.

"Please sit, and let my attendant pour you some wine," Hadila said.

"Thank you," Ebony said, lowering herself into her seat.

"So, what are you looking to trade?"

"Oh, just little things."

"Stop being so mysterious, and tell me what. I'm dying to know."

"I have gold."

Hadila laughed. "Gold? Where did you find that?"

"On a freighter that just got back from the Lupid Belt. A Cronish company that got wiped out by the war commissioned it. I don't have to tell you what's happened to the price of gold since the war started."

"No, you don't. I'm quite sure we can work something out."

"I'm also concerned about our long term prospects," Ebony said, picking up a piece of cheese.

"What are you scheming?"

"Do you think there's a market for land?"

"Where?"

"Here."

"On Bacchus?"

"If there was land somewhere on Bacchus, would people buy it, or are they happy living under the ocean?"

"I don't know. I haven't given it any thought."

"I could farm asteroids, herd them into orbit around Bacchus, and drop them into the ocean."

"Easier said than done. They tend to burn upon entry."

"But there are ways to slow them down, so they don't burn up, isn't there?"

"Perhaps, but think of the cost. I doubt it'd be profitable. Where would you get the freighters and excavators? The war destroyed most of them."

"I'm good at finding things."

"I can't argue with that, but I think you're biting off more than you can chew. Certainly, that's not what brought you here. You must be thrilled—such wonderful news. The war is over."

"I'm beside myself with joy."

"All this time, I thought Damascus was dead."

"He's pulled all of his troops out of Cronos."

"He's keeping Danae High, though."

"I guess he felt he had to give his people something. The cost in lives was high for both sides."

"And he has a new terraforming mirror."

"Yes. The ship that arrived here from Ziamli had a terraforming mirror built into it. It just needed to be deployed. It's working too. Atheni is getting warmer. Damascus was delighted and signed a peace treaty with the newly elected president of Cronos."

"I heard that your bother was killed. I'm so sorry for your loss."

"Thank you. I will miss him."

"One thing that puzzles me, though. I've heard from a reliable source that when the cyborgs went down to rescue Princess Charline, she was killed, and yet she appeared at the council meeting on Uras, and she was able to negotiate with Damascus on Ramus. How is that possible?"

"If I told you that the captain with the gold wouldn't sell to a Bacchian, what would you do?"

"I'd find a subsidiary to make the sale."

"Would you understand the importance of keeping the subsidiary at arm's length and completely secret?"

"Of course."

Ebony raised her eyebrows.

"Oh, I see. This was all your doing?"

"Just between you and me, I just happened to know someone that looked like the princess."

"Very clever. You're going to have to hope that no one finds out. The Athenians don't like being duped."

"Don't worry. My princess is well concealed."

"And what's this rumor I hear about the Messiah coming here from Uttara and performing a miracle?"

"He's not the Messiah, and he's not from Uttara. He's from Ziamli.

"I don't think that's quite right. Ziamli is mentioned in the Ancient Sacred Writings. It's a country on a planet called Earth in a solar system called Uttara." He smiled. "So the people on every planet are going to come to believe the story that the Messiah came here from Uttara and performed a miracle to stop the war, but what really happened is you orchestrated the whole thing. Not only did you find something to trade, but you found a substitute princess to negotiate the deal. I find it amazing. You weren't even in the army, yet you somehow accomplished the impossible. It's incredible."

"I can't take all the credit. I didn't know there was a terraforming mirror on the Messiah's ship. When the deal was made, I was just as surprised as anyone. But I was in the army. When I was on the *Resolution*, the freighter and its crew were conscripted."

"So, you were a conscript?"

"So were others."

"But you were the conscript that made plans and executed them. You're the conscript that's responsible for ending the war."

Ebony smiled. "I learned a valuable lesson. When you're negotiating a deal, don't lie."

"But sometimes you have to."

"If you have to lie, you shouldn't do the deal. Lies tend to grow in size and they're almost always discovered."

Hadila tilted his head to the side and pursed his lips. "I suppose that's true."

"Enough about the war. Let's talk gold."

Rose

Her entire body was shivering, her hands and feet were like ice cubes, and her core was frigid. She spread her fingers and lay them down on the hard surface beneath to try to warm them. When she opened her eyes, her vision was blurred with sapphire shapes blending to stark white. Her arms were stiff and heavy. She took a deep breath and felt the warmth of the air in her lungs. She frisked the white walls surrounding her and then let her hands fall to her chest. She felt wires and tore them off.

Where am I? she wondered, but she couldn't remember. She couldn't recall anything. It was frustrating. She had no idea where she was or why she was there.

She tried to sit up but didn't have the strength. She grabbed the sides of her chamber with both hands and pulled as hard as she could, but it was useless; she couldn't lift herself. She tried to roll over. It took three tries. She brought her knees up, rolled onto them, and pushed herself up so she could see over the chamber's side.

If her fuzzy vision could be trusted, the room was large. She rotated her head so that she could see the whole room. She gasped and held back a scream when she saw a woman was standing on the deck behind her, her body stiff, her skin a putrid yellow with black creases crisscrossing her face. *A Volian,* she thought. There was also a strange-looking bone sticking up from the floor with alien-looking symbols on its face.

Suddenly she felt nauseous and wanted to puke. She leaned over the side but couldn't get anything out. She carefully lay back down and stayed very still until the feeling passed.

Using all her strength and willpower, she got up again and put a leg over the chamber's side. She tried to stretch it down to the floor, but her arms weren't able to hold her weight, and she fell to the deck like a sack of potatoes. Her arm was crushed in the fall, and she squeezed her eyes shut and clenched her teeth. Before the pain was gone, she struggled to sit up and lean against the chamber. After a few minutes, the pain eased, and she rotated her arm to make sure it was okay. She tried to get up, but it was useless. She couldn't manage it.

Curious, she crawled over to the Volian and felt her legs. They were cold and hard.

Her heart skipped a beat when a section of the deck moved. She scrambled to get away. It went down and slid sideways, and a second chamber rose out of the floor. A stripe on the side of it turned orange. She watched and waited. The stripe turned red. She could feel the warmth of it and welcomed it.

She crawled over to the bone sticking up from the floor, grabbed on to it, and used all of her strength to pull herself up to a standing position. A zapping sound, coming from the new chamber, startled her. The lid opened, and steam rose. It zapped again.

From a distance, she tried to see into the chamber, but it was filled with smoke.

It zapped again and again.

She felt warmer now, and it was easier to move. She carefully took small steps and worked her way closer to the chamber. She brushed the smoke aside.

"Oh, by the gods of Uttara!" she whispered. The man in the chamber was black, like a gorilla with smooth skin and strong muscles.

She backed away, terrified.

The chamber zapped over and over again. The zapping went on, and on, and on, and it stopped. The lid closed, and the casket went back down beneath the deck. The deck slid out sideways from beneath the floor and moved up into place.

Another section of the deck slid sideways, and another chamber came up. The strip around it turned orange and then red. The zapping started. She moved up and swiped the smoke away. This one contained a muscle man, but white, ghostly looking.

The chamber zapped and zapped. The zapping stopped, and she thought she'd better get away from it before it, too, sank into the floor, but she realized the white man was staring at her, with blue eyes. She felt vulnerable.

He didn't move, just looked at her.

"Can you speak?" she asked.

The white man sat up.

She stepped away. *How could he do that so effortlessly?* she wondered, frightened.

He said something in a bizarre language. It was terrifying. She took a couple of quick breaths. "I don't understand you."

He didn't reply. He ripped the wires off his chest and got out of his chamber.

She tried to get away, but her legs wouldn't let her, and she fell.

He walked over to her.

She rolled onto her back and cowered like a child.

He extended a hand, and with the wiggle of his fingertips, beckoned to help her up.

She was afraid, but she reached out to him. He lifted her effortlessly, and in an instant, she was standing.

He walked over to the bone sticking up from the floor, stared at the scribblings, tapped it, and seemed to be reading from a small screen. He said nothing. He went to the Volian and unbuttoned her shirt.

"Don't do that," she scolded meekly, not knowing how she could possibly stop him. "Leave her alone."

He ignored her entirely and pushed his fingers into the skin on her stomach.

"Please stop it," she pleaded, but he buttoned her shirt back up.

The Volian suddenly came to life. "Hi, Rose," she said. "How are you?"

Surprised, Rose threw a hand to her chest. "You're an android?"

"I am Sopika."

The white man said something in his strange language. Sopika responded, speaking the same language.

"Who is he?" Rose asked, lifting her chin."

"That's Solin, your lover."

"My what?"

"You don't remember," she said. It was not a question.

"But he's white," Rose said, grimacing.

"He's human, and may the gods be my witness, that's all that's required."

Sopika spoke to the white man again, and he laughed. "Come," she said to Rose. "We must venture out and see where we are."

Solin put out an arm for Rose to hold. Reluctantly, she took it, and they made their way to the hatch and down a passageway. There were cabins, and beyond that, a bridge with large windows stretching across the front. Outside the window, there was a planet. The white man was staring at a large screen that displayed foreign words. He pressed icons on a console.

"What planet is this?" Rose asked.

"Earth," Sopika said.

"Is this my home planet?"

"Your home planet is Cronos. It's in another solar system."

"Where?"

"Far from here."

"How far?"

"Two thousand years."

Rose took a moment to digest that information. "That's not a distance," she said with a note of disdain.

"I know. It's probably a bit of a shock."

"What am I doing here?"

"That's a long and complicated story. This ship is equipped with highly sophisticated medical bays capable of doing things that aren't possible on Cronos. After you and Solin died, you were both operated on. Solin's wounds were patched up, and your blood was cleaned. You were both prepared for hibernation and put in a state of stasis."

"They killed me?"

"You needed to disappear. They figured Solin would want to go back to Earth, and given the circumstances, you'd probably want to go with him."

"Well, you were wrong. I don't want to be here. I want to go home."

Sopika quietly spoke to Solin.

He looked up, smiled, said something, and went back to reading.

"What did you tell him?" Rose asked.

"I told him that you didn't remember being in love with him and wanted to go home."

"And what did he say?"

"Ah, well, I don't think you would want me to repeat that."

"What did he say?" Rose demanded.

"He said he didn't remember being in love with you, and that he must have been desperate."

She took a quick breath and furrowed her brow. "What!"

"I told you you wouldn't like it."

Rose moved up to the window and looked down at the blue and white marble planet below. "What's down there?"

"I don't know. I rather think that no one's expecting us. I don't even know if there's any life on this planet. This ship left Earth twelve thousand years ago. Back then, the planet was in trouble."

"So, now what?"

"I'm not sure."

"Well, I'm not in love with the white man, that's for sure."

"He saved your life more than once. He taught you how not just to tolerate, but embrace people of different races and cultures. You were madly in love with him, and because of him, you were motivated to help stop a war and save your planet."

"But he's creepy looking," she said, her face contorted.

"That's your tribal nature. You instinctively fear anyone different from yourself. Give it time. You'll learn to like him."

Lightning Source UK Ltd.
Milton Keynes UK
UKHW011856161220
375343UK00001B/93